Jeff Sherratt

Cyanide Perfume

A Jimmy O'Brien Mystery

Innova Press edition 2013

ISBN:9780983873037

Library of Congress Number: 2013916937

Printed in the United States of America

Cover design by Karen Phillips

Edited by Mike Sirota

DEDICATION

Cyanide Perfume is dedicated to Jeff Sherratt
who died 100 pages shy of his "perfect" life.
Every adversity was seen by Jeff as a new
challenge, every challenge as a new adventure.

Cyanide Perfume was lovingly finished by his
wife, Judy, who was guided by their good friend
and author, Teresa Burrell.

Special thanks go to his editor, Mike Sirota,
whom Jeff adored.

Chapter One

Dead clients are definitely a cause for concern, I thought, as I sat in the stark attorney / client conference room at the Los Angeles County Jail focused on the guard sitting across from me.

The client that I came to see, one Henry "Buck" Simpson, was a career criminal. He had received his nickname from the Buck Knife he carried when rolling drunks late at night outside of trendy nightspots scattered around Hollywood.

Last month Simpson had been released from San Quentin on a conditional rehabilitation parole and assigned to a halfway house. However, around midnight a few nights ago, Buck had been caught with knife in hand lurking in the shadows outside of the Whiskey A Go-Go during a sold-out Johnny Rivers performance. Lurking with a weapon is a no-no for parolees and the Adult Correction Authority was about to revoke his get-out-of-jail-free card. I was assigned by the court to represent him at the parole hearing set for later in the month. Routine cases like this didn't pay much, but they helped defray the expenses of my small law firm.

Now instead of interviewing Buck here at the jail, I sat dumbfounded, looking at the twisted face of the jail guard sitting where my clients usually sat.

"What do you mean my client is dead?" I asked.

Seconds passed. The guard fidgeted and stared at the table. "It was a real stomach turner," he finally said. "The bastard had tied a bed sheet around an exposed pipe and hung himself. But, *Jesus,* the guy had shit his pants. Being new on the job, I'm the one who had to cut him down." He grimaced. "Eyeballs all bulging out, purple tongue as big as a bowling ball. He was blue, man, didn't look human. And the stink, *Christ*." The guard shook his head in disgust.

"Sounds nauseating."

"Comes with the job, I suppose." He sighed.

"Your first one?"

"I've only been out of the academy three weeks. They sent me to the jail to work as a guard. Never seen a dead body before."

"Yeah, rookies get assigned to the jail system right off the bat," I said. "You'll get used to it."

The brass hats wanted to expose the new recruits to the kind of scum they'll encounter later when patrolling the dark streets of L.A. County. Being an ex-cop I knew how the system worked.

"It's a lousy job," the guard said.

"Supposed to toughen you up, I guess."

"Man, I don't know how much more of this shit I can take. It's a freak show in here."

***

My windshield wipers beat back a torrent as I drove south on the Santa Ana Freeway heading back to my office in Downey. I sat in traffic listening as the radio played the latest hit by the Bee Gees, "Jive Talkin'." It was the fall of 1975 and the disco sound had taken over the airways. I loved music, but for some reason I couldn't fathom the appeal of disco—sappy vocals with a syncopated rhythm. I flicked off the radio and let my mind wander. I thought about Buck Simpson. In my first and only interview with him, he hadn't seemed depressed at all. When I explained that he'd probably be sent back to prison, he just nodded and said, "No sweat."

In fact, he seemed eager to get back to San Quentin. Buck had bragged about being a star on one of the prison's baseball teams, the Junk Yard Dogs. As the "big dog" on the team, he said he didn't want to miss the playoff game coming up against the black inmates, the Mother Fs. Yeah, I figured he wanted to go back and maybe that's why he didn't try to run when the cops spotted him outside of the nightclub. But now he was dead and they say he hung himself. Maybe he did—but maybe he had a little help.

I swung my Corvette into the parking spot in front of my office on Cecilia Street, just west of Lakewood Boulevard, and sat in the car for a moment watching the pelting squall whip across the lot. *Why did Buck Simpson die? How did it really happen?*

Holding my briefcase over my head, I sprinted through the rain to the front door of my office. After wiping the excess water from my briefcase onto the back of my pant leg, I opened the door and stepped into the outer office, shoes squishing with each step.

"Wet outside," I said to Mabel, our two-lawyer firm's secretary, receptionist, office manager, and resident nag.

She gave me a blank look, not responding to the obvious. Instead she said, "I gotta send the bill for your jail interview this morning. Gimme your timesheet."

I made my way to the coffee bar and poured a cup. "Simpson killed himself before I got there. Least that's what they told me, but anyway, he's dead."

"Yeah, well, we still have to bill the State for

your time."

"He's dead, Mabel."

"Okay, then we'll bill them half your normal rate."

Mabel, an outspoken woman in her middle fifties, ran our business affairs efficiently. At times, it seemed as if she were reading my mind. If I needed a letter typed, it would be completed before the words were out of my mouth.

Yeah, I was the boss, but Mabel was constantly on me about collections from my clients, always crabbing about money. What the hell, somebody had to worry about the cash flow and administrative hassles. I didn't want it to be me.

Holding the cup of coffee, I slipped into my office, set the cup on my desk, and leaned back in the chair, thinking again about the meeting with the guard. I knew how violent it was in the jail system. Murders happen on a regular basis, but suicide? Rarely.

I picked up the phone and dialed Steve Delacorte's direct line at the DA's office. Delacorte was the deputy DA handling the Simpson case. The so-called suicide wasn't any of my business, but I just couldn't let it go.

"Well, well, Jimmy O'Brien, friend of the downtrodden. What do you want now?" Delacorte said when he answered the phone.

"Steve, tell me what you know about the Simpson suicide."

"Nothing to tell. The guy hung himself. End of story, end of case." There was a pause on the line with neither of us saying anything. Finally: "Why do you care, anyway?"

4

"He was my client."

The deputy DA chuckled. "Yeah sure, your client, a hundred bucks to handle his arraignment."

"Steve, that's not fair. I was the last guy on his side...no, make that the *only* guy on his side. Besides, I kind of liked him." A baseball player can't be all bad, I thought.

"Look, if it will make you feel better I'll do a little checking and get back to you if I find anything that looks suspicious. But take my advice, just forget it."

Deputy DAs were constantly juggling a number of cases, and helping bemused defense attorneys wasn't in their job description. I doubted that Delacorte would call back. The L.A. Sheriff's Department, the organization that ran the county jails, would at times cover up a murder when a prominent or notorious prisoner got nailed while in their custody. It was terrible PR after all. But why would the sheriff's department cover up anything for a nobody like Buck Simpson?

Chapter Two

André, the maitre d', stood at his station by the entrance jotting a name in the reservation book when I walked into Rocco's restaurant. He looked up at me and waved as I strolled past him. André knew I was the only person Sol Silverman allowed to go to his booth unannounced.

Headquarters for Silverman Investigations on Florence Avenue in Downey took up the entire top floor of the office building that housed Rocco's Restaurant, and conveniently it was not far from my office. Sol had a large staff of operatives and secretaries on his payroll upstairs, but most of the time he hung out at the restaurant on the ground floor. Although he was twenty or so years older that I was, he was my mentor. More than that, my best friend. We had lunch together at the restaurant on a regular basis.

When I arrived at his booth Sol stood to greet me. "*Shalom*, my friend," he said. "Sit, and we'll enjoy a nice lunch."

He was taller sitting down than standing up, his chest was huge and matched his stomach, but his legs were short and skinny. His large round head hunkered down directly on his shoulders without a suggestion of a neck. Today he was wearing a rust colored turtleneck that fit tightly across his torso, but the folds of the sweater at the top were baggy and covered his chin. He tugged at his collar as he wedged back in his seat.

I slipped into the booth across from him. "Good seeing you, Sol. What's happening?"

"Not much with me, but I can see from the hang-dog look on your face that you have a problem," he said. "You need my help. Is that why you came to break bread with me?"

"I came to have lunch with my friend. What else?"

Buck's death still nagged at me. I thought about asking Sol to dig into it. He had contacts everywhere, his 'spies', and I knew he'd be able to get his hands on a copy of the sheriff department's report. Investigations were his business and people paid real money for his services. "Guy can't eat with a friend without needing something?" I asked.

"Of course, but I know you, Jimmy." He sighed.

"Yeah, I guess something's bugging me."

"Ah-ha, I knew it! A favor, that's what you want, a favor."

"No, Sol. I just found out about it. My client—"

His bushy eyebrows rose. "A client? You have a client?" The eyebrows fell. "Wait; is this a paying client or another one of your freebies?"

"The client is dead."

"A dead guy for a client. Hard to collect a fee from a dead guy."

Janine interrupted our conversation bringing a drink for Sol and a cup of coffee for me. She wore a new uniform more in keeping with the prevailing feminist movement than the low-cut miniskirt outfits that the waitresses had worn before. "Like the new getup?" Janine did a slow twirl showing off her loose-fitting white blouse buttoned at the neck, and her plain black skirt that covered her knees.

"Sweetheart, on you, a gunnysack would look sexy," Sol said.

"Oh, Sol, aren't you the sweetest thing." Janine

glanced at me. "How about you, good lookin'? Do you like it?"

Before I could answer, Sol piped up, "Why do you always call him good looking? I think you wore out that joke."

"Well..." Janine said, angling her head in my direction, "...he's got those baby-blues just like Paul Newman. Kinda looks like him too."

I'd been teased about the color of my eyes since my third birthday. It was embarrassing.

"Cut it out you guys," I said. "Let's order."

I ordered a hamburger and fries, and Sol had a veal dish served with some kind of French wine, a Château something or other. Sounded more like a fancy hotel than a bottle of the grape. The price of a room would have been cheaper.

"Now, Jimmy. What does this dead guy want me to do for him?" Sol asked.

I told him about Buck Simpson, and my hunch that I wasn't getting the truth. "Sol, the guard said Simpson committed suicide, but—"

"But what?"

"Suppose he didn't," I said.

"Suppose he did."

"He wasn't depressed at all. He had no reason to kill himself."

"How do you know that?" Sol asked. "How well did you know him?"

"I only met him once, at the initial jail interview. But damn it Sol, I knew enough about him to know he wasn't about to commit suicide."

"Take it from an expert, Jimmy, if you want to find out about a guy, you have to talk to his friends, people he knew. Go to his home and see how he lived. Did he have a girlfriend? Did she just dump him? How about his finances? You have to look into all kinds of stuff. I hate to tell you but you didn't know him at all. A thorough investigation takes time and money."

"Okay, but maybe you could find out what really happened, use your contacts at the Sheriff's Department," I said. "You have juice with them."

"Why should you care what happened?"

"I don't, Sol, but shouldn't somebody care?"

He raised his drink and took a long pull. "Look my young friend, the guy was a *goniff,* a *momzer* even. That's why he had no friends. He was a loser and the State was going to pay you a few bucks to appear at his hearing just to make sure his rights weren't violated. That's all."

"Yeah, now he's dead. What does that say about his rights?"

"Let's enjoy lunch. No more talk of dead guys, suicides, jails."

I felt a little down. I figured Sol didn't think the matter was important enough, or maybe he figured Buck's death wasn't worthy of his time.

Janine appeared with our lunch. We ate, and I listened as Sol rambled on about the food and the wine. He even talked about how great the damn salt was.

It was almost two o'clock by the time Sol had drained the last of his wine and I'd finished my third coffee refill. And after I made a halfhearted effort to grab the check and failed, I slid out of the booth and stood.

"Got to get back to the office. But, hey, thanks for lunch, Sol," I said.

"Thought you wanted to know about the dead guy."

"Well, yeah."

"Then sit down."

I sat across from Sol again as he asked a passing waiter to bring him a phone. An instant later the waiter returned and plugged it into an outlet located close to the booth.

Sol picked up the receiver and dialed his office. "Joyce," he said to his secretary, "call Bob Grimes at the Sheriff's Department in East L.A. and patch him through to me. I'll hold."

"Grimes?" I asked.

"The undersheriff, good friend, he'll tell us what he knows, but it'll cost me a dinner at La Scala. Expensive, but they got the greatest steak tartar, and you wouldn't believe the..." Sol stopped talking, raised his hand, and then, "Hey, Bobbo, my boy. I need a little help." He paused again briefly and nodded. "Thanks, you too." Another short delay. "Whaddya know about a con named Buck Simpson? Supposedly committed suicide in your jail last night."

After a few grunts, a couple of 'I understands', and one 'You know me, Bob, won't happen,' Sol hung up.

"What did he say?" I asked.

Sol took a sip of water, then picked up a napkin and wiped his mouth.

"The official line is that he committed suicide. Hung himself," Sol said, then stopped and said no more, but of course, I knew there was more.

The seconds ticked off as we sat and stared at each other. We were playing one of Sol's little games. I figured in a minute he'd order dessert or something, just to keep the suspense up before he told me what had really happened.

***

Then, after a moment or two, Sol fiddled with the napkin on the table and said, "He died hanging from a sheet, all right. Yep, sure did, dangling from a sheet...right after he was dragged to the laundry room and strung up by a couple of his friends."

Chapter Three

Mabel sat at her desk on the phone working the accounts receivables when I returned from lunch. She held up her hand, gesturing for me to wait. After a few seconds, she hung up.

"You took a check from Kangaroo Kelley. What were you thinking?"

"Did it bounce?"

"Bounce? Damn it, they charged him with check kiting. His checks are bouncing all over town."

"Okay, Mabel, next time I'll ask for cash."

"Tell him he's got to cover the stiff, before we help him again."

"I already told you I'd get the cash."

She turned back to her desk, thumbing invoices, mumbling under her breath, "Gotta make some changes around here. I'm tired of making excuses to creditors..."

Moving into my office, I walked to the window and looked out. The window was fogged over, but I could still see the traffic rushing by on Lakewood Boulevard. The cars were like speedboats on a lake as they sliced through the water overflowing from the storm drains.

I didn't mind rainy days. The air smelled good and I felt good. In spite of Mabel's grousing about money, I was satisfied with the way things were going lately. I was thirty-six, hadn't had a drink in five or six years, and I didn't brood about my failed marriage as much as I used to. Sure, I was still a little lonely, and money was tight. So what else was new? But overall, I was making progress rebuilding my life and that's what counted.

A tiny rap on the door. Rita, my colleague, walked in carrying a thick file across her chest. I wondered, for a moment, why women held files like that. I'd noticed that phenomenon while waiting in the hallways outside of courtrooms. Women usually held files wrapped in their arms up against their chests, while men held them cupped in their hands down at their sides. I don't know why I noticed those little details about women. "Hey, boss, got a minute?"

"Sure, Rita."

She laid the file on my desk and pulled a chair up close. I sat and looked at her. Rita was petite and graceful, a beauty with a nearly perfect figure. Her dark hair fell softly to her shoulders, and when she spoke, her large brown eyes danced, her face lit up and she smiled. She always smiled, and I like that. "Jimmy, guess what? I got a new client. And you won't believe what kind of case it is. Do you want to guess?"

"No."

"A bank robbery. Can you believe it? A bank robbery."

"My God, how could you get a case like that?"

Her voice became solemn. "Hey, Jimmy, a class B felony. That's big time."

Bank robbery was a federal crime and the case would be prosecuted by the U.S. Justice Department. They had an army of bright, capable attorneys. Even experienced criminal defense lawyers shuddered when they thought of facing these guys. Class B meant that there was a gun involved.

"Rita, do you think you can handle a case like that?"

"Sure, why not? I'm damn good and my client,

Charlie Busher, is innocent, but I have to get busy. I only have a couple of weeks to prepare before I go to trial."

"Wait a minute. How'd you get the case?"

"You know Bob Bonnet, don't you?"

I nodded. "Sure." Yeah, I knew Bob Bonnet, one of the sleaziest lawyers in Downey.

"Well, I bumped into him at lunch yesterday, and he's too busy to handle the Busher case. So after a bit of persuasion on my part, he gave it to me." She winked. "It's signed and sealed and filed with the court."

"Good for you Rita," I said, but alarm bells rang in my mind.

It was obvious how Rita got the case. Bonnet had given it to her, sure, but he did it for one of two reasons. Either he was too busy scamming little old ladies out of their Social Security checks, or Busher didn't have money to pay the fee. So at the last minute he palmed off the bank robbery on Rita. But she had the case now and was stuck with it. I didn't tell her my feelings about Bonnet, or why I thought he gave her the case. Maybe I should have, but she was so excited and I didn't want to dampen her enthusiasm, or her smile.

"Let me tell you about Charlie Busher and the supposed bank holdup," Rita said, leaning across my desk. She proceeded to tell me the essence of the case and summed it up by saying, "My client's just a misunderstood guy, Jimmy."

"They all are, Rita."

"Jimmy, he's not a crook, for crying out loud," she said. "He's from Texas, Muleshoe Texas."

"So?"

"Different kind of laws in Texas." Rita smiled. "Charlie told me that in Muleshoe everyone solves their hassles at the point of a gun. He said, 'It's no big deal. We don't need no stinkin' laws.'"

"Oh, I'm sure that's true, but around here when you walk into a bank with a gun in your hand and demand money they call it bank robbery."

"I know," she said. "But I studied the file and found mitigating circumstances. After interviewing Charlie at the jail, I think I can get him off on reasonable doubt."

My heart went out to Rita. Although we'd worked together on cases in the past, this was her first felony that she acquired all by herself. I knew how much she wanted to win. But just because I thought she was being overly optimistic, I wouldn't stand in her way.

I shook my head and smiled. "What the hell. Go for it then, Rita."

She beamed a smile as bright as the summer sun. "I don't have much time, Jimmy, Bonnet kind of handed it to me at the last minute," she said. "But Charlie's going to walk. You wait and see."

"He's very lucky to have you on his side, defending his case."

"Thanks. That's a very kind thing to say, Jimmy." She stood and walked to the door with her file held up to her chest.

With her hand on the doorknob, she looked at me over her shoulder. "Good luck," I said. Then a second later added, "Don't forget, if you need my help..." But she'd already left the room.

Chapter Four

When I awoke the next morning, I showered, climbed into my clothes, and headed for Dolan's Donuts. I picked up the morning *L.A. Times* from the rack just inside the door and grabbed a couple of glazed and a cup of coffee from the counter man. The rain had picked up overnight and developed into a tropical storm. People, bundled in raincoats, crowded the donut shop. They shook out their umbrellas, the dripping water forming small pools on the floor. I couldn't find a place to sit, so I drove to the office. I figured I'd have my breakfast there and relax and read the paper while waiting for Mabel to arrive and officially open the office.

I scanned the paper for any mention of Buck Simpson to no avail, and set the paper aside. Leaning back in my chair, I mulled over yesterday's meeting at the jail. I knew I should forget Buck Simpson, but the image of him hanging there dying while his murderers probably watched and laughed, haunted my mind. I had to decide if I would I pursue the matter further. Maybe if I found out more about the case, or if the sadistic bastards who'd killed him were caught and explained their motives, then maybe I could let it go. Sol said if I wanted to find out about Simpson I'd have to talk to people who knew him, go to where he lived, do a complete and thorough investigation. I sold my time for money, and money was dear right now, as Mabel constantly reminded me. But perhaps I could donate a little of my free time digging into the matter. It wouldn't cost the firm anything if I only worked on it between paying cases. I reached into my briefcase and pulled out the Simpson file.

Buck Simpson worked alone, as muggers often did. While in custody, except for the ball team, he stayed by himself and had been a model prisoner. Because of his good behavior he was released on special parole to St. Dismas Halfway House in La Puente. The file didn't mention whether Buck had a job or not. But to be eligible for the rehabilitation program Buck had to be gainfully employed. It was the responsibility of the halfway house to find work for prisoners before they'd be eligible for conditional parole.

When I had a moment, I figured I'd take a quick run out to St. Dismas and see what I could find out about Buck.

Finishing the donuts and coffee I started to put the report back in my briefcase when I heard the front door creak open. I walked into the outer office. Mabel was hanging up her coat.

"Did you hear? Rita's got a new client," I said.

"The guy hasn't got any money," she said, with a scowl.

"Yeah, I guess that's why he was robbing a bank." She didn't seem amused by my wry comment.

We spent a minute or two making the usual morning small talk. After that I explained to Mabel that I was going to look into Simpson's death, but only in my free time, mind you. I waited a moment for her response, but none was forthcoming. So I plowed ahead, "Can you get me the address of the St. Dismas Halfway House? It's in La Puente."

"Hey, the guy's dead, and that means he's no longer a client. Why screw around with it?"

"Just get me the address, please."

While she dialed Information, the other line buzzed. I dashed into my office and put the receiver to my ear. "Law office, O'Brien."

It was Geoff, one of my regulars. He was good for three or four thousand a year from his traffic offenses.

"Listen, Geoff, I got the report from the DA's office—"

"Hey, it was only a couple of beers," he said.

In the past, when I tried to explain the severity of driving while drunk, he'd interrupted me and wouldn't accept the harsh reality of his predicament. Now he was doing it again.

"Geoff, what do you mean just a couple of beers? You blew a two-point eight—three, they declare you legally dead. Looks like a weekend in jail."

Mabel walked in and handed me the halfway house address written on a slip of pink paper: 16250 Temple Ave.

I put my hand over the mouthpiece. "It's Geoff, the DUI," I whispered while Geoff continued to yammer about constitutional law, criminal justice as he saw it—a drunk's point of view, no less—the breathalyzer wasn't calibrated, the cops didn't read him his rights, the DA's a prick, and so on. I couldn't disagree with one of his points.

"Tell him to bring cash," Mabel said. "He still owes money from his last bender."

I nodded. "Yeah, okay."

"But anyway, you have a call holding on line two. Says her name's Laura."

I glanced at the blinking button on the phone.

"Yeah, Geoff, I understand, but they're getting a little hardnosed, buddy. Look, I've got a call on the other line. Be here today at three o'clock with a grand plus the five hundred you still owe and I'll see what I can do."

I punched the button for line two. "This is O'Brien."

"Hello Jimmy, this is Laura Woods. Do y'all remember me?"

I instantly recognized her lyrical southern drawl. "Laura, how could I forget you?"

Laura was a stunner, a gorgeous blonde. She'd been a client in the past. About a year ago, she'd gotten herself in a jam and I'd taken care of it for her.

"I need help, Jimmy. I think I'm in big trouble, again," Laura squeaked. She sounded like she had been crying.

"What kind of trouble?"

"I'm scared and I don't wanna talk about it on the phone." Her voice shook and lowered to a scratchy whisper. "Please help me. Please. It's an emergency. Oh my God. I need you. Quick!"

"I'm out the door. Take a deep breath, Laura. I'll be there as fast as I can."

"Oh, Jimmy, hurry, please. I can't be alone."

* * *

The street address Laura had given me was located in Trousdale Estates, definitely not the low-rent district. There must've been a drastic change in her lifestyle to be able to afford to live in the most exclusive area of Beverly Hills. When I handled her case before, she worked at a small nail salon on Reseda Boulevard in Van Nuys, and to make ends meet, did a little prostitution on the side. When she'd been arrested on a morals charge, it'd scared the hell out of her. She promised me in no uncertain terms that if I got her off without jail time she'd change and live the straight life from that moment on. A friendly judge and I worked out a deal: no jail if she performed twenty hours of community service counseling at a home for wayward girls. "Who better," I said, "than someone who's been there."

Now she was in trouble again. I wondered if she had slipped back into her old ways. But then I asked myself, did part time hookers make enough to live in a mansion in Beverly Hills?

I pulled up to the gate protecting 100 Ridgeview Drive at around ten-thirty and announced my name into a speaker box. When the baroque iron barrier swung slowly open, I drove up the curved brick driveway, past the manicured grounds, and parked in front of an imposing Greco-Roman style mansion. "Sorry, Buck," I said under my breath, as I climbed out of my car, "have to take care of business first."

Laura stood motionless, framed in the doorway, with her arms wrapped tightly around her lush terrycloth robe. She was in her mid or late twenties, young and beautiful, and her hair was long and silky with natural blonde waves floating over her shoulders.

The robe didn't quite obscure her dynamite figure, and besides, I recalled her shape from our previous meeting in the nail salon. There she wore a mini-skirt number that exposed her finely sculpted legs that seemed to go on forever.

"Oh, Jimmy, thank God you're here. I didn't know what to do, who to call. I didn't know if you'd come."

Climbing the porch steps I looked up at her face, at her full lips and high cheekbones, and into her gorgeous blue eyes wet from tears. She was still as beautiful as I had remembered her, but now there was something different. It was her eyes. The sparkle was gone, replaced by the hint of a dull sadness.

Laura rushed over and threw her arms around me. I could feel the beat of her heart. "I'm in bad trouble," she whispered.

"What kind of trouble?" I asked.

"Come in and see for yourself."

We walked into the house. The marble entry gleamed, wet looking, in the light shining down from a branched crystal chandelier. A curved staircase at the end of the entry soared to the upper floors. To my right, an arch opened into a formal living room. On my left was a pair of ornately carved doors, about ten feet high. Laura unlocked them and we moved into a cold dark room.

"The study," Laura choked.

Shadows filled the area and, as my eyes became accustomed to the dark, I could see a table, two chairs, and a sofa. I stepped around Laura and flipped on the light switch. My glance swept past the deep luster of the paneled walls and focused on the massive antique desk at the far end of the room. I turned back to Laura. She looked at me, terror in her eyes, and fled the room.

I faced the desk again and stared at the dead man slumped over it.

Chapter Five

Walking carefully across the room, I moved closer to the body. The head was turned sideways, resting in a pool of dark, coagulated blood. A black-edged hole appeared above and slightly behind his left ear, where the man's gray hair was cut short. I saw powder burns and gunshot residue on his scalp. The wound came from a shot fired at close range.

I leaned closer. The small muscles of his face and neck were beginning to stiffen, the first signs of *rigor mortis*. There was no sense taking his pulse or calling the paramedics. The guy had been dead for hours.

Stepping back, I quickly glanced around and spotted a .25 caliber semi-automatic pocket pistol lying on the carpet next to the desk. A small gun without much bang, which would explain why, more than likely, nobody heard the shot. With the thick walls in this mansion you wouldn't be able to hear the gunshot in the next room, much less next door.

Turning toward the antique credenza behind the body, I saw an electric typewriter with a note sticking out of it. I twisted my neck and read it without touching anything.

To my wife:
I can't possibly go on. This is the end. I'm sorry.
Arnie

Short and to the point, like a business memo. I felt relieved. Laura wasn't the shooter, and I wasn't there to defend a murder charge.

Pivoting to leave, I wondered why Laura hadn't called the police. I squinted at my watch. Two hours had gone by since she phoned my office. A small voice in my mind asked, could this possibly be a setup, another murder made to look like a suicide? I took another quick glance around the room: no signs of foul play. But what about Laura—could she have staged this?

Perhaps she just wanted to wait for me to arrive before involving the authorities. Why? If this is a suicide, not murder, why wait for a lawyer?

I'd noticed that Laura wore a wedding ring set. You'd have to be blind not to see the huge diamond glittering with brilliant points of light every time she moved her hand. Being married, she'd need a probate attorney not a criminal defense lawyer; that is if the dead guy at the desk were indeed her husband and he had killed himself.

The police needed to be called, but I wouldn't touch the phone or anything in the study. I'd make the call from somewhere else in the house. I walked across the hall, passed under the arch, and entered the living room.

Laura, sat on a white sectional sofa, leaning forward slightly with her knees pressed tightly together. I sat next to her. "I have to call the police," I said quietly.

She looked up at me, her eyes moist. "I'm scared," she said.

Laura laid her head on my chest, her body trembling. I put my arms around her and we sat in silence. A faint waft of her expensive perfume enveloped me and I held her a moment longer.

"Laura, I've got to make the call."

She pointed to a telephone on an end table. I

asked the operator to dial the Beverly Hills Police Department.

"I want to report a suicide," I said to the female voice that answered.

The phone line clicked and in an instant a deep male voice said, "Detectives. This is Sergeant Nick Pegis."

"My name is O'Brien. I'm a lawyer calling from 100 Ridgeview Drive. There's been a suicide here. A man shot himself. He's dead."

"You sure the guy's dead?"

"I used to be a cop. He's dead all right. *Rigor* has started to set in."

"A patrol car is on the way and I'm leaving now. I'll be there in a few minutes. Don't touch anything—and don't leave the scene."

I returned to Laura. She had her head down with her eyes focused on the white carpet. "We only have a few minutes before they arrive," I said. "Do you want me to represent you in this matter? Is that why you called me?"

She looked up at me. "Yes, you gotta help me. Please."

The police siren was close and getting closer.

"Of course I'll help you. Now listen..." I hurriedly gave her my usual spiel. "They'll want to question you. It's best if we cooperate, but I don't want you to answer unless I say it's okay, understand?"

"I'll do as I'm told."

I tilted my head toward the study. "That's your husband?"

"Was," she stammered.

"I'm very sorry, Laura."

Tears started to flow. "I don't know why he did this."

I remained silent for a few moments, then, "You know what, I don't even know your married name."

"Rosenthal," she replied and closed her eyes.

I walked to the front door and opened it. A black-and-white rushed up the driveway, swerved to miss my Corvette, and slammed to a stop in front of the house. The siren's howl reached a crescendo then died as two uniformed cops jumped out and stormed up the steps.

"Are you the person who called it in?" one of the officers asked.

"I'm Jimmy O'Brien. I phoned the station."

"Where's the body?"

"Follow me."

After escorting the cops to the death scene in the study, I returned to the living room and sat next to Laura again. "These guys are just uniforms. They're going to secure the area, but the detectives will be here shortly. They'll be the ones who'll question you."

She shook her head. "Jimmy, do I have to talk to them now?"

"No, you don't. I can stop them, but we want to cooperate. You have nothing to hide. It's a suicide."

Pausing, I waited for her reaction, a tic of her eye, a nervous twitch, something indicating that she knew more than she'd said. None was forthcoming. I continued: "I'll be right here and I *will* stop the questioning if I don't like the way it's going."

"My body's weak and I need peace and quiet. I can't stay here. Arnie's body and all. I'm dizzy. I feel like throwing up. I gotta get outta here, get a room somewheres."

Two men wearing gray slacks, navy blazers, and white dress shirts approached us and flashed their badges. Their outfits looked like uniforms for Guy Lombardo's band except for the fact that they wore different colored ties.

The detective with the light blue knit tie said, "I'm Sergeant Pegis." He pointed to the other cop. "That's Officer Barnes, my partner."

Barnes didn't say anything. He just marveled at the opulence in the room, focusing on the modern paintings hanging on the walls.

Impervious to the luxury surrounding him, Pegis started in. "You must be O'Brien, the lawyer."

I stood. "You got it."

He wiggled his fingers in a gimme manner. "Sir, I need to see I.D."

While I was digging out my credentials, Pegis said to Laura, "Ma'am, you live here?"

She nodded and meekly said, "Yes." Laura then told the detective that the deceased was her husband and his name was Arnie Rosenthal. The cop offered his condolences in a rote manner.

I gave him my credentials. He glanced at my bar card and driver's license and handed them back.

"Okay, wait here. I'm going to check the scene. I'll be back in shortly."

"We're not going anywhere."

The sergeant turned to his partner. "C'mon Barnes, let's go."

The cops headed for the other room, but Pegis stopped and turned back. He shouted to the uniformed policeman guarding the entrance to the study. "Hey,

Ryan, stay with these folks."

"Look, Sergeant," I said, "we don't need a babysitter. I'd like to talk with my client in private."

"Sorry, Mr. O'Brien, but it's routine." He hurried away.

For the next couple of hours, the mansion crawled with cops and a full crime scene squad darted in and out. Laura and I didn't have a chance for a private conversation about the legal process regarding her husband's death. Instead I tried to get her mind off the tragic events surrounding her by making inane small talk. There would be time for a serious discussion later.

"Nice paintings," I said, looking at the striking artwork covering the walls.

Laura wiped the tears from her eyes. "Arnie said they were Pop Art, something like that," she sniffled. "I wouldn't know Pop Art from Popeye. Although I kinda like that one over there."

I nodded as she pointed to a portrait of Marilyn Monroe painted by Andy Warhol. "But it would be better," she added, "if she didn't have such a lavender face."

"Yeah, I see what you mean," I said.

Not long after the medical examiner arrived, Sergeant Pegis stuck his head in the living room and gestured for me to join him in the hall.

"Where were you between twelve and four this morning?" he asked.

"Home in bed. Where else?"

"Yeah, guess so." He hesitated for a beat or two, then in a dry mechanical tone asked, "With who?"

"Alone."

"A guy like you. C'mon, O'Brien, I bet you're a

magnet for women."

"Hey, Pegis, what are you getting at?"

"That's your alibi? Home alone? Can you prove it?"

"What is this?" I asked.

He cranked his head toward the living room. "What about the blonde? You two an item?"

"You're beginning to piss me off, Pegis."

"You were a cop; you should have seen it," he said.

"Seen what?"

"You had ten years on the job; you should have put two and two together."

"What's going on?"

"When you called it in, you said the victim shot himself."

"That's right."

He pointed to the study. "Wrong, mister. That guy was murdered."

Chapter Six

Before I could respond, Sergeant Pegis motioned me back into the living room. Laura had left, and the uniformed officer sat thumbing through one of the coffee-table books.

"Where'd she go?" Pegis asked the guard.

The uniformed cop stood. "She went to her room, said she wanted to pack some bags."

"Well, go stand outside of her door, for *chrissakes*."

"Which room? There's a lot of rooms."

"Do you know where her bedroom is, O'Brien?"

"Of course not."

He waited a moment, cocking an eyebrow at me before turning to the uniform. "Knock on the upstairs doors until you find it."

The officer fled and the sergeant sat in one of the matching Chippendale chairs next to an old grandfather clock. He sat in a stern manner, hands placed firmly on his knees.

"Sit down. We have to talk," he said.

"You're saying Rosenthal didn't kill himself?"

"There's no doubt in my mind that he was murdered, shot at close range. And you, an ex-cop, tried to tell us it was a suicide. I wonder why?"

"Look, Sergeant, I worked the streets as a beat cop, not a detective. And anyway I didn't do a thorough investigation with crime scene techs all over the place like you just did. Now suppose you tell me why you think the guy was murdered."

"The killer botched it. Too many details don't fit."

"Like what?"

"Well, for one thing the amount of gunshot residue surrounding the site of the entry wound indicates that the weapon was held too far from his head to be a suicide."

"According to your experts, how far was the gun held away from his head?"

"Between a foot and eighteen inches. People usually shoot themselves with the gun held right up against their temple, forehead, or in their mouth. Don't want to take any chances on missing."

"That's hardly proof. What about gunshot residue on the dead man's hand, the one that held the gun?"

"We've bagged his hands. The lab boys will confirm that they're clean and that's all the proof we'll need."

"So as of this moment you can't say with absolute certainty that the cause of death was nothing more than it appears to be—a suicide."

"There's more evidence but I'm keeping the rest of it to myself."

Was he bluffing? Did he really have evidence that suggested murder? Or was he baiting me, trying to get me to say something that maybe I knew about the homicide but was keeping to myself? I didn't reply. I waited for him to continue.

"Yeah, she botched it all right," he said.

My antenna beeped red alert. I knew what his implication meant. "What do you mean, *she*? You have evidence that the killer was a woman?"

"C'mon, O'Brien, you know ninety percent of the time, the loving wife—"

"Hold it, Pegis." I stood. "Are you saying that Rosenthal was murdered and she's a suspect?"

He also stood. "That's right. What about it?"

"I'll tell you right now," I said. "Even if it was a murder, you don't have a damn bit of evidence that points to her. We both know that."

"Look, O'Brien, let's say I give you the benefit of the doubt, that means it could go either way. If the guy offed himself then that's how it will go down. But if he didn't and she pulled the trigger, or had help, we'll find that out too. And I think that's what this is all about—murder. I've seen it all too many times, especially in this town with all these men of substance, all these rich horny bastards out looking." The detective stiffened. "Oh, yeah, these women are like the dew on the morning meadow. They smell sweet and pure, but their perfume is cyanide. Pity the men who fall."

He gave a quick jerk of his head and ran his fingers through his hair. Obviously this wasn't his first case of a rich older husband dying at the hands of a young beautiful wife. In Beverly Hills there were plenty of sad stories about women who'd married for money. Not each ended in murder, though a few did. But he was a professional and had probably investigated many marital homicides. Truth be told, it had to be more than another dead husband with an attractive wife that had sparked his fierce reaction. This was personal. Perhaps something from his own past. I felt a slight flush of anger at his remarks, but in these circumstances, I knew it was better to keep my mouth shut about his misogynic attitude.

"She's not some bimbo just out for the money. She really loved the guy." I said, not knowing whether she loved him or not. But I had to say something.

He took a breath and said, "Okay, now how about you and the widow lady coming to headquarters for a little sit down?"

"No way. Mrs. Rosenthal isn't talking to anyone until I've seen the police report."

"You'll get a copy of the police report *after* I've arrested her. The DA will hand it over. But you're not getting it until then and you're not getting it from me."

Pegis stood motionless next to the antique chair and stared at me. I stared back.

"I think you're involved," he murmured. "I think you two cooked this up, bumped off the old guy."

I inched closer to Pegis. "Do I laugh now, or wait until you put on the clown suit?"

"All that money and a dame like her—hard to turn down."

"Hey, Pegis," I said. "Mrs. Rosenthal isn't a *dame*; she's a lady, a respected member of the community. How about giving the grieving widow the respect she deserves?"

I didn't tell him that when I first met Laura she was a part-time hooker, arrested and charged with prostitution. Didn't think it would help the situation. Being her lawyer I figured I'd keep that tidbit to myself.

"Now suppose you check me out," I added. "Call Lieutenant Hodges, South Gate P.D."

"I already ran you through the system. Oh yeah, you're clean as far as the records show, but I think you're dirty." He leaned into me. "I think you're sleeping with the lady, and I'm going to prove it."

"Take your best shot, buddy," I said.

His remark didn't trouble me. I could easily establish that I wasn't involved with her in any way other than professionally. His comment was simply a cop trick—make an absurd charge and maybe the person will say something incriminating out of anger or shock.

Laura stuck her head around the arch and caught my eye. I turned away from Pegis and walked into the hallway. She stood between two brand-new, expensive looking suitcases. Her hair was swept back, pulled tight, and tied with a large red bow. She had on slim fitting jeans, a white blouse fastened at the collar, and a full-length soft leather coat. The uniformed cop who was supposed to be guarding her stood off to the side and shrugged.

"Please, Jimmy, I gotta get outta here before I go crazy." Laura put her hands to her ears and shook her head vigorously as she burst out crying. "I can't stand it anymore. I can't stand being in this place another minute! Take me away from here, Jimmy."

I grabbed her shoulders, and turned her until she faced me. "Look at me Laura, please." I held her tight. "Hold it together. As hard as it is, hold it together."

Her body went limp and she took several deep breaths.

"Are you going to be okay?" I asked.

"I don't wanna be here with Arnie's body in the other room, cops all over the place. Take me to a hotel. I've gotta get away from all this."

Investigators wandered in carrying various implements related to their work. Strident calls on police radios squawked from squad cars parked outside and echoed throughout the house. Cops scurried to and fro stringing yellow crime scene tape around the grounds. Bright camera flashes and muffled talk of death, murder, bullet fragments, and words like *livor mortis* or *blood lividity* were being bandied about. This would be enough to make any person distressed, and it could only be worse if the police were discussing your dead spouse.

Pegis leaned against the arch. "You two going someplace?" he asked.

I let go of Laura and now she stood in a daze, frozen like a statue with her arms straight down at her sides.

"Yeah, my client is in a state of shock. She needs rest, and she obviously can't get it here."

"I have a right to question her—material witness," he said in a stilted voice.

"Won't work, Pegis. You already told me that she's a suspect. That means she's not required to talk to the police. And if you want to hold her, you'll have to arrest her."

He looked at me as if I had just shot his dog. "O'Brien, you know I don't have enough to haul her in. But I'll tell you this: if I find even the slightest bit of incriminating evidence, she'll be in cuffs so fast she won't know what hit her."

I wasn't being reckless by challenging Pegis to arrest her. I knew that the DA would not bring a murder charge against Laura without hard facts—suspicions and personal feelings don't count for squat. And by declaring up front that Laura was a suspect, he avoided being accused of circumventing her rights under Miranda. But that meant he couldn't interrogate her against her will. We would cooperate, but first I wanted to have a chance to talk to her at length before I let the police tear into her. However, there was a flipside to my stalling tactic. She might have information that would help the police find the real killer. With criminal investigations, and especially murder cases, the trail grows colder as time goes on. The first forty-eight hours were crucial. Still, there was no chance that I'd let the police question Laura in her present emotional state.

"Sergeant, look, we want to cooperate," I said, toning down my rhetoric. "After she has rested up, say, tomorrow morning around ten-thirty, we'll drop by headquarters and she'll give a statement for the record."

Pegis knew that he had no real choice in the matter. Nevertheless, he wanted to know where she would be staying. After a moment or two of discussion with Laura, I told him the Bel-Air Hotel. It was close and she would be available when needed, but I warned him emphatically that under no circumstances would he be allowed to talk to my client without me being present.

I grabbed her luggage and loaded the bags into my Corvette. She squeezed into the passenger seat, a tight fit with the suitcases. Starting the car, I nodded at Pegis. He stood there on the front porch staring at me with his hands in his pockets.

"Hey, Pegis," I yelled. "I'll save you the trouble. If you're going to tail us, after I drop the lady at the hotel I'm heading to my apartment in Downey and tonight I'll be snug in bed, *alone*."

He flipped me the bird.

"Alone, Jimmy?" she asked.

"Alone," I answered.

As we pulled away, I knew this wasn't over by a long shot and figured that Laura could find herself in deep trouble.

"You've been to the Bel-Air before?" I asked.

She turned away from the window and looked at me, eyes welling up again. "Oh yes, with Arnie many times. We had dinner there several times a week. And we stayed at the hotel while Arnie had the house redone. He was nice like that. He wanted to make the house special for me."

A few seconds of silence passed, than I said, "Laura, you have to tell me everything you know about what happened last night."

She turned back and stared out the passenger window again. "I don't want to think about it right now."

"Laura, we have to talk—"

"We'll talk at the hotel, okay? My stomach's queasy. Maybe we can have a bite to eat, okay?"

I drove slowly down the twisting, slippery Coldwater Canyon Drive. With only the sibilant sound of tires rolling on wet pavement and the rhythmic clacking of wipers, I let my thoughts wander. By the time I turned right on Sunset Blvd. my mind was playing a numerical odds game.

First, Buck Simpson, and now the possibility of another murder made to look like a suicide. What was the likelihood of that? I had no reason to think it was anything other than a coincidence, but the improbability of me being involved with two similar crimes in the same day rattled me just the same.

Chapter Seven

The storm had tapered off by the time we drove through the scrolled, wrought iron gates and onto the grounds of the Hotel Bel-Air. We left the car with the valet and Laura and I walked over the stone bridge spanning a small lake nestled amid the densely landscaped grounds. A flock of elegant swans drifted silently under the bridge. A pen, with her cygnets following in a row, stretched her long neck and hissed at me.

"The Bel-Air has a certain *je ne sais quoi*, don't you think?" Laura said.

"What does that mean?" I asked.

"I dunno. Arnie's son said that when we came here for his birthday a few months ago."

"Your husband has a son?"

"Yes. His name is Richie."

"Where is he now?"

"He lives back east. I called him from the house and he's catching the next flight to LAX, should be in late tonight. He'll be handling the arrangements," she said. "When do you think the coroner will release Arnie's body?"

"I'm not sure, Laura. Could take some time. They might hold the body if they think it has any evidentiary value."

"Meaning?" she asked.

"It could take a while."

We continued along the brick path that led to the lobby located in the pink, mission-style main building. At the check-in counter she flipped out her gold American Express card and requested the Chalon Suite.

"Mrs. Rosenthal, as always, it's a pleasure to serve you," said the tall, distinguished clerk, obsequious in his impeccable business suit. The clerk gave me a wry look over the rim of his spectacles then turned back to Laura. "Will Mr. Rosenthal be joining us later?"

"Well," I said, "Mr. Rosenthal is dead. So, I guess the answer is no."

The clerk didn't look up from his paperwork. "Of course. Perhaps next time then."

He handed Laura her key, then rang for the bell captain to handle her luggage. Laura and I agreed to meet back in the hotel restaurant in twenty minutes. She wanted to freshen up and I needed to call my office.

At the concierge desk, I asked the elegant lady in attendance to direct me to a payphone. She pointed to a desk phone across the lobby, resting on an ornate credenza flanked by a brown leather armchair. I explained I had to make a toll call across town to Downey. She just smiled and said that would be fine.

I walked to the phone and dialed my office. "Mabel, I won't be back today before we close. Cancel all my appointments."

"Fine time to tell me now. You should've called earlier."

"Mabel, please."

"That drunken bum, Geoff, your DUI client came by. He was upset when you weren't here. He left and guess what—he did *not* leave any damn money."

"Call the bar at the Regency and ask him to reschedule his appointment," I said.

"Okay. But don't hang up. Rita wants to talk to you. I'll get her." While on hold I sat back and sank into the soft leather chair. I checked my watch—3:14. I hadn't had lunch, only those donuts for breakfast, and I was starved. I hoped Laura wouldn't keep me waiting at the restaurant.

"Hey, boss," Rita said when she came on the line.

"Hi Rita. What's up?"

"Mabel's all over me about getting money from Charlie Busher."

"Yeah, I know Rita, she can be tough. But cash is getting tight. We've been there before and it'll work out. But it would help if you get a little something from your client."

"Charlie has money, but it's all tied up at that stupid bank. He inherited twenty-five thousand and bought a certificate of deposit with it. You know, can't get your money out without a thirty-day notice."

"He put his inheritance in the same bank that he robbed?" I asked. That's incredible, I thought. The guy's not only a crook; he's a half-wit, as well.

"Yes, same bank. But then the next day he wanted to buy a used car for his girlfriend. So he went to the bank to withdraw fifteen hundred dollars from his account. They told him to come back in thirty days. He didn't wait, he came back later with a gun and demanded the fifteen hundred. The teller gave him all the money in her drawer. But listen to this, he gave the teller back everything over the fifteen hundred that she'd handed him."

The guy's worse that a half-wit, maybe a quarter-wit. "Is that your position, Rita, a simple withdrawal?" I sighed.

"Well, the bank and the FBI don't see it that way."

"They're funny about things like that."

"I thought about what you told me, about putting out a feeler. But the U.S. attorneys won't make a deal. I'm going to have to convince a jury that Charlie's not a bank robber."

"I'm sure you'll do fine," I said, but inside I knew Rita was facing an impossible battle. United States attorneys were the brightest of the bright, appointed by the president, with a great deal of trial experience under their belts. And with the Busher case, they had eyewitnesses and the gun. Not to mention the fact that they had an unlimited budget.

"Boss, I've got an idea. And if it works I think I can get some money for us. It will also get Charlie off the hook."

"Yeah, what's your idea?"

"I don't want to say anything until my plan works. But can you get Mabel off my case for a few days?"

"I guess so, Rita. I'll talk to her when I get back."

I hung up and wandered into the hotel restaurant. The waiter immediately escorted me to a table overlooking the gardens. Crystal glassware, bone china, and about a ton of silver were placed on the bright white linen that draped the tables. Every table was resplendent with an elaborate arrangement of fresh-cut flowers in the center. Each flower arrangement probably cost more than my total food expense for the week.

I stood and pulled out a chair for Laura when she arrived.

A suggestion of a smile brightened her lovely

face. "My, aren't y'all a gentleman," she drawled.

A waiter dressed in formal attire handed us each a small menu. Although I was starved, I set the menu aside. "Laura, I'm afraid I'll have to lay it on the line. The police figure your husband's death was murder, not suicide. Right now you're their only suspect."

Laura turned her head and signaled the waiter, then turned back to me. "I hope it's okay to order before this discussion gets too heavy?"

The waiter rushed over. Laura asked for some kind of fancy tea with a name I couldn't pronounce and cucumber finger sandwiches to go with her beverage. I picked up the menu and glanced at it. I turned it over once or twice to be sure. Was someone putting me on? Finger sandwiches and several exotic brands of hot tea. Eighteen bucks.

"And you, sir?" the waiter asked, poised with pencil and pad at the ready.

I held up the menu. "This is it? Hot tea and little sandwiches?"

"Afternoon tea, sir, three to five."

"No steak?"

"Afraid not."

"Coffee?"

"No."

"Bring me a glass of water."

"Perrier?"

"Excuse me?"

"What kind of water?"

"Wet."

"Excellent choice," he said, and scurried away.

Chapter Eight

The waiter appeared with our order. He set a silver tea service on the table, filled Laura's cup, and placed the plate of finger sandwiches in front of her. He also set my glass of iced bubbly water on the table with the partially filled bottle next to it. Then he silently slipped away. Laura fussed with her tea, ignoring the small sandwiches fanned out on the plate.

Other than her teary-eyed demeanor at the mansion before the police had arrived and her outburst before we left for the hotel, Laura had not shown any signs of real emotion, or even a reaction to the fact that she was the prime suspect.

"I didn't do it, Jimmy," she said while rummaging through her purse and finding what she was searching for, an opened pack of Virginia Slims.

"I didn't ask if you did."

She put a cigarette in her mouth and glanced up at me. "But, Jimmy, you gotta know that I'm no murderer. I'd never do anything like that." The waiter rushed over and flicked a lighter under the cigarette.

"How long were you married?"

She held the cigarette straight out in front of her face, the smoke rising and swirling at the tip of her fingers.

"Six months." She took a quick puff and coughed lightly after exhaling.

I remained silent and let her continue.

"I met Arnie at a meat packer's convention in San Francisco. I guess you could call it love at first sight. . ." Her voice trailed off and she pushed the small sandwich wedges around the plate. "At first sight for *him* anyway."

"You didn't love him?"

A look of defiance flashed in her eyes. "I married him for his money." She focused on me, searching for a sign of disapproval.

I didn't give her one.

Laura stubbed out the cigarette repeatedly in a crystal ashtray. "Jimmy, I've done a lot of crazy things in my life that I'm ashamed of, but with Arnie I thought I could make a new start. No one had ever cared about me before. I was a left over kid. Never knew my dad, and my mother left me with whoever when she went on her binges. I've been on my own since I was fourteen. It felt good to have someone treat me special. Arnie knew about my past and he didn't care. He was a nice guy, but I didn't love him. Not at first, anyway."

She went on to explain that her husband had owned a large meat company in Vernon: Farmer Fred's Wieners. He was the local hot dog king. I knew of the company; everybody who lived in Los Angeles did. If you weren't sealed in a vacuum, you would have heard of Farmer Fred and his wieners. The company advertised heavily on TV. Laura told me that she was working as an escort at the convention in San Francisco and had gone out on a date with an employee of Arnie's. They were having dinner at the Blue Fox Restaurant when Arnie joined them at the table.

"And the rest, as they say, is history." Laura took a sip of tea and glanced at me over the rim of her cup. There was a glint in her deep blue eyes. "We were married three days later."

With that beautiful face, her amazing figure, and that marvelous smile, I had no problem believing that

Arnie would fall for her so hard and so fast.

"Why did you call me?" I asked. "There must be a hundred topnotch lawyers within a few miles of your home."

"I didn't know who else to call. Arnie had an attorney, but he was just his business lawyer. He wouldn't know what to do about this."

"You called me before the police arrived. Before they determined it was murder, not suicide."

"Oh, I knew he was murdered."

"Really? How'd you know?"

"We went to a party the night before and got home about one. I went up to the bedroom. Arnie said he had a few things to attend to and he'd be up in a while. I fell asleep, and when I awoke the next morning around 7:30, Arnie hadn't been to bed. I found him in the study just as you saw him." Laura stopped talking. She frowned and looked away.

"You didn't think it was suicide? Even with the note and everything?"

She looked back at me, shaking her head. "Of course not, Jimmy. Arnie wouldn't kill himself. *My God*, he loved life. Not only that, he didn't type that phony suicide note. Why, he couldn't type a word. The typewriter was for his personal secretary. She comes in once a week to pay the bills, type his letters, that sort of thing."

"Was he depressed at all?"

"Just the opposite. He was excited about a new breakthrough at his business. I'll admit he was in some financial trouble, but he seemed to have it under control."

"You found the body at 7:30, but you didn't

call me until after 8:30."

"You don't believe me, Jimmy?" she asked.

"Laura, the cops are going to ask a lot of questions and I have to have answers. I'll need to be prepared when we talk to them tomorrow."

"I don't know what I can tell you. I was sleepin' and heard nothing."

She glanced around the restaurant, spotted the waiter, and nodded slightly. She turned back to me. "Would'ya please take me to my suite? I need to rest."

She signed the check and we left the restaurant and walked along a picturesque pathway shaded by a row of mature sycamore trees. Laura's suite was snuggled among the lavish foliage and trickling fountains of the Bel-Air's garden setting.

We arrived at her suite and she unlocked the door. "Do you wanna to come in?" she asked.

I checked the time: almost five, rush hour traffic. The Santa Ana Freeway would be jammed. I figured I may as well stay a while longer. Besides, I had a few more questions that needed answers.

"We still have a few things to go over," I said and followed Laura into the room.

Laura sat in one of the overstuffed chairs resting in the corner next to a fireplace. I sat in an armchair facing her. The fireplace was set with a gentle wood-burning fire that cast the room in a warm glow. The designer had spared no expense. I didn't know much about furniture designs or styles, but I knew you couldn't buy this kind of stuff at Sears.

"Do you have someone special waiting for you at home?" she asked.

"Not really."

"Everybody should have someone, Jimmy. You were alone when I met you before."

"Yeah, Laura, but I'm working on it."

"Why don't you order a couple of steak sandwiches from room service, while I change?"

Hungry as I was, I didn't have to be asked twice. I picked up the phone sitting on an antique desk and ordered. Laura wanted a split of cabernet with her sandwich, and it was coffee for me. The clerk said the meal would arrive within twenty minutes.

Laura left for the bedroom to change, and I walked to the French doors on the other side of the living room. A faint hint of jasmine drifted in the gentle breeze as I wandered out onto an intimate terrace. While sitting at a round patio table and listening to the calming sound of a Jacuzzi bubbling at the far end of the tiled courtyard, I thought about what Laura had said, *someone waiting at home.*

I recalled the happy times, the times when I *did* have someone waiting for me at home. I thought about the first few years of my marriage, before the job on the force wore me down, before the drinking began, and before Barbara finally gave up on me. Why did I let her go? Why didn't I fight for her?

"It's wonderful out here. Let's eat on the patio."

Laura's voice caught me off guard. I jumped with a start.

"I didn't mean to startle you," she said, taking a chair next to me at the table.

She had on a pink robe with the hotel's logo embroidered on it. The loosely cinched terrycloth fell away, exposing a lovely thigh when she sat and crossed her legs.

"Laura, we have to talk about the case."

"What is there to talk about? I told you everything I know. I was asleep when whoever it was came in and shot him. I can't tell you more than I know, which is nothing."

"You didn't hear the shot?"

"No! I told you a thousand times, no."

The door chime sounded. I went to answer it. A waiter entered pushing a cart. Laura and I dined in the courtyard, as she had suggested. The steaks were superb, tender, and cooked to perfection. The waiter adjusted the music system before he left. The soft Brazilian sound of Stan Getz and Astrud Gilberto's smooth rendition of "Quiet Nights of Quiet Stars" floated in the air.

I reached across the table, refilled Laura's wine glass, poured myself another cup of coffee, and said, "Laura, back to the case."

"I don't know anything. I swear."

"Did he have enemies?"

"He must've."

"Who?"

"For God's sake, Jimmy, the guy who shot him. That's who."

"Please, Laura, think back. Do you know of anyone who'd want to see him dead? Or any reason why?"

"I really didn't know him that well. I mean, I knew him on a personal basis, but I didn't know anything about his business. I hadn't met many of his friends, except a few of his poker buddies, and his grouchy lawyer, once or twice. But that's about it."

"What about his secretary? You said she came

by to pay his bills. Maybe she was a jealous of you and—"

Shaking her head, she chuckled. "Mrs. Schroder? My God, she's seventy-eight years old, worked for Arnie forever."

"The cops will check; did you and Arnie ever have a fight, an argument, in public?"

"We never had an argument, period!"

"Can you think of anything that might shed some light on what had happened?"

"Oh *Lord*, Jimmy, I don't know anything. How many times do I have to tell ya that? Besides, I know you'll handle the police and their questions."

She rose from the table, picked up her glass, and sauntered toward the outdoor spa.

My eyes followed her movement. From her languid demeanor it was obvious that there would be no more discussion of her husband's murder, not tonight anyway.

"I'll pick you up at 10:15 tomorrow morning," I said, turning to leave.

Halfway across the patio, I stopped and glanced back at Laura. She dropped her robe and quietly slipped into the foaming warmth of the hot tub and began to weep.

Two minutes later, as I handed the valet the parking stub, I thought, such a beautiful woman, and so all alone.

Chapter Nine

Being on time for a change, I picked up Laura at 10:15 the next morning at the Bel-Air. She wore a conservative black business suit and smiled at the parking valet as she climbed into the car. She could have been any young professional instead of a murder suspect on her way to the police station to be grilled by detectives.

Overnight her mood had improved immensely. When I reiterated the ground rules regarding today's interrogation—never answer a question until I give my approval, and so on—she laughed. "Oh, Jimmy, I've been arrested before, as you well know. I'll be a good little girl." She crossed her heart. "I promise."

"Are you holding up okay?" I asked.

"I loved Arnie and I'm terrified about his death. I pray this will be over soon."

I didn't tell her what I thought about it being over soon. I figured there was a high probability that Laura would be arrested at any moment. She gave me nothing that would help with her defense and I feared she would appear cold to the prosecutors. But maybe what she told me was true. Maybe she simply went to bed and heard nothing, and maybe, as she said, she knew nothing about Arnie's outside world. It could be possible for Laura not to know what her husband was involved in, who his friends and associates were, and what he did all day. After all, they were only married six months. Then I thought about my failed marriage and all the things Barbara never knew about me. At least, I didn't think she knew.

"Anything else," I said to Laura, "that you want

to tell me before we're grilled by the cops?"

She looked at me, sighed, and turned away.

***

Pegis met us in the lobby of the old Spanish Renaissance city hall and escorted us to the antiquated police department. We walked through the detective squad room and arrived at a door with the word INTERROGATION stenciled in block letters on its frosted glass window. The place reminded me of the police stations shown in crime movies of the 1940s, films set in the world of dark shadows and loose morals where cops sweated the bad guys, rubber hoses flailing.

I almost expected to find Humphrey Bogart, trench coat and all, standing there when we entered. Instead, I saw a plain conference table with four hardback chairs drawn up to it resting in the center of an otherwise empty room. The room had a mirror running along one wall, a two-way mirror, obviously.

Laura and I sat next to each other and Sergeant Pegis straddled a chair across from us. He removed a mini-tape recorder from his outside jacket pocket, set it on the table, and pushed the start button.

I stood. "Let's go, Mrs. Rosenthal. Interview's over." I was bluffing, of course. It really didn't matter if the meeting was recorded or not. Anything Laura said could be used against her anyway, and I wouldn't let her say anything incriminating. But I wanted Pegis to know, right from the start, just who was in charge of the interview.

Laura stood, nodded at Pegis, and smiled politely. She hooked her arm in mine. We turned to leave.

"Hold it. What's the matter?" Pegis yelled at our backs.

I turned to him, still straddling the chair. "Turn it off, Pegis, and the other recorder that you have hidden, or we walk."

Pegis's eyes bored into me. "O'Brien, I've probably got enough to book her right now."

Laura looked at me. Her smile vanished like a vapor.

"Goodbye, Pegis."

"Okay, wait. I'll turn it off, but anything she says—"

"Yeah I know. But one more thing, if this gets out of hand and you try to twist her words I'll shut down this interview as fast as a Bo Diddley riff."

"Yeah, sure. Now, suppose we get down to business."

The cop turned off the recorder and put it back into his pocket. I nodded to Laura and we returned to the table. I pulled out the chair for her when she sat.

"I'll get to the point," Sergeant Pegis said, addressing his remarks to Laura. "You're our prime suspect."

"Of course, detective, I know that. The wife is always the suspect at first—"

I interrupted her. "Mrs. Rosenthal, please don't answer, until I say it's okay."

"You're going to play it that way?" Pegis asked.

"Only way to play it."

He got up and paced the small room. "O'Brien, I know you're involved." He was standing behind Laura giving me his hard-nosed cop look. "Don't think that I'm through with you. I haven't even started."

"Don't give me that chest-pounding, tough-guy act, Pegis. You know damn well I've got nothing to do with his murder."

Laura turned around and looked at the cop. I couldn't see the reaction on her face. "Whatever do you mean? What about Jimmy?" she asked him.

Pegis didn't say anything, and Laura turned back to me. "Jimmy, why would the detective say such a thing about you?"

"He's says we were together in this, a conspiracy, having an affair."

Laura looked down and away, saying, "Why, Sergeant Pegis, I haven't seen Jimmy since—"

"Mrs. Rosenthal, Please! Let me do the talking." I didn't want Laura to mention her past arrest on the prostitution charge. The police would find out about that soon enough. But, in the meantime, I didn't want their investigation to veer off course, keeping them from pursuing other possible theories or suspects.

Pegis walked to the other side of the table and stood facing us. "Why don't you let her talk, O'Brien?"

I ignored the question, but said, "Listen Pegis, I met Mrs. Rosenthal some time ago, before she was married, and I haven't seen her since. That is, until yesterday."

"That's why you were sitting in her house when I arrived?"

"I'm a lawyer. She needed advice relating to her husband's suicide."

"Murder."

I stood and faced him across the table. "She thought it was a suicide."

Pegis looked intently at Laura. "If it was a suicide, Mrs. Rosenthal, was O'Brien already there? Or did you call him when you discovered the body?"

Laura started to say something. I held up my hand. Sergeant Pegis asked her one of those when-did-you-stop-beating-your-wife questions. There were two ways to answer, and both were incriminating. If Laura answered truthfully and said she called me, a criminal defense lawyer, before she called police, it would appear that she knew it wasn't suicide and that she had something to hide. But obviously, if she said I just happened to be there when the body was discovered, the answer would fuel Pegis's conspiracy hypothesis.

"I'll answer the question," I said. "When she called my office, Mrs. Rosenthal asked me to call the police. I told her I'd call it in myself when I got there."

Pegis shook his head. "Why did she think she needed a lawyer if she thought the guy had killed himself?"

"C'mon, Pegis, you know how it is in this town. These people call a lawyer when their coffee's too hot, for *chrissakes*." I looked at Laura. "No offense, Mrs. Rosenthal," I said, and turned back to Pegis. "But I damn sure wasn't going to call you guys until I got there. Didn't want you questioning my client and twisting her words."

The detective grimaced. "Hey, O'Brien. I don't like that crack."

We've got to get out of there, I thought. *My God*, what are we doing? What we're saying is only making Pegis more suspicious. "We're going to wrap this up, Sergeant," I said. "Mrs. Rosenthal will give her statement and then we're leaving." I turned to Laura and whispered in her ear. "Tell him what you told me, where you were at the time, and how you discovered your husband's body. But that's all, don't embellish."

Laura told Sergeant Pegis basically what she told me but this time her story was cleaned up, sterilized and shrink-wrapped, packaged like a pack of Arnie's hot dogs. They got home from the party at about one a.m. Her husband went to the study. She went to bed and when she woke up the next morning she found him dead at the desk. She saw the note and knew that he'd shot himself. Laura told the cop that she was in a state of shock, but had managed to call me *immediately*. If this ever got to trial, I may not allow Laura to testify. While I didn't think the time she placed the phone call was a big deal, I couldn't knowingly put her on the stand and allow her to commit perjury. But I did wonder why she waited an hour before she made the call.

Pegis asked her about the card party they had attended that night. With my approval, Laura told him that the party was held at Danny Moyer's home on Roxbury Drive, not far from the Rosenthals' place. Moyer was the general manager of Rosenthal's meat company and ran the day-to-day operations of the firm. On most Tuesday nights, several of Moyer's friends and business associates got together for a game of poker. Sometimes they brought their wives, and when they did, the women mingled in another part of the house while their husbands retreated to the study for the high-stakes game. But on this particular night there were only two women present, Laura and Evie Moyer. Laura told Pegis that they went to the pool house to work on a paint by numbers canvas of some old master.

The card game had started at eight and ended at 12:30. The Rosenthals left the Moyer residence and were home by around one. Pegis wanted the names of the people who attended the poker game. Laura wrote out a list and gave it to him.

* * *

After the interrogation, Laura and I headed to Nate 'n Al's, the famous New York-style deli in downtown Beverly Hills. The deli was jammed and after a twenty-minute wait, Laura and I were shown to a tufted leather booth up front by the window. She ordered a glass of water, and I ordered a Reuben, potato pancakes, and coffee.

The waitress left and I placed the napkin on my lap, and leaned across the table. "Laura, why'd you tell Sergeant Pegis that you phoned me immediately when you actually called an hour after you'd found your husband's body?"

"I was scared to tell them the truth, Jimmy. I figured they'd blame me. You know, the wife thing."

"Okay," I said. But why *didn't* you make the call as soon as you found him in the study? What were you doing during that hour?"

"*Good Lord*, Jimmy, I didn't want to call the cops. With my record I knew they'd haul my fanny to jail and the case would be closed. I was in a panic, circling the house, and talking nonsense to myself. My thoughts were on a loop, playing the scene over and over. I knew I had to call someone. I thought of Arnie's lawyer, but he doesn't like me. I didn't know what to do. I sank to the floor and stared at him thinking of all the fun we had, the love that was developing, our future. I started to cry. I didn't know how long I sat there sobbing. Finally, I remembered how you had helped me before and I knew you'd help me again."

"Yeah, Arnie's lawyer is probably a business attorney," I said. "But he could've advised you at this point. In the event of an arrest, I'm sure he would've recommended a first-rate criminal defense lawyer." I looked at her, still perplexed. "Why do you think he doesn't like you?"

"I don't know, but I can tell. Women can tell things like that."

"What was his name?"

"Mr. Goldfarb."

"Herbie Goldfarb?" I asked.

"Yes, that's him. Do you know Mr. Goldfarb?"

I didn't make the connection before. Although there are more lawyers per capita in Southern California than anywhere on the planet, I knew Herbie Goldfarb, an old-timer who'd been haunting the L.A. courts forever.

"Laura, he doesn't dislike you. He's just a cranky old guy who was probably jealous of Arnie's happiness."

Herbie had been practicing law in and around the meat packing district for years. He'd made it big during World War II defending meat companies accused of selling on the black market. Then in the late forties, Herbie had taken his profits from the war years and invested them in blue-chip stocks like GM, IBM, and Xerox. In other words, he was rich.

He was a widower who doesn't live lavishly and certainly didn't need the income from his law practice.

When I met him, Herbie was old and worn out and ready to give up the sweat and stress that comes with being a high-voltage street lawyer.

A friend of mine from my days as a beat-cop introduced me to him shortly after I passed the bar and set up my practice. Times were hard. I was churning for clients and Herbie had a few he wanted to dump. The cases he shifted my way were small-time, a few misdemeanors: a pickpocket, a kid accused of stealing his girlfriend's bicycle, and a lady shoplifter. The pickpocket skipped without paying his bill. The kid with the bike had made up with his girlfriend before his parents got around to paying me a retainer. And the woman accused of shoplifting—well, she'd stole food to feed her children. I ended up giving her money.

"Arnie told Mr. Goldfarb all about me, even my past." Laura looked away. "I'm sure he disapproves of me."

I let the remark pass. It wasn't important and I had other things to cover before I took her back to the hotel.

The waitress returned with our order. My sandwich was enormous. I had a decent appetite, but I didn't think I could eat the whole Reuben and the potato pancakes as well.

"Miss, please bring another plate," I said to the waitress, then to Laura, "Hey, you can eat half of this sandwich, can't you?"

Laura smiled and nodded. "I think I'm hungry after all. Sure, I'll share the sandwich."

"I hate to bring this up Laura," I said when the waitress left to fetch the plate. "But how are you fixed for money? If you're charged with a crime, it'll be expensive. You won't be able to use Arnie's assets. Everything will be tied up, even your allowance."

"Do you think they're going to arrest me?"

"I hope not, but it's best to be prepared."

She folded her hands on the table and thought before she said, "I have a checking account with maybe ten or twelve thousand in it, left over from my allowance. Of course, I have some jewelry and furs and the Mercedes is in my name. It's paid for. Well, I guess when you add it all up it could be about fifty or sixty thousand." Laura lowered her head, hesitated, and then continued, "How much do I owe you so far?"

"Don't worry about that right now. I'm not charging you for today or yesterday." In my mind, I could see Mabel standing there with her hands on her hips admonishing me. "But if this goes any further I'll have to bill you for my time."

Laura gave me a puzzled look. "Gosh, do you think it will cost more than that?"

I reached across the table and took her hand in mine. "For now, let's just concentrate on keeping you out of jail."

I didn't tell her my fee wasn't the only expense associated with a murder case. A typical case like this, if it went to trial—with expert witnesses, private investigators, and other important incidentals that always came up—could easily run four or five hundred thousand. And, if she were lucky enough to be granted bail, the bond would cost maybe another hundred thousand. In the criminal defense business, justice was costly and you got what you paid for. As a British politician once said, "If you pay peanuts, you get monkeys."

Chapter Ten

During the drive back to Laura's hotel, I asked her if she had any close relatives. She said no, that the only person who cared about her at all was her stepson, Richie, Arnie's only child.

"Richie's in business for himself," Laura said. "I called him and he volunteered to look into Arnie's company, maybe take on some of Arnie's responsibilities for a while. He'll spend some time at the plant, checking on things."

"What type of business does Richie own in New York?" I asked.

"He's a hairdresser."

"Does he know anything about the meat business?"

"Oh, he'll do fine. He's a smart boy."

Just before I dropped Laura off at the hotel, she asked me if I believed that the police would hassle her again. I told her they wouldn't bug her anymore. I explained that they'd have to call me first, and we were through cooperating. What I didn't tell her was that the police would not phone me ahead of time if they arrested her.

"At this point it's more or less wait and see," I said. "I have a friend who has connections. I'll try to get a copy of the police report and we'll go from there."

Laura promised she'd call me if anything came up. But she was also concerned about the hotel and how long she could stay there. The American Express card that she used to check in belonged to the meat company. Herbie Goldfarb happened to be the executor of the estate and Laura felt that he'd most likely cancel the card as soon as he found out she was still using it.

"Don't worry about that kind of stuff right now," I said. "I'm sure something can be worked out."

I then told her I'd check with Herbie to find out what her position with the estate was. Herbie could be heartless at times, but I didn't think he could be that cold-blooded. I didn't feel that he'd cancel the card and toss his client's widow out of the hotel, at least until the probate was settled. My God, I thought, Arnie's ghost would haunt his every minute if he did.

It was still early and if I were lucky, I'd have the whole afternoon free before anything more developed with Laura. I decided to continue where I left off on the Buck Simpson matter. At this time of day I'd beat the traffic to La Puente, and be there within the hour.

I caught the Hollywood Freeway, shot east on the 60, and exited at Hacienda Boulevard. Cruising alongside the railroad tracks, I drove past dozens of industrial tilt-up buildings. The structures all looked alike, big concrete boxes all painted the same putrid color. When this area was developed there must have been a run on mustard-yellow paint.

There wasn't a sign outside the address I had for St. Dismas Halfway House, just a tumbledown brick wall with a broken chain-link gate shoved open and hanging loose. I drove up a small dirt road toward an old Victorian house looming above on a small rise. The grounds, about an acre or two, weren't landscaped. Hardscrabble weed-infested dirt surrounded the rundown mansion and the two smaller buildings that sat close to it. One of the buildings, unpainted stucco, was long and narrow and was probably used as a bunkhouse.

The other building was a dilapidated barn with a rusty sign nailed up advertising Indian Chief Chewing Tobacco. The chief, in war paint and wearing a full headdress, gave me an evil eye as I parked my Corvette in the mud, got out, and climbed the rickety porch steps of the main house.

I walked a few feet to the double doors and couldn't find a bell, so I knocked a few times. No answer. I went down the steps and around the side to the back of the house.

Two guys were sipping cans of Rocky Mountain Gold, the beer that won the west. They had on coveralls and were sitting on a paint-splotched canvas tarp spread out on the ground next to a white Styrofoam cooler. Paint cans, brushes, and paint rollers were scattered about on the tarp. The painters drank and stared at the side of the building and the ladders that were leaning up against it. They looked at me as I approached them.

"The boss around?" I asked.

"Who wants to know?" one of them asked as the other got up and walked to the cooler.

"Name's O'Brien. I was a friend of Buck Simpson."

The guy doing the talking crushed a beer can with his meaty hand and stood. He was massive, and I had to look up at him. "Buck had no friends," he said and moved toward the cooler.

The other painter popped the top of his beer and took a long pull. He belched and wiped his mouth. "You a cop? Trying to find out who punched Buck's ticket?" he asked.

"Nah, I was his lawyer."

"That's why you want to see Willie. You're

trying to get somebody to pay your fee."

"Hey fella, I'm here to tie up some loose ends, that's all. Is this Willie guy the boss?"

"He thinks he is," the tall guy said.

"Where is he?"

The guy nodded to his left, toward the long narrow building. "Can't go in there. Wait here." He turned to the short painter. "Get the boss man, Smokey Bear."

Smokey Bear mumbled something unintelligible and rambled off.

"Smokey Bear?" I said.

"Used to be an arsonist before he was rehabbed out here."

The halfway house director, Willie Chavez, came out to meet me. He was a big guy too, smaller than Godzilla, but not by much. He walked with a shuffle, dragging his left foot as he escorted me to his office. Willie had on well-worn loafers and he'd stop every few steps to put his foot back into the shoe that slipped off while he walked.

We entered his domain and I studied the room. His desk was heaped with bulging files and trays of documents. Two wooden folding chairs, facing the desk, were also covered with paperwork. In fact, the file cabinets and all the furniture, including a brown sofa resting against the far wall, served as a repository for folders, files, and different sized boxes and cartons.

"Take a load off, O'Brien," Willie said. He went behind the desk and pulled out his chair. The chair groaned and sagged under Willie's mass when he flopped down on it.

Willie saw me standing there looking for a place

to sit. He waved at one of the folding chairs. "Just toss the files on the floor."

I moved the papers, sat on the chair, and looked across at Willie. He reached into the pocket of his red-checkered Pendleton shirt and pulled out a pack of Camels. Without taking his eyes off me, he tapped out a cigarette. He held up the pack. "You smoke?"

"Nope."

"Hmm, you don't smoke," Willie said, sizing me up. "Did you know Adolf Hitler didn't smoke either, Mr. O'Brien?"

"Neither does Mother Teresa," I said.

He burst out laughing and chortling. I didn't think the remark was very funny, but Willie continued to laugh until it turned into a cough. "Got me there, Mr. O," he said between coughs. "Now, Smokey Bear told me you're a lawyer. Tell me, where do you guys fit into society?"

"It depends on how you look at it."

"Really?"

"Depends whether they're on your side or against you."

"I feel that." Willie lit his Camel with a plastic lighter he found hidden under a pile of papers. "I deal with screwed up people out here, O'Brien. Maybe you can tell me what the secret to a good life is?"

"Breathing."

Willie laughed again, "Oh, you're a riot, should take your show on the road."

"Look, Willie, the reason I'm here—"

"You're here about Buck, aren't you?" He spoke with a weak voice, somewhat high pitched for a guy his size.

"Yeah, I need a bit of information."

Willie's cigarette dangled out of his mouth, Bogart style. "Gonna sue us?" he asked.

"No, I—"

"Just fishin' for information, is that it?" When Willie spoke, the cigarette tip bobbed up and down slightly, and the rising smoke drifted into his right eye, causing him to squint.

"Well, yeah. Maybe you could tell me—"

"Can't tell you much, not much to tell." Without touching the cigarette, Willie inhaled deeply, and exhaled through his nose.

"Look here, Willie, you've got to—"

"Why'd you really come here anyway?" He coughed again, coughed hard. The cigarette flew out of his mouth and landed among the heap of papers on his desk.

"If you want to play twenty questions why don't you wait until I nod or shake my head before you ask the next one?" I said.

"Sorry, Mr. O, just a habit, I guess." He stood and his gaze scanned the top of his desk. He seemed to be looking for the wayward cigarette. "The cons around here don't talk much. Anything I want to know I have to dig it out."

"I'm not a con."

He stopped looking at the desk and shifted his gazed to me. "The Bible says, and I quote, 'The truth shall set you free.' Now, Mr. O, why don't you unburden your soul and tell me why you're really here."

I began to think I was dealing with a nutcase. "Look, I'm telling you. I'm not here to sue, collect a fee, or cause problems. I just want information about

Buck. Maybe it'll help me find out why he died."

Willie peered at me like I was stupid. "He died because he hung himself. That's what happens when you tie a rolled up sheet around your neck, attach the other end to a pipe, then take a nose-dive off a laundry cart." He shook his head as if to say I was somewhat slow on the uptake.

Willie already knew the official line about Buck Simpson's death, and I was careful not to leak the fact that Buck hadn't committed suicide. That he was murdered. I had to keep that information confidential to protect Sol's source. To do so, I had to be careful how I phrased my questions.

"Maybe he was into something. Maybe something nasty," I said. "Maybe some bad guys were after him and he took the easy way out," I said.

Willie shook his head. "Nah, he was solo. Didn't make friends, didn't make enemies. See, I'd know if he was pulling down." He plopped down on the chair again.

"He was arrested in the middle of the night, out on Sunset Boulevard. Did you know he was violating his parole then?"

Willie jumped out of his chair like he was spring-loaded. "*Goddamn, son-of-a-bitch!*"

He started to pound furiously on the desk with his dilapidated loafer. Cussing and shouting, he repeatedly beat a small flame that had erupted, setting fire to the papers there. He finally extinguished the fire, but the room held the stench of charred paper and ash. Willie put his shoe back on and waved his hands through the air a few times. "Damn," he said, falling back into his chair.

I nodded at the small pile of incinerated documents on his desk. "Were those papers important?"

"Nah, don't worry about it. Just some forms from the State. I toss most of them anyway," he said. "Now, where were we?"

"I asked you about Buck, about his running around after curfew with a knife. I asked about your controls—"

"Hey, O'Brien," Willie said, interrupting again, "I'm the director of the program, not a den mother and these guys aren't Cub Scouts. We're on the honor system around here. Sometimes stuff slips through the cracks." He spread out his arms. "What can I say?"

"Those guys in back are drinking beer. Isn't that a parole violation as well, alcoholic beverages?"

"Big deal. A few bottles of suds. The stuff is donated by one of our placements, a beer distributor in Lakewood. Keeps the cons happy, and besides, the inspectors who are supposed to monitor our program never show up. That means I'm in charge. Hell, call me loco, but beer is okay with me."

"Did Simpson have a job?"

"It's part of the deal. Guy can't get out of the slam until we have a job lined up for him."

"Where'd he work?"

"Nowhere. After he'd been assigned here, he never showed up at the job. He disappeared."

"How does this program work anyhow? And how'd you get the job as the director?"

Willie struggled out of the chair and slowly rose to his feet. "C'mon, I'll give you the nickel tour." He took the pack of Camels out of his pocket and put another cigarette in his mouth.

"You not going to light that thing, are you?"

"Bother you?"

"No, not at all. I just thought you could wait until I leave before you burn down the place," I said.

Willie laughed and then coughed.

We walked out of his office, which was just off the parlor, through a small living room crammed with a mishmash of furniture, and looked at the convicts' sleeping quarters. After that Willie escorted me into a restaurant-sized kitchen. The kitchen was dirty. The tile on the counter was chipped and cracked, dishes were piled in the sink, and it didn't appear as if the floor had been scrubbed in ages.

From there we moved into the dining room and sat at a wooden table covered with a stained oilcloth. One of the parolees, dressed in filthy white pants and a sleeveless T-shirt, his arms covered with tattoos, brought us a cup of coffee. While we drank our coffee, Willie told me how the program got started.

"When you're in the joint, you have nothin' but time to think about stuff. I got a lot of friends on the outside, you know, homies, ex-roomies, that care about me. So, when I was made trustee at Vacaville and seen how terrible the overcrowding was, I hatched a plan to help these poor stiffs."

"You're a regular caped crusader," I chimed in.

"I got this plan to start a rehab half-way house. This chica, DeeDee, came to the prison to give English classes, and she helped me with a letter-writing campaign. That got the attention of this assembly lady, Mattie Niles."

Willie explained that because of his newfound political connection, he was released from Vacaville and appointed as the program's first director at a nominal salary. Willie said the money didn't matter that much as long as he was out of the joint and could help his *compadres.*

"The program must cost a lot of money," I said.

"Not really." Willie's face seemed to brighten. He took a BIC pen from his pocket, grabbed a paper, and started to write on it. "Looky here."

I took a sip of my coffee and glanced at the paper.

"We take prisoners that didn't have a shittin' chance for parole, and get 'em jobs," he said.

"Must be hard to find work for these guys, being convicts and all."

"Nah, that's the beautiful part. The companies—we call them our placements—hire the parolees and pay them minimum wage, about three dollars an hour. The employers agree to keep the cons on the payroll for six months—the worker's training period—and each week the State refunds back to the placements fifty percent of the wages that was paid to the trainees. Big incentive for the companies."

"How much does that cost the State?"

Willie's ballpoint flew across the paper, scribbling numbers all over it.

"Check the numbers; they don't lie," he said. "Instead of costing the State twenty-four thousand dollars a year to keep a guy locked up, it only cost sixty bucks a week, around three grand a year. Saves the State of California over twenty big ones for each guy I take. Not too shabby."

"How about the businesses, can they handle the convicts?"

"Hell, we have counselors on the road constantly. They help our placements work with the program. These guys are real pros."

Willie threw the pen on the table, and looked up at me. "So there, Mr. O, see what kinda guy I am?" He leaned back and crossed his arms over his huge belly. "Hell, helping the government like that? Yep, that's me, just good ol' Willie, just a good citizen. And that's a fact."

"You got a lot of convicts on the program?"

"Damn straight, and the Department of Corrections wants me to take more." Willie stood and gazed at the ceiling. "Take them all, I say, take them all." He was almost shouting. "We have two acres here, and we're building more bunkhouses on the grounds. Look around, whaddya see? I'll tell you what you see: you see a lean, mean, well-oiled rehab machine."

"Amazing," I said.

Willie continued: "Got an option on some property up by Fresno and we've started negotiating for some land in San Diego County. Shit. We'll be statewide soon."

"Sounds like you're expanding fast. Can you handle it?" I asked.

"Sure. Why not?"

"You'll have a chain of rehab centers. Like a franchise deal," I said.

Willie looked at me and scratched his head. "Yeah, I guess you could say that."

"Con in the Box," I said.

More laughing, chortling, and coughing from Willie.

Chapter Eleven

The sun had set by the time I finally arrived back at my office at 7:30. I didn't know a whole lot more about Buck's murder, but now I knew a whole lot more about Willie and St. Dismas. I wondered why the state would put an ex-con in charge of a prisoner rehab center. Not only that, it didn't appear that Willie possessed the management skills required to run a huge rehabilitation program, but then again, who was I to judge? What did I know about rehabilitation? Most of the cons I met, my clients, mostly repeat offenders, were people who couldn't be rehabbed if you hit them on the head with a Louisville Slugger.

Mabel had left a few phone messages and a note on my desk. The messages were routine, mostly solicitation calls, but no new clients. She also left a nasty letter from the bank about my car insurance lapsing, and a notice from the phone company about a rate increase. I tossed the mail and pink message slips in the wastebasket and read Mabel's note:

Tomorrow is Friday. Payday. I'll make out the checks in the morning. Will overdraw the bank. But your client, Geoff the boozer, will be here at 10:00 a.m. with money. Don't be late. Also, I'll need your time sheets for the last two days, so I can send out the bills.

Signed, Mabel.

P.S. Rita's client hasn't given us any money. Please talk to her about that.

Rita drew smiley faces on her notes. There were none on Mabel's.

I'd have to tell Mabel that I had no billable hours for the last two days. However, in addition to

Geoff's cash, with a little luck, we'd get a couple of checks in the mail. Maybe one from the State.

I stopped at Luigi's Italian Deli on my way home to make some notes on Buck's murder. Dining at Luigi's felt as if you were in an authentic old country restaurant. Colorful maps of Italy lined the walls, empty Chianti bottles sporting drippy wax candles sat in the center of each table, and the pungent aroma of Italian cheeses and dried salami filled the air. I sat at a table with a red checkered tablecloth and the owner, Luigi, waddled over.

"Hey *goombah*," he said.

He had short legs, stood only five-foot six, and with his massive belly, he weighed in at about 250 pounds. He had a big happy face, and his olive tone complexion went well with just about any garment color. This was perfect for Luigi, because he wore a white apron splattered with red tomato sauce, smears of yellow cheese, and bits of green pepper. From a distance when you saw him walking, he looked like a huge colorful beach ball bouncing along.

"Hey, Luigi, I'll have the usual."

"Saw you in the parking lot. It's already ordered. Number six pie with extra anchovies."

"Sounds good."

"Hear you got a new client, a murder case," Luigi said.

"Yeah, she's a lady in Beverly Hills." How'd he know? I wondered. Small town gossip, I guess.

While waiting for my pizza, thoughts of Buck ran through my mind. I figured I had hit a dead end investigating his supposed suicide. Without the sheriff's department doing some kind of real investigation I knew I'd never find the truth. As far as they were concerned the case was closed. Maybe I should just back off and worry about finding new clients. As Mabel said, pursuing jailhouse murders won't put money in the bank.

Besides, I now had a paying client, a woman who actually needed my help. Tomorrow, I'd try to get my hands on a copy of the police report. I needed to know if the police were looking at suspects other than Laura. Pegis told me he wouldn't hand it over, but there could be another way.

After I ate, there was still a half a pizza staring me in the face. Luigi packed it in a takeout bag and I headed home to my new two-bedroom apartment on Fifth St.

I figured, when I had the time, I'd convert the extra bedroom into an office; perhaps do a little paperwork at home. I'd get a desk, some filing cabinets, shelves, and maybe a stereo system. Meanwhile, I used the extra room to store the odd and ends that had been boxed up ever since Barbara kicked me out of the house. I knew that someday I'd have to sort through all that stuff, but I never seemed to get around to it.

I was *not* enamored with the idea of spending hours rummaging around in those boxes. As the days and months passed, I got more and more bugged. Finally, I called Goodwill and in less than an hour they came and hauled everything away. Except, that is, for one straight-back chair, which I placed in the center of the room. In the evenings when alone and bored I'd sit in the chair and practice singing aloud while strumming my guitar. I wasn't very good, just determined. Tonight in the living room I fiddled with the TV, thinking I might get it to work. It was Thursday, and I wanted to catch an episode of the detective series, *Harry O*. The TV Guide blurb said the plot had to do with a San Diego cop's effort to clear a woman accused of murder. Who knows, I thought, maybe I'll learn something.

I hooked up a wire coat hanger to the broken rabbit-ears antenna, and to my amazement the picture actually came on. I settled into my beanbag chair with a bowl of popcorn resting on my lap, but before the show had ended I dozed off.

I awoke with a start in the middle of the night, the phone ringing in my ear. I jumped to my feet, popcorn spilling across the floor, and raced to the kitchen.

"Jimmy. Oh, God. Help me," Laura screamed. "They've arrested me for murder."

Chapter Twelve

"Laura, are you okay?" In the background, I heard the clanking sound of metal banging metal and muffled cries of desperation echoing in the concrete halls. I knew this call would eventually come, and I'd dreaded the thought of it.

"I'm in jail! I'm in jail! Oh, God!" Her voice was hysterical. She was having a meltdown. And who could blame her?

"Laura, calm down—"

"They said I killed Arnie. I told them—I told them over and over I didn't do it. I loved Arnie. I really loved him. They're not hearing me. I told—"

"Laura, breathe! Calm down and listen. This is important. Don't say anything to anybody. Not a word. Understand?"

"Jimmy, I'll try, but I'm scared."

"They're going to arraign you in the morning. I'll get the details and meet you at the court. We'll go over everything then. I know it's hard, but try to be brave and, Laura, please remember, keep your mouth shut."

"Please, Jimmy, please get me outta here? I'll go crazy in this horrible place."

"There's generally no bail for a murder charge. But, anyway, I'll request it at the arraignment. It's a long shot, but I'll try."

I didn't have to explain the arraignment process. Laura had been there before. But I did tell her that after the "not guilty" plea was entered the judge would set a future date for the preliminary hearing. Then, if bail was a possibility, that's when a new judge would most likely grant it.

* * *

Without stopping at the office the next morning, I shot directly to the arraignment court located on the corner of Spring and Temple in downtown L.A. When I entered the building and approached Division 60, I saw a reporter lurking in the hall outside of the courtroom. I didn't know his name, but I nodded as I walked past him. I'd seen him hanging around the Criminal Courts in the past, always scrounging for a story. Inside the courtroom, the clerk sat alone behind her desk perched at the foot of the judge's bench. I walked through the bar that separates the spectators from the business end of the room and gave her my card.

"The judge is running a little late," the clerk said. "We'll be starting the arraignment at ten."

The judge was late and I was early. What a switch. "I'd like to see my client," I said.

"Wait here."

The clerk got up and moved through a door to the right of the bench. She returned a moment later accompanied by a bailiff.

"Your client's in the holding cell. Take your seat and we'll bring her out," the bailiff said.

About five minutes later, the bailiff and another L.A. County deputy sheriff returned with Laura between them. She had on a jail-issued orange jumpsuit, and cuffs hooked to a belly chain shackled her hands. She looked wasted and exhausted. Her eyes were red-rimmed, mascara ran down her face, and her once beautiful hair was now matted and tangled. I reasoned, after they picked her up and hauled her to Sybil Brand, processed her, fed her a stale sandwich, and put her back on the Sheriff's Department bus, she couldn't have gotten any rest at all.

When the guards brought her to the defense table, I stood and pulled a chair out for her. Laura awkwardly collapsed in the chair next to me. I put my arm around her shoulders and she bowed her head and started to sob quietly.

I asked the guards to remove the handcuffs.

"Can't do it. Security."

"She isn't going anywhere. Look at her, she's wiped out."

He paused. "Sorry, counselor, but I think I'd better leave 'em on."

"C'mon, officer," I said. "You guys, two trained police officers, can't handle a 110-pound woman?"

The deputies looked at each other, then glanced down at Laura. One of them unlocked the cuffs. Laura didn't say anything. She just peered at the deputy and rubbed her wrists. The guards walked around behind us and stood with their arms across their chests, their eyes fixed firmly on Laura.

She stared at me, her eyes wide with fear. She struggled to choke out the words. "Jimmy, before this starts, I beg you to believe me. I'm innocent."

"Of course, I believe you. And I'll get you out of this mess, but it's going to take some time. Trust me and we'll get through this together."

I believed her, but it didn't matter. I would defend her anyway.

The rear courtroom door swung open, and the deputy district attorney rushed in and plopped his briefcase on the prosecutor's table. He snapped open the case and spread documents out in front of him.

A moment later the bailiff walked to the front of the courtroom. "All rise. The court is now in session. The honorable Judge Belford presiding."

The judge entered from a door to the left of the bench and ascended to her throne. The proceedings were underway. Judge Belford, an attractive black woman, appeared to be thirty-five, but I knew better. She was closer to fifty.

Laura and I stood and faced forward. Judge Belford, looking down, arranging her desk, gestured with a finger wave to the clerk. The clerk, a prim woman in her forties, stepped up and handed a file to the judge.

Judge Belford looked up at me with the file in her hand. "Reading waived?"

She was referring to the details contained in the complaint filed by the district attorney's office. "O'Brien for the defense. And yes, Your Honor, reading waived."

"All right then, let's get started." She glanced at the deputy DA. "And you are?"

"Mark Webster for the People, Your Honor."

"Very well, Mr. Webster. Now, will everyone please be seated?" The judge turned to the clerk. "Evelyn, read the charge."

The clerk stood and in a loud voice announced, "Docket 75-3325, the People of The State of California versus Laura Rosenthal. Penal Code section 187, murder in the first degree."

"Mrs. Rosenthal, how do you plead?"

I tapped Laura on the shoulder and we both

stood again. "Your Honor, my client pleads not guilty."

Judge Belford marked her calendar and set the preliminary hearing for ten days in advance in Division 102. The judge raised her gavel. She was about to adjourn the arraignment proceeding.

"Bail, Your Honor?" I called out.

Webster jumped to his feet. "Your Honor, the People request that bail be denied."

"Judge, the DA's case is extremely weak," I said. "The evidence against my client is circumstantial, and besides, Mrs. Rosenthal is not a flight risk. She has strong ties to the community."

"Your Honor," Webster said. "The defendant has priors—"

"Objection!" I shouted. So, they finally got around to running Laura's name and prints through the Records and Identification Bureau. I wondered what took them so long.

"Sit down, Mr. O'Brien." The judge glared at me. "You know better. This is a first-degree murder case, and the law states that bail is to be denied."

"Judge, you have the prerogative to grant bail when the district attorney has failed to present compelling evidence that a crime had been committed, and evidence that the person charged had in fact committed the crime."

Webster started to say something. The judge gave him a dismissive wave, and said to me, "That will be decided at the preliminary hearing. You can request bail then, but for now bail is denied."

Before I could say anything else, Judge Belford pounded the gavel, walked off the bench, and without looking back disappeared through her chamber door.

The arraignment proceeding was adjourned.

Laura and I remained standing. The bailiff and the deputy came around the table and cuffed Laura's hands. They started to frog-march her back to the door leading to the holding cells. She glanced at me over her shoulder. "*Jimmy*—"

"Hold up guys. Give me a moment with my client."

"Go see Richie," she said. "He's probably at the meat plant. Tell him I've been arrested."

They dragged her away. Her voice trailed behind her, echoing in the courtroom.

"Please, for *God sakes*, tell him I did not kill his father!"

Chapter Thirteen

I ran to catch up with Mark Webster in the hallway outside of Division 60. "Hold up, Webster," I hollered.

He stopped and looked back at me. When I caught up with him I said, "Hey, Mark, why don't you tell Pegis to go find the real killer? Someone you can convict? You've got nothing on my client."

"O'Brien, you're lucky we haven't charged you too. You were at the scene when the police arrived and you stayed with her at the Bel-Air."

"Who, me? I didn't—"

"Not that I blame you," he interrupted. "But you've got to know how it looks."

He started to walk down the corridor again. I stayed with him. "C'mon, Webster, you don't actually believe I'm involved and had anything to do with her husband's murder?"

He stopped and turned to me. "Okay, I've checked you out. Lieutenant Hodges, South Gate P.D. says you're a stand-up guy."

"Thanks."

"But hey, the fact is normal law-abiding guys have done crazier things for women like her."

"You've been watching too many movies."

"Ever seen *The Postman Always Rings Twice*?" Webster asked.

"The movie? Give me a break." I started to laugh. "You're not thinking that I'm involved in a murder because you saw an old movie, and my client looks a lot like Lana Turner, are you?"

"Could be. Same M.O."

My jaw dropped. "Are you nuts? Same M.O. as

a *movie*?"

"That's the way Nick Pegis figures it. But we've got nothing on you. Just the babe."

We arrived at the elevator. Webster pushed the button for the first floor.

"There's a snack bar on the ground floor," I said. "I'll buy you a cup of coffee."

"Why not? I'm not too proud to drink coffee with a criminal lawyer."

"As long as he's buying?"

"As long as he throws in a Danish."

"You got it."

We walked into the small snack area. Webster found a spot to sit, and I got in the food line. It wasn't crowded at that time of the day and in a few moments I placed the coffee and pastry on the table and sat across from Webster.

He took a bite of the Danish and a sip of his coffee. "All this generosity, I figure you want something."

"Nothing I'm not entitled to, like for instance, a copy of the police report." I held my breath waiting for the deputy DA to reply.

"I don't have to turn over any information until fifteen days after the prelim."

"Yeah sure," I said. "We can play it strictly by the book. I'll file a bunch of motions at the last minute. You'll stay up all night preparing documents to submit. We'll run back and forth to the judge down here where the parking is bad and the blueberry Danish tastes like cardboard, or we can just help each other right here, right now, and save the hassle."

"I'll give you this one, O'Brien." He dropped

the pastry on the table, reached into his briefcase, pulled out a file. He slid it over to me. "Maybe I should've held out for lunch at the Bistro in Beverly Hills," he said.

"At those prices, I'd expect a dismissal." I laughed a little as I casually laid my forearm across the file, as if to protect it from magically flying away.

Webster wiped his hands on a napkin. "Now that we're buddies, how about giving me the skinny on your client? I'll bet she's a firecracker in bed."

"Nice try, Webster, but leave the detective work to the cops. Now here's the truth. Our relationship is strictly professional."

He gave me a sidelong glance and laughed. "That's too bad."

After Webster left, I sipped a second cup of coffee and quickly scanned the police report. There didn't seem to be much in it. I set the photos and list of exhibits aside. Then I studied Pegis's remarks at the end of the file. He noted: *Two people walked into the house late at night, Arnie and Laura Rosenthal. They were alone, nobody else came in, a gun was fired, and only one person ended up alive. And that person was Laura Rosenthal, a woman of questionable character with prior convictions.* The investigation was finished. There were no other suspects.

Pegis's statement summed up his view of the case. I knew the simplistic theory didn't really provide justification for Laura's arrest. The DA had to have more. I was sure of it.

I closed the file, left the snack area, and entered the building's lobby. I needed to get back to the office and sign the paychecks, but first I had to phone Arnie's son. Weaving through the crowd, I found a bank of pay phones around the corner from the restrooms. I dropped a dime and dialed the meat company.

At first Richie must've thought I was calling about the coroner releasing Arnie's body, or the funeral. Because before I could say anything, he started to rattle on about how he's been spending his time since he's been in L.A. He spoke in a quick, disjointed manner as people without enough sleep often do.

From what I could understand, Richie made all the funeral arrangements and gave the name of the mortuary to the authorities just as he was instructed. The funeral director was to notify him when the body was to be released. He also said that he hadn't had a chance to grieve his loss. Richie was running around helping Laura cope, and now he was troubled by what he was finding out about his father's company.

"Something is going on—"

I interrupted him. "Richie, hold on a second. I have something important to tell you." He stopped talking and I quickly explained what had happened to Laura.

He kept silent for a moment. Then his anger flared.

"Laura? Laura didn't do it. *Damn it*, those idiots," he sputtered.

"Do you know Laura well?"

"People around here might be listening, so I have to speak softly. But yeah, I know her well. She's an exceptional person. What she did for my dad..."

He paused again. It was quiet and I heard whisper-soft breathing on the other end. I assumed Richie was trying to control his rage. I kept still and waited for him to gather his thoughts.

After what seemed like a long time, Richie said in a slow and steady voice, "Let me tell you about my dad and Laura."

According to Richie, after his mother died his father had gone to pieces, his life shattered. He felt he had nothing to live for. Arnie didn't leave his house for weeks, not even to go to the meat company that he loved. He barely ate and began losing a lot of weight.

Richie continued. "I flew out from New York, tried to help, but all we did was bicker. Eventually, I forced him to go back to work, get his mind off my mother. He went back, all right, but, *damn*, he was just going through the motions."

Richie didn't know what the original spark was that triggered his father's attraction for Laura. But she was like a strong magnet that pulled him back together and made him a whole person again.

"They were inseparable. The two of them went everywhere together, Lakers games, the Rams, romantic dinners at fine restaurants, you name it," he said. "In fact, they had just recently returned from a month-long vacation in Europe."

"How'd you feel about your dad marrying a much younger woman?"

"At first I thought she was just after his money. It's only natural that I'd think that. But I didn't care. He was happy."

"Still think she was after his money?"

"There's more to life than money."

Not for everyone, I said to myself. Just walk into any courtroom. "Yeah, I guess so."

"Laura loved my dad," Richie continued. "I

could tell. The way they acted together, like high school kids, holding hands, giving each other those looks. Does that sound like she wanted my father dead, Mr. O'Brien?"

"No, not at all," I answered.

I explained that I needed to speak with him in person about his dad and the case and go over the details of Laura's arrest. "Do you have an office at the plant where we can talk?"

"Yeah, but right now I'm on the factory floor, a direct line to the outside. This line is reserved for the USDA inspectors. I didn't want to use the office phones to take your call. They go through the switchboard."

"I understand." I assumed he wanted to keep his personal life private.

"Anyway, I can't talk here." There was silence on the line for a few seconds. "Can we meet tomorrow, Saturday?" he said in a hushed voice.

"Of course."

"I won't be coming to the plant. While in California, I'm staying on the company's boat down in Newport. We own a weekend cottage on Lido Isle, but it's rented out right now. The boat is parked at the dock in the back."

"What time do you want me to be there?"

"How's ten o'clock in the morning sound?"

"That's fine." He gave me the address, Via Lido something. I wrote it on the back of my business card.

"Mr. O'Brien, what I'm going to tell you could mean trouble."

"What kind of trouble?"

"*Oh Christ*, he's watching me."

The phone went dead in my hand.

Chapter Fourteen

Driving back to the office, the thought of Mabel's disappointment weighed heavily on my mind. I knew she'd browbeat the hell out of me for standing up my client without even calling in. Geoff had to be pissed, probably had a new lawyer by now. Not only that, I failed to ask Rita to pressure Charlie Busher, her bank robber client, into coughing up a small retainer. Yeah, it would be hard to face Mabel. I'd have to be real creative to come up with an excuse that would overcome all of that. The last few didn't seem to work.

When it came to finances Mabel could be exasperating, constantly hounding me about money. But, of course, we needed cash to stay in business and it was her job to protect my back. Still, did she have to do it so well?

I swung into the parking lot, climbed out of my Corvette, and trudged up the steps to the office.

Slowly opening the door, I braced for Mabel's tirade. But instead I heard laughter coming from within. I peeked around the doorsill. Mabel and Rita sat at the reception room desk, chattering and laughing while counting and stacking hundred-dollar bills. There had to be thousands of dollars spread out in front of them.

I stepped in and Rita noticed me standing there, wide eyed. "Oh, Jimmy, look at this," she said, pointing at the money. "My plan is working."

"My God," I said. "Where'd all that cash come from?"

"It's Charlie's. There's over twenty thousand here. He's paying us five thousand to handle his defense. We get two thousand now and another three when I get him off at the trial next week. The rest we're putting into the trust account for Charlie."

Mabel jumped in. "Some lawyers around here have clients that actually pay up."

I let the smart-assed remark pass. "That's incredible, Rita."

"Yes it is. If I don't mind my saying so," Rita said. "I forced the bank to release the funds that Charlie had in his CD without waiting the mandatory thirty days. They deducted some charges, the fifteen hundred he took that day, and gave me a cashier's check for the balance made out to Charlie. I copied the check for our files. He endorsed the original and I cashed it." She held out her hands, palms up. "Easy as pie."

"Rita, that's fantastic! Your plan worked."

"Not yet, Boss. That's only half the plan."

"What's the other half?" I asked with caution.

"I'll tell you all about it when I get Charlie off at the trial next week."

I wondered how Rita aimed to prove that Charlie Busher was not guilty. The prosecutor had an open-and-shut case. They had the gun, a dozen witnesses, and a note in his own handwriting. Charlie wasn't a career criminal, so she might get him a reduced sentence, but to get him off scot-free—no way. The FBI frowns upon people walking into a bank, waving a gun around, and demanding money.

"That's the other half of the plan?" I asked with a smile. "Getting Charlie off?"

"Jimmy, quit bugging Rita. She's doing her job," Mabel said. "By the way, your client, Geoff the drunk, cancelled his appointment. Said he was sorry he couldn't make it. Called at the last minute, sounded plastered."

As the old saying goes, *Make me lucky, not smart*. "Yeah, Mabel, I figured he wouldn't show this morning. That's why I didn't call in. The police arrested Laura Rosenthal last night and I handled her arraignment. I'll get you my time sheet later."

"Things are looking up."

Not for Laura, I thought.

"I put the paychecks on your desk," Mabel said. "Oh, and while you were out a package came for you. I signed for it and put the box in the storage closet."

"What is it?"

"Came from the jail. It's Buck Simpson's personal effects. The clothing he was wearing when he was arrested and stuff. He had no relatives and you're his attorney of record, so they sent the package to you."

"I guess we can give the clothing to Goodwill."

"Mabel and I are going to lunch at the Regency to celebrate my deal with Charlie," Rita said. "Why don't you come with us?"

"You two go on and have fun." I held up the file. "I've got to go over the Rosenthal police report."

Mabel raised her eyebrows. "Oh yeah, the report about the Wienie Widow case. It was all over the news." She looked at Rita, and they both giggled.

Wienie Widow, Christ, I should've known the media would lay a tag like that on Laura because of her dead husband being the hotdog king. But I wondered what else they'd cooked up. "Did they say anything about me?"

Now they both laughed out loud.

"Oh, Boss, we didn't know about your secret life. Having a wild fling with the Wienie Widow."

"Hey guys, not funny. That could damage my reputation."

"Oh, I don't think so," Mabel said.

"Yep, you might be surprised, Jimmy," Rita said. "Women love a guy who'll go all out for them and take a personal interest in their needs."

"That's not what I mean. Give me a break."

"C'mon, Boss, come to lunch with us," Rita said.

I should probably be there to celebrate Rita's first big retainer. The file could wait a couple of hours. "Okay, I'll go. But I don't want to hear another word about the Wienie Widow and any of that stuff about me and her. I mean it!"

They both cracked up.

"And no laughing, understood?"

They nodded, pretending to be solemn.

We stopped at the bank and deposited Charlie's money. The girls managed to control themselves all the way to the Regency. No mention was made about the news release.

When we arrived at the restaurant, Marilee the hostess escorted us to a booth in the main dining room just to the right of the bar.

Everyone in Downey seemed to have heard the news, but of course, no one believed the story. Even Dwayne, the bartender, came over to our booth to let me know he didn't buy a word of it.

"I knew it wasn't true the minute I heard it on the radio," he said, shaking his head. "Nope. Me and the boys at the bar laughed. Can't be true, we all said. A doll like that, rich and gorgeous, nah, she'd never fall for a guy like O'Brien."

"Gee thanks, Dwayne."

"Although Shirley—you know her, the looker that always sits alone at the bar?" Dwayne made an outline of a woman's figure with his hands and whistled softly. Then he glanced at Mabel and Rita. "Whoops, sorry ladies." Dwayne turned back to me. "You know who I mean."

"Yeah, I know Shirley."

"Well, she wants to go out with you."

"She does?"

"Yeah, she told me to ask you. Said you didn't even have to knock off her husband. Just rough him up a little."

"Ha, ha," I answered sarcastically.

During the meal I mentioned that with funds no longer an issue, I could probably spend time looking into Buck Simpson's murder. Mabel shot me a voiceless look that meant to say, *You're really pissing me off, buster.*

It seemed to me that she wasn't exactly wild about my idea.

Chapter Fifteen

It was dark outside when Rita and Mabel left for the day. I remained holed up in the office scrutinizing Sergeant Pegis's police report. First, I carefully went through the report word for word, looking for anything on which I could hang a defense.

The prosecution had three facts that pointed to Laura as the killer, but only one posed a real problem. *Money.* And they'd beat that fact like a drum until it reverberated in the jury's mind, blocking any doubt about Laura's innocence. Juries understood money. Oh, how they understood money.

If Laura beat the charge, she'd be independently wealthy—quite wealthy, indeed. Shortly after their marriage, Arnie took out a life insurance policy, naming Laura as the sole beneficiary. And now that the police ruled that murder was the cause of death, not suicide, they'd have to part with the money. The payout: *ten million tax-free dollars.* I leaned back in my chair and slowly said, "Ten million bucks." Said it a couple of times. I let the number roll around on my tongue, trying to get my mind focused on all those zeros. *Christ*, I thought, half the jurors would knock off their own loving spouses for that kind of dough.

The second fact was important, but I figured I could get it blocked. They'd dug out Laura's past record, the arrest relating to the prostitution charge, and it was obvious what the jury would infer from that. I'd file a motion to suppress. The fact that she'd led a checkered life, which had nothing to do with the case, would unfairly prejudice the jurors' minds. I figured the judge would go along with me on that one.

The third point was conjecture on Pegis's part. He stated that Laura had been seen arguing with her husband earlier that night. The sergeant said he had witnesses. No conjecture there if he had witnesses, but he also added, *"Two people walked into the house that night and only one person ended up alive. Mrs. Rosenthal had been the only other person present at the time her husband, Arnold J. Rosenthal was murdered in cold blood."* He went on to describe how painstakingly the police investigated the scene in an effort to discover if there had been any sort of break-in, any possible way an intruder could have entered the premises. There was none.

What a bunch of crap, I thought as I got up and walked around the office. Of course Laura was in the house at the time. We wouldn't deny that point. She lived there. But just because the cops couldn't find evidence that someone else was in the house when Arnie was killed didn't mean it was so. However, Laura and Arnie's so-called "argument" that night bugged me. It was a loose end, a dangling loose end. A loose end like that could end up dangling around Laura's neck— like a noose.

But if it were true what Pegis had said in the report, that there was no possibility an intruder had broken into the house that night, could that mean that Arnie himself had let the killer in? I sat back and threw my pencil down. If he let him in, then it was obvious: he knew the guy.

I scribbled O'Brien's Rule Number One on my tablet: *When invoking the reasonable doubt defense, blame the crime on someone else. Someone the jury would hate. Someone they'd hate more than they hated your client.* I underlined *someone the jury would hate.* But who?

That's where I'd start, I figured. I'd find someone else to blame. I'd check Arnie's known acquaintances, business associates and friends, starting with the poker players.

I dug out the list and studied it again. There was Herbie, Arnie's lawyer. He was at the game, but he was harmless. No, Herbie didn't kill Arnie. If he picked up a gun he'd probably shoot himself with it.

But there were others at the poker game that night, a salesman who supplied some kind of cereal filler for the wieners, the insurance broker who wrote the meat company's policies, and of course, Danny Moyer, the company manager. He hosted the game.

The police identified Moyer and the insurance broker as the witnesses to Laura and Arnie's argument. So it seems that Moyer and the other guy were going to be witnesses for the prosecution. I picked up the report again and flipped back a few pages. They didn't say what the argument was about. They told the cops they couldn't remember. Maybe they made the whole thing up. Maybe the insurance guy and Moyer were lying. Maybe they were trying to make Laura look bad, trying to set her up. Laura said she had been in the house, but she didn't mention an argument. During the game, Laura said she came into the house to make sure Arnie ate something because he needed medicine that had to be taken with food. Evie Moyer, the only other woman at the game, stayed at the pool house because she was worried that her paint would dry up before she could apply it to her paint by number canvas. Evie said she never talked to the guys until it was time to leave. She had confided in Laura that Danny snored and kept odd hours, so she had her own bedroom on the opposite of the house. But Laura thought Evie probably avoided Danny because of his girlfriend, Honey.

Maybe one of them had a motive. Lots of *maybes*—maybe I was reaching. Anyway, what kind of motive could an insurance guy have? True, some insurance guys will kill you; bore you to death with their actuary tables. But I never heard of one shooting a good client in the head.

Did Moyer want to control the business? Could that be his motive? Could the motive have something else to do with the meat company? I'll have to check with Richie Rosenthal. He'd tell me what he knew about these two people.

The rest of the report was routine. The photos of Arnie's body showed nothing that I didn't already know. I had seen the body when I was at the house. There was no physical evidence to worry about. The forensic team had lifted prints from all over the house and grounds. As one would expect, Laura's and Arnie's were there, and of course, the maid's and his secretary's. Several other prints were found but were not identified in the report. There were always prints at a scene with no matches from friends, delivery people, and others. It would be impossible for the police to take sample prints from everyone who had entered the home. There was nothing else significant.

The report also stated that Laura and I had left the scene when the detectives arrived and refused to cooperate, therefore, a paraffin test of Laura's hands was not performed. I'd contest that. We hung around for a while. On cross, I'd get Pegis to admit that he hadn't asked Laura for the test. The detective knew I would have objected to the test if he asked, but I wouldn't tell the jury that.

That was it. That was their case. I had the basics down, and now I needed someone who would fit the requirement of O'Brien's Rule Number One, somebody to blame, someone who had motive, means, and opportunity.

That would be the hard part: finding the bastard who had murdered Arnie in cold blood.

And by now the killer had to know I was looking for him.

Chapter Sixteen

At the Arches Overpass in Newport Beach, I turned off of Pacific Coast Highway and swung around to Newport Boulevard. I drove south about a half mile, turned left at Via Lido, and entered the village next to Lido Isle. I cruised past a movie theater and glanced at the marquee: *Three Days of the Condor*, a spy thriller with Robert Redford. I made a mental note to see the movie when it came to Downey.

Crossing a small bridge spanning a narrow portion of Balboa Bay, I rolled onto Lido Isle and veered right then left, ending up on Via Lido Nord. A moment later I pulled up to the address Richie had given me. The house wasn't much different from the others on the island—no front yard and short driveways in front of three-car garages. From the street, the homes appeared to be small and practically jammed on top of one another. But this was no low-priced, high-density housing tract. Most of the homes on my right, the ones perched on the edge of the bay, had sailing-yacht masts reaching for the sky behind them and the driveways held pricey imported cars.

"Found the place, I see," a guy standing in the cobblestone driveway next to a gray Buick Skylark said after I parked my Corvette at the curb and climbed out.

"Yeah, no problem. You Richie?"

"That's me. C'mon, we can talk on the boat."

Richie Rosenthal, a tall lanky guy in his late twenties, had dark hair covering his ears, reminiscent of the early Beatles mop style. He had a long brooding face, but his clothing reflected a more casual attitude— tight fitting white jeans, a sleeveless light-blue T-shirt, and pale deck shoes with no socks.

I followed him along a curved flagstone path leading to the back of the house. The backyard was mostly patio with a fire pit and a scattering of outdoor furniture. A gleaming white sport-fishing yacht moored to a dock beyond the yard loomed in front of us. Slowing, I gazed out at the stunning view, Balboa Bay in the foreground with magnificent homes perched on the bluffs across the sparkling water. World-class yachts and sailboats of all sizes cruised gracefully through the harbor. Cigarette-type racers, fishing boats, and even a few inflatable dinghies bobbed in their slips lining the water's edge.

We walked down a gangway to the dock and climbed aboard the *Hatteras*. The craft was rigged for serious fishing. A dozen poles lined up and polished like sentries at the ready were clamped to the back of the cabin. A couple of them had reels bigger than volleyballs.

Richie opened the sliding hatch door and we stepped down into the salon. I sat in one of the captain chairs facing a small glass-covered mahogany coffee table heaped with neatly stacked files and ledgers.

"Nice boat," I said making conversation.

He looked around the cabin, appearing as if he'd never seen it before. "Yeah, guess so, if you like this sort of thing. To me it's a big hole in the water that sucks up money."

"You don't like boats? Fishing?"

"Hell no. My dad made me drive this tub since I was twelve years old, but I would get seasick. And I hated fishing; the stink, the blood, the guts. That's one of the reasons I became a vegetarian. I'm just staying here because it's too painful to stay at the Beverly Hills house."

"I guess you don't like boats, but it's still nice."

"Get you a drink?" Richie said moving toward the galley. "We have just about anything."

"Coffee?"

"Sure, just made a pot. It's a special blend. I have a coffee designer in New York. She blends my coffee according to my moods. Brought some with me."

Richie poured us both a cup. I took a sip; delicious. No doubt about it, the coffee designer knew her stuff.

"Coffee's outstanding. What is it?"

"Depressed," he said.

"Depressed? It tastes great."

"No, that's the name of the blend, *Depressed*. I drink it when I'm feeling low. Then my mood changes and I feel better."

"What kind of coffee do you drink when you're in a good mood?"

"Maxwell House." Richie chuckled at his little joke. The caffeine must've been kicking in.

He sat on a couch upholstered with a blue fabric that had little anchors printed all over it. He crossed his legs, leaned back, and took a sip of his coffee.

"Yesterday on the phone you told me someone was watching you," I said, figuring I'd get right to the point. "You seemed nervous."

He squeezed the bridge of his nose with his thumb and forefinger. "Yeah, Danny Moyer, vice president of the company. I think he's having me watched all the time."

"Why would he do that?"

"He knows I'm looking into the way he's running the business."

"There's something wrong at the plant?"

"I've been poring over the company's records." He pointed to the documents resting on the coffee table. "I discovered some alarming irregularities, and I'm shocked. Just more to be upset about on top of everything else."

"What did you find out?"

"The company's a mess. I don't mean the plant's a mess, although it is filthy—somebody should call the USDA—I mean the company is a financial disaster. Practically bankrupt. And it's Moyer's fault."

"Can you tell me about it?"

"I have to tell someone or I'll go berserk."

"I'm listening."

"I'll admit part of the problem was my dad's personal spending habits, and the company *did* spend money on his crazy ideas—like chicken wieners. *Christ.*" He rolled his eyes. "But that's only a small part of it."

Richie went on to explain about the meat company's financial difficulties. He said the bank accounts were depleted; the expenses were out of sight, the debt load crushing.

"And that's not all," he added. "The payroll's bloated. There are more guys standing around doing nothing than Zsa Zsa Gabor has ex-husbands."

"Why is all that Moyer's fault?"

"When my mother died, my father went into a funk. He just sat around and moped. He quit going to work and forgot about his company, the business he built and loved. At that point Moyer took a greater role in managing the corporation and has been running it ever since."

"So that means Moyer is to blame?"

"Yeah, even with falling sales he's hired a lot of new people, guys that answered only to him. He also increased the advertising budget. I think Moyer's robbing the company. Take the cottage here at Balboa, for example." He pointed at the home behind us. "Moyer has it leased to his girlfriend, Honey, from his ad campaign for two hundred a month." He shook his head. "The place is worth a half-million and he's got it leased for two hundred a month."

"Not much of a return," I said.

"No, and I found out Moyer had forced Dad to take out a mortgage on the home in Beverly Hills. Two million bucks at twelve percent and payments are over twenty thousand per month. The house isn't even worth that much. With Dad gone, the bank will foreclose."

"Maybe the girlfriend is blackmailing him. Do you have evidence that Moyer is somehow defrauding the company?"

"No, not yet, but I'm going to get to the bottom of it. I'll prove that he's stealing from the business. How else could things get so bad in such a short period of time? As to the girlfriend, Evie Moyer could care less. Everyone knows about his 'Honey.' I think Evie is glad to have him off her back as long as her money is still coming in."

"Do you think Moyer would resort to violence to keep you from digging deeper?"

"I don't know him that well. Don't know what he's capable of. But the whole affair stinks and it has me on edge."

Through the open hatchway I looked out at the bay. An old wooden sloop cut silently through the water. With the wind at her stern a huge yellow and blue spinnaker ballooned out in front of the sailboat's bow. As I gazed at the serene setting I wondered if Moyer might be the alternate suspect that I could present to the jury in Laura's reasonable doubt defense. Richie might be handing me a fall guy on a silver platter.

Richie had no proof that Moyer was guilty of wrongdoing. At this point it was just his gut feeling. I couldn't present evidence during the trial based on a hunch. My reasonable doubt theory of the case would have to be rock solid, or the judge would slap me down quicker than a short-fuse bomb goes boom. But even if Moyer stole money, it didn't mean he killed Arnie. Accusing him of murder could be a minefield loaded with peril. I'd have to step lightly with that or the accusation could blow up in my face.

If someone had, in fact, been looting the company, it's also entirely possible that the person doing the pillaging was Richie's father. Arnie must've needed cash like an addict needs a fix. He spent lavishly, a luxury European vacation with Laura, showering her with cash, furs, valuable jewelry, and God knows what else. Not only that, upkeep on two expensive homes must've cost a small fortune.

Yeah, I thought, if I used Moyer as the fall guy the DA could easily turn it back on me. Make it appear that somehow Laura had manipulated poor Arnie into fleecing his own company for *her* personal gain, then murdered him for the insurance money when there was nothing left to steal.

With high-priced gifts and the life insurance policy rattling around in the jurors' minds, they wouldn't even leave the jury box after the prosecutor's closing remarks at the end of the trial. They'd jump to their feet and shout out in unison, "*Guilty!*"

Could Richie's assertion that Moyer was the cause of the company's troubles stem from a desire, maybe subconscious, to protect his dead father's image?

"What about your relationship with your father? Did you two get along okay?"

"We got along great when I was a kid."

"And later?"

"Everything changed when I went to college. He sent me to Stanford to study business, and after graduation I was supposed to come back, help him run the plant, someday take over the company."

"But you didn't do that."

"No. I quit college in my senior year. I hated it: debentures, barrier options, all that crap, and the thought of the meat company made me want to gag. Which was another reason I became a vegetarian. I guess it was my way of rebelling, letting him know that I wanted no part of his plan."

He looked away, not focusing on anything, just a long blank stare. I kept still and let him gather his thoughts.

"I ran off to New York, bummed around for a while, then signed up for beauty school. It didn't take me long to know that I'd found my calling."

"It must've been hard for him to take, his only son quitting Stanford and heading for New York."

"Oh, *damn*, he was devastated. He didn't agree

with my lifestyle."

We sat quietly as the boat rocked in the gentle swell of a passing trawler.

"I just couldn't go back," he finally said. "New York is alive and vibrant, and it's intoxicating to hang with such creative and talented people."

"You have to live your life, Richie."

He ignored my trite remark and continued. "But even though we were hardly speaking, when I opened my first beauty salon later on, my dad backed me financially. His attorney set it up, strictly business." He hung his head.

"It's working out for you?"

"I'm doing okay. I have a loft in the Village and two salons now, one on the Upper West Side, the other on 57th, Midtown East. But even with a bit of success, my dad would have nothing to do with me. I'd hurt him terribly."

There are times when it is wise to keep one's mouth shut, and this was one of those times.

After a short time he said, "But when Laura came along, Jimmy, my dad became a new person." His face brightened. "She was a godsend. Laura was his wife, but I think he felt like he had a new kid to show off. Everything was new to her and he got joy out of seeing her so happy."

"Laura can have that effect on men," I said.

"By then my dad had just started to come around. He was still depressed, but he began to attend meetings at the plant, take trips for the company, that sort of thing. That's how he met Laura, at a meat convention in San Francisco."

"I know," I said. "She told me he fell in love

with her at first sight."

"She helped him come to terms with my lifestyle. Because of Laura my dad and I became close again. Laura brought us back together." He sat back and glanced out the porthole. Then he stared at his shoes and said nothing. Finally, he looked up at me again and shouted, "No, damn it! She didn't kill my dad. For *Christ's* sake, she loved him."

He sat for a moment, then walked to the galley, grabbed the coffeepot, and held it up to me with a questioning look.

"No thanks. I'm fine," I said.

After pouring himself another cup, he sat on the couch and silently sipped his coffee.

"Richie, I'm trying to find out as much as I can about that awful night. It might help with Laura's defense."

"I don't know much," Richie said. "Laura told me that she and Dad came home from a card game and later someone must have entered his study and murdered him. Laura was upstairs asleep when it happened. That's about all I know. Who knows? Maybe it was Moyer, maybe not."

I pulled the list of Arnie's poker buddies out of my pocket. "Help me with this, okay?" I unfolded the paper and handed it to him. "These are the four guys who were at the game with your dad that night. One of them is Moyer. But tell me about the other three."

He set his coffee cup on the table, leaned forward, and focused on the paper.

"Well, Herbie Goldfarb was Dad's attorney. Herbie, playing poker?" Richie chuckled. "That had to be a laugh. And David Lawrence is an insurance guy.

Did a lot of business with the company." He looked up. "Sorry, Jimmy, I don't know Mr. Lawrence that well. I only met him once or twice. But he seems okay, I guess."

"What about the fourth guy?"

Richie looked at the list again. "Hmm, Joe Short. Your list says he sells ingredients. Don't know him at all, I'm afraid."

I hadn't found out much about the people on the list, with the exception of Moyer, of course. But I wouldn't say that the trip was wasted. I knew now that Richie would make an excellent witness at Laura's trial.

"I appreciate all your help," I said, standing to leave. "We'll be in touch."

"Hold on a second, Jimmy." He disappeared for a few seconds, returning with an envelope. He handed it to me. "This is for you," he said.

I opened the flap and glanced inside: a cashier's check, ten thousand. Stunned, I looked at Richie.

"I'm not a wealthy person, but I do okay," he said. "It's a retainer for Laura. She trusts you, and so do I."

"I'll do my very best, Richie. I promise she'll go free," I said as I tucked the envelope into my jacket pocket.

Chapter Seventeen

Sunday morning the wind whipped around from the east and hot air from the Mojave Desert roared in through the mountain passes and chased the smog out to sea. The sky was bright. The torrid Santa Ana winds were with us and woke me before six with the sound of their howling in my ears.

I showered and shaved, pulled on an old pair of Levis, and at 6:20 jumped in my Vette. Although it was Sunday, I knew I had to work on some motions for Laura's case; a motion for a bill of particulars, a motion to set bail, a motion to reduce charges, a motion for discovery, a motion to preserve evidence, a motion to examine police personnel file, a motion for a speedy trial, and a slew of others. I figured I'd file them all and see which ones, if any, stuck.

I headed out for breakfast at Dolan's Donuts. At this hour the donut shop was about as crowded as a karate class for Quakers. I pulled the *L.A. Times* from a rack and grabbed up a couple of glazed and coffee from the counter man. I spent the next fifteen minutes enjoying my breakfast and scanning the paper. To my relief, there was no mention of the Rosenthal murder case, or me.

Arriving at the office I went straight to the storage closet to get some blank legal forms. When I opened the door, I noticed the package that Mabel had stowed there, the box containing Buck Simpson's personal effects. I opened it and pulled out his stuff—a dirty, white, work uniform of some sort, heavy-soled black shoes stuffed with filthy white socks, Simpson's six-inch Buck knife, and thirty-five cents.

I laid the knife on my desk, put the change in my pocket, folded the clothes and placed them back into the box. Leaning back in my chair it occurred to me that white clothing would be a strange outfit for a guy who made his living lurking in dark shadows waiting for victims. White pants and a white shirt wouldn't be my wardrobe *du jour* if I were a midnight mugger.

Opening the top desk drawer, I put the knife away and took out the Rosenthal police report. I leafed through it again, looking for something, anything that might suggest Moyer or someone at the game, or anyone else for that matter, could have been the guilty party. I needed a strong motive, not one based on hunches, and I'd have to back it up with something tangible.

Moyer and Lawrence, the insurance guy, had said they saw Laura and Arnie arguing at the party. Why didn't the other two men at the game that night say anything about an argument? One way to find out. I got Herbie Goldfarb's home number from the report, grabbed the phone, and dialed.

While the phone rang, I thought again about Buck's white clothes. The outfit could be the uniform of a milkman, baker, or perhaps a medical orderly. But Willie at the rehab center said Buck didn't have a job. Strange.

After a number of rings with no answer, I hung up.

Next I tried the number of the fourth guy: Joe Short, the salesman. I got an answer this time.

"This is Joe."

"Good morning, Mr. Short. I hate to disturb you.

I'm Jimmy O'Brien, the lawyer defending Mrs. Rosenthal."

"Yeah sure, the murder." He paused for a beat. "Man, that's heavy. A bummer. But I don't know how I can help. I did business with Arnie, know what I mean, but I wasn't a close friend. I'll say this, though; his wife is some kind of somethin'. Know what I mean?"

"She's that, all right, and she's a good person, too. But I've got a question."

"Shoot."

"A couple of the guys at the game, David Lawrence and Danny Moyer, said that Arnie and his wife were arguing before they headed home that night. Did you see or hear an argument?

"Nah, left early. Got cleaned out and split around eleven."

"Did you notice anything that might indicate they were upset with each other?"

"No, in fact, doll face seemed pleasant. While I was there she treated Arnie nice, nothing lovey-dovey, nothing like that. Know what I mean? But the looks they exchanged when she brought him sandwiches and stuff said it all. Of course that could've changed after I left. You know how women are."

"Thanks, Mr. Short. I guess—"

"Hey, if you want to verify Moyer's and Lawrence's story," he said, "why not ask the other two guys who were at the game?"

"You mean the other one guy, Herbie Goldfarb. I tried, he's not home."

"Well, there was another guy. He came late." He paused. "Let's see. I think he was Moyer's pal. Or maybe David Lawrence's amigo? I dunno."

What is this guy talking about? I thought. I hadn't heard that anyone else was at the game that night.

"Other than Arnie and you, I only have three other names on the list, Moyer, Lawrence, and Herbie Goldfarb," I said.

"Some big Mexican guy showed up later. Seemed like a groovy cat. His name was Guillermo, I think. Yeah, that's it, Guillermo. Don't know his last name."

"Laura gave the police a list of people at the game. She didn't mention anyone named Guillermo."

"Like I said, he showed up late. Maybe she didn't see him. Mrs. Rosenthal was probably outside clucking with Mrs. Moyer. You know how the ladies can gab."

"Guess so."

"Or maybe she lied. Know what I mean?" he said.

Chapter Eighteen

Farmer Fred's wiener factory, located in Vernon, took up an entire city block. When I drove there the next morning trucks of all sizes and types—tractors with forty-foot refrigerated trailers, bobtails, and even pickups—jammed the loading dock area in front of the plant. The stench of pig manure hung in the air. The vehicles blocked the visitors' parking area, overflowed into the street and hindered the flow of traffic. Around the corner on Union Avenue, in front of the main office, a large mob milled about, some with raised fists, some shouting obscenities.

I wondered what the hell was going on as I slowly wormed my way through the traffic, searching for a place to park. Finally, I found a spot on Olympic, five blocks away.

In the sweltering heat I hoofed it back to the wiener factory, then elbowed my way through the crowd and climbed the steps to the main office. Someone had woven a heavy steel chain with a brass padlock through the handles of the main door, locking down the facility.

Sweating like one of Farmer Fred's pigs, I made my way all the way around to the north side of the building and saw a door opening cut into the brick wall. With caution, I turned the knob on the metal door and was surprised when it opened. I quietly slipped through the doorway and entered what appeared to be a production office.

Inside, more angry people were pushing and shoving, trying to get the attention of a fat guy in a white uniform sitting behind a glassed-in reception counter. I knew it would be pointless to try to muscle my way through the irate mob, so I withdrew and marched back down Union Avenue.

After walking several hundred feet along the ten-foot high wall surrounding the plant, I came to a guard shack at the cattle-truck entrance to the yard behind the building. As I trudged through an open gate adjacent to the shack, the security guard, perched on a tall stool inside, scrambled to his feet and stuck his head out the sliding window.

"Hey, Mac, where'd ya think you're going?"

I stopped walking and surveyed the yard. About fifty feet in front of me, beyond an expanse of blacktop, a semi-trailer truck, loaded with bellowing cows, slowly backed up to a fenced-in holding pen attached to the plant. I turned to the guard and pointed to the massive red brick building.

"Going to the plant. Have to see Moyer."

The guard, dressed in a dark-blue uniform with a badge, but no gun, stepped out of the shack.

"Got a pass? Nobody gets in here without a pass," he said.

"Look, I'm a lawyer—"

"Nobody gets in here without a pass. Especially lawyers, understand?"

I stood there wondering what the guy would do if I just took off running for the building. Would he chase me? Probably. Would he catch me? Probably.

We both heard it at the same time. A loud noise, the rapid discharge of high-pressure air from the tractor-trailer's brakes followed by a jarring crunch. The truck had backed into the cows' holding pen. The driver jumped out of the truck's cab and darted around his trailer.

"What the hell," the guard shouted and started running toward the truck.

The semi must have knocked down the holding pen fence, because ten or twelve black-and-white cows spilled out from around the back of the trailer. They ran wild, picking up speed as they broke for the open gate directly behind me. An instant later the half-ton animals were racing at full gallop. The cows charged straight at me as I stood frozen in the middle of their path to freedom.

The guard ran back and dove for the shack.

At the last second, I jumped out of the way and pressed my body tight against the wall of the guard shack. The frightened cows, chased by a couple of workers and the truck driver, escaped through the gate and raced out into the street. The herd turned and stampeded down Union Avenue. They ran uncontrolled, wild, like the running of the bulls in Pamplona, Spain.

I jerked my attention away from the raging herd and focused on the security guard. He had a phone receiver gripped tightly in his hand. His face took on a fire-engine hue as he yelled into the receiver, making it clear in harsh tones that the cow breakout was not his "*damn*" fault. The argument got hotter. When he went ballistic and started pounding the desk with his fist, I made my move and lit out for the rear of the meat plant. As I got closer to the building, I took a quick glance back at the guard. He was out of the shack now, mumbling as he dragged the gate across the pavement.

I found an entrance marked: USDA OFFICE, NO ADMITTANCE. I slowly turned the knob. It wasn't locked. Why lock the door; who could get past the guard? Glancing from side to side, and seeing no one, I slipped inside. I scanned the room; the inspector must be out to lunch. I hadn't given much thought about what I'd say if he were actually there sitting at his desk. Tell him I got lost looking for the little boys' room, I suppose.

Across the small unadorned office I spotted an exit that I hoped led to the rest of the plant. Next to the exit door a sign read, *"Federal law requires that white lab coats must be worn beyond this point."* Grabbing one from the rack, I shrugged into it, and with apprehension opened the door.

"God almighty!" I shouted. The blaring racket, stench, and blood splatter in the cold bright room was nothing compared to the sight of a dozen or more dead cows. They hung upside down from their hind legs. Their mouths were open wide and their swollen tongues dangled out, scraping the floor as they moved along on a chain conveyor suspended from the ceiling.

Workers dressed in blood-soaked, white uniforms and wearing black rubber boots were slipping and sliding all over the wet concrete as they flashed sharp knives and buzzing saws, hacking away at the hanging carcasses.

A wave of nausea overcame me and I vowed I'd never eat a piece of meat again. But then what did I expect? Sirloin steak, prime rib, and all-beef franks didn't grow on trees.

I stayed put, trying to figure a way to get across the kill-floor without getting tossed out on my can. Suddenly, a man dashed into the room and shouted to the workers, "Cows are loose. Let's go!"

Instantly, the men dropped their cutting tools

and headed toward an exit. One of the guys, a big Latino, ran to the far wall and snatched a rifle mounted there next to a fire extinguisher and a first-aid kit. He darted out the door, racing after his buddies waving the gun over his head.

I edged along the wall, pushed open a metal swinging door, and entered a long, dimly-lit hallway packed with people in work clothes moving from one processing room to another. Navigating through the crowd, I headed toward the front of the building. The workers smiled at me and politely stepped aside as I moved through them.

At first I thought it strange that no one asked what I was doing inside the plant. But then I noticed a small silver badge pinned on the outside of the white lab coat that I'd snatched from the office: *USDA Federal Inspector*. I'd have to ditch the coat as soon as I got to Moyer's office, before I got caught impersonating a government official, but for now the badge would help get me through the plant without being hassled.

After navigating through a maze of rooms where hundreds of employees turned slabs of cow meat into all-beef smoked franks, I finally found the main office. I stepped into a large area with a linoleum floor and fluorescent lighting. Twenty or thirty desks were jammed together in the room, staffed with people pounding business machines and answering the constantly ringing phones. A bright-eyed young woman with a chubby face directed me to Moyer's office.

The company vice president stood behind his desk with a phone in his hand. He held the receiver a couple of inches away from his face as he screamed into it. One look at Danny Moyer's bulbous nose and reddish face with its broken spider veins told me he enjoyed a stiff belt or two every now and then.

I stood silently in the open doorway until he finally looked my way. His face contorted as he cupped the receiver with his hand and waved me in. "Get in here, goddamn it," he said to me. "I want to talk to you." Then he faced the wall and started yelling into the phone again.

Entering the office, I noticed a half-empty bottle of Old Grand Dad sitting on his desk next to a well-worn paper cup. From the appearance of his prodigious belly, drooping sloppily over his green gabardine slacks, it didn't look like he wasted any of his drinking time hanging out at the gym.

Moyer continued to shout into the phone, getting hotter by the moment. His outburst had something to do with the company's bank overdraft, three-hundred thousand. He slammed the phone down yelling, "Bankers, those *cocksuckers*, have liquid nitrogen in their veins."

He turned toward me standing there. "It's your *goddamn* fault." He said, jabbing his fat finger at my face. "*Damn it*, I want this fucking plant opened. And I mean now! Those jobbers out front are ready to tear this place apart. They'll riot if we can't ship their *goddamn* orders."

"Me? What do I have to do with any of this?" It was then that I noticed two big thugs slouched on a couch that was shoved in the corner, giving me the eye.

"We cleaned up the place." Moyer took a deep breath. "Look around, *Goddamn it*! Go ahead, do your inspection." With labored breathing, he kept rattling on.

"Who called your headquarters anyway? If I find the son-of-a-bitch that reported us, I'll—" He stopped in mid-sentence, exhaled, and reached for a pack of Rolaids sitting on his desk next to the bottle of whiskey.

"Look, Moyer, I don't know what you're talking about. I'm here about Arnie Rosenthal's murder. I have nothing to do with. . ." God, the lab coat with the inspector's badge. I'm dead meat now, I thought.

As I started to remove the white coat, a guy stuck his head in the door and grabbed Moyer's attention.

"Hey boss," the guy said, "Manny's been arrested."

"Manny? Who the fuck is Manny?" Moyer shouted.

"He's the union rep. We can't run the kill-floor without Manny," the guy said.

"*Aw Christ*. Why was he arrested?"

"It seems some cows got loose. Manny was chasing them down, riding in the back of the company pickup truck, when..."

"Get to the point! *Jesus*."

"Yeah well," the guy sighed. "It seems that he was shooting over the cows' heads trying to turn them back, and well. . .I mean, he. . ." His trembling voice trailed off. It appeared as if being the messenger bearing bad news made the guy anxious to say the least. But then again, the look on Moyer's face would scare the bejesus out of a marble statue.

"*Goddammit*, Freddie—"

"Hit a cop car."

"He did *what*?"

"Nobody was hurt, but the cops cuffed Manny

and took him in."

Moyer yanked a white handkerchief from his pocket and mopped his sweaty face. "Call a bail bondsman," he said to Freddie. "Get his ass back here."

"Okay, boss."

"After that, call David Davis. Tell him to get the cops off our back. And, damn it, keep them off. Tell him to do what it takes, but get it fixed."

Before Freddie could react, Moyer spun around and pointed at me. "And while you have Davis on the phone, let him know this asshole here shut down my plant. And I want it back up and running, immediately. If not sooner."

"I'll get on it right away," Freddie said eagerly, then hesitated. "Who's David Davis?"

"Chet Hatfield's administrative assistant."

Freddy didn't budge.

"The congressman, you jerk!"

Freddy disappeared. Moyer, with his chin jutted out, now focused on me. "Well, are you going to open the plant or do you want to wait for the call from my guy on the Hill?" he said, the words slithering out through his malicious grimace.

"Moyer, listen. I'm not a meat inspector." I searched for somewhere to hang the lab coat while keeping sight of the two bruisers sprawled on the couch. "Mr. Moyer, I'm sorry, but I'm a lawyer. Name's O'Brien. I'm representing—"

Moyer's red face turned blue. Arteries on his forehead pulsed irregularly like Morse code—*danger ahead*.

"What! A *goddamn* lawyer? How the hell did you get in here? Get out. *Goddamn* it!"

I dropped the coat. It landed at my feet. "You were at the poker game—"

"I said get the hell outta here." Moyer moved fast, charging out from behind his desk; halfway he stopped. He snapped his fingers at the two bruisers on the couch, "Hey, you guys throw the bum out," he yelled.

Both gorillas slowly lifted their fat backsides off the couch, rising to their feet. The guy on the left puffed his chest. The other guy, striking a pose, flexed the muscles in his massive arms. Testosterone reeked.

"Hey, Moyer," one of the thugs said, dusting imaginary lint off his silk shirt. "We don't work for you. You want the asshole outta here, throw him out yourself."

If they didn't work for him, I wondered what the goons were doing in his office. These guys weren't there to sell Tupperware. From their appearance I figured they were professional leg breakers. Maybe he owed a debt to folks of an unsavory nature.

At that point, Moyer ran his eyes over the length of my body. "Okay. You got five seconds," Moyer said. "On second thought, just get the hell outta here. Right now, before I call Freddy."

I wondered if he was talking about Freddy, the pipsqueak who was just at the door.

"Where's Richie?" I asked. "Maybe I can talk to him. That is, if you're too busy at the moment. I've got a couple of things about the murder that I need to clear up."

He gave me an ugly sneer. "Richie? *Christ*, the nutcase is on the loading dock with a bunch of truckers, chanting."

"Chanting?"

"Yeah, *ommm, om nah ring nah choe.* Some kind of crazy shit like that. Can't get him to stop. He's got everybody buggy. *Goddammit,* he's Arnie's son, for *chrissakes.*"

With all the turmoil, chanting didn't sound like a bad idea to me; get everyone to simmer down until calmer heads prevailed.

"Maybe he thinks it'll help," I said. "Maybe relieve some of the stress around here."

"There is only one *goddamn* thing that'll help. And that is getting the inspectors off my ass and getting this *goddamn* plant back open."

With trouble surrounding Moyer like a heavy shroud it didn't seem as if I'd get a chance to have a serious discussion with him. I figured I could catch him later, someplace where he'd be able to loosen up and talk freely like a cocktail lounge. He'd go for that.

I started for the door, but a thought suddenly hit me. All the workers around here wore white uniforms like the one in Buck Simpson's effects. With all the commotion, I failed to make the connection until now.

"One question, then I'll go," I said turning toward Moyer. "Did Henry 'Buck' Simpson ever work here?"

Moyer remained silent for the first time since I arrived in his office.

"C'mon, Moyer. Did he, *or did he not* work here?"

"Never worked here. Now get out, *goddammit!*"

I started to leave again, but stopped at the doorway and shot him one last question: "Tell me about Guillermo."

Moyer froze for an instant, turned to the thugs, turned back, and jammed his finger at me, sputtering. Then he fell into his chair. While reaching across his desk for the bottle of booze, he mumbled, "Leave me alone, *please*."

I did as he asked. I left him alone. I had the answers to my questions.

Chapter Nineteen

I darted out of the meat company and hightailed it back to Union Avenue, looking for a phone booth along the way.

As I hurried up the street, I thought about Moyer's response when asked about Buck Simpson working at the plant. From the size of the company, there had to be at least five or six hundred people employed there. Moyer didn't even know that the union rep, a key figure in his operation, was named Manny. It would have been improbable that he would know, off the top of his head, if a lowly employee like Buck Simpson had ever been on the payroll. The obvious answer should've been, "I have no idea." But he didn't say that. He gave me an explicit response: *"Never worked here."*

I found a pay phone at a gas station on the corner of Union and Soto and called my office.

Mabel answered on the first ring. "Law office."

"Mabel, I—"

"If you're calling about the motions, don't worry. I've already re-typed the forms and served the DA's office this morning."

"Thanks, Mabel." I don't know why I bothered to spend Sunday afternoon typing the things. It probably took Mabel less than ten minutes. "Great, but listen," I said. "I've got an idea."

"Uh-oh."

"Do you remember Buck's clothes? Came in the box that you stashed in the storage closet."

"Of course."

"See if the clothing has a laundry mark on it. Or

the name of a uniform supply company, something like that."

"You want to find out where Simpson might've worked?"

"Yeah, in the meantime, I'm going across town to see an insurance man."

"Lucky you," Mabel said.

***

After a grueling forty-five minute ride through the streets of LA, I walked into the steel-and-glass high-rise tower at 1900 Avenue of the Stars in Century City and rode the elevator to the fourteenth floor. I entered the suite occupied by Lawrence and Associates and stopped at the receptionist's desk. Handing the attractive young woman my card, I asked to speak with Mr. Lawrence about an important legal matter. She said she'd check to see if he was available.

Lawrence stepped into the artfully decorated waiting room. The receptionist handed him my card, and with a toothpaste-commercial smile he escorted me to his office. He had steel-blue eyes and a long straight nose, which highlighted his thin, rather pale face. He wore an expensive light gray suit, the color of which matched his razor-cut and blow-dried hair.

He moved with confidence in long strides and spoke in a subdued and polite, yet commanding tone. His bearing suggested that he was a man of confidence and authority.

Leaning over, Lawrence opened the door, "After you," he said taking a slight bow with his arm out. I walked into a huge expanse of Persian carpeted luxury.

My God, I thought, he didn't rent this space by the square foot. He leased it by the acre.

Lawrence followed me in and marched to his desk, located in the south forty. He stopped at an overstuffed armchair facing the desk, patted it lightly, and said, "Take a seat here, Mr. O'Brien, and we'll talk in a moment. Forgive me," he said while putting on his reading glasses. "I must clear up a couple of pressing matters."

I sank into the chair and my nose came up to the edge of his desk. Uncomfortable, I decided to stand while waiting for Lawrence to finish fiddling with his papers, and strolled around the office.

Awards, certificates, and photos of him standing next to a number of entertainment celebrities, a few sports figures and, of course, the obligatory politician or two adorned the insurance man's trophy wall.

In one picture Lawrence was laughing it up with Ol' Blue Eyes himself, Frank Sinatra. In another he had his arm around Mattie Niles, the dynamic assemblywoman from the Fairfax district. I paused. Hanging next to the Niles photo was a shot of former Governor Reagan and Lawrence taken at the Reagan Ranch. They were perched atop palomino riding ponies—just a couple of old buckaroos, I thought, straddling their cayuses, *riding to the ridge where the west commences*...

Moving along the wall, I noticed a small triangular banner with red letters, GCYC, circled in the center against a blue background. The small flag, mounted on a plaque, hung on the wall next to a framed portrait of an expensive yacht.

"My yacht club burgee." I turned. Lawrence

had quietly moved up behind me. "Gold Coast Yacht Club in Newport. I'm a commodore."

"A commodore. Why, that's impressive." Commodore, I thought, sounds like a military rank of some sort. What does a commodore of a yacht club do, drill the rich guys on how to engage in naval gunnery without spilling their martinis?

"Yes, I'm a founding member and the honor came to me out of longevity, not because of my seafaring prowess, I must admit." He chuckled at his insincere self-deprecating remark.

I pointed to the picture of the vessel. "And that's your boat?"

He beamed. "My one indulgence. She's a custom built Rybovich, sixty-five feet of the finest craftsmanship...named her *Double Indemnity*." He hesitated. "Insurance, get it? He paused again. "Double indemnity. Twin Detroit diesel engines—"

"Like the movie," I said.

"Movie?"

"Yeah. Fred MacMurray has the hots for Barbara Stanwyck and bumps off her husband."

"I don't have time for movies." Lawrence turned and moved back to his desk.

"Too bad. It's a good one," I said, following. "But this is real. A beautiful young woman's wealthy husband has been murdered."

He sat behind the desk and leaned back with his arms folded across his chest.

"Yes, I know," he said.

"I'd like to ask you about something."

"Of course." His polished smile hadn't diminished since I arrived. Either he found me amusing, or the smile had been surgically planted on his face.

"I'm representing Mrs. Rosenthal. I'm her defense attorney, and I'm trying to piece together the events that transpired on the night of the murder."

"Tragic affair. Very unfortunate." Lawrence bowed his head in silence for a second or two.

"Yes, but she's innocent and I'm going to do everything I can to prove it," I said. "Regardless of what it takes."

"Mr. O'Brien, I'm impressed with your commitment. I'm sure Laura made the right choice when she retained you. And I believe she's innocent, as well," he said in a sincere manner. "For the life of me, I can't understand why the police have arrested her."

"Here's one reason. You told the cops that she quarreled with her husband on the night of the murder. The report says that you're going to testify as a witness for the prosecution?"

"The police questioned me intensely for over an hour, wanted every detail about what happened at the game that night. They finally wore me down and, well, I guess I did mention the argument. But I told the detectives that they were a loving couple and all married people occasionally have little spats." He leaned back in his chair and put his fingers to his lips, deep in thought.

"Just a little spat?"

"Yes, and that's hardly evidence she's a murderess."

"Do you happen to know what the 'little spat' was about?" I asked.

"No, but it was nothing, I'm sure."

"No slapping or shoving?"

"Of course not!"

The police report stated that the quarrel had been described as boisterous, but I didn't want to delve into that right then. Lawrence wasn't under oath and he could say anything he pleased without repercussions. I'd cover the argument later when I took his deposition. Today I wanted to focus on information that might help with my reasonable doubt defense. I needed to know about the guy who showed up at the game late that night. I wanted to find out exactly who he was and why was he there. He wasn't a regular. Joe Short would have known him if he was.

"A guy came late to the game," I said. "I think his name is Guillermo. What can you tell me about him?"

The lines at the edge of Lawrence's smile tightened almost imperceptibly. "Let's see, a man by the name of Guillermo. At the poker game?

"Yeah, the poker game."

"I don't know..." His voice trailed off and he looked at me over the top of his tortoise shell reading glasses.

I looked back, giving him my best cynical look. The one I'd practiced—right eyebrow raised, head tilted sideways with a callous frown on my face. I figured the look would come in handy when cross-examining reluctant witnesses.

He got up and moved to the floor-to-ceiling window behind his desk. He stood there with his back to me gazing out at the view that overlooked the city, Santa Monica Bay, and Malibu across an expanse of the Pacific Ocean.

"Oh yes, I remember, now," he said as he spun

around. "There was a gentleman who came later. And, if memory serves me, he *did* introduce himself as Guillermo. I thought it was a strange name."

The look worked. I'll be damned.

"Are you the one who invited him to the game?" I asked.

A dim shadow crossed his eyes and vanished just as fast. "No, of course not. He may have been an acquaintance of Arnie. I don't know."

He slipped back into his executive desk chair and adjusted a silver letter opener resting on his leather desk pad, moving it about a millimeter.

"Ever seen him before? Around the meat plant, at the house?" I asked.

"I told you, I don't know him." His face cracked. If this kept up his smile would disappear and he'd have to call the surgeon.

I gave him the look again, but his polished, professional smile remained. Maybe the look wasn't foolproof. "So you don't know the guy, huh?"

Lawrence stood. "I really want to help Mrs. Rosenthal. But, unfortunately, I have a very hectic day ahead of me. Perhaps you can arrange an appointment with Miriam, my private secretary."

"One more thing. You write all the insurance for the meat company, is that correct?"

"Yes, we've been very fortunate. It's a good account." He came from behind his desk with his hand out. "Now, it's been nice meeting you, and—"

I didn't move. "Workers' comp, health insurance, stuff like that?"

His hand dropped. "Yes, now if you'll excuse me—"

"You want to help Mrs. Rosenthal, don't you? Don't forget when this is all over she'll be a major shareholder in the company, your big customer."

"Certainly, I want to help all that I can, but right now—"

"Check your workers' comp insurance files," I said. "See if a Henry 'Buck' Simpson has worked at Farmer Fred's in the last couple of months."

"Who?"

"Buck Simpson. Now please, check your files. Henry Buck Simpson."

"That would be impossible."

"Why?"

"I'm terribly sorry, Mr. O'Brien, but I must ask you to leave."

"What about the files?"

"I don't see how that would help her."

I stood there a moment knowing I'd get nothing more out of Lawrence today. He seemed sincere when he said he didn't know anything about the mystery man, Guillermo. But I wondered why he wouldn't ask someone on his staff to check the agency's workers' comp files to see if Buck had ever worked at the plant. He didn't know why I needed the information, but he knew I was defending Laura and if he wanted to help, then that would've been reason enough.

However, even if Buck had worked there, I still didn't know what his murder had to do with Arnie's death. But my gut told me it wasn't just a coincidence.

"Sorry to intrude, Mr. Lawrence." I walked to the door, opened it, and glanced back at him standing by his desk staring at my card in his hand. He looked up; the smile was gone.

Chapter Twenty

I patted my jacket pocket where Richie's check rested. With an air of self-satisfaction, I dropped the envelope on Mabel's desk.

She looked up from her number crunching. "What's that?"

"Open it and see."

She pulled out the check. Her eyes lit up. "God Almighty," she said. "Is this for real?"

"Yes, ma'am. As real as it gets," I replied with a bit of smugness in my tone.

"It must be snowing in hell."

I didn't want to dampen her spirits by mentioning the fact that ten grand wouldn't make much of a dent in the expenses that would probably accrue by the time Laura's case went to trial. I'd think of a way to handle the cost later.

She started to gather her things.

"Where are you going?" I asked.

"To the bank before he puts a stop-payment on the check when he figures out we're really not that good."

Knowing Mabel's sarcastic wit, I let the remark pass. She was kidding; at least I hoped she was kidding.

"Wait, Mabel. Did you find out anything about Buck's uniform?"

She reached for a scrap of paper on her desk. "You were right. He worked at the wiener factory."

"How'd you know I figured he worked there?" She gave me a blank stare. I shouldn't have asked.

"A label sewn inside the pants and shirt had a serial number and a company name, Industrial United

Supply. They supply uniforms to all the meat companies in town, something about their detergent being USDA approved." She shrugged. "Anyway, the uniforms are rented to businesses like Farmer Fred's. Every week the supply company exchanges the dirty uniforms for fresh ones. If an employee is laid off or quits and fails to turn in his uniform, they bill the customer for the missing outfit."

"Obviously Buck's wasn't turned back in," I said.

"Obviously not. Every month quite a few go missing. But anyway, I called Industrial United. They traced the number printed on Buck's uniform through their system."

"And they found his uniform number?"

"Damn right. The one we have here in the closet, the one Buck Simpson had on when he was arrested, had been issued to Farmer Fred's Meat Company."

"That's great, Mabel, it proves—"

"Let me finish, damn it," she said. "While you were out dilly-dallying with the insurance guy I drove to the uniform supply company and gave the clerk fifteen dollars and change. I told him we wanted to keep the uniform. He naturally figured I was from Farmer Fred's. Now here's the good part."

"What?"

"The guy gave me a receipt."

"Well, of course. You gave him money and—"

"You don't understand. The guy made the receipt out to Farmer Fred's. Can you believe that?"

"And, of course, you didn't correct him."

"No way, José. We now have the uniform with

the laundry number, the letter from the jail, and a receipt made out to Farmer Fred's for Buck's uniform. I'd say that's proof that he worked there."

"It's proof all right. If needed, I can use it in court."

"Only one hitch," Mabel said.

"What's that?"

"When Farmer Fred's gets their monthly statement from the uniform supply company they'll see the payment listed and know that someone outside the company had paid for Buck's uniform. They won't know who paid for it, but they'll know somebody made the connection."

"Oh, I think they already know who made the connection," I said.

"Jimmy, you didn't!"

"Yeah, I kinda tipped my hand."

Mabel shot me a hard look. "*Goddammit,* Jimmy."

"What?' I asked.

"Just be careful, will you?"

"Yeah, sure."

She tucked Richie's check in her purse, snapped it closed then looked at me for a long moment.

"What's the matter, Mabel?"

"Jimmy, remember: two people are already dead."

Chapter Twenty-one

The next morning I drove to the United States District Court in downtown LA. Rita's first solo trial, the Busher bank robbery case, would be heard in Judge Cyrus Buckner's courtroom at nine a.m. I wanted be there as a friend just in case she needed me. I knew Rita would be nervous and perhaps a little frightened. And I figured she'd be disappointed when she lost and might need a shoulder to cry on.

I didn't think the trial would last more than a day or two. The assistant United States attorneys would parade their eyewitnesses in front of the jury: the bank employees and customers who were there at the time, the FBI agents who arrested Charlie with the money and the gun in his pocket, and the teller who had the pistol pointed in her face as she dished out the cash. The jury wouldn't take long to decide the case. Maybe an hour.

Rita didn't have any witnesses to call that I knew of, other than Charlie. But if she put him on the stand, and he tried to worm his way out of it by saying he just wanted his money back, the Feds would chew him up. No, I thought, the whole thing will turn out pretty grim.

Slipping into the courtroom, I took a seat in the third row of the visitors' section.

Judge Buckner pounded his gavel and the proceedings began. With no jury challenges the selection was completed in record time. The federal prosecutors gave their opening remarks, highlighting all the damning evidence that would put Charlie away for twenty years.

Rita's turn came next. She rose from the defense attorney's table, spotted me, and with a breezy smile winked. Then she marched purposefully to the jury box. She looked terrific in her new black suit and white pleated blouse specifically bought for this occasion.

"Ladies and gentlemen, good morning," Rita said pleasantly. She had the jury's attention. A couple of jurors even nodded and smiled. Then she turned and pointed to Charlie sitting at the defense table, hanging his head. "My client, Charlie, did not rob the bank."

Rita used his first name—good ol' Charlie, smooth Rita.

"He made a withdrawal of his own money." Rita walked back to the defense table and took her seat.

That's it? I thought. It didn't seem to be much of an opening statement. When she had the jury's attention maybe she should've expanded on the *good ol' Charlie* thing.

The U.S. Attorneys began presenting their case, calling their witnesses to the stand, one after another, and when asked who held the gun that day the customers and employees all turned and pointed at Charlie. One of the loan officers shook a finger at Rita's client and I thought I heard her say, "Naughty-naughty, Charlie." But I could've been mistaken.

Rita didn't move. She sat at the table staring straight ahead with her hands folded in front of her. She didn't object once, not even when the prosecutor was obviously leading a witness. She didn't cross-examine any of the witnesses either. She didn't even say a word when the government called Mrs. Spiels, the operations manager. Mrs. Spiels testified that during the robbery she stayed at her desk the whole time. Yet later she said that she saw Charlie get into his car and drive away. I asked myself, how could she have seen the car if she stayed at her desk the whole time?

"I'd like to call Mr. Brandworthy," the lead prosecutor announced.

"Counselor, it's close to lunch," the judge said. "How long is Mr. Brandworthy going to be on the stand?"

The government attorney glanced at the clock mounted on the wall. "Not long, Judge. The witness is the branch manager of the bank, and we merely need to verify the amount that the defendant stole."

"Call your witness."

The judge leaned back in his chair, took off his watch, and started to wind the stem. There couldn't be any doubt now in the jurors' minds about Charlie's guilt. The banker's testimony would just be a technicality, tedious and boring.

As the banker walked to the witness stand, I glanced at the defense table. Charlie sat stoically with his chin on his chest, as he had all through the trial. Rita continued to stare straight ahead. They looked like two people sitting on a bench waiting for a bus.

Sympathy for Rita tugged at my heart. A couple of days ago she had spent hours lining up an anger management therapist for Charlie. After that she had to persuade Charlie to use some of his inheritance to attend the sessions. He finally agreed when she promised that she'd win the case and he'd be released. It appeared now that Charlie would spend the next twenty years in federal penitentiary and treatment would no longer be an option.

Mr. Brandworthy was sworn in and took a seat

in the witness chair. With prompting from the prosecutor the banker gave a deliberate and mind-numbing explanation about the bank's accounting procedures. The system was foolproof. The bank's figures were accurate.

The prosecutor had no additional questions and Mr. Brandworthy stood and started to step down.

Rita raised her arm. "Your Honor, I have a question for the witness."

The judge looked down at Rita, perturbed. "Hmm, a question?" He glanced at his watch. "Can't it wait until after lunch?"

Rita grabbed a paper from her briefcase and walked boldly forward. "Only take a few moments, Your Honor. Sit down, Mr. Brandworthy," she demanded.

The judge rolled his eyes. "Proceed."

The two prosecutors stopped stuffing papers into their briefcases and looked up at the judge. He shrugged. They sat and focused on Rita and Brandworthy.

"This is a letter that my client received from your bank." Rita handed the paper to the witness. "Is that your signature on the bottom?"

Brandworthy took a passing glance at the document. "Yes, it is."

"Did you write the letter?"

"Well, my secretary—"

"Yes, or no. Did you dictate or write that letter?"

"Yes."

Rita took the letter from Brandworthy and walked to her table. She picked up another document and showed it to the witness. "Is this a copy of a cashier's check that you sent with the letter?"

"Well, yes."

"Your signature?"

"Yes."

The lead prosecutor stood. "Your Honor, I don't see the relevance of—"

"Let her finish. The young lady said it would only take a moment."

Rita previously had given the federal attorneys copies of these documents and now they were digging through their briefcases, trying to find them.

"Mr. Brandworthy, will you please tell the jury the dollar value of the check."

The banker stated the amount then went on to explain how the bank had arrived at the figure. He told the jury that Charlie Busher had a certificate of deposit on account with the bank. The bank promptly refunded the principal and accumulated interest, he said, but they deducted a few small handling charges, a charge for processing the check, and a penalty for early withdrawal. It was all perfectly legal. The bank, Brandworthy noted, also deducted the amount that Charlie stole that day.

Rita took back the copy of the check and handed Brandworthy the letter again.

"All the deductions are explained in your letter. Is that correct?"

"I believe so."

"Now, regarding the deductions. In the letter, which is a legal document signed by you, how did you classify the last deduction on the page, the amount handed to Charlie on the day in question?"

"What do you mean?" Brandworthy asked.

"Here, I'll show you," Rita said. "Do you see in the letter where you guys deducted fifty-seven dollars for penalties?"

Mr. Brandworthy held the letter in his two hands and stared at it intently. "Yes, I see it, and it's very clear why we deducted that amount."

"Of course. And next to the amount, you described the reason for the deduction. Early withdrawal penalty. Is that correct?"

"That's the reason we deducted the fifty-seven dollars. Early withdrawal penalty."

"Fine; now, how did you describe the fifteen hundred dollars that was given to Charlie?"

"You mean the money he took?"

"Your teller gave Charlie the money and he took it, of course. Now please, tell the jury how the letter describes the deduction."

Brandworthy didn't speak. He looked up at the judge, and getting no reaction he focused on the letter in his hand.

"Please, Mr. Brandworthy, we'd all like to go to lunch. Tell us what it says," Rita said.

"Withdrawal. Fifteen hundred dollars."

"You included a copy of the withdrawal receipt with the letter?"

"Yes."

Rita turned to Judge Buckner. "Your Honor, I'd like to make a motion for a directed verdict of not guilty."

The judge sat straight up in his chair. "On what grounds?"

"The crime of bank robbery, as charged in the

indictment, has four essential elements. The government must prove that all four had occurred," Rita said. She held her hand in the air and counted off the points on her fingers. "One: the defendant took the money in the presence of another that belonged, or was in the custody of the bank. Two: such taking was by force. Three: the defendant, while taking the money, had used a deadly weapon. And number four—"

"We get the point, counselor," the judge said. "I think we all know the law."

"Of course, Your Honor, but I wanted to establish—"

"Hold on a second." The judge turned and peered at Brandworthy. "Are you telling this court that the transaction was a withdrawal? That the money belonged to the defendant? And then you deducted the amount he took at the point of a gun from his certificate of deposit when you sent him a refund?"

"Well, yes, but—"

The two Fed's were on their feet. "Your Honor," the lead attorney said, "even if the money belonged to the defendant, the indictment clearly states that at the time of the robbery the money was in the custody of the bank. Custody fulfills the requirement of element one, as the defense attorney has pointed out."

The prosecutors sat at their table, smiled at each other, and nodded their heads confidently. Any moment now, I figured they'd clap themselves on the back and do a little victory fandango.

Rita glanced at the prosecutors, waited a moment, and turned back to Judge Buckner. "Your Honor, will the assistant U.S. attorneys stipulate that the money in question came from Charlie's certificate of deposit? Because if it didn't come from his CD, then the bank stole the money from my client. They deducted the money from his refund, but Charlie hadn't been proven guilty of any crime."

The two prosecutors huddled, whispered, and in a few seconds, they sat back in their chairs. The lead attorney slowly climbed out of his chair, waffling his hand as he stood. "Your Honor," he said in a slow condescending manner, "it doesn't matter if it was his money or not. Like I said, the money was in the custody of the bank and the defendant used deadly force—"

The judge pointed his gavel and shook it at him. "Did the money come from the CD? That's what the young lady wants to know."

"I suppose so. But—"

"You *suppose* so?" the judge growled.

"All right, it came from the CD, so stipulated." The attorney sat in his chair.

Rita patiently waited until the exchange was completed and then said, "Your Honor, I again request that the court dismiss the charges against Charlie."

The judge sighed. "The government has made its point, Miss Flores. The law is clear. Even though the money came from the defendant's CD, it was still in the custody of the bank at the time. And I think there is probable cause that the defendant used force. There's testimony that he had a weapon."

"Okay," she said. "I'd like to ask the witness one more question," Rita turned to Mr. Brandworthy. "Sir, are your certificates of deposit—specifically the type of CD that Charlie owned—insured by the Federal Deposit Insurance Corporation?"

"Checking accounts, passbook accounts, and

some certificates are, but Charlie Busher's certificate of deposit paid a high interest rate..." he paused.

Rita glowered at him with her hands on her hips. "Please, Mr. Brandworthy, just answer the question."

"Okay, the answer is no. That particular type of CD isn't insured by the government."

An audible groan came from the prosecutor's table. The lead government attorney put his head in his hands and the other one slouched back in his chair.

"What'd I say?" The bank manager glanced around, then twisted in his chair and faced the judge.

"Bank robbery is a federal crime and the crime has four elements," the judge said to Brandworthy. "Element four of the crime states that the bank's funds, the money that the defendant took, must be insured by the Federal Deposit Insurance Corporation."

"Thank you, Your Honor. Now, about my motion?"

The judge held his palm out at Rita, like a traffic cop. He glared at Frick and Frack, my new name for the federal lawyers.

"Did the government include any lesser charges, like, for example, one or more weapons and firearm violations in the indictment?" The judge made a show of picking up the copy of the indictment documents, flipping the pages back and forth. "Funny, I don't see it listed here if you did."

Frick and Frack stood and desperately shuffled through their papers. "Well, did you?" the judge growled again.

I took a quick look at Rita. She stood calmly at the defense table with her hands folded in front of her. I saw a hint of a smile blossom on her angelic face as she gazed mindlessly at the ceiling. I knew it. Everyone knew it. She had won the case.

"I can't *hear* you," the judge chanted, aiming his venom at the Feds.

"I-I don't think so," one of the prosecutors mumbled.

"Don't think so? My God, who are you guys?" The judge pounded his gavel.

Frick and Frack didn't speak. They just sank slowly into their seats.

The case was dismissed, and the judge sternly admonished the prosecutors for their failure to charge Charlie with any firearm statutes that he'd violated. Due to Charlie's rights under the Fifth Amendment— the doctrine of double jeopardy—he couldn't be charged with these crimes again, at least not in federal court. He was free to go.

While waiting for Rita and Charlie to complete the final paperwork with the court clerk, I called the office from a pay phone in the hall, telling Mabel the good news.

"I'll have champagne on ice, and I'll call Luigi's Deli and ask them to send over some pizza and a platter of goodies. We'll have a little celebration here in the office. Sound good?"

"You bet," I said.

Twenty minutes later, Rita walked out of the courtroom with Charlie at her side. As they came through the door, Rita was in the middle of giving Charlie a stern reminder about the anger management therapist. He nodded meekly at every word.

She saw me and raised her arms. "We won! Jimmy, we won."

"I know you did, Rita. You pulled it off. You did an amazing job. No lawyer could've handled the case better. Not even a man."

At first she glowered at me. Then she laughed. We all laughed.

Chapter Twenty-two

As I drove up Florence Avenue heading for the office, I mulled over Rita's victory and her trial. At Lakewood Boulevard, it hit me: the gun. All the witnesses were questioned about the gun. The prosecutors kept referring to the gun in Charlie's hand. The holdup weapon was a key point in their case. The Rosenthal murder scene flashed in my mind and I felt like a fool. Pegis's homicide report contained no mention of the firearm lying on the carpet. A first-year law student would have seen it. The murder weapon found at the scene wasn't listed in the evidence report. For crying out loud, anyone that ever watched Perry Mason on TV would've noticed the glaring omission.

Who owned the gun? Arnie, Laura, the intruder?

When I walked in the front door, Mabel stood on a stepstool, stapling a six-foot-long banner to the wall. Printed on it were the words:

CONGRATULATIONS—IT'S A BOY.

"Don't say anything," she said, as she climbed down from the stool. "They didn't have anything at the stationery store that said, 'congratulations, you freed a bank robber.'"

I let the remark pass and viewed the outer office. Colorful balloons, tied to the chairs by crepe streamers, hovered just below the ceiling. A couple bottles of domestic champagne, chilling in cardboard ice buckets, a platter of cold cuts, and an open box of pizza covered the top of Mabel's desk.

"Nice going, Mabel. Rita will be thrilled." I nodded toward my office. "I'll be right back. I have to make an important call."

I stepped into my office, grabbed the phone, and dialed the district attorney's office. "Mark Webster, please. Jimmy O'Brien calling."

While I waited for Webster to come on the line I opened the top desk drawer, pushed Simpson's Buck knife aside and pulled out the police report. I had no use for the knife. I made a mental note to give it to Luigi. Perhaps he can use it to chop garlic or something.

"This is Webster."

"Hey, Steve, I got Pegis's report in front of me. Guess what, there is nothing in it about the gun."

"What gun?"

"What do you mean, *what gun*? The murder weapon used to kill Rosenthal, the .25 on the floor by the body? There's nothing in the report about it."

"Are you accusing Pegis of falsifying the report?'

"No, Mark, for chrissakes, gimme a break. I'm just saying there's nothing in the report about the murder weapon, that's all."

"Look, O'Brien, when Pegis wrote the report, he hadn't received the details from ballistics. The weapon hadn't been tested. You wanted the report fast, so—"

"Okay, but I'm sure the gun has been tested by now."

"Yeah, I'm sure it has," the deputy D.A. said.

"And?"

"The .25 found at the scene was the gun used to kill him, okay. The details will be in the information that I'll file after the prelim. Now I've got to get back to court, afternoon session is about to begin."

"Hold it, Mark. Whose gun is it?"

"We don't know."

"Didn't you run the serial number?"

"I gotta go, O'Brien."

"Are you holding out on me?"

There was a short pause on the line. "There you go again."

"What about the serial number?"

"It was removed, filed off, not a trace. Look, I can't talk anymore. I'm late for court. See you around, O'Brien."

I leaned back in the chair and put my feet on the desk. Webster said, *not a trace* of the serial number remained on the gun. That meant the number had to have been removed by a professional. That fact will play well before the jury. Laura wouldn't have had the ability to remove the serial number completely. If an amateur filed the number down far enough so that you couldn't see it with the naked eye, the impression would still be imbedded in the molecular structure of the gun's metal. The number could be detected by a sophisticated crime lab. The .25 used to murder Arnie was a professional hit piece, altered by someone who was proficient and had the necessary tools to do the job. I was sure of it.

Mabel stuck her head in the door. "Party's starting. Sol's on his way too."

I moved to the outer office and poured a cup of coffee. Rita, Mabel, and Charlie were sipping champagne and chatting. I raised my cup high in the air.

"To Rita," I said in a loud voice. "And to her hard-fought victory."

They cheered, clicked their glasses together, and drank.

"I knew all along she'd win the case," I added.

"Boss, I told you I had an idea. When the bank sent Charlie that letter, I knew right then that I could nail them. I didn't do anything so great, they did it to themselves."

"Rita, it was brilliant how you got the bank to send that letter in the first place. Take the credit. You deserve it."

Her smile grew wider. "Thanks, Jimmy, I will. But if Mabel hadn't been hounding me to get some money from Charlie, who knows." Rita tilted her glass to Mabel. "Thanks."

As Charlie and I added to Rita's praise of Mabel, the door flew open. Sol burst in carrying a large bouquet of yellow roses in one hand and a little white box in the other.

"Congratulations, you little *bubeleh*," he said, placing the flowers and the package on an end table. He then rushed over and hugged Rita. When he pulled away he saw Charlie standing alone by the desk. "C'mon here and shake my hand, Charlie."

Charlie shuffled over to Sol and stuck out his hand. "Hey, Mr. Silverman."

"Hey to you, Charlie." Sol pumped his hand. "You know something, you got guts, and I liked the way you handle a gun. You take those therapy sessions Jimmy told me about, and when you're ready, come and see me. Might have a job for you around the place. Is that a deal?" Sol patted him on the back.

Charlie's grin stretched from one side of his face to the other, exposing a few missing teeth.

"It's a deal," Charlie said. "But I gotta tell ya ahead of time: can't count on me for no fancy shootin'. The boys at the jail took my old .44 away. And Rita said I can't have one no more."

"That's okay, Charlie, anyone can shoot. We need someone who can keep our cars in tiptop shape, washed and polished and ready to go at a moment's notice. Can you handle that?"

"You're darn tootin'. I got experience, worked at Downey Car Wash."

They shook hands again. "It's a deal then," Sol said.

Mabel handed Sol a glass of champagne. He took it and held it up to the light. "Interesting. Yellow champagne." Sol took a sip, set the plastic glass down, and picked up the little white box he brought with him. "Rita, my dear, this is for you, but you can't open it until you get home. Promise?"

"Oh, Sol, thank you. How sweet."

I remembered the reason that Charlie needed money when he walked into the bank that day. His girlfriend had to have a car. When I was able to get Rita alone for a moment, I asked her what'd happened to Charlie's girl.

"As soon as he left the bank," Rita said, "before the police caught up with him, he gave her the fifteen hundred so she could buy a car. He hasn't seen her since."

"Poor guy. Now that he's been acquitted, maybe she'll come back."

"Get real, boss."

Fifteen minutes later, after Sol had polished off half the pizza and made a sizable dent in the platter of cold cuts, we retreated to my office. I needed help with the Rosenthal case, and Sol's expertise would help immensely.

I hated the idea of imposing on Sol again, and I couldn't guarantee that money would be available for even a cut-rate fee, but I didn't have much choice and I knew it wouldn't hurt our friendship to ask Sol for help with Laura's arrest.

We made small talk for a bit then I brought up Laura's predicament. "Laura's arrest is complicated and I sure could use your expertise, Sol."

"Tell me about the case," Sol said.

Sol and I had worked *pro bono* cases together in the past, but now with all the malarkey coming from the ever-present media about the Wienie Widow and the fortune at stake, I didn't think he'd provide his services without some sort of payment up front. He was in business, after all, with a huge overhead to worry about. His staff was superlative, his operatives unparalleled, and he paid them accordingly.

"Sol, there's not much money available. Arnie's estate is frozen and Laura doesn't have a lot."

His bushy eyebrows arched. "Who said anything about money? I just asked how it's going. Didn't ask to be cut in."

"I want you involved," I said.

"Nah, you're just saying that."

I held my arms out. "Look at me, I'm begging," I said, with a smile.

"You're just trying to make me feel better. I won't take your kind offer."

I reached in my drawer, and pulled out my checkbook. "Richie, her stepson, gave me ten thousand—"

"Put the checkbook away," he said, now serious. "When I take a case, I work for the client. I get paid by the client, not you. Besides, with a murder rap you'll need every dime of that money, and probably a lot more."

"Sol, I know your clients normally pay their fees up front, but with this case there will be nothing available for starters. Unless she walks, of course, then she'll have a large life insurance settlement."

"You'd have to win the case. Otherwise the insurance goes away. Your client would have to be completely exonerated. No plea bargain, lesser charges, or anything like that."

"I know, but this is a murder-one case. I'll have to keep the plea option open. It might be the only way to save her from doing life without parole and get her a reduced sentence."

"That means at the last minute, after we've spent hours working on her behalf, you could decide not to go to trial and accept a plea. If that happens we'd get nothing. Is that the way it's going to be?" Sol asked.

"That's the way it's *got* to be," I answered.

"And you're satisfied with that deal?"

"She's my client and needs my help. If she's innocent, I'll get her off, but—"

"Count me in. Jimmy. Goddamn it, I've never turned you down. Have I?"

Sol picked up his drink and raised the glass to the light, pretending to examine the small bubbles.

"But I feel like I'm taking advantage of our friendship."

With a deliberate motion, Sol set his glass down on my desk. "Jimmy, I thought I taught you better than that."

"What do you mean?"

"If you can't stick it to your friends, who can you stick it to?"

I laughed. "That's right. I remember. Sol's Rule Number One."

"Now it's Jimmy's Rule Number One."

"No. It's Jimmy's Rule Number Two," I said.

"What's Jimmy's Rule Number One?"

"Always come back for more."

He laughed, then became serious again, his business side kicking in. "So, here's the way I figure it: if you win the case Laura goes free and we get paid. But if you lose, well..." Sol pulled a cigar from his breast pocket and fiddled with the wrapper. "Well, it won't change *my* lifestyle."

"I won't lose...I may not win, but I won't lose."

Sol smiled. "Irish logic," he said, and shook his head.

Chapter Twenty-three

I brought Sol up to speed, telling him about the serial number on the Rosenthal murder gun being filed off by a professional. Then I went on to explain what was discussed during my visits with Richie, Moyer, and David Lawrence. I laid out what Mabel had discovered about Buck's uniform. How I thought the two cases might be related, and how Moyer lied when I asked if Buck Simpson ever worked there. I told him how stunned Moyer looked when I mentioned Guillermo.

"Jimmy, I'm still not convinced that Buck's murder is tied in, but I'm getting the idea that you think Moyer had Arnie knocked off, then framed Laura," Sol said. "And the gun makes it a professional hit. That he hired this Guillermo guy to do the job. Is that what you're thinking?"

"It'd make sense, if I could find a motive."

"What about the insurance guy, Lawrence? What's your take on him?"

"He's working with the DA and not really cooperating with me. But I've got a gut feeling that Moyer told him to keep quiet about Guillermo showing up at the game. He makes good money writing the insurance for Farmer Fred's. Moyer runs the company. So I figure Lawrence is just doing what he's been told to do."

"You think Lawrence makes enough dough from the meat company to lie about a murder investigation?"

"He's lying to me, not the police or the DA's office. The cops don't know about Guillermo. He wasn't mentioned in the police report, so obviously they didn't ask Lawrence about him. Besides, I highly doubt that Moyer would tell Lawrence anything about Guillermo, who he is or why he was at the game. I think he just told Lawrence to keep quiet about him."

"So, you figure he's not an accomplice?"

"I don't think Lawrence has a clue as to who murdered Arnie."

Sol's eyes went from the wine glass to me. "Don't you think he'd be a tad suspicious? A stranger shows up at the game. Later Arnie is murdered and Moyer tells him to keep his trap shut?"

"Lawrence is kind of egotistical. He probably didn't give it a second thought."

"Maybe he thinks Laura did it."

"I don't think he cares, just as long as he gets to write the company's insurance. He agreed to see me; didn't have to. He's hedging his bet. If Laura is set free, then she takes over the company and decides who is going to write their insurance. But if she's put away, Richie will head back to New York and Moyer will continue to run Farmer Fred's."

Sol drained his glass and set it on my desk. "So you think Moyer hired Guillermo to do the job?"

"It adds up."

Sol paused to collect his thoughts. "Would Rosenthal let someone in his house at one in the morning? Someone he didn't know?"

"Moyer could've brought Guillermo to the game," I said, "introduced him to Arnie, and later, Guillermo could have wormed an invitation to go to Arnie's house on some pretext. Then..." I made a gun with my fingers and pointed at my head. "...bang."

"Jimmy, you go public with this hit man theory

and you'll be making the DA's case against Laura. They'd figure, with her background, she'd know some lowlife in the business that could do the job."

"Yeah, I thought of that. The cops would think Laura hired the killer and let him in the house that night."

Sol made a steeple with his fingers. "Jimmy, I've gotta tell you something."

"What?"

"I haven't been sitting on my *toches*, you know. I figured you were going to ask for help."

"Wait a minute. How'd you—"

"And I've been doing a little digging."

"You made me go through my whole spiel, no money, all that stuff, and you were going to help me anyway?"

Sol grinned. "Of course, haven't I always?"

"Yeah, but—"

"Shut up and listen. I have information that might go to motive. It's a stretch, but who knows?"

At that moment, the door flew open and Mabel swept in holding the almost empty bottle of champagne. "You want to finish this Sol? Hate to toss it out."

"Thanks, you big beautiful creature." Sol stood and took the bottle from Mabel. "If I were six months younger, sweetheart, you wouldn't stand a chance."

Mabel laughed. "Sol, did you inherit that line of bullshit or did you find it lying in the street?"

"Oh, you sweet talker, you." Sol filled his glass, raised it to Mabel in a mock toast, and swallowed the wine in one gulp.

"Did Rita leave?" I asked.

"Yeah, she drove Charlie home. Said to tell you

goodbye." Mabel pointed at Sol. "And she said to tell the aging lothario sitting there, thanks again for the gift. Rita can't wait to get home and open it. Now, if you two boys will excuse me, I'm gonna tidy up a bit then I'm gone too."

Sol filled his glass with the last of the champagne. He picked up the empty bottle, scrutinizing the label. "No offense, Jimmy, but where did you get this stuff?"

"Sol, forget the champagne. Tell me what you found out."

He leaned back and wrapped his arms around his massive chest. "We pulled the records. Richie's right. Financially, the meat company is in the toilet. It's going downhill fast."

"How do you think the company's money problems ties in?"

"We dug a little deeper."

"And?"

"Moyer's a heavy gambler with big losses. I think he's tapping the company."

"Think so?"

"Yeah, and I think he knows you're on to him."

Chapter Twenty-four

Sol left, and I hung around the office jotting notes about our discussion. Sol thought Moyer was tapping the company to cover his gambling losses. He figured Arnie caught him at it. And that would be the powerful motive that I needed in my reasonable doubt defense.

I walked around trying to figure out the DA's response when I dropped this bomb on the jury. I knew what I would ask if I were the DA. The question would be simple: if Arnie found out his trusted employee was stealing money from him, why would he casually sit down with the guy for a friendly game of poker?

Sitting at my desk again, I picked up my pen and doodled on my yellow legal tablet. Another question dogged me and I couldn't shake it loose. I threw down my pen and assumed my thinking posture, leaning back with my feet on the desk. The image of Buck hanging from a sheet in the jail laundry played in the back of my mind like a ghostly film clip on a never-ending loop. And a question rattled in my brain—why did Moyer lie about Buck working at the plant?

I was on a panel of court appointed attorneys who represented indigent prisoners and parole violators. I drew Buck as a client a few days before Laura called me. Could it be just a coincidence that Buck worked at Farmer Fred's, or could his death be somehow tied into the Rosenthal case? Sol didn't think so. Mabel said it would be a waste of time chasing after Buck's killers. But I just couldn't let it go.

The day drifted into evening. I put my notes away, rinsed out the coffeepot, and opened the office door to leave. Outside in the parking lot, dimmed by the evening twilight, I caught a glimpse of a black Ford LTD idling in Rita's spot. I hunched over, fumbling with my keys.

The air trembled! A gunshot!

The slug slammed into the door, just missing my head.

I caught a glimpse of the shooter. Like a scene in slow motion he came toward me, walking slower with each exaggerated step.

Move, Jimmy, move. My shoes were lead; my arms hung useless at my side, dangling like a puppet's with the strings cut.

Then, an adrenaline rush kicked in. I jerked the door open, and in a maneuver I didn't know existed, twisted back into the office.

Scared shitless, I slammed the door shut, hugged the wall and waited...

A hissing whack followed twice in rapid succession. Two more shots tore through the door.

And then silence.

Five, ten, fifteen seconds I stood in the silent darkness. Silent, except for the pounding in my chest and the blood roaring through my veins. I took quick breaths, inhaled deep, and exhaled until oxygen neutralized the adrenaline. I had to keep my cool. I had to *think*. In my mind, I saw the shooter outside. His arms were extended, his hands held an automatic, and he moved around the back of the Ford with his gun pointed at me.

Think, Jimmy. The gun had a silencer on it. Nobody beyond a hundred feet would hear the shot. And no one would see him; the streets were basically deserted. Silencer! He's a pro. Means he won't quit.

He's going to come through the door.

I raced to the phone on Mabel's desk. Dead. He cut the line.

Charging into my inner office, I locked the door, and in the darkness, found the way to my desk. I yanked open the top drawer and grabbed Buck's knife.

Me with a knife against a professional killer with a gun. Didn't seem fair.

Think, Jimmy. Was the guy alone? I only saw him for an instant. There could've been another guy in the car. I didn't know.

"Why is this happening?" I whispered to myself.

I heard the shot that blasted the front door lock. The shooter was in the outer office now.

In seconds, he'd be in here. I darted across the room and flattened myself against the wall next to the door. I raised the knife in front of my face.

Under my breath I said, "Come through that door, you son of a bitch! I'm waiting."

My eyes became used to the darkness; I reached over and quietly unlatched the lock.

Light from the outer office seeped in from the gap under the door. Within a few heartbeats, the knob turned. The door opened about three inches, and a hand, holding the gun, slowly poked through the slot.

My nerves were on fire. I felt as if I'd been jabbed with an electric prod. *Keep calm, keep calm,* I chanted silently. A few more seconds and I'll make my move.

I stared at the opening, sweat pouring from my face. The door creaked open a few more inches, and the shooter's head followed the gun into the room.

Come in, just a little more, *please.* The shooter

moved faster now, but his eyes weren't accustomed to the dark. He stopped halfway.

I squeezed the knife tightly. With caution, he stepped into the room.

Like lightning, I moved from behind the door, grabbed his hair with my left hand, and shoved the blade up under his jaw with my right. I didn't push it in all the way, but I cut him and blood flowed. I felt the warm sticky fluid trickle over my hand and run down my arm.

"Drop the gun, asshole!" I screamed in his face.

"*Jesus*, I'm bleeding."

"Drop it! Now!"

The gun clattered to the floor. "Kick it across the room," I shouted. He did, and the gun slid under the desk.

I pushed the guy back into the outer office, and swung him around until I was behind him, the knife pressed firmly against his spinal column. A flick of my wrist and it's lights out.

He had on a black sweatshirt and black Levi's. The guy was taller than me by a couple of inches, and he outweighed me a good thirty or forty pounds.

At first, I thought the guy might be Guillermo, but Joe Short said Guillermo was a Latino, and in the light of Mabel's office I could see the bastard was an Anglo.

With his arms raised, I saw a symbolic jailhouse tattoo etched on the back of his right hand. The asshole had done prison time.

The blood from under his chin, where I nicked him, dripped to the carpet. Mabel would be pissed about that.

"Who sent you?"

The bastard didn't speak.

I pushed the blade in a little into the hard flesh of his back. It had to hurt like hell.

"*Goddammit*, who sent you?"

"Go ahead; shove it in all the way. I don't give a shit. I ain't talking."

He's one tough son-of-a-bitch, I thought as I marched him through the shattered front door and out into the parking lot. I took a quick glance at the Ford LTD. Nobody there. I shoved him toward the corner gas station where a horrified passerby ran screaming to call the police.

First, I heard sirens wailing in the distance. Then I saw traffic on Lakewood start to slow, the cars pulling to the side of the road. Black and whites converged on us from all directions with their lights flashing and their sirens screaming.

I glanced over my shoulder. One of the cop cars raced up behind us and slid to a stop about ten feet away. I looked to my right. Two more cruisers charged up Lakewood, side by side, zooming past vehicles stopped at the curb. Straight ahead, a squad car swerved to miss a Volkswagen and skidded to a dead stop five feet in front of us.

Police officers bolted from their vehicles with revolvers and shotguns drawn. The cops flashed a spot on us. From behind one of the cars came an amplified voice that reverberated through the night.

"Drop the weapon. Now!" the faceless voice demanded.

I whirled us around. Surrounded. We stood in a circle of bright light and eight or ten cops had us in their sights. I kept the knife pressed against the guy's back. The entire time he hadn't moved a muscle. He stood in the bright light like a propped-up mummy on display.

"Bring the cuffs. I've got him under control," I yelled.

I wondered, *why all the firepower?* The thug was unarmed and I had a knife against his back.

"Last chance! Drop the knife and raise your hands." I heard the ratcheting sound of a couple of shotguns.

I did both, the knife fell to the ground, and my arms shot up into the air. Instantly I was huddled in the middle of dark blue uniforms. One cop grabbed my arms and forced them behind my back while another snapped the cuffs on my wrists. I was jostled toward one of the police cars and felt a hand pushing on the top of my head as the cop forced me into the back seat.

As we sped away, I looked back and saw two plainclothes officers talking to the guy who tried to kill me, but *he wasn't cuffed.* I fumed inside, but I kept quiet on the way to the station.

Totally pissed off, with my shoulders and wrists sore as hell, I sat cuffed and alone for over forty-five minutes locked in an interrogation room. Finally the door opened and two detectives came in. One, wearing a beat-up checkered sport coat, stayed by the door and kept quiet.

The other, a big black man, wore a short-sleeve white shirt with a purple knit tie loosely knotted at his neck. He had a friendly face, but from his commanding demeanor, I figured he was the type of cop that didn't take any crap. I figured he played it right down the middle.

He came over and unlocked the handcuffs. "Sorry about the misunderstanding, O'Brien," he said.

"You know who I am?"

"Yeah, a couple of our men recognized you when we brought you in. Said you're the Wienie Widow's lawyer. I went to the scene. Saw the bullet holes in your office, the phone line cut. I can add one and one."

"I guess that makes you the department's math whiz," I said, rubbing my wrists.

"Can't blame you for being a little hot, but think about it. You used to be on the job. What would you do? Guy with a knife and all that."

"Did you hold the knuckle-dragger or did you let him walk?"

"We spotted the tattoo. He's in the lock-up now. Won't talk, but we're running his prints."

"Got any coffee?"

The detective nodded and turned to the other cop in the room. "Deter, get O'Brien a cup."

"Thanks," I said.

He turned back to me. "I'm Sergeant Trayvon Stinnett. I caught the call on this one. Now suppose you tell me what it's all about."

I told Stinnett the short version. The scene in the parking lot, the Ford LTD, and how the gunman came into my office. I explained why there happened to be a knife in the drawer without going into detail about Buck's murder. I just said that the jail had sent me his effects. I didn't get into anything related to the Rosenthal case.

"You're not giving me much, O'Brien." Stinnett

sat across from me with both hands on the table. He fussed with his simple gold wedding band while he spoke. "Does this have anything to do with your client, the babe who whacked her old man?"

"You know I can't talk about her. Attorney-client privilege."

"Why'd the bad guy come after you, anyway?"

"Maybe he doesn't like lawyers. Maybe I just pissed him off. Christ, how in the hell am I supposed to know why the son-of-a-bitch tried to kill me?"

"I'm sure you piss off a lot of people, O'Brien, because you're beginning to piss me off." Sergeant Stinnett stood, turned to the two-way mirror on the far wall, and made a slight gesture with his head.

Deter came back with the coffee. I took a sip and winced. I set the cup on the table.

"Is this how you get suspects to talk? Force them to drink this battery acid until they confess? Go back to the rubber hoses, Stinnett, more humane."

I nodded at the cup of coffee. "Give it to the shooter, he'll talk."

"Oh, he already talked." Stinnett said. "Wants me to tell you next time they won't miss."

Chapter Twenty-five

After a couple of hours spent filling out forms at the police station, I finally got home at about two a.m. I felt exhausted, the effects of coming down from the adrenaline high finally kicking in. When I hit the sack I tossed and turned, tangled the sheets, and after hours staring at the ceiling I finally climbed out of bed, showered, and drove to Dolan's Donuts.

With morning sunlight drifting over the mountains in the east, giving light to a cloudless sky, the day promised to be pleasant. I felt refreshed in the misty cool air and kept my car's windows open as I drove. Arriving at the donut shop, I ordered a jumbo coffee and sat in my car sipping it while waiting for the world to come alive.

I stayed in my Corvette for about an hour, swallowing aspirins and drinking coffee refills. At six-fifty, after the sun had risen completely and a vivid hue of yellow-orange reflected in the donut shop window, I walked to the pay phone on the corner and dropped a dime in the slot.

She answered on the second ring. "Speak," Mabel said.

"I hate to wake you—"

"No you didn't or you wouldn't have called."

"Something came up."

"I'm listening."

I told her about my night's escapade, the shooter, the cops, and even my restless attempt at sleeping.

I rattled on until she interrupted me, asking, "Do the cops know who the bad guy is?"

"Downey PD sent the prints to Washington. It will take four or five days for the FBI to I.D. the guy. The Ford was stolen, and the plates were switched with a car parked at Long Beach Airport. But I doubt the cops will tell me anything they find out about the guy."

Mabel remained silent, probably thinking the same thing I was. It might happen again.

"Now listen," I said. "Call Rita. Tell her to take a few days off. You can work at home too. Order a new door for the office, and call the phone company. The line is cut. We'll lay low until this thing blows over."

"If his buddies show up at the office when I'm there I'll be ready. I've got a gun in my purse next to the pepper spray," Mabel said. "Nobody's running me out of my office."

"The office is a crime scene and a mess, Mabel, so stay at home with your arsenal."

"Where will you be in case anything comes up?"

"I'm heading to Sol's. I think he's got a spare office that I can use for a while." As an afterthought I added, "Laura Rosenthal's prelim is Monday. I've got to be prepared."

***

Driving to my office to pick up the Rosenthal files, I slowed as I approached the building. Not seeing any suspicious cars parked close by, I pulled into the lot, ducked under the yellow police tape, and darted inside. I glanced at the bullet holes in the door, but didn't dwell on the shootout. I was angry and depressed enough and didn't want to sink any deeper.

At eight o'clock I arrived at Sol's building and rode the elevator to the top floor. I told the new receptionist my name and asked to speak with Sol's personal assistant, Joyce. I knew Sol wouldn't be in for at least another few hours.

Joyce walked through the door a few moments later. I asked her if the company could spare an office for a few days.

She said, "Yes, of course, Jimmy."

I then told her what'd happened, why I needed to hole up there for a while.

"That's horrible. You poor thing. Are you all right?"

"I'm fine. Just a little tired."

Following Joyce out of the lobby past the company's control center, we rounded a corner, moved beyond the employees' cafeteria, and ended up at a large, lavish office at the end of the hall.

"Sol's brother-in-law used this office, but he's no longer with the firm. It's yours for as long as you need it." Joyce didn't elaborate on why the brother-in-law left the company. I didn't ask for an explanation.

I explored the room. At the far end, behind a polished desk and matching credenza, a picture window overlooked downtown Downey. A round conference table rested in the center, and a built-in wet bar stood in the corner opposite the window. Knowing Sol, I presumed it was fully stocked. Perhaps that's why Sol's brother-in-law was no longer with the company. Maybe he spent too much time at the office.

"This is more than I need, just a cubby-hole would be fine," I said.

"I'm sure Sol would want you to have a nice

office. He thinks very highly of you, Jimmy."

"Thanks, Joyce. The feeling is mutual. Tell Sol I appreciate the favor."

When Joyce left, I set the files on the table, walked around the desk, and sank into the big chair. I put my feet up, crossed them, and leaned back. "So this is how it feels to be a big shot," I murmured under my breath. In less than fifteen seconds I fell asleep.

***

"Hey you. This isn't a goddamn motel."

The booming voice jilted me awake and I almost fell out of the chair. "What in the hell?" I shouted. Rubbing my eyes, I tried to regain my composure.

Sol stood in front of me with his hands on his hips, laughing.

"My God, Sol, you almost gave me a heart attack."

"Aw Jimmy, my boy, sleeping on the job."

"Thanks for the office," I said meekly.

Joyce had already told Sol about the attempt on my life. I added the part about the phone line being cut and how I'd spent hours at the police station. But I didn't embellish or mention the threat that the thug had made after he'd been locked up: *the next time they wouldn't miss.* The guy was probably blowing smoke, shamed by the fact that I got the jump on him. A professional goon taken down by a lawyer wouldn't look good on his gangster résumé. I just told Sol how I had to be prepared for Laura's hearing.

"That's why I need the space, Sol."

"Keeping you out of trouble is like trying to keep frogs in a bucket," Sol said.

"The cops sent the gun to ballistics," I said, moving the conversation back to what had happened last night. "They should know something in a couple of days. The gun had a silencer. It looked like it was made by a pro, but I don't think the cops will tell me much about him. They weren't too friendly."

"You were lucky, Jimmy. A professional hit man rarely misses."

Sol's words sank in, and my morning coffee felt like lead in my stomach.

"He didn't miss by much, and the guy had guts, coming after me the way he did, walking into a dark office."

"That doesn't sound like a pro to me," added Sol. "But, hey, he was determined. I don't think they'll stop there. They might send someone else."

Silence filled the room as I wrapped my mind around what Sol had just implied. From this point on I'd always have to be on guard.

Sol grabbed a sweet roll that one of his staff brought in, leaned back, and took a bite. "Oh man, this is good. The baker knows his stuff. Did you get a load of that cheese filling, Jimmy?"

"I don't care about the coffee and rolls," I said.

Sol looked a little hurt. "You don't *care*?"

"Sol, no...I mean, yes, I mean the rolls are great. But listen, *please*. The shooter had a strange-looking tattoo on the back of his hand."

Sol quickly finished off the sweet roll, wiped his hands on a napkin, and leaned forward. "Yeah, what did it look like?"

"Like a jailhouse tattoo," I said.

"Could be a gang symbol. Tell me about it."

"Kind of like a bird. You know, like a stylized Phoenix, but it had the number twenty-one under it."

"Hmm, twenty-one." Sol silently counted on his fingers. "Stands for the letter 'U'."

"What's that mean?"

"I think I know what it means, but I'm going to find out for sure."

I didn't say anything. I just looked into Sol's eyes. His mind seemed to have wandered. After a moment, he pushed his chair back and started to get up. "Jimmy, it's almost lunch time." He pointed to a door on the other side of the office. "There's a bathroom over there. Why don't you clean up a little? And then we'll go to lunch downstairs at Rocco's. In the meantime, I'll make a phone call. Might find out something about the shooter. Maybe we can figure out who sent him."

"That would be great."

"I'll make the call," Sol said. "But first, I've got something else to tell you."

The expression on his face changed. I didn't like the look of his mischievous grin.

"Yeah, what?"

He sat again and moved his hands in front of him like a baseball umpire—safe at first. "Now, don't get upset."

"Sol—"

"There's someone joining us for lunch, someone I want you to meet."

I knew what he had on his mind. "*Ah*, Sol, not again."

"She's attractive. And, hey, you two have a lot

in common."

"Yeah, like what?"

"Well, she's divorced, like you."

"Sol, please tell me you're not trying to fix me up again. Especially today."

"Look, Jimmy, it's been a long time since your divorce. And, it's been a while since you broke up with Bobbi."

Bobbi Allen was the prosecutor on a big case I had in the past. After the case was wrapped up, Bobbie and I started to date, and soon we were engaged. During our brief engagement, Hoot Stephens, an assemblyman in our area, died in office. Because of Bobbi's excellent record in the DA's office, and perhaps because she was the only Democrat willing to run in the heavily Republican district, the central party endorsed her for the vacant seat in a special election. Bobbi jumped into the race with all she had. We put our wedding on hold, and unbelievably she beat the odds, winning by a small margin. Somehow our wedding was never taken off hold. I didn't fit in with the politicos, and shortly after her victory, we officially broke off the engagement. We stayed friends, though. I even planned to vote for her in the next general election.

"It hasn't been that long," I said.

"Jimmy, you're thirty-seven years old. It's just not natural. It's time for you to find someone."

"I've gone out with a lot of girls since Bobbi."

"Well, what is it with you then?"

I started to squirm. "What do you mean?"

"Are you afraid to get married again, or what?"

"No, that's not it," I said. "I'm not afraid to get married or anything. It's just...I just don't like to get involved."

"Don't like to get involved? What kind of crap is that?"

"God sakes, Sol—"

"Jimmy, you'll want to get involved with this girl. I guarantee it."

Sol climbed out of the chair. "Seriously, Jimmy, just meet her for lunch. She's an attractive woman. My wife's niece. Name's Deborah. I told Sylvia I'd introduce her to you."

"This is *another* one of your wife's picks? Gimme a break."

"Deborah works for one of those stock brokerage outfits. Just transferred to L.A. from New York. If you don't hit it off, well, what can I say? But you could do worse."

"Okay, I'll meet her, just to get Sylvia off your back, but that's it."

Sol hunched his shoulders. "Would I ask more?"

Sol left to make the telephone call about the tattoo, and I tried to pull myself together. The restroom was fully stocked with the finest brands of men's toiletries. It even had a small shower stall.

I took a shower, shaved for the second time that day, and waited for Sol in the office. When he returned, we took the elevator to Rocco's on the ground floor.

On the way down, I asked Sol if he made the phone call about the shooter.

"Yeah, I did. You and I have an appointment with Lola, a very special lady. She owns Lola's Tortilla Factory in East L.A. We'll head over there after lunch."

"A lady who owns a tortilla factory?"

"Yeah, we'll talk about it after we eat. Now

forget about last night, and try to be pleasant to Deborah. Who knows? Maybe..."

"For chrissakes, Sol, I'm just having lunch with you and her. And, damn it, that's it!"

Chapter Twenty-six

We walked into the restaurant and André escorted us to Sol's private booth at the back of the dining room. Janine, our waitress, rushed over and Sol demanded, "The best champagne, Janine. A lovely young lady will be joining us and it will be a great day for you know who." Their eyes shifted to me. Janine winked.

"Hope you get lucky," she said.

Sol flashed a grin, showing a lot of teeth, and Jeanie nodded knowingly. I picked up the menu. "I'll have coffee."

After a few moments Janine returned with a bottle of Hiedsieck Champagne, chilling in an ice bucket. She also brought my coffee. She filled Sol's glass. He sipped, nodded, and she left again.

At 12:30 on the dot, André brought Deborah to our booth. I stood to say hello and suddenly all my cares and concerns—the shooter, the cops, and even my worries about the case—vanished. A dream had just walked into my life.

When Deborah looked at me and smiled, my heart flipped and the blood in my veins reversed its flow causing me to become lightheaded. Her face glowed sending a shiver through me that I felt to the tips of my toes. Tiny flecks of gold danced in her hazel eyes and her dark and wavy hair flowed beyond her shoulders. She had a slim figure, and I was overwhelmed by the thought of just being with her.

"Uncle Sol told me so much about you, Jimmy; I feel as if I already know you." Her voice was warm and soft, and she seemed genuinely interested in me as she spoke.

"Ah yeah, Uncle Sol. Yep, Uncle Sol." I stood there stammering like a school kid and hoped that Deborah couldn't hear my heart pounding.

Sol came to my rescue. "Deb, honey, why don't you sit in the middle? Between Jimmy and me. That is if Jimmy will get out of your way."

I didn't move at first, but finally I realized I was gawking at her. Then I stumbled over my own feet as I stepped aside.

"Thank you for inviting me today," Deborah told Sol as she slipped into the booth. Then she turned and looked up at me. I was still standing there like a fool. "Isn't he wonderful?" she asked.

"Wonderful...Yep, that's Sol all right, wonderful." I sounded like an idiot, but she didn't seem to notice or care.

"Sit down, Jimmy," Sol said. "You look like a *shmegegi* standing there."

I slid into the booth and gulped some coffee. Sol poured champagne into Deborah's glass. She took a sip, and when she looked my way and smiled again a warm wave of euphoria washed over me. I wanted to make her laugh, hear her speak, and I wanted to be smooth and charming and brilliant with just a touch of elegance. Instead I spilled coffee all over the front of my shirt.

Grabbing a napkin from the table, I furiously wiped at the spreading stain. Sol and Deborah carried on a conversation, catching up on family matters. Neither seemed to be aware of the clumsy oaf I'd become.

Sol ordered lunch for the three of us, but I couldn't focus on the meal or anything in the restaurant other than Deborah. After a few minutes, I'd regained my composure somewhat: however, I remained self-conscious about everything I did and said. Deborah was lovely, witty, and intelligent, the epitome of grace. I felt like a clown.

Perhaps I was emotionally vulnerable at that moment, given the shooting at my office, the complexities of the case, and my increased loneliness over the past few years. Or maybe I just never met anyone like her. I didn't know how it happened or why, I just wanted to be with this girl forever.

"Jimmy, Deb, I've got a surprise for you two," Sol said.

"What kind of surprise?" I asked.

"I pulled some strings and got two tickets for you guys—Friday night, best seats. You'll love it." He had the tickets in his hand, waving them in the air. "Now, Jimmy, why don't you ask Deb if she'll go out with you?"

"Deborah, would you care to go out with me Friday evening?" I said with the greatest sincerity.

"Of course Jimmy, provided you really want to. Not just because Uncle Sol—"

"No! I really want to take you out."

"I'd love to then. Where are you taking me?"

We both turned to Sol.

"*La Bohemé,*" he said.

"What's that?" I asked.

"Opera."

Oh my God, opera! I thought.

"Wonderful, I love the opera," Deborah said. "Do you enjoy opera, Jimmy?"

I had never been to an opera—the fat lady and

all that—and I couldn't think of anything worse to do on a Friday night, or any night.

"Love it, Deborah," I said.

I could've killed Sol right then. Opera, of all things! *Three Days of the Condor* just opened at the Showcase Cinema. Ray Charles was in town. I could even stomach the Ice Capades. But he pops up with opera tickets. Sol said something about the opera being a special performance, straight from the Met in New York. I wondered if I had to wear a tux to the damn thing or what. But then I glanced at Deborah and the thought of being with her all evening thrilled me and the dread of attending an opera melted away.

"Don't you just love Puccini?" Deborah asked.

"Yep, have it all the time," I said.

Deborah smiled at me and I smiled at her.

The lunch ended all too soon. But it ended better for me than it began. Toward the end of the meal, I started to behave somewhat normally. I laughed and finally admitted to Deborah that I really didn't know anything about opera, but I'd be willing to give it a try.

As I walked Deborah to her car I gave her my phone number. I didn't need to ask for hers since she would be staying with her Uncle Sol and Aunt Sylvia until she could get set up in a place of her own.

I floated back in the restaurant just as Sol finished his second helping of dessert.

"Sol, why didn't you tell me you had a niece like Deborah?"

"Would you've listened?"

"But, Christ Almighty, the opera?"

"Now look, Jimmy, Deborah is a very classy lady, and if you want to take her out you'll have to learn to appreciate some of that cultural stuff."

"No kidding?"

"Yeah, when Sylvia told me she'd bought the opera tickets and wanted me to go with her, I immediately thought of you. I told her we'd have to make a little sacrifice, give the tickets to you and Deb, and we'd go to see *Three Days of the Condor*."

Sol sat there shaking his head. His sorrow was unbearable. "Sol, you phony—"

"Hey, it worked out, didn't it?" he said.

I couldn't argue with that.

Chapter Twenty-seven

Sol and I sat in the backseat of his big limo as the car cruised along the Santa Ana Freeway heading toward East L.A. It was still early afternoon and rush hour traffic hadn't hit yet. With an uncluttered ribbon of concrete in from of him, Cubby, Sol's driver, didn't spare the horsepower. We exited the freeway, hung a right on Brooklyn Avenue, and pulled into a dirt parking lot next to Lola's *Tortilleria* in less than fifteen minutes.

The factory, a large two-story red brick structure, had to have been built before the earthquake codes went into effect shortly after a six-point something tremor in 1933 that destroyed half of Long Beach. Bricks seemed to be stacked helter-skelter with crevasses and cracks between them. Steel T-bar braces were bolted to the walls here and there in a herculean effort to hold the plant together. It appeared to me that the factory would be nothing but a pile of rubble after the next big one hit.

A small retail Mexican deli attached to the front of the building sold fresh tortillas and *comida* prepared in Lola's *cocina*. A profusion of scents wafted from boiling pots filled with chilies and spices, while marinated meat grilled over an open flame.

Sol asked the busy Latina behind the counter to let Lola know that we were there. The girl used a phone on the wall behind her to make a call.

"Lola asked me to show you to her office," the girl said, nervously looking around the deli at customers waiting to be served.

"No sweetheart, that won't be necessary. I know

177

the way. But gracias," Sol said. "C'mon, Jimmy. Let's go."

Earlier, while on the drive to the factory, I'd asked Sol why we were meeting Lola and what did tortillas have to do with anything.

"Let me tell you a little about her," Sol said. "It goes back almost fourteen years..." He then went on to explain how he'd been called in by a criminal attorney to handle the investigation of a homicide case he was defending. A young Latino had been charged with murder and the lawyer wanted Sol to find out if the truth matched the DA's allegations as filed in the criminal complaint.

"It was a typical gang-related drive-by shooting," Sol said. "The police had a couple of witnesses who identified the client. The lowlifes said he was one of the guys in the car at the time the shooting went down. I won't bore you with the details, but I proved that the kid was innocent."

"He wasn't a member of the gang that did the shooting?"

"Oh, the kid was in the gang, all right. His homies called him Galco-Greyhound because he could run fast. But this time he wasn't in the car when the murder happened," Sol said. "Arturo, the kid, is Lola's son."

I followed Sol through the back door of the deli and into the tortilla production area. We walked past ten or twelve rows of shiny stainless steel tunnel ovens and tortilla packing conveyors lined up in a row. A handful of workers were cleaning machines and hosing down the red tile floor. The sweet fragrance of corn simmering in steel tanks drifted through the area just waiting to be ground into *masa* and shaped into tortillas.

At the rear of the plant, we climbed an unpainted wooden staircase to an office at the end of a long corridor. The door was open.

Sol held his arms out wide. "*Hola, mi amor*," he said to the small woman who jumped up and rushed toward him. While hugging Sol said, "Lola, you haven't changed. You're as beautiful as ever."

The office was plain, but neat and functional. Clipboards with order sheets hung in a row above the desk and gray metal file cabinets flanked an inside window overlooking the production area. The walls were bare and an old sofa and chair sat sadly against the far wall.

Sol turned to me. "Jimmy, I want you to meet the love of my life. Say hello to Lola."

We shook hands. "Any friend of Sol's is always welcome here," she said. "Please sit and tell me how I can help you."

Lola had a lovely smile, but it seemed to hide a hint of sadness. In times past she must have been very attractive. But it seemed the years of working so hard had captured her vitality. Webs of worry lines spread from the corners of her troubled dark eyes, and her voice sounded weak and tired.

Lola returned to her desk. I sat on a sofa against the wall and Sol moved to the armchair facing her. He picked up a sombrero resting there and placed it on his head.

Lola laughed. "Sol, take that stupid thing off. You look like a giant mushroom."

"But my sweet, you love mushrooms.

Remember how you used to prepare *setas* with garlic and white wine?" Sol winked, took the hat off, and sat in the chair. "Lola, maybe you, and perhaps Art, can help us."

"*Por supuesto*. Of course."

Sol told Lola about the attempt on my life and about the tattoo on the gunman's hand. "I got a feeling it's some kind of gang logo," he added.

"Sounds like it, all right," she said.

"Lola, you and Arturo know more about gang violence than any two people on the planet," Sol said. "I need to know which gang we're dealing with here."

She stood. "My son will know. I'll get him. He is in the production area," she said as she left the room.

"Christ, she lets her son work here? The guy who likes to kill people?"

"I didn't finish telling you about Lola and Art. He was only ten years old when his papa died. Arturo, growing up in the barrio with little parental guidance, ran wild in the streets and soon fell in with a gang. And then within a few years he had the murder rap hanging around his neck."

"That's when you met Lola?"

"Yeah, you can't imagine how she felt. But she didn't give up on him. She scraped together enough to hire a decent lawyer who retained my services."

"And then, of course, you proved he wasn't guilty."

"Damn right," he said. "But it took a while to prove it. Art stayed in jail almost a year."

"What happened when he got out?" I asked.

"Lola made his life miserable until he gave in and went back to school. He got his high school diploma, gained confidence, and for the first time in his life felt that he could make it on his own. He realized he didn't need the gang and their bullshit. He eventually graduated from UCLA with honors. He's quite a kid."

"They're good people, Jimmy. And they're working on community service projects for kids in the barrio financed with profits from the tortilla factory. What could be more important than giving kids a chance?"

"Sounds like she's a special lady, Sol."

We stopped talking as the door opened and Lola walked in with Arturo, a tall man in his late twenties dressed in jeans and black cowboy boots.,

"*Jefe*, good to see you." Arturo draped an arm around Sol as they shook hands.

"*Me alegro de verte también, amigo*," Sol said, with a seriousness in his voice that I rarely heard. "Art, I want you to meet my dear friend, Jimmy O'Brien."

As Arturo and I shook hands, Sol reiterated what he'd told his mother earlier about the gunman and his tattoo.

Lola handed me a yellow tablet and a pen. "Please, Jimmy, make a sketch of the tattoo for Art. Maybe he will recognize something about it."

I drew a fairly good representation, but of course without all the flourishes, just the basic design— a circle wrapped around a phoenix with the number 21 under it.

He studied the drawing for a moment, then without moving his head shifted his eyes and looked at me over the edge of the pad.

"You're telling me a guy with this tattoo came after you?"

"I'm afraid so."

"Was he a big guy?"

I looked at Sol and then back at Art. "Well, he didn't need a gun; he could've thrown a cement truck at me." I was the only one in the room who chuckled.

He raised his head slowly, as if he picked up the distant thunder of peril inching closer.

"Jimmy, Sol, listen up. This is serious."

Chapter Twenty-eight

Lola's pager beeped and she had to leave the office, something about a truckload of corn. Arturo grabbed the desk chair and pulled it over to the couch. Sol moved his chair closer and huddled together.

"Jimmy, look at me. Look into my eyes. I'm not fucking around. There's some serious shit going down here."

I didn't like what I heard or the concern in his eyes.

"What do you mean?"

"You've been green-lighted."

"Green-lighted?"

"Means they want you dead."

"Who?"

"Let me give you a little background," he said. "There are two big Latino gangs that control things around here—the *Sureños*, the Southern California gang. They call themselves *La Eme*, means 'M' in Spanish. And the *Norteños*, or the Northern gang. You'll see the letter 'N' in their tats and graffiti. The two gangs are fighting over drug turf. Each formed alliances. The southern guys, *La Eme*, aligned with the old Italian Mafia, *La Costa Nostra. The Black Guerilla Family* and other black gangsters united with the *Norteños*."

Sol leaned back and locked his hands behind his head. "But the guy that attacked Jimmy had a tattoo with the number twenty-one in it. Could that stand for the letter 'U'?"

"Yeah, I'm afraid so."

I didn't like the look on Arturo's face. "What's

the big deal about a 'U'?" I asked.

"The letter 'U' means the guy is a member of a new gang, a third one. Believe it or not, it's more violent than the other two. Pretends to be Latino, but they'll let anybody in, provided they are big, mean, and have a felony record."

"Never heard anything about these guys," Sol said.

"They call themselves *La Familia Unidos*—The United Family. And you're right, Sol. A capital 'U' is their symbol, the twenty-first letter of the alphabet."

"Where did they come from?" I asked.

"They must have crawled out of the sewer." Arturo had a disgusted look on his face. He was silent a moment before he continued. "Actually, nobody seems to know for sure who these guys are. Started about three years ago. We know they're well funded with strong political ties. They're heavy into violent crime, contract murder, armed robbery, you name it. The gang has a large army, all experienced ex-cons. But they don't have a drug distribution system and they're desperate to get into the drug racket."

"What are they doing about it?"

"There's a rumor floating around."

"Yeah, like what?"

"They want to unite the Northern and Southern gangs, take over the marijuana trade, and expand into cocaine and heroin."

"Is anyone trying to stop them?" asked Sol.

"If there's even a hint, and I mean just a hint that someone is a threat to their plans, they'll slaughter him and anybody that happens to be nearby without batting an eye."

Arturo's eyes flicked back and forth between Sol and me, looking for a reaction to what he'd just said. We didn't give him one.

"They must think I'm a threat," I finally said

"Looks that way," Arturo said in a voice just above a whisper.

"So far, *La Familia Unidos* hasn't been able to merge the two gangs and take over, but they're causing rifts, stirring things up. Some of the *soldados* are signing up with the new guys. And lately, the Aryan Brotherhood has aligned with them."

When Arturo mentioned the neo-Nazi gang, Sol started pacing and turned back to Arturo, his eyes blazing. "Tell me more about these cocksuckers."

"*La Familia Unidos* is organized in the traditional military manner, Sol. You know, a general directly under the supreme leader that gives orders to his captains. The captains have lieutenants that control the neighborhood gangs. Then, of course, like any gang, there are the soldiers, *los soldados.* But these guys also have squads of enforcers that report directly to the general, specialists: killers, arsonists, vicious bastards who love to torture." Arturo then turned to me. "It was one of these deranged assholes that paid you a visit, Jimmy."

"Why would they send one of their storm troopers after Jimmy?"

"He probably stumbled onto something. So why take a chance? But they underestimated him. That won't happen again. They sent one guy—he failed. They'll send more."

"You don't think the guy was just trying to scare me? Maybe giving me a warning?" I asked.

"They don't give warnings."

Sol continued to pace the room.

Arturo sat with his head down.

I felt like a condemned prisoner with no court of appeals for this death sentence.

No one spoke for a few minutes. I figured they were all thinking the same thing—Jimmy's a goner.

Finally, Sol turned and said to Arturo, "Who are we up against? Who are the leaders of this new gang of *momzer* freaks?"

"No one knows who organized and funded the gang. People have died when they asked too many questions. I've tried to find out and so far I've failed." He paused as if he was thinking. "I don't know if this will help or not, but I discovered the name of the general."

"Could be a start," Sol said. "What is it?"

"His name is Guillermo."

Chapter Twenty-nine

We had remained at the plant late, past the evening rush hour traffic. Arturo agreed to keep us informed if he heard any rumors on the street relating to the case or me. The thought of Sol protecting me eased my mind a bit. It felt good having a professional of his stature with me.

As we wheeled along on the freeway towards Downey, Sol's solemn face glimmered in the red taillights of cars rushing by as he stared out the window. During the ride he remained as quiet as a mime.

"Sol," I said, breaking the silence. "Got an idea. I might be on to something."

He turned toward me. "What?"

"I was thinking about Buck."

"The dead guy again?"

"Yeah, the dead guy. He'd worked at Farmer Fred's. I know that because of his work uniform, but when he'd been released on parole originally he was assigned to a halfway house."

"So?"

"A guy by the name of Willie Chavez runs the halfway house. He gets the parolees jobs. And that means Willie is connected to Arnie, and Buck."

"Where are you going with this?"

"Don't you see the connection?"

Sol didn't say anything.

"Listen, Sol, the name of the gang leader is Guillermo, and a guy named Guillermo was at the poker game."

"Guillermo is a common Spanish name," Sol

said, playing the devil's advocate.

"Yeah, but hear me out. Guillermo means William in English. And one of the nicknames for William is Willie."

"Hold on, Jimmy. Are you saying that Guillermo, the guy at the poker game, is this Willie character, the guy who runs the halfway house? And on top of that, he's the general of the *La Familia Unidos* gang?"

"I don't know for sure, Sol. But if he *is* the general, then it ties everything together."

Sol chuckled. "That would be a wild coincidence now, wouldn't it?"

"A coincidence? What are you talking about? *Christ*, what are the odds of all that happening? A trillion to one? A guy named Guillermo came to the poker game the night Arnie was murdered. Willie's linked to Arnie through Buck, and Buck was killed in jail at about the same time. I think the two murders are connected."

Sol shook his head. "Sounds like a real long shot to me."

The more I thought about Willie and Guillermo being one and the same, the more excited I became. "Ever bet a long shot at the track, Sol?"

"Only if I have good information."

"Okay, let's get the good information."

"Maybe you've got a point." Sol pulled a pen out of his pocket and started to write on a business card he'd removed from his wallet.

"Willie Chavez and his halfway house. Okay, we'll run him through our enhanced assessment protocol."

"You'll check him out?"
"Yeah, that's what I said."
"Couldn't hurt."

***

The limo pulled into the underground parking garage at Sol's office building. I opened the door and started to climb out. Being distraught and exhausted, I wanted to get home fast, slip under the covers and hide there until this all went away. But I'd settle for a hot shower and a good night's sleep.

"Talk to you later, Sol."

"Where in the hell do you think you're going?" he boomed.

"Home, I guess. Why?"

"No way."

"What do you mean, *no way*?"

"If you think I'm going to let you wander around so anyone can take potshots at you, think again. You heard what Art said. Those bastards are coming back and next time it won't be pleasant."

"It wasn't pleasant last time."

"You're coming with me," Sol said as he took my arm and guided me to the garage elevator. We rode it to the top floor, Sol's headquarters. The night man on duty at the reception desk jumped to his feet and tried to look busy when we entered. He moved a clipboard from one side of the counter to the other and back again.

"Get Jack Fox and the Deacon on the horn," Sol snapped at the guy. "I want them in my office in twenty minutes."

Sol's office looked more like a cocktail lounge than a business office. Sure, a desk rested at the far end of the large room with several telephones scattered across the top of it. But the remainder of the office had been set up as a place for drinking and relaxing. A classic bar counter with leather padding and a brass foot rail ran the length of one wall. Bottles of Chivas, Beefeaters, Stolichnaya Vodka, and others stood like soldiers at attention on glass shelves behind the bar. Instead of a conference table, a large cocktail table with eight tufted leather chairs took up space in the center of the room.

Sol walked behind the bar, put an ice cube into a tall class, and filled it with gin. He grabbed me a Coke and came to the table.

"The Deacon and Jack Fox are two of my best security men. Each guy, starting tonight, will work one twelve-hour shift. Wherever you go, one of these guys will be at your side." Sol explained the routine in a perfunctory manner. "And when you have to go someplace, you'll take one of the company's limos. They're equipped with two-way radios. *Fershtay?*"

"Yeah, I guess." I took a long pull on my Coke. I'll admit I was nervous. Who wouldn't be with depraved gangsters trying to mow you down? But I didn't like the idea of someone hovering over me twenty-four hours a day. I set my drink on the table and started to climb out of my chair.

"I don't know about this, Sol."

"What's to know? Guys are shooting at you. You need help. Now sit down."

I sat for a moment and thought. Arturo's words freewheeled in my mind. Could what he said possibly be true? It sounded a little over the top to me: murder squads, monsters with swastikas and strange tattoos, coming at me from all directions brandishing automatic weapons.

But what if only half of what he said were true? The thug who came after me at my office was very real. And maybe, as Arturo said, the gang would try again.

I cherished my privacy. But did I want to be constantly looking over my shoulder? Did I want to sleep with one eye open, waiting in the dark? Could I count on being able to duck in time? Yeah, it might be a good idea to listen to Sol. He's an expert in this sort of thing and maybe his offer of protection wouldn't hurt.

"Okay, Sol, I guess you're right."

"Of course I'm right. Now, here's the deal," he said, rubbing his hands. "Jack Fox will work the day shift. He's top notch. Pinkerton snatched him from the FBI and I hired him away from Pinkerton."

"What about the other guy?"

Sol sipped his drink and chuckled. "The Deacon? A Special Forces officer in Vietnam, decorated for valor—but more importantly, a former Secret Service guard who I was lucky enough to hire. He will do night duty."

Two big guys came into the office. Each wore a conventional business suit. Except for the quickness of their step and their ominous bearing, they could have been salesmen for IBM. Sol and I stood to greet them.

"Chief, you wanted to see us?" one of the guys asked.

"Yeah, thanks for getting here fast," he said turning to introduce me. "Deacon, Jack, meet Jimmy O'Brien. He's a criminal defense lawyer and he's got a little problem."

I shook hands with the two men. Jack Fox, tall and lanky with red hair, had a long face and a broad chin that stuck out like Dudley Do-Right's. But this guy was no cartoon character. He looked tough and seriously capable. The Deacon, a big-shouldered black guy, was no slouch either. He had the build of an NFL linebacker. He stood about six-three and weighed in at around two-twenty. His suit coat fit tight around his chest and his biceps bulged and looked as if they might rip through the sleeves. The Deacon seemed to roll on his toes when he walked toward me to shake hands.

"We're going to set up a twenty-four hour close protection program for Jimmy. Starting right now," Sol said. "He's already had one incident. The word's out that next time the bad guys will have automatic weapons."

"Who we dealing with?" Deacon asked.

"New kids on the block. Pretend to be a Latino gang. They call themselves *La Familia Unidos*, don't know too much about them, but I know they're a gang of experienced, hard-core felons."

While Sol spoke, the two bodyguards kept their eyes focused on me, appraising me as if I were a valuable porcelain sculpture.

"We'll take care of him, Chief," Jack Fox said.

"Don't get the wrong idea. O'Brien's no wimp. He's ex-LAPD," Sol said. "He took on the last guy, a big son-of-a-bitch armed with a handgun. Jimmy only had a knife, but he brought the asshole to his knees."

Jack's and the Deacon's eyebrows arched. Were they impressed or thinking I was stupid?

Sol told me his company kept a one-bedroom

suite here at headquarters for emergencies, and for a few days it would be best if I stayed here knowing full well how restrictive the program would be.

Jack Fox left to get some sleep. He'd take over the babysitting duties from the Deacon in the morning at six. The Deacon drove to my apartment to pick up a few of my things and when he left, Sol escorted me to the bedroom suite. He then ran around like an enthusiastic hotel bellhop, showing me the closets, the mini-bar, and he even fiddled with the TV, explaining how it worked. The accommodations reminded me of a suite at the Hyatt, only theirs had windows.

Sol put his hand on my shoulder. "Jimmy," he said, "this won't last forever. We're going to nail their asses to the wall."

Shortly, the Deacon returned with my stuff: a change of clothes, shaving gear, and a couple of books lying on my nightstand. He also brought my guitar.

"Found this in the empty room. Can you play the thing?" he asked me.

"No, not really. I just like to fool around."

"Hmm, a Gibson." He ran his eyes over the instrument. "Mind if I give it a try? Used to be a plank-spanker myself, messed with one of these when I was a kid."

"Sure, why not."

He held the guitar across his chest, finger-plucking the strings, tuning it. Then with his eyes closed, he leaned his head forward. His big body hunched over, and his fingers were a blur as they worked their magic. "*The thrill is gone, babe...the thrill is gone away for...*" He finished his song and abruptly handed me the guitar.

Sol and I stood there in silence, our mouths agape. My god, the hairs on my arms stood on end. The guy had an awesome talent and I knew that Sol thought the same thing.

"Lost my touch," he said, and plopped down on the sofa. He picked up the TV remote control and starting flipping through the channels.

"Jimmy's been practicing for years," Sol said. "Show the Deacon what you can do, Jimmy."

"I'll pass," I stammered. I scurried into the bedroom with the guitar and buried it in the closet.

Sol left and Deacon asked, "Anything you want to watch, Mr. O.?"

"Not really, Deacon. I think I'll turn in. It's been a day."

"Yeah, I'll bet."

"But first, I've got to ask a question," I said.

"Shoot."

"You're just going to sit here all night with nothing to do?"

"The job is ninety-nine percent boredom," he said. "And the other one percent...well, you get the idea."

"Right," I said, and moved to the bedroom. The other one percent—a little excitement for the Deacon, a bomb exploding in my car, or guys with machine guns blasting away at me.

Chapter Thirty

I woke up to a murmur of voices coming from the other room. For an instant, I didn't remember where I was, but then it all came back. It came back too fast. The clock read six a.m. I stumbled out of bed and stuck my head in the sitting room. Jack Fox and the Deacon were discussing the shift change. I showered, dressed, and in fifteen minutes I was sitting at the table with Jack. He'd already set up an automatic coffee maker, and on his way to the suite he'd stopped at Dolan's and picked up a dozen assorted donuts.

After grabbing a glazed I thanked Jack.

"Sol mentioned that you go to Dolan's every morning for breakfast."

"That's what I do, all right."

"No more," he said. "Going to change your habits. From now on we'll bring the donuts here to you."

"C'mon Jack. Let's go," I said.

He took his eyes off the TV and gave me a questioning look. "You want to go someplace? Where?"

"To Dolan's. I go there every day and I'm not changing. I'll stick with the program to a point, but I'm not going to be a prisoner." I started to head for the door.

Jack Fox scrambled to his feet. He could tell from my decisive tone that I wasn't kidding. My mind was set. I'd go the donut shop with him or alone. Perhaps I was being foolish, but I wanted to establish the ground rules before the program got out of hand.

"Afraid not, Jimmy," said Jack. "You're not

going anywhere. You're my duck now."

"Duck?"

"Your code name."

Was I the duck? A pigeon maybe, but a duck? I felt more like a turkey. "Jack, what is all this duck business about, anyway?" I asked.

Jack looked at me. "Acronym, DUC—means, designee under close protection. We dropped the letter P at the end. Otherwise, it would've been 'duck-pee'. The short version is that you only go out when necessary."

Hell, this guy wasn't joking. I guess I wasn't going anywhere for now.

***

Joyce stuck her head in the door and said the phones in my law office had been repaired. She pulled some strings at the phone company, and now any calls that came in over there could be patched through to me here. I thanked her, picked up the receiver and dialed my office.

Mabel answered on the first ring. "Law office."

"Just checking in, Mabel. I'm here at Sol's."

"You called just in time. Laura Rosenthal is on the other line. She called collect and said it's urgent that she speak with you."

Oh Christ, what now? "Do you know how to patch the call through to me?"

"Of course. Hold on."

Within five seconds, Laura's voice was on the line. She sounded defeated. "I gotta tell you something, Jimmy, but I don't know how to say it."

"Just say it for crying out loud."

"I no longer need you as my lawyer. Goodbye."

"Hey, hey, hold on. What in the hell are you talking about?"

"I'm gonna plead guilty at the hearing, so I don't need you anymore."

"*My God*, Laura, what is this all about?"

"Jimmy, that's it," she whispered barely audible. "You're fired!"

"Laura, you listen to me—"

She hung up.

Chapter Thirty-one

Sybil Brand Institute, the central holding jail for women, was located in Monterey Park, across the San Bernardino Freeway from Cal State University. When the freeways ran unencumbered it took only twenty minutes to drive from Downey to the jail, but in the morning rush hour it took us over an hour. At ten past nine we pulled into the parking lot. Cubby weaved the limo slowly through an assortment of bizarre vehicles, cars, trucks, even buses. Some had psychedelic paint schemes and all were modified in some way. A few were chopped and channeled and lowered so much that they could barely cross over the speed bumps in the parking lot. We wheeled into a loading zone close to the entrance and stopped. The clamor of rock 'n roll and soul music blasting from high-amp speakers in the waiting vehicles could raise a deaf person's hackles.

"What the hell is going on?" Cubby shouted above the racket that flooded the limousine, even with the windows rolled up.

"I guess you don't take many trips to jail in the morning," I said to Cubby, leaning forward and almost shouting in his ear.

"No sir, first time."

Jack flashed a wide grin and said, "You're in for a treat."

"A treat? How's that?"

Obviously Jack had been around law enforcement in the past, and knew that at nine each morning the guards opened the doors and released the prostitutes that had been rounded up the night before. The tricked-out vehicles in the lot belonged to their pimps waiting for their release.

"We've got prime seats for the parade," Jack said.

Cubby still hadn't made the connection, but then the jail doors burst open.

"Holy shit!" he shouted.

Ladies of the evening flooded the parking lot and scurried to the cars. The lovelies were dressed in the outlandish costumes they'd worn while walking the streets during the night. One young thing in a leopard-print miniskirt had a purple feather boa wrapped around her neck with the end of it trailing behind, collecting debris in the dirty parking lot as she hobbled on five-inch spike heels heading to her pimp's car. Except for the Day-Glo heels that seemed to be *de rigueur*, the others weren't so elegant. Most of the working girls wore short-shorts with the bottoms of their fannies hanging out. Baggy and torn fishnet stockings, and cut off tops with spangles stitched on them glittered in the harsh morning sunlight—*haute couture pageant de la bizarre.*

After the last of the women paraded past us, Jack Fox climbed out of the limo and leaned against the fender.

Finally the lot had quieted down, the pimps had left, and only a few cars remained. I stepped out onto the parking lot and glanced around. Jack, seeing me standing outside the limo, walked over.

"Do you see them?" he said.

I didn't notice anyone in particular. "Who?"

"Get your head down. Stay behind the car."

I ducked below the top of the limo and looked up at Jack. "Who's out there?"

"Two gangbangers in a lowered metallic-blue Chevy over by the tree," Jack said. "They've been pinning us the whole time we've been here."

"Think they're gunning for me?"

"If they are, they won't try anything here. Too many cops. They'd never get away."

"Maybe they're not gang guys. Maybe they're just waiting for one of their buddies to be released."

"Yeah, could be. Go on into the jail, see your client, but stay down until you get inside. You'll be safe in there. I'll stay here and keep an eye on them. I can't take a weapon inside the building anyway."

I moved inside the fortress-like structure, walked up to the attorney check-in counter, filled out the visitor request form, and handed it to the guard. She glanced at it and asked me to take a seat. In a short while, the guard called out my name. I walked back to the counter.

"The prisoner refuses to see you. Says you're no longer her lawyer."

Laura's attitude was starting to piss me off. But regardless of her wishes she couldn't relieve me without the judge's approval. I'd still have to be present at the preliminary hearing. Due to a conflict with her attorney, her guilty plea wouldn't be accepted. At the hearing she could request a change of counsel. I didn't know what the judge would do, but I hoped he'd grant a continuance. He might do that if the DA didn't fight it.

"I'm her attorney of record until a judge says otherwise."

"She doesn't want to talk to you. Nothing I can do about it."

"Look, officer, my client has a hearing Monday

and I think she's had a breakdown or something. I have to see her to assess her condition."

The guard held the form up to the wire mesh screen and jabbed her finger at Laura's signature on the line that said VISITOR DENIED. "The form is signed by the inmate. There is nothing I can do. Can't you understand what I'm saying?"

I took a deep breath and stared at the guard. I knew they couldn't force Laura to see me against her will, but her sudden decision to plead guilty, and the fact that she refused to talk to me, felt like a punch in the stomach.

"You about through here?" the guard said.

I turned and started to leave the building, but I stopped at a pay phone by the exit. I called Farmer Fred's Meat Company and asked to speak with Richie Rosenthal. Maybe he could talk to Laura and find out what the hell was going on.

"I'm sorry, sir, Mr. Rosenthal is not in today."

"Will he be in later?"

"Mr. Rosenthal doesn't keep regular hours. He hasn't been in for a couple of days, and I have no idea when he will return."

I hung up and walked back out to the parking lot. The metallic-blue Chevy had left. Jack said he called on the limo's radio and ran the plates on the car while I was inside the building. The guys in the Chevy were gangbangers all right. The car was registered to a known member of *La Eme*. I felt a little relieved. The car's owner wasn't from *La Familia Unidos*, the gang that green-lighted me.

"Back to headquarters, sir?" Cubby asked as I climbed into the back seat.

"No, we have to go to Newport Beach, Lido Isle."

We jumped on the Long Beach Freeway and headed south, made the transition to the 405 and continued on toward Newport. We exited the freeway at Beach Boulevard, drove south past miles of automobile dealers' lots, and turned left at Pacific Coast Highway. We cruised through downtown Huntington Beach, and soon entered the city limits of Newport Beach. Moments after driving over the bridge at Lido Isle, we parked at the curb in front of the house on Via Lido Nord.

Jack and I walked around to the boat slip in the back. The yacht wasn't there.

"Guess he must've taken the boat out," Jack said. We walked back to the front and glanced up and down the block. Across the street, I spotted an unoccupied gray Buick Skylark parked at the curb. With decals stuck to the windshield, the car appeared to be a rental.

I glanced back at the house. "Someone inside might have seen if Richie had been on the boat when it left the dock. I'll check it out."

A thought flashed in my mind when Jack said Richie took the boat out. But it came and went too fast to grasp and hang onto. I continued to look at the car across the street, thinking I may have seen it before.

"The Skylark across the street might be his rental. Why don't you run the plates?"

"Good idea," Jack said.

I knocked on the door and Jack waited by the limo with the radio mike in his hand. I knocked harder, and when no one answered I walked back to the limo.

Jack received a call on the limo's radio.

"*The Buick Skylark is registered to Hertz*," the static-filled voice called out. "*And it's presently rented to one Rosenthal, Richard.*"

"Roger, limo one out," Jack said.

Suddenly it dawned on me; when I met Richie on the boat, he told me that he hated the ocean, and fishing, and got seasick. There was no way in hell he would've taken the boat out of his own accord. Yet it was gone. And his rental car was still in front of the house. On top of that the receptionist at the meat company said she hadn't seen him in a couple of days. I began to get concerned. What had happened to Richie?

***

We arrived back at Sol's headquarters at noon. When we walked into my office, Jack—knowing that the building had tight security—left me alone and went to grab a sandwich in the executive lunchroom.

I was about to check my messages when Joyce stuck her head into the office. "Sol's at his booth in Rocco's and would like you to join him for a bite."

"Okay, thanks, Joyce," I said. "Tell Jack Fox where I'll be."

I snuck into the restaurant via the delivery door. Walking through the kitchen, I darted past cooks and their prep tables, as I made my way to the dining room. I felt like a thief in the night.

When Sol saw me coming he slipped out of his seat and stood. "*Vos tut zich*, Jimmy my boy. Let's sit, eat, then a little business."

I edged into the booth. Sol took a sip of his

drink, and I leaned across the table.

"Sol, the hell with your rule about business discussions during lunch. I've got to talk to you right now. Everything has gone to hell. Laura wants to fire me. She's going to change her plea. She won't even see me."

"Whoa, slow down, *boitshick*," he said. "Now, what in the hell are you talking about?"

"Laura called and wants to plead guilty. I tried to talk to her, tried to find out what's going on, but she hung up on me. I thought maybe Richie could talk some sense into her, but he's not around."

"Where'd he go?"

"I don't know, but we got to find him."

Janine brought me a cup of coffee and started to leave.

"Hold on, sweetheart," Sol said. "Jimmy's going to order something." He turned and glanced at me. "I think he's getting a little skinny, Janine. What do you think?"

She leaned back, gave me the once-over, and smiled. "Looks pretty damn good to me."

"Sol, I weigh one-eighty-five. Same as always."

"When was the last time you weighed yourself?"

"Okay, for chrissakes. Bring me a hamburger, Janine."

Janine turned to Sol with her order pad handy.

"My wife put me on a strict diet," he said. "So I'll just have a small dish of cottage cheese and some of those rye crackers that taste like cardboard."

"That's it?"

"Actually, it's a protein diet. Better bring a New

York steak on the side, but trim the fat."

"Okay, but salad is good when you're on a diet."

"True. Bring a salad also with that special Roquefort dressing I taught the chef to make."

Janine didn't say anything. She just waited.

"Not healthy to skip carbohydrates, better put a baked potato with the order," Sol said.

"Sour cream and chives, or butter?"

"Yeah, I guess I'll have that. How many calories in asparagus?"

"Not many."

"Okay, but put a little hollandaise sauce on them. And instead of the crackers, bring me a loaf of warm sourdough."

"Still want the cottage cheese?"

"Nah, I'll make the sacrifice."

"Dessert?"

"We'll talk about that later. It's got to be low cal, though. I promised my wife I'd stay on the diet."

"She'd be proud," Janine said.

Chapter Thirty-two

The butterflies in my stomach were doing acrobatics. I wanted to talk about the case, and Sol kept going on about his special salad dressing. I should've known better than to talk business while he ate, but I was upset and worried. Not just about getting shot at, but about the way the situation had gotten out of hand so fast.

"Sol," I said. "Is it okay to talk about my case now?"

"Of course, I'm here to help, aren't I?"

"We've got to find Richie. He's got to talk to Laura."

"We can run a preliminary skip-trace this afternoon. Show if he's used his credit cards, gas, hotel, things like that."

"It's got to be fast."

"Leave it to me," Sol said.

"Did you find out anything about Willie Chavez, the guy at St. Dismas Halfway House?"

"Yeah, we sure did. On the surface he seems to be straight as an arrow. They tell me his plan to rehabilitate hard-core cons is working out just fine. Very few of his parolees get sent back to the slammer. Buck Simpson was an exception. They say Chavez is doing a great job."

The restaurant was busy. Businessmen were making deals over lunch. Mayor Joe Di Loreto was eating with the owner of Paramount Chevrolet, probably trying to get his support in the next city council race. Waiters and waitresses were scurrying about with food trays on their arms, serving customers. Everything was normal in their world. In my world it seemed as if the air had been sucked out of the room.

"Sol, if Willie isn't Guillermo, where does that leave us now?"

"You didn't hear me. I said, *on the surface* Willie seems legit. We're digging deeper, but we're having a hard time getting details about the program. He's got powerful friends."

"Yeah, like who?"

"Politicians and business people. Willie supplies low-paid workers to the business community, and they donate money back to the pols. Everyone's happy, so naturally the program works."

André came to our booth and Sol asked him to bring a plug-in telephone. When the phone arrived, he called upstairs and told Joyce to run a fast skip-trace on Richie. In less than five minutes, Joyce called back.

"Okay, thanks Joyce," Sol hung up. "Richie bought gas at Mike's Texaco Station in Vernon, Tuesday morning."

"That was quick. How'd you get that information so fast?"

"Yeah, it's incredible. We leased a new IBM model 135 computer. It cost a fortune and if it doesn't keep breaking down, it'll pay for itself in the long run. The guy told me it has 96,000 bytes."

"What does that mean?"

"I have no idea, but it sounds like a lot, doesn't it?"

I started to ask Sol what else we could do to find Richie when Janine rushed to our booth.

"The TV in the bar is saying something about the Rosenthal murder," she said.

Sol and I charged into the lounge. The TV was

tuned to the Midday News on Channel Five. News anchor, Stan Chambers, read the bulletin: "...*fifty-three-foot Hatteras fishing yacht was found drifting about five miles south of Catalina Island earlier this morning. According to a Coast Guard spokesperson, the yacht was abandoned. There did not appear to be any evidence of foul play or signs of a struggle, and they have no information as to what happened to the person or persons on board the boat prior to its discovery. The luxury yacht, owned by Farmer Fred's Meat Company, is being towed to a dry dock in Long Beach. The investigation is continuing.*"

The TV cut to a commercial and Joey the bartender flicked off the set with a remote control.

"Hey, Joey," I said. "What did the news guy say before we got here?"

"Chambers said the Coast Guard had called Farmer Fred's, and someone there said that Richard Rosenthal, only son of Arnold Rosenthal, the guy who had been murdered, was staying on the boat. The Coast Guard found it drifting out by Catalina—"

"Yeah, we heard that part. Thanks."

"Are you thinking the same thing I am?" I said.

"Yeah, the cocksuckers snatched Richie and they're trying to make it look like another suicide," Sol said.

Chapter Thirty-three

"C'mon, we're going to my office, right now," Sol said, shouting. "We're going to get some answers. I'm tired of the bullshit."

We darted out of the restaurant, rode the elevator, and sprinted to his office.

"Joyce," Sol yelled. "Get my friend, Bob Grimes, the undersheriff, on the phone."

Less than a minute later a button on Sol's phone lit up. He grabbed the receiver.

"Bob, I'm fuming. Buck Simpson—the guy murdered in your jail, the guy that you're telling the press was a suicide—was killed by the *Familia Unidos* gang. I know it, and you know it. So let's quit playing games. I need to know what in hell is going on."

Sol sat quietly for a moment before he exploded. "Damn it! Cut the crap. It's a gang murder. It's tied into a case O'Brien's working on and now he's in danger. If you don't help me on this, I swear I'll go to the media."

He paused again for a few seconds. "Bob, don't treat me like a *schmuck*. I got you your promotion. Where would you be without me? Ever think of that?"

After a pause a grin surfaced on Sol's face. "Sure, Bobbo, we'll be there, five-thirty on the dot." He slowly placed the receiver in its cradle, and turned back to me.

"We're meeting Grimes later at the Hearth Restaurant on Florence Avenue. I'm cashing in a few chips. He'll tell us what he knows."

At five-fifteen, I met Sol in the underground parking lot. Earlier, Sol and I had discussed the need for absolute secrecy regarding the meeting with Grimes. It wouldn't help Grimes's career, and it wouldn't do us any good if word got out that the undersheriff agreed to meet with a criminal defense lawyer to pass along sensitive information. We decided not to drive to the restaurant in the big limo, too conspicuous. Instead we took a white Chevrolet Impala that was used for stakeouts and surveillance.

Sol tossed me the keys and nodded toward one of the white Impalas parked at the end of a small row of identical Chevys. Jack Fox rode shotgun. Pulling out of the lot, I turned left on Florence and stopped for a red light at Paramount Boulevard. It felt good to be out riding again.

"Sol, I think it would be better for us to always use one of these Chevys instead of cruising around in the limo all the time," I said. "I'll admit my red Corvette is too noticeable, but I feel uncomfortable in the limo. It's too big of a target."

"Keep the keys to this one. But please...." Sol paused for a beat and placed his arm on my shoulder. "I'm worried about you. You have to let Jack Fox or the Deacon go with you. Don't go anywhere alone."

"Yeah, okay Sol."

The light changed, and we continued west on Florence.

"But Jimmy, when you go out with Deb tomorrow night take the limo. It's safer and won't be out of place at the opera."

I could hardly wait to be with Deborah, but with gangsters gunning for me, it might be too dangerous for her to be at my side in public. I was dying to see her again, and I knew she had her heart set on the opera, and frankly I was starving for female companionship.

"Do you think I should still take her out? Does she know what's going on?"

"Of course she knows. We've discussed it. We agreed it would be okay. You'll have the Deacon with you, and I'll assign Cubby, our best driver. He's also licensed to carry. Jimmy, she'd be very disappointed if you cancelled," Sol added. "I think you made a hell of an impression on her."

"Really? What did she say?"

"Sorry, my boy, I can't tell what she said to me in confidence. But I guess you've got something after all. To me, it seemed like you acted like a blithering idiot at lunch. But knowing how you are, I figured you did that helpless *shtick* on purpose just to get her sympathy." He poked me playfully in the ribs. "I don't know about you, you rascal."

I slowed the Impala and turned into the restaurant parking lot. We circled once and didn't spot any suspicious cars or people hanging around, so I parked in a stall not far from the entrance. Jack Fox remained with the car.

The Hearth Restaurant had been in Downey for as long as I could remember. It was one of those old clubby type places, dark with red-leather booths and faux-stone covered walls. The old geezers who waited tables wore red vests and had white towels folded on their arms. A brass hearth set with artificial logs and a gas fire flickered at the end of the dining room, and an old-fashioned organ pumped out the latest Jerome Kern hits while you dined on huge fat-rimmed T-bone steaks.

"Grimes chose this place, because he doesn't want to be recognized. Knows cops don't hang out here," Sol said. "In fact, nobody hangs out here." He opened the door and we entered the restaurant.

"Did you make reservations?"

"I'm sure they can fit us in," Sol said.

One of the elderly gents wearing a white dinner jacket with a pink carnation pinned on the lapel met us at the edge of the dining room. "Good evening, Mr. Silverman. Welcome to the Hearth. It's nice seeing you again. I'll take you to your usual booth."

"I haven't been in this place in a hundred years, and the guy remembers my name. Go figure," Sol whispered to me as we slowly followed behind the maitre d' heading toward a booth in the back of the dim room.

A long bar ran down the far side of the dining room. Its faded elegance was a throwback to a time when guys like William Powell in *The Thin Man* drank their martinis made with two parts gin and one part vermouth.

We arrived at the booth and Sol slipped the maitre d' a folded bill. "Thanks, ah..."

"My name is Humphrey," he said.

"Yes, of course, Humphrey. A guy will be joining us soon. He's tall and kind of beefy, know what I mean?"

"I'll show him to the table, sir. Now, can I get you gentlemen something from the bar?"

"A Coke for me," I said.

"Bring me a Beefeaters on the rocks."

Humphrey left, and I glanced around the restaurant. My eyes were becoming accustomed to the dark, and I noticed we were the only customers under eighty in the place. Except for the staff, the restaurant was practically empty. A bald man, who appeared to be pushing eighty himself, stood behind the bar polishing a wine glass, staring off into space while he wiped the glass over and over and over again. A waiter old enough to be the bartender's grandfather stood by the fireplace warming his backside, and the woman at the organ, who looked like a schoolmarm from the Old West, granny dress and all, was pounding out a laborious rendition of "Long Ago (and Far Away)."

"I feel like I'm at a funeral," Sol said.

"It's not your kind of place, but like you said, nobody will spot us here."

Humphrey returned with the drinks, set them down, and wandered away. A few minutes later he came back escorting a tall, beefy man with dark penetrating eyes, black hair swept back, and a prevalent five-o'clock shadow. The man, who I assumed was Bob Grimes, fidgeted with the top button of his white shirt and yanked off his red tie, stuffing it in his jacket pocket. "Too goddamn hot in here," he mumbled, as he struggled out of his jacket and tossed it onto the booth's seat next to Sol.

"Jimmy, meet Bob Grimes," Sol said.

"Hello, Bob."

Grimes, ignoring me, glanced quickly around the dining room and snapped his fingers at Humphrey. When the waiter appeared at our table, Grimes ordered a Jim Beam on the rocks. Humphrey left to fetch his drink.

The undersheriff leaned into the table. "Sol, if the word got out that I'm talking to you guys about the Simpson murder, I'll be in deep shit with the chief."

"What do you mean, *you'd* be in trouble?

Jimmy's got thugs shooting at him," Sol said.

Grimes glanced at me and nodded. "Yeah, I heard." He took a nervous look around again. "How many people know I'm here?"

"Just us. Not even my personal secretary knows," Sol said. "Now damn it, tell us what the hell is going on."

Grimes started to say something, but stopped when Humphrey appeared with a drink and three menus tucked under his arm.

"We won't be eating, Humphrey. We're just having a little chat," Sol said.

Humphrey's face fell, but only slightly. It couldn't get much lower. "Of course." He turned and wandered toward the fireplace.

"Okay, Bob," Sol said, "tell us why you're covering up Buck Simpson's murder."

Grimes hesitated a moment, then in a lowered voice said, "The DA was negotiating a deal with Simpson. He had information about alleged illegal activity at a halfway house where he'd been assigned."

"Wait a minute," I said, "the DA was talking to my client without me being present?"

The undersheriff's face reddened. "I'll admit it was unusual, but—"

"Unusual, hell, it's illegal for chrissakes!" I settled back in the booth. I started to do a slow burn, but I didn't want to stop the flow of information from Grimes. "Well anyway, that's in the past. Go on about the halfway house."

"Simpson told us the program was a fraud. Said he could prove it, had evidence."

"What kind of evidence?" I asked.

"We never got that far. Simpson wanted to be placed in the witness protection program. But damn it, his testimony about a simple fraud wouldn't justify releasing a violent felon."

"Sounds like there's more going on out there than simple fraud," Sol said.

"I agree," Grimes said. "The grapevine has it that Simpson was whacked by a member of *La Familia Unidos*. We figured the halfway house, St. Dismas, might have something to do with the gang, but we don't know how, or even for sure if they're connected."

Grimes looked over his shoulder at the front door as it opened and two little old ladies walked in. He turned his attention back to us.

"God, if this gets out..." Grimes paused, looked down at his Jim Beam, and picked it up slowly. He held the drink in his hand for a moment before he took a swallow. "It's a sensitive issue, politically."

Sol leaned into Grimes. "You're talking to me, Bob. Nobody knows we're here, and I don't leak."

"Yeah, I know, Sol, but if anything got out it could cost one of our men his life."

"What do you mean?"

"We've got an undercover operation going on at the halfway house."

"You've got a cop out there posing as a con?"

"Don't ask me his name, but yeah. He's one of our best guys."

"We don't want to know his name. We just want to know what he's found out so far."

"So far everything at St. Dismas is disorganized and difficult to read. But our man has only been there a few days. It's too early to tell."

215

"You'll let us know if your guy turns up anything?" Sol asked.

"It's a two-way street, Sol," Grimes said.

"I have a client-privilege issue," I said. "I can't tell you what information I have about the case right now. But I'll tell you this: I think the Simpson and Rosenthal murders are connected. After Mrs. Rosenthal is released, I'll turn my case files over to you—with her approval, of course."

Grimes's eyebrows ratcheted up a notch. He looked at me with a glimmer of surprise. "You think Simpson's death is connected to the Rosenthal murder?"

"Of course he does! That's why the gang is trying to silence him," Sol said.

Grimes kept pinning me. His expression of surprise turned to doubt. "What did you find out?"

"Jimmy said he can't tell you anything right now," Sol said. "But listen, Bob, here's something else you don't know. We have solid evidence connecting the gang to Richie Rosenthal's disappearance."

Sol was pouring it on a little thick. We had our suspicions that Richie had been kidnapped by Rosenthal's killer, but no evidence, solid or otherwise.

"Jesus, are you now saying that Rosenthal's son is missing, and that *La Familia Unidos* has something to do with it?" Grimes wiped a hand across his brow. "Is this on the level?"

"Richie disappeared. His boat was found in the middle of the ocean. The kid wasn't just out for a morning swim," Sol said.

"I get the point," Grimes said.

An idea came to me. If I could get a copy of

Willie's mug shot, then I could show the photo to Herbie Goldfarb and maybe he could positively identify Willie as Guillermo, the fifth guy at the poker game.

"I'll need a copy of the Willie Chavez mug shot," I said to Grimes.

The undersheriff took another sip of his drink and turned to me. The look he gave me wasn't all smiles.

"You aren't telling me anything, O'Brien, why should I help you?"

"Because I'm going to prove Mrs. Rosenthal is innocent and her husband's murder was gang related." At that moment, I didn't know exactly how I was going to prove *anything*. Laura wasn't talking to me. She planned to plead guilty at the next hearing and the only person who could possibly change her mind had disappeared.

Grimes finished his whiskey and thought for a moment. "Look, you guys, you're wacko if you think I'm getting involved in this heap of political bullshit without a hundred and ten percent solid evidence."

"Get me the mug shot. I'll get the evidence," I said.

"Sol, I trust you, but I don't want any cowboy crap from this guy," Grimes said, nodding at me.

"Hey Bob, Jimmy's heads up. C'mon man, I'm vouching for him."

"All right, I'll send the mug shots to your office tomorrow morning, Sol. But remember, damn it, don't screw with my investigation."

Humphrey appeared and asked if we'd care for another round of drinks. Grimes grabbed his coat and slid out of the booth. "Not for me. I got to get going."

Sol waved Humphrey away and focused on Grimes.

"Thanks Bob, but if you hear anything about Richie, let me know. Okay?"

"Yeah," Grimes said. "But if this shit gets out, we're through. Understand? And you know what that means, Sol."

"Yeah, Grimes, I know exactly what it means."

Chapter Thirty-four

The next morning, with Jack Fox riding shotgun, I drove the Impala south on the 605 Freeway heading toward the city of Long Beach.

The authorities had impounded the yacht and placed it in dry dock at Alamitos Shipyard on Marina Drive pending further investigation. The police said there was no evidence of foul play, no blood or signs of a struggle on the vessel, but that opinion had been formed with just a cursory examination. I wanted to get on board, have a look around, and see for myself.

If Richie couldn't be found right away, then teams of crime scene investigators would climb all over the boat and tear the interior apart looking for anything that might suggest a crime had taken place, a minute particle of blood that may have dripped between the duckboards, a fragment of torn clothing, or anything that may have been disrupted during a struggle. They would dust for prints and take dozens of photos and perform a myriad of tests before they were through. In the meantime the boat would be sealed and a uniformed police officer would most likely be guarding the yacht. I'd been on board before, and there might be something that would spark my memory and give me a hint as to what had happened to Richie. I couldn't wait for the police to release their final report; time was my enemy now. By all odds I'd find nothing, but I had to look anyway.

"The police will have the boat sealed," Jack said.

"Ever do a B and E, Jack?"

"Breaking and entering?"

"That's right."

"Isn't that illegal, Mr. Lawyer?" Jack asked, mockingly.

"According to the Code of Regulations, Rule Number One—"

"Yeah, I know. Only if you get caught."

"That's right, Rule Number One."

Richie told me he was looking for evidence that Moyer had been looting the company. I had a hunch that he had found something. My hunch told me that Richie's discovery could be the reason he disappeared.

But hunches were like shells: every nut had one. I had hunches almost every day and most of them were dead wrong. But every once in a while a hunch paid off—just often enough to make a hunch something I couldn't ignore completely.

However, what if Arnie's killer was holding Richie captive and he was being used as a hostage to force Laura to change her plea, dangling him like a worm on a hook? Wouldn't the kidnapper need him alive in case Laura demanded proof? If so, then it meant Richie might still be alive.

These questions about Richie's fate gave me goose bumps. The killer would not want a witness, that's for sure. Damn it, couldn't Laura figure that out? Richie would be kept alive only until Laura's guilty plea was entered and the case was closed. Then it would be too late for both of them. This time I hoped my hunch was wrong.

My plan for getting on the yacht was simple. "Jack, you divert the attention of any cop guarding the boat or any workers in the yard, while I sneak on board. I don't know what we'll find, maybe nothing, but there might be a clue as to what Richie discovered about Moyer."

"It will be risky, breaking a police seal and climbing on board," Jack cautioned.

"I don't care. The result of getting caught and getting slapped with a misdemeanor pales in comparison to the consequences of doing nothing at all."

Jack winked. "Gotcha covered, Boss Man."

A warm salt-tinged breeze carrying the scent of industrial solvents from the boatyard and seaweed drying on the dock wafted over us as Jack and I came up behind a chain-link fence bordering the yard. I stepped over a coil of rusted steel cable lying on the ground and peeked around the gate. The coast was clear. We slipped into the yard and walked past a beat-up sign that read: KEEP OUT! THIS MEANS YOU!

Large pleasure boats of every type were scattered about the yard. A couple of the larger ones sat mounted on huge wooden cradles. Some looked brand new with their paint gleaming in the sun. A few old rusting hulks lay on their sides in the dirt, derelicts being scavenged for parts.

Down by the water's edge three workers jumped around, guiding a crane that held a large cabin cruiser suspended by a sling underneath it. One of the men studied us as we approached them.

"You guys cops?" he shouted above the crunching noise of the crane as we moved closer.

I shouted back, "We're looking for the Farmer Fred's yacht."

The cables holding the wooden craft groaned under the weight, and the worker turned his attention back to his job. After a moment, satisfied that everything was okay, he glanced at us again and pointed to the *Hatteras* resting on a frame about fifty feet to his left. Without saying anything, Jack and I spun around and headed for the boat.

In the water, the yacht looked big, but sitting on the ground in a cradle, with the draft and freeboard exposed, it was huge. Stapled to the massive wooden supports holding the boat upright was a sign posted by the L.A. County Sheriff's Department. The sign, a warning, said that anyone caught doing exactly what I planned to do was breaking the law, and any person or persons would be severely punished.

We stood at the base of the boat and looked up. I needed a ladder to get onto the deck, a big one, and there wasn't one on either side.

Jack removed his jacket and folded it over one of the support beams. The brown leather straps of his shoulder holster had wrinkled his shirt, and the butt of the .45 facing out left a small oil stain on the white fabric.

He adjusted his belt and glanced around the yard. "Wait here," he said to me. "Hey guys, we need a ladder over here, pronto," I heard him shout as he walked toward the men working by the crane.

A few minutes later, two men pushed an A-frame ladder up next to the *Hatteras*.

"Thanks," Jack said. "We'll be finished here in about ten minutes, and then you can have the ladder back. But in the meantime, keep everyone away from us. Got that?"

The two guys nodded and left. Before I climbed the ladder I motioned to Jack to stand watch. I whispered to him to pound the hull if he spotted any cops coming our way.

Climbing aboard, I crossed the deck and opened the cabin door. Just as the news guy on TV had said, there was no sign of a struggle inside the boat. At least, not in the main salon where I now stood.

After about five minutes of searching the galley and the navigation station, rifling quickly through drawers, cubbyholes, and even the storage lockers under the seat cushions, I found nothing relevant to the case. I descended a few steps and rushed through an oak-lined corridor toward the bow of the boat. I stuck my head inside the guest quarters—nothing. I opened the door to the master cabin. A doublewide unmade bed practically filled the whole space. Blankets, sheets, and pillows were disheveled, and a fancy bedspread heaped on the floor.

Picking up a corner of the bedspread I uncovered a stack of self-help books, and a four-inch thick stack of green-lined computer paper. Suddenly, I heard three loud thumps on the hull.

"Shit." Jack's signal. Cops!

Spinning around, I started to leave but stopped to look at the stack of computer paper. It was too cumbersome to take the whole pile. The cops would be here any minute. I ripped off a few sheets of the printout, raced through the main salon, and darted out onto the afterdeck.

I peered over the side of the boat by the ladder. Seeing no one, Jack, workers, or cops, I crawled to the other side of the boat, raised my head, and looked down over the edge.

A uniformed cop stood at the bottom of the hull,

talking to the workman who had brought us the ladder. I moved back to the other side of the boat, hopped over the side, and hustled down the ladder.

I got about halfway to the ground when the police officer rounded the transom and came toward me. I jumped, or maybe fell the remaining distance to the ground with the sheets of computer paper in my hand.

"Find anything, detective?" the cop said.

I froze for an instant. Then I exhaled slowly. "Yeah, some computer papers." I waved the printout in the air. "Don't know if it's anything, but we'll see."

"Your partner said he'd meet you at your unit in the parking lot out front. He's in a hurry, said your lieutenant wants you back at the station."

I started to walk toward the parking lot. "Yeah, got to get back right away. But anyway, keep everyone off the boat, understand?"

"Yes, sir. That's why I'm here."

"Where were you when we arrived?" I asked, trying to keep cool.

The cop shrugged. "Got to go once in a while. You know how it is, all that coffee."

"Believe me, I've been there before." I continued to walk away at an easy but steady pace.

"Hold it a minute," the uniform shouted.

My heart thumped. I turned halfway and gave him a sidelong glance. "What do you need?"

"Got to have your name." He held up a clipboard. "For the report."

"Grimes. Detective Bob Grimes." I turned back and walked to the car.

Chapter Thirty-five

"Payroll report."

"What?" Jack asked.

"It's a payroll report, that's all. We took a risk and all I got are a few pages of a Farmer Fred's payroll report."

Jack drove the Chevy as we headed back to Sol's office. I sat in front scanning the report. But if there were irregularities, I didn't find them. The report consisted of row after row of names, numbers, and amounts, a typical corporate accounting of a weekly payroll.

"Shit," I mumbled as we rolled along in silence back to the office.

The receptionist in Sol's lobby handed me an envelope that had been couriered over from the Sheriff's Department. I ripped the top off and pulled out two mug shots of Willie, front and side views.

By showing the mug shots to Herbie Goldfarb, Arnie's attorney, I hoped he could confirm that Willie was in fact Guillermo, and it was Willie who came to the poker game. Yet even if Willie and Guillermo were one and the same, it still wouldn't prove that he was the general of *La Familia Unidos*. It wouldn't prove that he was a murderer, and it wouldn't prove that Laura was innocent of killing her husband. But it would give me a starting point. I had nothing else to go on, and I needed something, *anything*, desperately.

I handed the computer printout to the receptionist and told her I'd pick up the papers later. I gestured to Jack, who leaned against the wall. "Let's go."

"Where to now?"

"Herbie Goldfarb's office in Vernon."

"Who's he?"

"Arnie's lawyer," I said.

At Herbie's office we pulled into a parking stall and parked next to a pre-World War II Cadillac sedan with dents and dings and a crumpled fender. The car in its faded glory sat there like an aging lothario—still raring to get up and go, but without any horsepower.

Jack motioned for me to stay in the Chevy while he scanned the area outside. A moment later, he gave me an "all safe" thumbs up. I hadn't seen anyone who looked remotely like a gangster since the office shooting. After my date with Deb tonight I'll tell Sol I'll take my chances without protection. The babysitting routine was starting to grate on my nerves.

Goldfarb Law Center sat in the heart of the meatpacking district on the corner of Soto and Vernon Avenue, across the street and kitty-corner from a big pork processor. Herbie's office was located in the middle of a row of tired and sagging one-story stucco structures built in the 1920s and, like Herbie, the building had seen better days.

Betty, Herbie's gray-haired assistant, sat behind her desk with her back facing me when I entered the law office. A little bell nailed to the doorframe jingled and Betty's swivel-chair squealed when she spun around. "Yes?" she said.

"I'd like to see Mr. Goldfarb."

"Is he expecting you?"

"No, but it's important, Betty. I'm Jimmy O'Brien. Do you remember me?"

She titled her head sideways and studied me for

a moment. "Why, yes of course, Jimmy. Just a moment, I'll see if he's in."

When Betty opened the door and walked into the private office, I caught a glimpse of Herbie. He sat at his desk playing solitaire.

In a few seconds, she returned. "He said to tell you that he'll see you when he's off the phone." She smiled, shook her head, returned to her desk and started to pound the keys of an old Underwood.

I sat in a metal folding chair and waited politely.

"Send him in," Herbie shouted through the closed door.

I walked in and sank into a cracked and worn leather armchair facing Herbie's desk.

He leaned his head back and peered at me through his reading glasses. "Hello Jimmy," he said. "Haven't seen you in a while."

Herbie's face held an impish grin. He nodded his bald head slightly, as if he knew a bit of wisdom that the rest of us could only wonder about.

"I'm here about Arnie."

"Arnie's dead. Hard to believe, but. . ." His voice trailed off, his words disappearing like a whiff of smoke.

I stared at a little six-inch plastic bobble-head doll sitting on Herbie's desk. The doll, an English barrister, held a law book under one arm and except for the wig, it had a striking resemblance to Herbie, impish grin and all. Inscribed on the doll's base were the words: *Sue the bastards*. For Herbie's wayward clients, I imagined the doll and inscription were more reassuring than a Harvard diploma hanging on the wall.

"Maybe you can help me." I handed Herbie

Willie's mug shots. "Was this guy at the poker game?"

Herbie held the pictures at arm's length and squinted at them over the top of his glasses. "Looks a little fuzzy."

"Adjust your glasses," I said.

He shifted his gaze and peered at me. "Don't get smart with me young man."

Herbie set the pictures on his desk, opened a drawer and took out a large magnifying glass. He ran it over the photos. "You representing this guy?" he asked with his head bent down, his eyes gazing through the glass.

"No, I'm representing—"

"Hope you do a better job with this guy than you did with the cases I gave you," he said.

Using solid judgment, I kept my mouth shut.

"What did this guy do? Never mind, I know what he did and he's guilty as sin. Don't let him fool you, he's guilty. Just plead him out. That's my advice."

"Have you ever seen him before?" I said, as I picked up the mug shots.

This wasn't getting me anywhere. Poor Herbie, I thought. He's over the hill, but I had to hand it to him. He still suited up and came to his office every day to fight the battles, even if they were imaginary ones. I stuffed the pictures into my shirt pocket and stood to leave.

Then Herbie piped up, "The guy in the mug shot is Guillermo. He was at the poker game."

Chapter Thirty-six

Jack and I grabbed a bite at Angelo's Fat Burgers before heading to my real office on Cecilia Street. It was Friday and I had to sign the girls' paychecks.

Jack stood guard at the front door and Mabel sat at the reception desk preparing the payroll while mumbling with frustration that she wasn't ready yet.

"Go to your office and get out of my hair, Jimmy. With all the deductions it will take a while to finish the checks." She started back on her work and began to complain again. "First the taxes, then the damn insurance, disability, workers' comp, unemployment, social security. God, they make me take the money right out of your check. Don't ask if you want it, they just . . ."

Mabel continued to ramble on and I slipped into my office to go over the mail. Rita stepped in and sat in the chair next to me.

"Hey, boss, good to see you again," she said, her smile as bright as ever.

It felt good to be here, I thought as I leaned back in my chair and looked at Rita's pretty face. Yeah, the routine with Sol would change starting tomorrow. I'll keep Jack and the Deacon around. But I figured I'd move back into my apartment and work out of my own office again.

"It's good to be back, Rita."

"There is something we've got to talk about. I don't know how to say it."

"You know you can talk to me about anything."

"It's about your client..."

"Yeah?"

"The DUI, Geoff."

Oh Christ, I thought, not that asshole again. I've got too much on my plate to worry about him. If it wasn't for his money—

"Jimmy, I guess I'd better come right out with it. He wants me to handle his cases from now on. He's upset because you stood him up a few times. I know he's your client and—"

"Is that so? That's an ethical violation, you know, poaching my clients."

"Oh Jimmy, I'd never, ever—"

I laughed. "Rita, I'm kidding. You're helping me by getting him off my back. But get money up front from the guy."

"He mailed us a check for a thousand, only to be cashed if I represent him."

"A thousand! Well, what the hell. Go for it!"

"Unless he quits drinking and joins AA, I won't handle his drunk-driving arrests anymore. I'll only represent Geoff if he agrees to stay on the program. Otherwise he can find someone else. That's what I'm going to tell him." Rita glanced at her watch. "He'll be here at three."

"Just have Mabel cash the check first."

We both fell silent and just looked at each other for a few moments then Rita said, "I have a little time before Geoff's appointment if you want to chat a bit."

I started to talk, telling Rita about the halfway house, the gangs, and Willie being Guillermo. I told her my hunch that Richie had been kidnapped and was being held hostage to force Laura to change her plea. I said I believed the gang would keep Richie alive only long enough to prove to Laura that they had him, but I was sure he would be killed once she pled guilty and the case was closed.

Straying off on tangents, I didn't present the facts in any logical order. Continuing to ramble on in a stream of consciousness, I didn't lay out the case as I would to a jury, no conclusions to be drawn, and no embellishments. It felt good to talk, and Rita was a good listener. She didn't interrupt. She just sat there with her hands folded in her lap, her face blank.

Once, during my long-winded monologue, Mabel stuck her head around the door and saw me running off at the mouth. I suppose the scene appeared serious, because she quietly slipped back into the outer office.

I stopped for a moment, walked to the office window, and gazed at the traffic rushing by on Lakewood. A guy at the Union gas station across the street stood on a ladder changing the sign that posted current gas prices, 59.9 cents a gallon. God, can you imagine paying that much for gas?

But what did the inflated price of gas have to do with my case? I guess I was tired of constantly thinking about it. Maybe I was tired of the whole thing, tired of worrying about Laura and Richie. Tired of Moyer, Guillermo, and the gang. What the hell, maybe I was just tired.

"Moyer is the weak link."

I heard what Rita said, but it didn't register. I turned back to her. "What did you say, Rita?"

"If the two murders are tied together then whoever arranged to have Buck murdered also killed Arnie. Then, of course, he's probably the one who grabbed Richie. It could be Guillermo—Willie. But

Moyer is certainly involved, and that could mean Moyer is Willie's stooge."

I hadn't thought of it that way, Moyer being on the hook to Willie. And if both murders were linked, then what Rita said made a lot of sense.

"Rita, I think you nailed it. Maybe Danny Moyer didn't hire Willie to eliminate Arnie." I walked back to my desk and sat on the edge. "It might be the other way around. Maybe Willie has Moyer under his thumb."

"Suppose Moyer's scared. Suppose he's in over his head," Rita said.

"Yeah, could be. If Willie is, in fact, the general of a gang of vicious thugs, I wouldn't blame Moyer for being scared."

Rita stood and looked at her watch. "Got to run. Got to go meet my client."

"If you need any help, call me," I shouted to her back as she rushed across the office.

Rita turned in mid-step. She looked back at me over her shoulder and smiled. "Sure, Jimmy, I'll call you." She opened the door and left.

Chapter Thirty-seven

The curtain dropped. After several bows from the performers and bravos from the audience, *La Bohème* was over. Deborah and I worked our way through the crowd toward the exit and wandered out onto the plaza, taking in the streaming colorful banners and the fountain with its dark reflecting pool. The night air was cool and refreshing and a slight breeze rustled through the lighted trees.

While walking hand in hand, we wandered toward an angry bronze sculpture dedicated to World Peace. Deborah said the sculpture looked like a stylized Madonna reaching for a dove. To me it looked like a train wreck standing on end.

We continued on our way, walking leisurely and moving closer to the limousine waiting in the valet parking area adjacent to Hope St.

"Well?" Deborah asked.

"I'll admit the music was beautiful, but the story—I don't know, I guess, it seemed a little cornball."

"You weren't moved a little? Come on, Jimmy." She gave me a slight nudge in the ribs. "Big macho guy like you not touched at all by the sad story of young love lost. Is that it?"

"No, Deb, that's not it. But really, Rodolfo and a couple of other young horny guys moping around their Paris flat, no job, no money, raging jealousy...sounded like me when I was a kid."

"There you go, timeless story. Any tears for Mimi?"

I thought about the girl, young and pretty. And I

thought about her dying at the end. I glanced at Deborah. "I guess she moved me a little."

We walked quietly for a moment. Deborah put her arm around my waist and pulled me a little closer. "Want a hankie?"

I laughed. "Well, at least I didn't embarrass you by dozing off and snoring during the boring parts."

"Do you snore, Jimmy?"

"Now that I think about it, I don't know."

"No one has told you that you snore?" Deborah asked playfully.

"Deborah, I'm not going with anyone."

"I'm sorry. I didn't mean to pry, I—"

"I know you didn't, but I *wanted* you to know that I'm not seeing anyone right now." I paused, and when Deborah didn't say anything, I asked, "How about you? Are you going with anyone? Anyone special?"

Deborah looked down and fiddled with the clasp on her clutch purse. "It's only been a few months since my divorce, and the move here...well, I just haven't had a chance—"

"Good. I mean it's not good that you're...what I'm trying to say is—"

"Jimmy, I know what you're asking and I think you're sweet. You seem like a good guy. Uncle Sol's told me a lot of things about you. Nice things."

We paused and Deborah looked away, gazing at the waxing crescent moon low in the west. She turned and faced me again "But I've never gone out with a guy in a limo with two bodyguards before."

"Deborah, I have to be honest with you. The big limo, guns, bodyguards, and all that isn't really me. I'm more down to earth, a normal guy with a routine job, a lawyer with lots of forms to fill out and an occasional trial. I could learn to enjoy an opera or an art opening occasionally, but right now I guess I'm your average movie and popcorn type of guy."

"So, you like movies."

"Good movies. The old black and white film noir movies are my favorite."

"Oh, I love film noir. Have you seen *Out of the Past*?"

"Robert Mitchum and Jane Greer. Mitchum is Jeff Bailey and she plays Kathie Moffett, a girl with a heart of lead."

"Hey, you really do know the old films," Deborah said.

"It's a classic. From the novel *Build My Gallows High* by Geoffrey Homes," I said, showing off a little.

Deborah smiled at me. "His real name was Daniel Mainwaring."

"Whose name?"

"Geoffrey Homes, the guy who wrote the novel."

"Are you showing off?" I said, and we both laughed.

We stopped and faced the Dorothy Chandler Pavilion, as if bidding our farewell to the grand lady, glittering in lighted glory.

While Deborah admired a colorful three-story banner hanging on the façade, announcing the next performance, I looked back over my shoulder. Through the crowd I spotted the black limousine parked across the plaza at the curb. The Deacon stood by the passenger door. He didn't see me. He was busy checking his weapon. He ejected the clip, examined the bullets then pushed it back into the handle of the automatic. He did this twice in rapid succession. Cubby followed our every step, a few discreet paces behind.

"Your Music Center is beautiful," Deborah said, and we turned and started to walk again.

As we approached the limo the Deacon stood ramrod straight with his jacket unbuttoned, exposing the holstered .45 dangling from his shoulder. He peered about menacingly, and people wandering by were held at bay by his outstretched arms.

Cubby rushed around us and opened the rear passenger door, and the small crowd that gathered there must have wondered who we were. At first I felt slightly embarrassed by all the hoopla. But down deep I actually enjoyed the fantasy.

The Deacon gestured to Cubby, motioning him to get behind the wheel and start the car. Deborah and I slipped into the backseat. Deacon climbed in the front passenger seat and soon we were driving south on the Santa Ana Freeway.

Deborah sat close to me. I had my arm around her and she rested her head on my shoulder. Deacon turned and held up one of my music cassettes. I nodded and he popped the tape in the stereo. Softly, Billie Holiday's smooth and haunting version of "Body and Soul" filled the limo.

"Did you have a nice evening?" Deborah whispered to me.

"I hope it's not over, but yes, it's been one of the best nights of my life."

She snuggled a little closer. "Me too."

Lady Day's mellow torch songs continued as we rolled through the night. Deborah shifted her body and I felt the steady beat of her heart, her breasts warm against my chest. We were quiet now, and I looked into the stirring passion in her eyes, searching. She tilted her head slightly, and I leaned into her.

We kissed, and it lingered for a moment. Deborah pulled back, smiled, and rested her head on my chest again.

The big limo slowed as we rounded the curve where the San Bernardino Freeway splits off from the Santa Ana and heads toward the Inland Empire. Deacon leaned close to Cubby and said something I couldn't hear over the music.

The limo instantly accelerated and surged into the middle lane of the freeway. We heaved and pitched with the wheels squealing, and the limo, moving fast now, shot around a truck carrying a load of pipe.

Something was up!

I turned and took a quick look out the rear window.

A pair of headlights careened around the truck we had just passed.

The vehicle closed in on us rapidly.

Deborah must have sensed my anxiety. She started to straighten up; she turned her head to me and, for an instant, our eyes locked.

I snapped my head to my left and saw it at the same time Cubby did.

The limo swerved again, the car beside us now. A gun, a rifle barrel, sticking out the window.

I shoved Deborah to the floor, covered her body with mine. Shots tore through the limo. Automatic gunfire. A short burst, and then another, and then nothing.

I felt the cold air rushing through the shattered windows, and I felt Deborah trembling beneath me.

It's funny what you think about at a time like that.

I heard Billie Holiday's voice, and in my mind, I saw her dying in the Paris flat surrounded by Mimi, Rodolfo, and me.

A line from *Out of the Past* drifted in my mind *"They say when you die, your name is written on a cloud."*

"Who says?" Did Deborah ask that?

"They. . ." It was then that I realized I had been hit.

Chapter Thirty-eight

I'm dead.

"No you're not, *damn it*! I won't allow it."

Did I say I'm dead? Where am I? Why all the bright lights? I'm so cold.

"He's slipping off again," someone said.

I opened my eyes. The room was awash in sunlight. A phone rang. I tried to raise my head and a wave of nausea engulfed me. I lay back down and heard myself moan. I was in pain, but didn't know exactly where I hurt.

"He's awake again now, I think." Rita's face appeared above me and she held the phone receiver to her ear. "His eyes are open, but I don't think he can talk." She hung up the phone.

I raised my head again. This time I didn't feel as queasy, but my arm was sore as hell.

"Lie down, Boss. Everything is okay."

It all came back, and it came back too fast. I was sick again, and I lowered my head to the pillow. "Deborah?"

"She's fine, a little shook up, that's all. She wanted to be here, but Sol insisted that she go back to his place. You know how he can be."

"The Deacon? Cubby?"

"Deacon wasn't hit. Cubby took two, but he had surgery and he's feeling okay now. The doctors say he'll be fine," Rita said. "He's a tough guy. He took two bullets and still managed to drive to the hospital."

"Where am I?"

"Downey Medical Center. It was the closest hospital with an emergency room. They say Cubby did a fantastic job driving here. You were losing blood, and he had to go over a hundred miles an hour to get you here in time."

Again, I rose up. I fought nausea, and focused on the room and Rita. She looked cute in cut-off jeans and a white sleeveless pullover. A lock of her hair had fallen onto her forehead. She brushed it back with her hand.

I didn't see a clock in the room, but I knew it was daytime. Light streamed in from the window. "What time is it?" I asked.

"Ten-thirty," Rita said. "Sol's here. Stayed practically the whole time. He just left to get something to eat. Mabel's called a dozen times."

Ten-thirty. The shooting started about midnight. I did the math. At least my brain worked. "I've been here over ten hours, Rita."

"No boss, it's Sunday not Saturday. You've been in and out of it a few times. You don't remember?"

"No, Rita, not much. I remember seeing a car. . . a blue Chevy, I think."

"You lost a lot of blood and went into shock. Your shoulder was a mess. They had to pin it. But the doctor did a first-class job. He used titanium instead of steel. Hey, it won't rust." Rita smiled and brushed back the wayward lock again. "Anyway, Sol called me about six, Saturday morning. When I got to the hospital you were still in the recovery room. After a while, they brought you in here, a private room. Sol insisted. They let me in to see you, but you slept most of the day."

"I didn't wake up? I slept around the clock?"

"No, you woke up at dinnertime last night. The

nurse brought some yucky food, but you were too sick to eat. They gave you a shot of Demerol, and you went out like a light."

"You also woke up a couple of times during the night, mumbled some stuff, and they gave you another shot. Oh boss, and then you told me. . ." She brought her hands to her mouth, and her face glowed like the cherry on top of an ice cream sundae. "Demerol is a truth serum, Jimmy."

"What did I say?"

"I'll never tell." The mischievous look in Rita's eyes told me more than I wanted to know.

"You were here all day and night?"

"I had nothing else to do. Besides, I wanted to be with you."

"Oh, Rita."

"Your doctor was here this morning, said he'd be back. His name's Dr. Bone. He's an orthopedic guy."

"Dr. Bone, an orthopedic guy? A bone doctor named Bone? Are you sure that's his name?"

Rita nodded. "That's what he said."

"Dr. Bone, that's rich."

A nurse, wearing starched whites and a stiff attitude, filed into the room. She held up a syringe to the light and squeezed off a few drops. "Time for our shot."

In a single motion, the nurse whipped off my cover, rolled me on my side, and jabbed the needle in my ass.

"Oh my," Rita said.

"Ouch," I said.

The nurse pulled the covers back and turned to

leave, saying, "Doctor will be here shortly."

"Lawyer will be waiting," I answered.

Sol came bouncing in, one hand loaded with flowers, and the other holding a wooden box of chocolate bars. Rita took the flowers and went to the nurse's station to ask for a vase.

Sol put the box of candy on my food table and took out one of the bars. After unwrapping it, he broke off a piece for me.

I took a bite. "God Almighty, Sol," I said. "This is no Hershey Bar." The chocolate was overwhelmingly strong and somewhat bitter.

"Of course not. It's a limited edition, Valrhona Chuao Bar, made in France. Sixty-five percent cocoa, and sweetened with brown sugar. Got a whole box full."

"Why not a box of See's Candy, like everyone else? Where do you find this stuff?" I regretted what I said as soon as I said it. Sol's face fell. He was just being Sol, and that meant showing off a little.

"I don't know, the stuff finds me, I guess."

"Well, thanks Sol," I muttered. "I'm a wee bit crabby, that's all."

He plopped down in one of the chairs and started to munch on the chocolate bar. "See if you can get the game on TV."

After several attempts fumbling with the remote control, I hit the right button. The TV lit up. But I couldn't get it to change stations. Sol came over to help. It was no use. The TV was stuck on a channel that showed an Asian guy in a chef's hat selling steak knives. Sol went back to the chair and watched the commercial.

Rita came back with the flowers in a plastic water pitcher, kissed me on the cheek, and said she'd see me later. She was tired and needed some sleep.

Ten minutes later a doctor stuck his head in the room. At least I figured he was a doctor, the stethoscope hanging from his neck and all. "You awake?"

"Yeah, come on in."

Sol dozed in the chair. The doctor looked at him then grabbed my chart from the end of the bed. The guy on the TV was still pitching the steak knives. He was now cutting beer cans in two.

"How bad was it?" I asked the doctor.

"The bullet tore up your shoulder." He shook his head and frowned. "Cases like this can be tough. You'll be all right in time. Just remember, nothing strenuous for a while."

"How long will I be here, Dr. Bone?"

"Dr. Bone?"

"Isn't that your name?"

"My name is Bowen, B-O-W-E-N." We both laughed. "We'll see how you do in the next couple of days," Dr. Bowen said as he exited.

Sol woke up from his nap, stretched, and started in on the candy bar again. "What was that all about?" he said between bites.

"It was nothing. Listen, I've got to get out of here. I've got Laura's hearing coming up tomorrow morning and we still haven't found Richie."

I tried to rise up and immediately became woozy. I plopped back down. "Laura's going to try to change her plea. I've got to try to block it."

Sol pushed himself out of the chair, came over,

and took another chocolate bar out of the box. He started to unwrap it.

"You're not going anywhere," he said. "Rita's taking your place tomorrow. It's all set. She'll get the continuance, and you'll stay here until you're better."

I figured Sol might be right. My shoulder throbbed, and maybe it would be for the best if I stayed put for a day or two. Rita could handle the hearing, no problem. In fact, with me in the hospital it would be hard for the DA to object to an extension.

"Yeah," I said. "The judge should grant the continuance. Maybe a week or so. But we've got to find Richie before the extension runs out."

"We don't know who's got him, much less where they've taken him. Assuming he's still alive," Sol interjected.

"To keep Laura in line they would have to prove to her that he's alive, but after the hearing, he'll be a goner."

"That is, if your theory about his disappearance is correct."

"It has to be. Willie is a convicted felon, and with the halfway house, it would be simple for him to form a gang. A guy like Willie would have the guts and wherewithal to kidnap Richie. I think he has his clutches in the meat company, and I think Moyer's the weak link. I figure Moyer is being used by Willie, and he might know where Richie is stashed."

"You could be right," Sol said, "but even if so, it won't be easy to get Moyer to talk. He saw what happened to Buck, Arnie, and now Richie."

"We've only got a few days. I need to get out of here."

Chapter Thirty-nine

Finally it quieted down and I must have dozed off. But when I opened my eyes I heard soft sniffling coming from across the room. I lifted my head and the sound stopped.

"Jimmy, are you awake?" Deborah asked in a gentle voice, just above a whisper.

Scanning the room, I saw her standing in the far corner with her head bowed. She stood silently with her hands held together as in prayer, covering her mouth.

"Deborah, come here. Let me look at you."

She didn't move and she didn't look at me. I started to tremble; I knew something was wrong. But her demeanor wasn't really a surprise. I figured she must be terribly upset with me because of the shooting. I should've known better than to take her out in public under the circumstances.

"Deb, I'm so sorry about what happened. Please forgive me."

She looked up. "It wasn't your fault. Sol explained the risk and I was willing to take it to be with you."

"Please come here beside me. I want to talk. I want to promise you that it will never happen again. And I want to talk about us."

"I'll never forget how you saved my life. And I'll never forget how much being with you meant to me."

"We'll have many nights together," I said. "It's just a matter of time before this case is behind me. Then everything will be back to normal."

"I'm leaving."

"What do you mean?"

"I'm going back to New York. I'm catching the red-eye tonight. But I just had to say goodbye in person."

"How long will you be gone?"

"I don't know."

"Deborah, why? I promise that the bad guys will not—"

"No, Jimmy that's not why I'm leaving." She came to me and held my hand. "I haven't been completely honest with you."

"What do you mean?"

"I'm still married."

Her words hit like a bowling ball slamming into my gut.

"You lied to me?"

"Rodger and I are separated and I thought it was settled. He agreed, but changed his mind and now he won't go through with the divorce."

"Divorce him anyway."

"I can't, Jimmy. Unlike California, New York doesn't have no-fault divorce. That means I have to go back home, hire an attorney, and go through the whole mess all over again. But he wants to see me right away. He said if I talk to him in person, maybe he'll change his mind about granting the divorce."

What she said sounded like a crock—not the part about her filing for divorce. Maybe she thought she wanted one, but then again down deep maybe she still loved the guy. Rushing off to see her husband on such short notice seemed as if she actually wanted to work out their problems. A beautiful woman of such breathless charm—a married woman.

So goodbye Deborah, I said to myself. I'll dream of you from time to time, I'm sure. But there will be no regrets and I won't hang around panting and moaning like a lonely hound waiting for your return. There's someone out there who I'll meet, a woman who'll want me for who I am and enjoy what I enjoy and I'll find her someday.

Laying there I looked into Deborah's eyes until she turned away. "Do what you have to do," I said.

She faced me again. "Will you wait for me?"

"I'm not going anywhere."

She bent down and gave me a light kiss, turned, and rushed out of the room—and out of my life. She didn't look back.

***

I waited for my dinner to arrive. I hadn't eaten anything since I'd been in the hospital and I was famished. They say if you're hungry you must be getting better. I felt good about that.

A candy striper wearing a perky barber pole uniform finally came into the room carrying my dinner. She set the tray on the portable dining table, whipped off the plate cover, and pulled the table stand over me.

Disappointed, I looked down at my food: a slice of pressed beef drenched in some pasty gravy, a handful of cold peas, and a cup of coffee. The dinner didn't strike me as a gourmet feast, but on the side sat a small plastic cup of rice pudding. The pudding looked pretty good.

I took a sip of coffee—as bad as Dolan's, just

the way I liked it. I set the cup on the tray, and just then Jack Fox stuck his head in through the door.

"Hey, O'Brien, there's a couple of cops out here. I had a little chat with them about the shooting. Now they want your side. Do you feel up to talking?"

The pain had subsided. But it hurt when I scooted myself up in bed trying to raise my body to a full sitting position. I shoved the food tray out of the way.

"Okay, Jack, send them in. May as well get this over with."

Jack pushed the door open all the way and two tall men walked in. Each had short hair and a trimmed mustache. They wore plaid sport coats and dark slacks. I didn't need to see any badges. Their wardrobe and demeanor identified the men as cops better than any brass shield.

The detectives circled the bed, one standing on each side. The cop on my right told me his name, Sergeant Ray Brent, LAPD Robbery Homicide. He nodded at the cop on the other side of the bed. "My partner, Kenneth Stokes."

"You're here about the drive-by."

"You got it. Now suppose you tell us exactly how it went down."

"Well—"

Stokes piped up, "Don't leave anything out."

"Guys driving a metallic-blue Chevy opened up on us as we headed back to Downey. It happened somewhere on the Santa Ana Freeway, I think."

"Could you ID the shooter if you saw him again?"

"No, it was dark and it happened fast. The

incident was over in seconds."

"What else can you tell us?"

"Look, Detective, the whole thing is a bit fuzzy. Anyway—"

"How many guys in the car?"

"I don't know. At least two, the guy driving and the guy with the gun."

"Your bodyguard out there," Brent's gaze shifted to the door, "said the rifle used in the drive-by was a SIG SG 510. Does that sound about right?"

"What the hell kind of gun is that?"

"Military automatic rifle. Made in Switzerland. The guns are all over the streets now. The SG 510 was the military's weapon of choice in the Chilean coup d'état a couple of years ago. The rifles were supplied by ITT."

"Is that some kind of government agency, like the CIA?

"Nah, it's a US conglomerate, International Telephone and Telegraph."

"Maybe the Chilean government didn't pay their phone bill," I said.

"That's the only possible explanation," the sergeant said. "But anyway, the slugs recovered from the vehicle are consistent with what your bodyguard reported."

"How did Jack know what kind of gun the shooter had? Like I said it was over in a flash."

"He knows his weapons."

"Guess so," I said.

"Anything else you recall?" Brent asked.

"You haven't told us much," Stokes added.

"Not much to tell, but there is one thing…"

"Yeah and what's that?"

"Jack and I were at Sybil Brand the other day; saw a metallic-blue Chevy in the lot. Might be the same one. Jack ran the plates, registered to a member of *La Eme*."

"Yeah, he told us about the car and turned over the owner's name and address. The address is phony. That is, unless the guy lives at the mayor's mansion."

"Highly unlikely," I said.

"Why would a member of *La Eme* take potshots at you?" Stokes asked.

"Just random, I guess."

"It wasn't random. And I think you know why," Sergeant Brent said.

"Suppose the reason had to do with the attorney/client privilege."

"The Wienie Widow case?"

I said nothing, just stared at him. A few seconds went by and Brent and I were locked into a game of eyeball-to-eyeball.

He blinked. "Okay, that's it for me. You want to ask him anything else, Kenny?"

His partner moved in closer. "Yeah," he said. "You gonna eat that pudding?"

Before I could answer, he reached out and swiped the plastic cup off my tray.

The phone rang. Brent picked up the receiver and handed it to me.

"Hi, Sol. Police are here."

"Why are they there?"

"They came for the pudding."

"Get rid of the cops. I've got something to tell you."

I put my hand over the receiver. "You guys about done? Private call."

Detective Stokes grabbed my spoon and both cops sauntered out of the room.

"What's up, Sol?"

"Nobody else in the room?"

"Nobody's here."

"Door closed?"

"Yeah, it's closed. What's going on, Sol?"

"This morning a couple of my guys snatched Danny Moyer and took him for a ride."

I lurched forward. Pain shot through my shoulder. "*Jesus H. Christ*, Sol! You kidnapped Moyer?"

"Well, if you want to get fussy, I guess you could call it that."

Chapter Forty

"Tell me you didn't kidnap him!" I said. "My God, Sol, that's a serious felony. What were you thinking?"

"It's not as bad as all that."

"What the hell happened?"

"Yesterday morning a couple of my men went to Moyer's house and staked it out. He stayed inside all day and all night Saturday, didn't budge. But this morning he came out to pick up the Sunday paper and, bam, that's when my guys grabbed him and took him for a little ride. Went down without a hitch, smooth. My guys are—"

"*Christ*! They forced him into a car?"

"Jimmy, I thought it over and I got pissed. And when I get pissed I don't sit around and debate the finer points of legal canons. I get my ass in gear."

"Yeah, but Sol—"

"Calm down. It's no problem. My boys just drove him around for a few hours. They didn't hurt him none. Shook him up a little, that's about it. Then they let him go. But first, they leaned on him a bit. My guys can be intimidating, if you get my drift."

I thought of Jack Fox and the Deacon. It wouldn't be healthy to be on the bad side of those two bruisers. And I knew Sol had several other guys just as tough on his payroll.

"Yeah, Sol, I know what you mean," I said, "but I'm an officer of the court. I don't know if I should be listening to this."

"Cut the holier-than-thou crap and hear me out."

Laura and Richie flashed in my mind. Richie could be dead, for all I knew. Maybe Sol's right, I thought. I'll follow the rules when it comes to parking tickets and pickpockets, but now lives are at stake.

"Okay, Sol, I'm listening."

"Jimmy, Moyer is terrified of Willie's thugs. Said they had him by the *beitzim*. He said Willie's got a whole gang of thugs living at the halfway house. He gets the cons out of jail, and then he gets them jobs, but the jobs are just for show. No telling how deep this thing goes. You were right after all."

"What else did he say?"

"Not much. Moyer is scared, and he knows if he talks they'll kill him."

"Did he say anything about Richie? Does he know where he is?"

"Said he didn't know anything about Richie. Believe me, my guys pounded him hard about that. They feel he's telling the truth."

"Think so?"

"Yeah. It stands to reason. Willie doesn't confide in Moyer, he's just using him."

Just because Moyer didn't know about Richie's disappearance didn't mean that the gang hadn't kidnapped him. But wait, the sheriff had an undercover man at the halfway house, and if the gang took Richie there the cop would have tipped off Grimes.

"Jimmy, you still with me?"

"Yeah just thinking, that's all. You've got to call Grimes."

"Already called him. Phoned him at home a little while ago. Told him about the shooting, Moyer, everything."

"You told him your guys kidnapped Moyer?"

"Told him Moyer decided to take a Sunday

morning drive with my boys. I didn't tell him *why* he decided to go, just that he went. But Grimes said that even if Moyer squeals, which he won't, it's still not enough to bust Willie. Got to have hard evidence."

"Yeah, Grimes is not about to go out on a limb. And the district attorney will take forever to get anything that will hold up in court. I know how the system works. Court orders for wiretaps, probable cause for search warrants, and all the rest of it. They won't put the bastards out of business in time to save Richie, or even Laura for that matter."

"You should know. You're usually on the side of the bad guys," Sol said.

His remark stung, but I didn't say anything. He was right, but this was different.

"Okay, let me get this straight. Richie figured Moyer was looting the company. And now we know the gang is ripping off Moyer." I paused for an instant, and thought. "Richie must have found out about the gang and how they're getting the money from the company." I tensed and felt a chill in my spine. "Are you thinking what I'm thinking, Sol?"

"I'm afraid so," Sol said. "If Richie found out the gang is involved with Farmer Fred's then maybe they shut him up—permanently. They might have tossed him off the boat out in the Catalina Channel. He might be swimming to Avalon with cement water wings."

"Wait a minute, Sol. If that were the case, Richie would already be dead. The gang would have nothing to hold over Laura. She wouldn't change her plea. No, we're back to where we started. That's why the gang has to get rid of me. They probably figure I'm standing in the way of Laura's guilty plea. If I'm gone..." My voice trailed off. I didn't want to dwell on that possibility.

"Yeah, you're the fly in the ointment. And you know what they do about flies."

"Call in an exterminator."

"Unless you buzz off."

"What do you mean?" I asked.

"If you let Laura take the fall your *tsoris* will go away. It will be done, finished, kaput. They'll call off the shooters and you're off the hook."

"Looks that way," I said.

"Sooner or later, the cops will close them down."

"Yeah, I'm sure they would."

"Well what about it?" Sol asked.

"What about what?"

I held the receiver in my hand, waiting for Sol to say something. Finally the line erupted: "Listen up, Jimmy. Here's the plan. We're going to find Richie and shut those homicidal bastards down. We're going to stomp 'em like cockroaches. And we're going to do it now!"

Sol was getting pissed again.

Chapter Forty-one

Daytime slipped away and the evening turned to night. It must have been around eight-thirty or nine, and my room was dim with a yellow-orange glow shining from the nightlight beside my bed. I'd clicked off the TV earlier and now it was finally peaceful. But the door was open and the hustle and clamor of the hospital staff drifted in from beyond my room.

"Hey, boss." Rita peeked in from the doorway. "How long are you going to lie around, anyway?"

She walked in carrying a white paper sack. I could smell the hamburger and fries clear across the room. "Rita. You sweetheart, you stopped at Angelo's." I grabbed the control and groaned as I raised my bed to the sitting position.

Rita tore open the sack, arranged the burger, fries, and Coke on my portable table, and moved it over to me. "Thought you might be hungry. I saw the food that they serve here, yuck."

"Rita, you're a lifesaver. How did I ever get along without you?"

"You didn't," she said.

I laughed a little inside. She's right, I thought, as I dug into the hamburger. How could I get along without her? She had been with me since the day I hung out my shingle. I had just rented a two-room storefront and was throwing a coat of paint on the walls trying to convert the space into a law office. Rita, walking by outside, stuck her pretty head in the door and asked if I needed any help. Before I could say anything, she grabbed a brush and started painting. I was practically broke and had few prospects, but there was something about her cheerful smile and vibrant personality that I couldn't resist. Two days later we opened the office and Rita was my brand new legal secretary, soon to be an associate.

Rita filched a French fry and popped it into her mouth. "Umm, good, but I didn't come by just to keep you from starving to death," she said. "I want to go over the hearing." She pulled a chair close to the bed and sat next to me.

"There's not much to it, Rita. I don't have anything to present. You have to get a continuance, that's all. With me in the hospital, I don't think the deputy DA will object."

"Does Laura have another attorney lined up? The judge won't accept her guilty plea unless she has a lawyer."

"I don't know. She won't talk to me, but even if she has one, it's imperative that we stay on the case and get some time to work it out. We need the extension."

"Maybe Laura will talk to me. You know, kind of girl-to-girl."

"Yeah, maybe so. If she talks to you, tell her we know about Richie, and tell her not to worry. Sol and I have a plan. Tell her to hold off on the guilty plea, give us more time."

"You and Sol have a plan?"

"Not yet, but we will. Just tell her that."

"All right. If you say so."

The night shift nurse came to the door. "Thought I heard talking in here. It's after visiting hours." She shooed out Rita as she collected the food wrappers on the table.

The nurse replaced my chart and gave me a

haughty look as she rushed toward the door. I heard her voice reverberating in the hall. "I'll put a stop to this. You'll see." The voice of doom. I laughed. Her threat paled compared the real threats coming my way from Willie and his gang of vicious killers.

Chapter Forty-two

Time stood still in the darkened hospital room. It had to be about three a.m. and I couldn't sleep. I was cold, on edge, and wrung out. I couldn't get comfortable. Of course, I worried about Richie, Laura, and the case, but it was more than that. I knew I was coming down from the effects of all the drugs, and I supposed it would be a day or two before I was anywhere close to normal. It would probably take an additional few weeks for my shoulder to heal, but I couldn't let my injury slow me down. Finding Richie and ending this horrible mess before the extension ran out, assuming the judge would grant one, was my number one priority.

My thoughts drifted to Deborah. I relived the moment of our affectionate embrace. I felt her in my arms, her warmth, and I thought about the kiss. Suddenly, the shooting flashed before my eyes. I started to tremble: the automatic gunfire, Deborah screaming, and then the silence.

What was I thinking, taking her out? It was a foolish risk. How could I have been so stupid placing her in jeopardy? I'd destroyed any chance I had with her. Who could blame her if she hated me? What chance did I have with her anyway? Why would a sophisticated city girl like Deborah settle for a second-rate lawyer with an unfurnished two-bedroom apartment in a small town like Downey?

With a sip of water, I swallowed the sleeping pill the nurse had left on the table beside the bed.

***

"Wake up! It's time for your sponge bath."

I opened my eyes and blinked. A rotund nurse with a bucket in her hand walked into the room and snapped on the lights.

"What time is it?" I said, squinting from the bright lights shining in my eyes.

"Six o'clock already. Rise and shine. We've got a busy schedule."

"Why don't we skip it today?"

My eyes adjusted and the look on the nurse's face convinced me that skipping my sponge bath was not an option. Maybe I should threaten to sue.

"Okay, I'm awake. Let's get it over with."

The nurse propped me up and removed my hospital gown. After I was completely bare, she went to work on me with a coarse, cold wash rag.

"Why, Jimmy, you've never looked better."

I glanced over my shoulder. Mabel stood in the room with papers in her hands. The nurse didn't slow down. "Raise your arm, your good one," she said.

"Mabel, what are you doing here so early?"

She set the papers on the end table and sat on the edge of the bed. "Came by for the show."

I gave her a look that would halt a charging rhino.

"S'cuse me, Mr. O'Brien," Mabel said, not bothering to hide the sarcasm in her voice. "I bust my ass to get here early with your mail and stuff so you won't be bored, and that's the thanks I get." Mabel moved closer and pulled up a chair. "I also brought the papers you left at Sol's."

"Okay, Mabel." I turned and looked at the nurse. "I'll go over the stuff when this woman is through torturing me." It felt like she was trying to scrape off the outer layer of my skin.

"There, now you're squeaky clean for the doctor." The nurse dropped the rag in a bucket of sudsy water and left.

A few minutes later Dr. Bowen walked into the room as I was struggling to get back into the hospital gown. "How are you feeling today?" he asked.

Mabel stood up and waved at me while walking to the door. "I'll wait in the hall," she said.

"Doc, I've got to get out of here right now," I said. "I've got important legal matters pending, life and death ones."

"I wouldn't advise your leaving, but I can't stop you. Too many things can go wrong at this critical stage of your recovery."

"I didn't think you could."

"I won't be responsible, understand? You'll have to sign papers indemnifying me and the hospital."

I signed the necessary releases. Mabel went down to the cashier and paid the bill, which took a sizeable chunk out of the ten thousand advanced by Richie. Jack Fox pushed me in a wheelchair to the car and drove me back to my suite at Sol's headquarters.

Once back, he helped position me on the couch, and at noon, he left to grab a snack in the executive dining room. It was quiet and I felt bone tired.

Before leaving the hospital, the nurse said it would be advisable for me to stay down for at least a week. The pain in my shoulder increased, and I wanted to take a couple of aspirins and lie down for a nap, but first I needed to hear from Rita.

I wondered why it was taking her so long to call

me. The hearing must've been over hours ago. I'd left word at the hospital switchboard to have her call me here.

I noticed the papers Mabel had brought into the hospital, which were now sitting on the coffee table next to the couch. I figured this would be as good a time as any to look them over. Worry had made it impossible to sleep anyway.

I tossed the bills in a pile. I was depressed enough and didn't want to make it worse by opening them. The advertisements I threw away. Included in the stack of papers were a bunch of phone message slips. They could wait until I felt better. That left the payroll report I had taken from the yacht. I'd more or less forgotten about the report, but now I remembered I had given it to the receptionist at Sol's office. She must have given it to Mabel, and Mabel must have thought the printout was important. She was good that way.

I unfolded the sheets of paper and set them on the couch. I was curious to see what workers at the meat company earned. With union scale and benefits that butchers got these days, I imagined they made a whole lot more than I did.

Before I could peruse them, the phone rang and I tried to get up. The second and third ring went by and I was still struggling on the couch. Finally, I got to my feet, but feeling woozy I leaned against a chair on my way to the phone in the kitchenette. I stood there through two more rings. Slowly I moved and the ringing continued.

"Please, Rita, don't hang up," I said out loud.

Inching along, I managed to make it all the way across the living room. I stopped with my right hand braced against the door jam. The ringing continued.

"I'm coming!" I shouted. When I was an arm's length from the telephone, I reached out and grabbed the receiver.

"O'Brien," I blurted out breathlessly. There was silence on the other end. "Hello," I said, and hearing nothing, I started to hang up.

"Boss?" I put the phone back to my ear. "Are you there, Jimmy?"

"Yeah, is that you, Rita?"

"You'll have to speak a little louder," she said. "I can hardly hear you."

Speaking barely above a whisper, I realized I was a lot worse off than I thought. I had trouble just standing there. Clearing my throat, I spoke louder. "Rita, tell me how it went in court."

"Jimmy, you sound terrible. You shouldn't have left the hospital. Hang in there. I'll be there in ten minutes." Rita hung up before I could get my answers.

With great effort, I worked my way back to the couch, plopped down, and leaned my head against the cushions. Sitting there, shoulder throbbing, I couldn't get Laura and Richie out of my mind. But how could I do my job feeling the way I did? I knew if I quit the case Richie would die and Laura would be sent to prison for the rest of her life. To hell with my shoulder, I had to get a grip and start sorting out the case again right away.

Suddenly, the door opened and Rita walked in carrying a large brown paper bag. "Hey boss. I stopped at Foxy's and picked up some chicken soup."

She scurried to the kitchen and a moment later returned with a steaming bowl on a tray. I sat up as much as I could. Rita put the tray on my lap.

"Do I have to feed you as well?"

"Thanks, Rita." I smiled. "You really take care of me, don't you?"

I picked up the spoon and sipped the soup. I didn't know if it was the soup or Rita, but I started feeling a whole lot better.

"Now, tell me about the hearing."

Chapter Forty-three

"We didn't win," Rita said.

"God," I sighed.

"No. But we didn't lose."

"Okay, Rita, did we get the continuance?"

"Yes and no."

"What does that mean?" I asked.

"We got fired," she said.

"Fired?"

"Yes, Laura already had a new lawyer. She signed over her Mercedes to this guy and he agreed to plead her out. But when the hearing started, I objected."

"On what grounds?"

"On the grounds that in order for Laura to plead guilty, the new lawyer would have to review the case. To do that he'd need to see our files. Then I said, unfortunately Mr. O'Brien—that's you—is in the hospital suffering from a gunshot wound and would need at least a week to prepare the files before he could turn them over."

"The judge went for that."

"At first Laura's new lawyer wanted to object, but when he heard that we were willing to quit the case and turn over the files without a hassle he sat down."

"Yeah," I said. "He'd want to see the files if he was going to try for a plea bargain."

"Funny thing—and I may be wrong—but I didn't think the guy was interested in any kind of plea deal. I think he just wanted to get it over with and drive away in his new car," Rita said.

"What about the deputy DA? What did he say?"

"He sat there and listened, but he didn't seem to

care. He knew he was going to get a guilty plea now that we're off the case."

"Yeah, and the judge wouldn't want this thing coming back and biting him on appeal based on incompetent representation."

"That's what I figured. I reminded the judge that this is a murder case, for crying out loud. How could Laura's new attorney assess mitigating circumstances without the files? I told him, one week wouldn't make that much of a difference when we're talking about a capital crime."

"The judge granted the continuance?"

"He postponed the hearing until next Monday, but he wants you to give the files to the new lawyer prior to the hearing."

She picked up the tray with the empty soup bowl, walked into the kitchen, and shouted from the other room. "The judge didn't say when we had to turn over the files. He just said 'before the hearing.' So that gives us a week. Then it's history, I guess."

"Did you get a chance to talk to Laura?" I shouted back.

Rita raised her voice over the sound of water running in the sink. "The new lawyer hovered over her and I couldn't get her alone. I guess he didn't want to give the Mercedes back. But before the hearing started I spoke to her at the defense table for a moment."

"What did she say?"

"After she told me about giving her car to the guy, she said to tell you to back off." Rita appeared at the kitchen doorway wiping her hands with a dishtowel. "Boss, Laura looked like hell." Rita shook her head slowly. "I think she's over the edge. She said she didn't care anymore. She just wanted it to end."

"Who's the new lawyer?"

Rita tossed the towel aside and walked back into the living room. "I've got his name here somewhere." After rummaging through the purse, she held up the lawyer's card. "Here it is. Guy's name is Walker, Johnny Walker." Rita glanced up at me. "Isn't that some kind of whiskey? Johnny Walker, I mean."

"Yeah, scotch whiskey."

"Is it any good?"

"It's not the best. But compared to Johnny Walker, the lawyer, the whiskey is liquid gold," I said.

I knew Walker by reputation. When they talked about shysters who cared only about their fee, not about what is best for their clients, they were talking about guys like Walker.

A few years back, he dodged a bullet that would've cost him a felony conviction. He made a bundle negotiating insurance settlements for a gang of tumblers and gymnasts, ex-circus performers, who were later convicted for what is known in the insurance rackets as hot jumping. These acrobats would jump in front of moving cars and then roll off and claim to be injured. Rumor had it that he was in on the scam. Some say he set the whole thing up.

Bunco squad detectives finally arrested the gang after an insurance company reported that over a two-year period they had paid a hundred forty-seven claims to one of the hot-jumpers. Walker wasn't charged in connection with the scam. In fact, the insurance companies put him on retainer in their efforts to curb fraud.

I wondered why Laura would choose Walker, a

personal injury attorney. He wouldn't have the experience needed to handle a murder case. Rita figured Laura just didn't care anymore. She just wanted it to end. Maybe Rita was right.

Rita stepped over and sat on the couch next to me. "What do we do now, boss? Want me to get the papers ready for the new guy?"

"I'm not giving Laura's file to anyone," I said in a stiff-necked manner.

"We have a week. Think it over, Jimmy, the judge—" Rita picked up the payroll report resting on the couch between us. "What's this?"

"Nothing. Just part of a payroll report that I found on Richie's boat."

Rita ran her eyes down the list of names. "What were you doing on the boat? Isn't it impounded?" She looked up at me and sighed. "I shouldn't have asked."

"It was risky, but I had to do something. A waste of time, nothing was there that would give us a hint as to what had happened to him."

"Just be careful, Jimmy. Where would we be without you?" Rita returned to the report still in her hands. "Hey, look at this. Farmer Fred uses a payroll service. A company that makes out the paychecks, handles the deductions, and prepares all the tax forms. Wonder what it costs? Maybe we could use them and you wouldn't have to worry about signing checks on Friday."

"God, Rita, we only have three weekly paychecks." That included mine, I thought, and I didn't always get one.

"APR Paycheck Services, name's on the top of the report. They're in Century City, 1900 Avenue of the

Stars. Sounds fancy."

"Should be Avenue of the Accountants," I said.

Rita continued to study the report. "Hey, boss, these workers don't make very much."

"Really? Let's see." I twisted a bit when I reached out for the report, and a jolt of nerve pain ran through my shoulder.

"I thought meat cutters made good money," Rita said. "These guys are only making minimum wage."

"Rita, can you get me a couple of aspirin, please? They're in the kitchen." I stifled an urge to groan.

"Oh, Jimmy," she said, and rushed away.

I picked up the payroll sheets for a closer look. Rita was right. The amounts paid to the workers were all the same. Minimum wage, three bucks per hour. Each employee worked forty hours, and netted exactly—after all the government and insurance deductions—one hundred dollars and thirty-five cents.

Rita came back with a glass half filled with water and a small bottle of aspirins. She handed me the water and shook out three pills. "Here, take these. The way you look, two won't do it."

I popped the pills in my mouth, took a sip, and swallowed. I handed the glass back to Rita. "You're right," I said. "about the workers getting paid minimum wage." I flipped through the pages. "They all make the same. Must be trainees."

Rita set the water glass on the coffee table and took the report from me. "Farmer Fred's must have a lot of trainees."

"That's for sure," I said. "They get them from Willie's halfway house. They're ex-cons. There must be seventy-five or more on these three pages alone."

After she set the report on the table, Rita said, "Here, boss, I think you'd better lie down. You don't look so good." She leaned over and started to shift my legs onto the couch.

"Wait a minute!" I shouted.

Rita dropped my legs and bolted upright. "Did I hurt you?"

"No, it's the report. Hand it to me, quick!" In my mind I saw the four-inch stack of computer paper that I'd left on the boat. A lot of trainees, indeed. A hell of a lot.

Rita gave me the report. "What's going on, Jimmy?"

Without saying anything, I ran my finger down the names on the paper. I didn't see Buck Simpson listed on the report. I didn't care. I wasn't looking for him. I was looking for something else, something that caught my eye, something that wasn't right. After a quick scan, I started in again. This time moving slowly down from the top. I had to be sure.

I set the report aside. I'd found what I was looking for. Now I knew why Richie had taken the report to the boat. I knew what he was searching for and I knew what he'd discovered.

Chapter Forty-four

Concentrating on what Richie must have discovered, I tried to piece it together in my mind. I heard Rita's voice, but at first it didn't register.

She repeated herself: "Hey boss! Jimmy, are you all right? Your face is white."

"Rita, I'm better than all right! Now listen, I think I've got those guys."

"Maybe you should lie down."

"No, let me show you."

"What?"

"Come here." I pointed to one of the employee names on the report. "Look at this guy's Social Security number."

"So what? Everybody has one."

"True, but look at this." I ran my finger down the list.

Rita focused on what I pointed out and glanced up at me with wide questioning eyes. "That's funny," she said. "I thought everyone's number is supposed to be different."

Two Social Security numbers were exactly the same, but with different names.

"Someone screwed up," I said.

"Think it's a typo?"

"No. I think the numbers are phony, probably the names as well."

Leaning back on the couch I formulated my thoughts for a moment. Rita started to say something, but I held up my hand and she remained silent.

"I think I know how to prove that the numbers are phony." I felt the sinews in my body compress as I tried to get to my feet.

"Jimmy, what are you doing?"

"Rita, help me get to the table over there." I pointed to the kitchenette. "And bring me the phone."

"Jimmy, you don't look so good. You just got out of the hospital—"

"Rita, please!"

"Okay, but after that I beg you to go to bed. The nurse said you should stay down at least a week."

With Rita's help I made it across the room. The telephone cord stretched tight from the counter to the table as she handed me the phone. I set the phone on the table and told her to run down to the lobby and ask the receptionist to loan us the La Puente phone book.

After Rita rushed away, I spread the payroll report on the kitchen table, dialed information, and got the number of the local Social Security Administration district office. I punched the number and a recorded message came on. "Due to a computer error, your checks will be mailed later than usual. Thank you for your patience and understanding." The line went dead.

I redialed the number and when the message played again I hit 'O' and a moment later a voice answered. "Good afternoon, Social Security. How may I help?"

"This is Detective O'Brien, homicide. I need to talk with someone in the fraud division." The line clicked. "Duffy, fraud division."

"Duffy, I need information about your number system."

"What's your name?"

"O'Brien."

"FBI?"

I didn't know where that question would lead. "No, local."

"You know better. We can't give out names or numbers. That's confidential information."

"I didn't ask for names. I just want to know how to spot fraudulent numbers."

"Should have asked for the information office."

"I did, but—"

"Give your address to the operator. She'll send you bulletin SSA 634 dash Q, which explains all about it." The line went dead.

Dialing the number a third time. I figured I'd try a different approach. "Yes, ma'am," I said to the woman who answered the phone. "My name is Jimmy, and I'm blind."

"Oh, I am so sorry. How can I help you?"

"You people sent me a bulletin, SSA 634 dash Q and I can't read it. What does it say?"

"Hold on a second. I think that bulletin came from our fraud division."

The line went dead again for a moment then a familiar voice came on the line. "Duffy, fraud."

"Can you read bulletin, SSA 634 dash Q to me?"

"The operator said you're blind."

"Yeah, I—"

"Didn't I just talk to you? You're the cop."

"Look, Duffy, just help me out here. I just need to know how to interpret the Social Security numbers. That's all."

"All right, all right," Duffy said. "The first three numbers are known as area numbers. They represent the geographical region where the cards were first issued. The second two are called the group numbers. They range from 01 to 99. The final set of digits is the serial number. The serial numbers are meaningless for your purposes."

"Okay," I said, recalling my own Social Security number. "If a card starts with 566, where is that from?"

"California."

Good, that's where I'm from. I ran my finger down the report and randomly stopped on a number. "How about 136?"

"New Jersey," Duffy said.

"Here's another, 255."

"That's Georgia. But where is this getting us?"

"687?"

"Look O'Brien, I haven't got time—what number did you say?"

"687."

"It's a phony. We don't use that series. Give me some more numbers."

I called out a dozen or so more and a pattern began to emerge. Some of the area numbers were in a series that were not used by the government and some of the legitimate area numbers didn't match the proper group number that corresponded to it. Someone had obviously just dreamt up the trainee's Social Security numbers. And I had a good idea who was responsible for gaming the system.

"Look, O'Brien," Duffy said. "I think you're on to something. What police department are you with? I'm going to send a field investigator out to see you. Give me your badge number."

The line went dead. I hung up.

Chapter Forty-five

Just as I got off the phone with the Social Security office, Rita walked back in carrying the La Puente white pages. I knew the numbers were bogus and now I wanted to check the names.

Rita laid the telephone book on the table, pulled up a chair, and sat next to me.

"Who are you going to call?" she asked.

I explained the false Social Security numbers, and told her how I hoped to prove the names were false as well.

"It's not difficult to make up numbers, but making up names that sound real is a lot more challenging," I said.

I could see the lights flashing in Rita's mind. "Yes, you're right. After Smith, Johnson, and maybe ten more it gets harder. They'd have to get creative," she said.

"And, if the scheme works the way I think it does, they'd have to come up with maybe a thousand names that wouldn't raise eyebrows."

"So that's why you wanted the phone book," Rita said. "If all the names on the list are in the La Puente book and the halfway house is in La Puente, it means—what does it mean?"

"Nothing, unless you tie it in with the phony Social Security numbers. Then it proves that someone in La Puente, probably Willie, picked the names at random right out of the book and gave them false numbers. It means the trainees don't exist. They're just names and numbers."

"You want me to check the book to see if the

names are there?"

"Yeah, I'll call them out, and you look in the book."

We spent the next twenty minutes cross checking the names on the report with the names in the phone book. My presumption was correct. Most of the names were in the book.

"Ghost workers," Rita said. "And the State's picking up the tab."

"The State pays back half of the gross payroll. About fifty dollars a week, each."

"Jeez, if they have a thousand ghost workers on the payroll, that's a lot of money."

"Yes, it is. And that's just Farmer Fred's. They'd need other companies in the program as well. Perhaps not as big, but it wouldn't look right unless they had some other businesses signed up."

There was a knock on the door. Rita ran to answer it.

Sol walked in carrying a portable tape recorder. "Rita, Jimmy, you got to hear this singer they hired at Rocco's bar," he said.

"Later, Sol. Jimmy has evidence about the trainees at Farmer Fred's," Rita said.

Sol set the recorder on the table and gave me a curious look. "Evidence, you have evidence?"

"You're damn right." I told Sol about the report, the counterfeit Social Security numbers, and the names right out of the phone book.

Sol picked up the report and ran his eyes quickly down the list of names. "*Oy vey!*" he exclaimed. "Jimmy, it looks like you've used your noodle for more than just an ear-spreader. Are all these numbers false?"

"Most of them are," Rita said. "And we've checked the names in the phone book." She handed the book to Sol. "Here, take a look."

Sol pushed his tape recorder out of the way, looked over the papers, and placed the report and the phone book back on the table. "Amazing!" he said. "With this I can force Grimes to get off his ass and move on the bastards."

"Rita called them ghost workers. I figure there could be close to a thousand names and numbers on Farmer Fred's payroll. But I was out at the halfway house and doubt that they could board more than forty or fifty convicts, tops."

"How can the people running this scheme get away with it? Isn't anybody checking on them?" Rita asked.

"Good question, Rita," I said. "When I was at the halfway house the parolees were drinking, a serious violation. Not only that, it looked like the records were a mess. I asked Willie about the booze and his files. He told me nobody checks on him. Now I believe it."

"You'd think someone, somewhere in the system would match the number of prisoners released with the number of payments made," Rita said.

"Look at it this way," Sol said. "The Adult Correctional Authority is happy to dump as many prisoners as they can. It cuts their budget, reduces overcrowding, and the politicians who passed the bill can show their constituents how much money they're spending on criminal rehabilitation. And of course, the State Welfare Department just dishes out the money as directed by the program. Everybody wants the program to succeed, but nothing is tied together. Willie knows the system and he knows how to bend it his way.

"But the gang has to figure that sooner or later they'd get caught. Don't you think?" Rita asked.

"Sure," Sol said. "But if they get away with the scam for just a few years they'll have raked in millions. Enough to take over the Mexican gangs and finance the drug distribution system they're trying to set up."

"Yeah, and when Willie feels the heat coming down, I'm sure he figures he can disappear, change his name, and run the drug business from Mexico for all we know," I said.

Sol crossed his arms. "There are other people involved. There have to be. Remember what Arturo said. *La Familia Unidos* is structured like the military, a general who is directly under the supreme leader. We know Willie's the general so, obviously, there has to be someone above Willie. Could be a whole group of people pulling his strings."

After a moment, Rita turned to me. "I suppose to make the scam work there has to be *so-called* honest citizens involved as well, people like Moyer, maybe others."

I nodded. "That's for sure. Moyer and businessmen like him would have to sign the false weekly payroll forms. Then when the company gets paid from the State, they could be forced to hand over most of the money to the gang."

"Willie is in a position of control with the blessing from the State. He's collecting the cash and building an army of hardened thugs," Sol said. "Don't forget, if he gives the word, the cons are back in the slam."

"That could be what happened to Buck Simpson. Maybe he didn't go along," Rita said.

"Sure, and when he threatened to talk in exchange for a deal, Willie had him killed," I chimed in.

Sol let out a dramatic sigh. "He'd have the necessary connections in jail to do the job. Inmates who want to get out. Guys who knew that Willie had the juice to get them paroled."

"Okay, I'll buy all that." Rita paused for a moment. "But why did they kill Arnie Rosenthal?"

Sol and I looked at each other. That was the big question, the sixty-four thousand dollar question, and I didn't have the answer. The fraud going on at the halfway house, the gangs and convicts and drugs, the conjecture about Willie, Moyer, the supreme leader, and even Richie still didn't prove that Laura was innocent.

I knew Willie had been at the poker game, same as Moyer, of course. And I knew that Buck Simpson had worked at Farmer Fred's for a short time before Arnie was killed. What I didn't know was how it all tied into Arnie Rosenthal's murder. And I had less than a week to find out.

Sol picked up the telephone book, the payroll report, and Rita's hand-written notes summarizing the fraud. "Get some rest, Jimmy," Sol said, "and I'll take the evidence you and Rita came up with and call Grimes at his home tonight. I hope he'll have enough evidence to get the warrants and put Willie and his gang out of business."

"Maybe you're right," I said. "I don't feel so great."

"Now listen, Jimmy," Sol said, "tomorrow morning at ten o'clock, if you're up to it, we'll meet in the conference room here at my office. By then we'll know what the cops are going to do and we can plan our next move."

"I'll be up to it."

I thought about what Sol had said. Grimes could order a raid on the halfway house, and by tomorrow night the gang could be in jail. The security routine would be over for me. I could move back into my apartment and get back to normal.

"I want to be in the meeting in the morning," Rita said. "I'll bring the donuts."

"I'd like you there, Rita," I said. "You've got to know what the plan is in case I'm not able to be at Laura's hearing next week." I didn't say anything about turning over the files to Laura's new lawyer and Rita didn't ask about it. If our plan worked, he'd have to give back the Mercedes.

"Fine with me, Rita. Bring the donuts and we'll see you there." Sol thought for a moment. "Make it jelly donuts." He turned and headed for the door with the phone book and papers in hand.

"Hey, wait!" I shouted. "You forgot your recorder."

Chapter Forty-six

The next morning I shuffled into the kitchenette and put on a pot. While waiting for the coffee, I attempted to fix the shoulder bandage that had come loose. The injured area looked grotesque, purple and yellow with thick black stitches that were like the scars on Frankenstein's monster. I had slept in and it was nine o'clock before I poured my first cup.

At around ten I stepped into Sol's conference room. He wasn't there yet but Jack Fox sat at the table in a casual manner with his arm resting on the back of a chair. He appeared to be flirting with Rita, who sat next to him. Rita didn't seem to mind, her smile was bright as ever. She flinched, however, when she saw me.

"How you feeling this morning, boss?" she asked.

"Much better. Thanks." I nodded hello to Jack, and gingerly poured another cup of coffee. Then I grabbed a jelly donut out of the box while grimacing to disguise my pain.

"Sol will be here shortly. He's running late," Jack Fox said stretching his long, muscular arms and yawning.

Sol thundered into the room. "We better get moving or we're doomed."

I didn't like the sound of his voice or the worried look on his face. Maybe the gang thing wasn't going to be wrapped up today after all. "Did you talk to Grimes?"

Sol picked up the box of donuts, brought it over, and sat beside me. "Afraid so," he said, taking a big bite of a jelly donut. The jam oozed out of the side and spilled onto the polished inlaid wood table. Sol dropped the donut back in the box and wiped his hands on a napkin.

"What did Grimes say?"

"I called him and laid out what you guys came up with, the phony names, the phony Social Security numbers. I told him, obviously, the evidence shows that Willie's running a racket at the halfway house. I told him to get a warrant and bust the place, put the gang out of business."

"He didn't go for it, did he?" I asked.

"No, he's sitting on his ass. He's the human equivalent of a potted geranium," Sol said. "The schmuck told me he believed our evidence, but it wasn't enough. He said it's circumstantial. He wants an eyewitness. He thinks his undercover man out there will turn up something, sooner or later—then he'll move on it."

"How long will that take?" Rita asked.

"He said the guy is making progress and now has a job at Farmer Fred's. Said he's keeping his eyes open. Grimes said to give him time, but he didn't say how much time."

"Could take forever the way they work," I said. "And we only have a few days left."

Jack took a sip of his coffee and glanced around the table. "Why don't we smoke 'em out?"

We turned to Jack. He took another sip and delicately set his cup down, folded his arms, and sat back.

"What do you mean?" Rita asked.

"Lay a trap," he said.

"What do you have in mind?" Sol asked.

"If the cops aren't going to do anything, we've got to bring them down ourselves."

"You might have something," Sol said. "We'll need the name of another company that has Willie's trainees on the payroll. Maybe we could persuade the management to talk."

"Do we have the names of any of those companies?" Rita asked.

"Jimmy, what about the other guy who was at the poker game? The cereal guy." Sol put his cup down. "You know, the salesman."

"Joe Short, but I've already thought of him. He's the guy that told me about Guillermo in the first place. Nope, if he were involved he wouldn't have mentioned him."

Sol glanced around the table. "Any more ideas?"

We sat around and tossed out ideas for an hour or so. None of them seemed workable. They were either too complicated, too obvious, or the ideas were so blatantly illegal that Rita said we'd be the ones in jail, not Willie.

"We've got to get an eyewitness, somebody who will talk. Then Grimes would have to move on the gang." Sol looked at his watch. "Look, it's lunchtime. Why don't we go down to Rocco's, grab a bite, and then come back and figure this thing out?"

Sol looked at me. "It'll have to be a fast lunch. We'll have steak sandwiches, and finish our brainstorming there. Sound good?" We all nodded, and Sol called the restaurant and told them to have our order ready.

Soon we were sitting in Sol's booth at the back

of Rocco's dining room. The steak sandwiches appeared, and Janine, the waitress, asked us what we'd like to drink. Sol ordered his usual Beefeater martini, Rita and Jack asked for iced tea. I paused, remembering something, and in a moment of inspirational recall shouted, "Beer, Rocky Mountain Gold!"

Rita turned my way. Her smile was gone. Sol looked at me, too, with a shocked expression on his face. "Is it your shoulder?" he said. "Are you in pain?"

Janine dropped her arms to her sides. "I thought—" she started to say something, but Sol interrupted her. "Janine, cancel my drink. I'll just have coffee."

"Are you going to start drinking again, Jimmy?" Rita asked.

"No, hell no. But beer is the answer," I said.

"What's the big deal?" Jack said. "What's wrong with beer?"

"Hey guys, what's the matter with you? I've got it, damn it. I've got it!" I exclaimed.

"Got what?" Sol asked.

"The plan. Rocky Mountain Gold. I can see it!"

I remembered Willie said he had a placement. I remember the word placement because it sounded odd. Anyway, one of the companies that used his trainees was a beer distributor in Lakewood. The business must have been a distributor for Rocky Mountain Gold. That was the brand the cons were drinking when I went to see Willie at the halfway house.

André rushed to our booth. He probably saw the look on Janine's face when she placed our order. "Is everything okay?"

"Where do you get your beer?" I asked. "Rocky

Mountain Gold?"

"From the bar."

"No, who do you buy it from, for the restaurant?"

"We order it from an outfit in Lakewood, Carriage Trade Distributors. Why, is something wrong?"

"Just the opposite," I said. "Everything's great."

And then I explained my plan.

Chapter Forty-seven

André had given us the owner's name and address of the beer distributor located in the city of Lakewood. Sol, Jack Fox, and I were in the Chevy Impala, driving south on Paramount Boulevard heading there now.

My plan was simple. The beer distributor had to be one of Willie's placements, a company on his trainee program. So I figured the odds were good that the distributor had ghost workers on the payroll. We'd talk with the owner, tell him that the cops were ready to pounce on the halfway house and if he turned state's evidence before the wheels came off, he'd stand a better chance of cutting a deal with the DA. If he agreed, his confession would nail Willie and the halfway house, and we'd have it all on the tape recorder Sol had tossed in the car.

As an added bonus, I'd volunteer to represent him in the negotiations with the DA without charge.

Right after lunch Rita headed off to Sybil Brand, the women's jail. She felt that if we came up with a witness against Willie, she could convince Laura to change her plea. I doubted that Laura would see her but agreed it was worth a try. Before she left, Rita asked, "What if the guy at the beer company is legitimate? Didn't cheat on the program?"

I said the afternoon wouldn't be a total waste. Jack and Sol could have a cool one with the owner and I'd have a better opinion of mankind.

After cruising through the town of Paramount we entered the city limits of Lakewood. A few miles farther along we turned left on E. Kessler Rd., close to Long Beach Airport. Carriage Trade Distributors was housed in a medium-sized concrete tilt-up building. A chain link fence surrounded the blacktop parking lot. We pulled in and parked in a slot reserved for visitors close to the front of the building. Farther down, a half dozen bobtail delivery trucks were backed into the side of the building. A large graphic representation of an idealized mountain scene with a bubbling stream running through it was painted on the side of the trucks. The words *Rocky Mountain Gold, The beer that won the west* surrounded the image.

A small door with a sign reading, EMPLOYEES ONLY was cut in the side of the building.

"Wait here, I'll check out the place," Jack Fox said.

Sol and I remained in the car while Jack slipped through the employee entrance and disappeared inside the building. Only three cars were parked in the lot, a beat-up Opel, a silver Honda, and a ten-year-old Buick Skylark.

A few minutes later Jack returned from the warehouse and gave us the thumbs up. "It's okay, just saw one old guy. He was sitting at a desk toward the back of the warehouse by the loading area. He's no gangster. Looks like a shipping clerk."

The three of us walked around the corner of the building to the front office and entered a small reception area through the main door. To our right, about halfway up the wall was a sliding glass window above a two-foot-wide counter. The window was closed but a push-top bell sat on the shelf. Sol pounded the knob. A few seconds later a pleasant looking woman in her thirties appeared and slid the window open.

"May I help you?" she asked.

"Yes," Sol said. "We're here to see Mr. Sullivan."

She turned her head and shouted, "Mike, there's some guys are out here to see you."

A shout returned: "What do they want?"

"How should I know?" she said and walked away.

The door to the interior offices opened and a man with red hair and a sizeable belly appeared. "You want to see me?"

I handed the guy my card. "It's extremely important that we have a few minutes of your time."

He glanced at the card then shifted his eyes to Jack. His hand holding the card trembled slightly. "What's this about?"

"We got a deal for you," Sol said. "You'll like our deal."

"Who are you?"

Sol stepped forward and put his arm around Sullivan and slowly edged him through the door leading to the interior. "Call me Sol. I'm a friend, and we're here to help. Let's talk in your office."

We moved down a hallway. Sullivan pointed to the left. We entered a stark office with a linoleum floor and no windows; the only decoration adorning the yellowing walls was a beer calendar with a picture of what I appeared to be the Rocky Mountains. Two white plastic visitor chairs faced a standard wooden desk.

"Was that your wife who greeted us in the lobby?" I asked.

"Yeah, how'd you know?"

"It figured."

"She helps out around here, but sometimes..."

Sullivan's voice trailed off. Then he said, "I'll have to get an extra chair."

Jack leaned in the doorway. "Never mind, I'll stand." Jack's suit coat hung open, his shoulder holster and gun clearly visible.

Sullivan sat behind his desk and picked up a pack of Winstons. "Mind if I smoke?"

He took a cigarette out and lit it before anyone could answer. Sullivan, clearly nervous, must have guessed we weren't there to buy beer.

He took a deep drag, exhaled, and nodded at Jack. "Is he a cop?"

"Why do you think that?" Sol asked.

"Well, the gun for one thing."

"You were expecting cops?" I asked.

Sullivan hung his head.

Sol pointed at me. "When the cops show up they won't have a defense lawyer with them. Meet Jimmy O'Brien. He'll get you out of the mess you're in."

"What mess?"

"Knock off the bullshit, Sullivan," Sol said. "You're in deep and you're about to get hammered."

"We know you've been padding the payroll reports, getting kickbacks from the state. But the scam is coming apart," I said. "The sheriff is about ready to take down the halfway house and bust everyone involved. If you're smart you'll cut a deal while there's still time."

Sullivan looked at us with bloodshot eyes. "Who are you guys, anyway?"

Sol told Sullivan about Richie and Laura and about the thugs coming after me. He didn't threaten him. That would be useless. Sullivan had to know that any threat from us would pale in comparison to what *La Familia Unidos* would do to him if he talked. No, the best approach was to have Sullivan work with us, help put the gang out of business, eliminate the fear of retaliation altogether.

"We need your statement to nail the bastards," I added when Sol finished speaking. "How'd you get involved with these crooks, anyway?"

Sullivan started to talk. The words and tears poured out of him as if they had been churning in his gut forever. They say confession is good for the soul; Sullivan's words proved that he still had one.

"Hold it," I said. "Jack, get the tape recorder out of the car." I turned to Sullivan, "I want to record this, if you don't mind."

While Jack was gone, Sullivan lowered his head and kept quiet. He appeared to be ashamed of what he had done, and I knew he would be uncomfortable discussing his complicity in Willie's criminal activities on tape.

"Listen to me, Sullivan," I said. "I'm not a judge. I'm a lawyer and I'm on your side. Believe me, Sol and I have heard it all, stuff a hell of a lot worse than picking up a couple of bucks on the side." I paused a moment to let him absorb what I was saying. "Don't forget, everything you tell me is privileged. That includes anything Sol hears. But privilege doesn't extend to Jack. We'll have him wait in the outer office if that's what you want and I won't use the tape without your permission. Is it a deal?"

His eyes left the table and focused on me. "I guess it's all going to come out anyway. Go ahead and record it. I don't care if the other guy stays."

Jack returned and started to hook up the recorder.

"Before you start recording, let me send my wife and the shipping clerk home."

Sullivan picked up the phone, punched a button. "Honey, tell Fred he can finish the paperwork tomorrow. You can leave too. I'll be home later." He paused for a moment. "Please, just do as I say." He paused a second time. "Goddammit, go home." He banged down the phone.

Everyone in the office heard Sullivan's wife cry out as she slammed the front door: "If you think I'm going to stick around for this, you're nuts."

Her words hung in the air.

"I don't care what they do to me," Sullivan cried. "I'll tell you everything I know."

Chapter Forty-eight

Mike Sullivan took a hit on his Winston and nervously watched Jack adjust the microphone on the desk. He glanced up at me, took another hit then stubbed out the cigarette. He cleared his throat; Jack stepped back, and Sullivan looked up at me. "Where do I start?"

"Why not the beginning?"

He leaned forward with his hands folded on the desk and his eyes shifted to the microphone. "I've got a small business here. Only seven real employees, not counting me and my wife Vicki."

He then focused on Sol and me. We nodded.

"Anyway, this type of business is low margin; the sales price is set by the brewery. If expenses get out of hand...you know how it is."

"Yeah, we know about that, Mike," Sol said. "Right, Jimmy?"

"That's business all right," I agreed. "Go on, Mike. Tell us how you got involved with the gang at the halfway house."

"One of my customers owns a chain of topless beer bars," he said, wincing. "The guy told me about the trainee program. Told me to call St. Dismas Halfway House. I wasn't interested. I didn't need trainees. I needed licensed truck drivers. Well, the bar owner kept pestering me. He's a good customer, so one day, to keep him happy, I called them."

"What happened then?"

"They sent out a couple of guys. Supposed to be counselors." Sullivan pushed his nose to one side with his finger. "Know what I mean?"

"Yeah," Sol said. "Broken noses. Goons with

scar tissue for brains."

"The thugs told me they'd send out a trainee and the State would pay half his wages. He could sweep the floor or something. They said they didn't care what he did. I figured I'd keep the guy a while, see how it goes. It would only cost me about sixty bucks a week."

"Did the guy show up?" I asked.

"Yeah he showed up, all right. Came the next day, two hours late. He brought a trainee form from the state. I filled it out and gave him a uniform and a broom and told him to sweep the warehouse. About an hour later I went to the back to see how the guy was doing. The floor wasn't swept. The nutcase just sat around drinking beer, hadn't done a damn thing."

"What did you do then?" Sol asked.

"Told him to get busy, what else? Told him if he didn't start working, I'd report him. He just gave me a smirk and continued drinking my beer. I went in the office and called the halfway house, told them what was going on."

"What did they do?" I asked.

"Nothing, told me they'd talk to him. I figured I'd give the guy one more day, and then that would be it. But the next day the guy didn't show up. So I called the halfway house to cancel out. The guy who answered said that's why it's a training program. I shouldn't worry. He said that sometimes the cons have a hard time adjusting. Then he told me to fill out the form, anyway. Go ahead and put forty hours worked on the report."

Sullivan stared off in the distance for a few seconds before he continued. "The guy disappeared with the uniform and a case of beer. I figured the State would pay me sixty bucks, cover my loss. So I agreed. The rest of the week I didn't think about it. Then Friday the same two big guys came back to pick up the form. They said I didn't have to pay the trainee anything. But I had to make out a paycheck, photocopy it for the records, then tear it up."

"They wanted you to sign the form stating that the guy worked forty hours, even though he hadn't worked at all. And you gave them a copy of the form and the phony paycheck. Is that what you're saying?" I wanted his actions to be perfectly clear on the recording.

"Yeah, I know it's stupid, but—"

"Mike," I said, "we all make dumb mistakes."

"Those guys were pretty intimidating."

"That's how it started?" Sol asked.

"Yeah, that's how it started," Sullivan said in a voice barely audible.

"What happened next?" I asked.

"I figured it was over, but I was wrong. Didn't hear anything from the bastards for a week. Then they came by again on payday, had a form already filled out. Five names on it."

"You signed it and gave them copies of some more phony checks," I said.

"Yeah, they said they had a quota to fill, had to show that they were getting the parolees jobs."

"You believed that quota thing?" I asked.

"No, not really." He started tapping a pencil on his desk. "I guess Artie and Flavio, the counselors, you know, were a little scary." He broke the pencil in half.

"They threatened you?"

"Not directly. Mostly intimidation. I just wanted

them out of my office." He nodded toward the door. "My wife was here."

"They came by every week with forms, and you signed them. Right?" Sol asked.

"One time I tried to stop but they got rough. Told me if I didn't cooperate they were going to hurt Vicki. Huh. I guess they did threaten me."

"What about the money from the state?" I asked.

"I was supposed to deposit the checks and give half to them."

"You did that. Didn't you?" I said. "You cashed the checks and gave them half."

"In the beginning, I just put the checks in the drawer, and gave them money out of my pocket. It was a few hundred a week. I thought I could handle it until I could figure a way out."

"It got worse, didn't it, Mike?" Sol asked.

"Yeah, they kept adding more names. I couldn't keep paying them. I'd go broke. Then they wanted a bigger cut."

"How big?" Sol said.

"They wanted it all. Plus I had to give them free beer. I had no choice. If I went to the cops, well, they told me what they'd do." He lit another cigarette. "I had to cash the checks. I knew that once I cashed the checks, I was just as guilty as they were."

He tried to place the cigarette on the rim of the ashtray, but his hand shook so hard that the cigarette slipped off and fell to the floor. He bent down, picked it up, and stubbed it out.

"I knew, sooner or later, the deal was going to fall apart and my name was the only one on the reports."

"Your wife knows what's going on?" I asked.

"She knows. This thing has practically ruined our marriage."

"How many ghost workers are on the list now?" Sol asked.

Sullivan looked at his shoes. "A hundred," he said.

Chapter Forty-nine

Reaching over, I turned off the tape recorder. The room fell quiet except for faint din of an air conditioner rattling in the background. Jack Fox stood in the doorway. Sol sat next to me. No one spoke. We thought about Sullivan, about how an innocent guy struggling to run a small business could get caught up in a nightmare like the one he was living now.

The silence was broken by a ringing phone.

Sullivan picked up the receiver. "This is Mike." He paused. "Okay, Vicki, just a minute." Sullivan put his hand over the mouthpiece. "It's my wife."

"We'll go in the other room. We've got things to talk over," I said.

As we stepped into the hall we heard Sullivan on the phone: "Vicki, they're here to help us. He's the Wienie Widow lawyer. Remember, in the paper? I trust them. I told them everything."

We walked into a small, tidy lunchroom furnished with a Formica table and four chairs. In addition to a full pot of coffee, a beer keg, tapped and ready to draw, sat on the counter.

Sol looked in the cupboard, found two pint glasses, and pulled a couple of beers, one for himself and one for Jack. I poured a cup of coffee. The three of us sat at the table.

"I think we have enough for Grimes," Sol said. "What do you think, Jimmy?"

My mind was elsewhere and I didn't answer. I just sat and gazed at the employee notices pinned to the wall, thinking. If Sullivan agreed to testify against the gang, the DA would have a good case and maybe the

Sullivan tape would get Grimes moving. But to get the district attorney's office to seek an indictment and order arrests before my deadline, I felt we needed more, something stronger. We needed to catch the thugs in the act and have their threats and extortion on tape.

Sol took a sip of his beer and set the glass on the table. "You seem far away, Jimmy. Is it your shoulder again?"

I felt a dull ache but it was no big deal. "Just thinking, Sol," I said.

"Notice you took off the sling," Jack said.

"Didn't really need it. The sling was only on there to keep my shoulder immobilized for a day or two."

Sol picked up his half-full beer glass, twirled it around, and watched the foam coat the inside of the glass. "Well, I think we got what we came for."

"We need more."

Sol and Jack took a sip of beer and looked at me with misgivings.

"Maybe Grimes will move, but maybe he'll wait for the DA. And the DA's office will want to start its own investigation. They'll want corroboration. Right now it's basically Sullivan's word against Willie's. And Willie has strong connections. Don't forget Richie's life is at stake."

"Then we're back where we started," Sol said.

"Not at all." I nodded at Jack. "We do just as Jack suggested back at the restaurant. We smoke them out—and I think I know how we can do it."

With a look of skepticism, Sol asked, "Yeah, how?"

"For their safety we'll stash Sullivan and his

wife in a hotel room somewhere, just for a day or so, just until the gang's behind bars."

I had their attention and I continued to talk. "I'll call the halfway house from here and tell them that I'm a new partner in the business. I'll let them know that I'll go to the cops immediately unless we get a cut of the payroll money. I'll say that we're taking the risk and want, oh, maybe seventy-five percent."

Sol was staring at me as if I were nuts.

I explained that a serious threat would bring Artie and Flavio out here for a showdown. "In the meantime," I said, "Sol, you take the tape with Sullivan's declaration to Grimes and let him hear what we've got."

Sol shook his head warily without saying anything. I sensed his concern for my safety. I knew I'd be at risk, but I didn't have a choice. We had to make our move. Time was running out. If the plan had any chance of success, I needed Sol's full cooperation.

"Jack will hide somewhere close by," I said, "and when the thugs show up and start hammering me, he'll appear and get the drop on them. Then, I'll call the cops and have the hoods arrested. We'll have the whole thing on a second tape, their threats, intimidation, and extortion."

"Crude," Sol said.

"But effective."

"And dangerous. What if one of the thugs recognizes you?"

"When I was at the halfway house, Willie said the counselors were constantly on the road working with his placements. Artie and Flavio are Sullivan's counselors. They weren't at the halfway house at the time." Willie also said the counselors were real pros. Now I knew what he meant: professional leg-breakers.

"I don't know—"

"Sol, what part about Richie's life being in danger don't you understand?"

"All right already. Tell me the rest of it."

"Grimes would have to move immediately, that is unless he wanted to blow his whole setup," I said. "He couldn't sit on it with Sullivan's statement and a couple of Willie's goons in custody with their threats and extortion recorded."

Sol turned to Jack. "What do you think? Artie and Flavio might be a couple of tough *momzers*. Think you could handle this or should we wait and get some back-up?"

"Sol." Jack's face was calm and he spoke slowly, but with determination. "I'm a pro. I'll do my job, and as Jimmy says, I'll have the drop on them. The more people we get involved the trickier it gets. Let's go with what Jimmy has laid out."

"It's up to Sullivan too. If the plan crashes, he and Vicki will be the ones going down in flames," I said.

"Yeah, guess so," Sol said. "But you're the one in immediate danger."

"It's my plan, I'll take the chance. Besides, I won't be alone."

I glanced at Jack, sitting cool and quiet. He looked at the rim of his beer glass, raised it to me and took a sip. If he were any more relaxed, I thought he might doze off.

"Don't forget, Sol, I want these guys off my back as well," I said.

Sol shot a quick look at Jack, who gave Sol an almost imperceptible nod.

"Okay," Sol said. "Let's go talk to Sullivan."

We walked back to Sullivan's office and explained the setup. He agreed to do anything we asked. He was scared, and worried about his wife, but he figured that one way or the other his nightmare would finally be over.

Chapter Fifty

"You have an extra piece?" Sol asked Jack Fox.

"Sure do." Jack bent over and pulled a small automatic out of his ankle holster.

"Give it to Jimmy."

"I'm not going to shoot anybody, Sol. That's not what this is about," I said.

"Keep it handy, Jimmy, just in case."

Sitting at the desk, I opened the top drawer and dropped in the gun along with the tape recorder loaded with a fresh blank cassette. I turned it on for a moment and left the drawer opened slightly.

"One, two, three, four, testing," Jack said a few times. I played it back. The recorder worked fine. I hit the stop button. I would start it again just before Artie and Flavio came in the office.

Sullivan called his wife and explained the situation, telling her to hurry, pack an overnight bag for both of them and he'd pick her up in a fifteen minutes.

After hanging up the phone, he viewed the office, a look of concern clouding his face. "But what about my business?"

"It'll be here. Quit worrying." Sol patted Sullivan on the back. "We'll get these animals locked up and your business will be better than ever. Now why don't you make a little vacation of it? Take your beautiful wife to Vegas for a couple of days. I'll call Morty at Caesar's. He'll fix you up, comp the whole thing."

"My God. How can I thank you guys?"

"Go on, get out of here, Mike." Sol practically shoved Sullivan toward the door. "Have a good time with your gorgeous wife."

Sullivan shook hands all around. He handed me the keys to the building and rushed off.

Jack dashed into the hall. In a moment he stuck his head back in the room. "There's a storage closet right across the hall. I'll go in and open the door a little. You and Sol say something. I'll see if I can hear you."

"Testing, one, two, three, four," Sol shouted.

"Sol, I can't shout at these guys. They'll think something's up and they'll be right."

Jack came back. "It'll work. I could hear Jimmy. But we'll need a code word. In case it goes wrong."

I was trying to think of a word that would come up in normal conversation when Sol yelled, "Help."

We laughed a little. It wasn't subtle, but if the situation got to the point where I needed Jack, *help* would work.

Jack told me not to worry. He'd be set and ready. As soon as the thugs arrived and went into the office, he would sneak out of the closet and stand against the wall right outside of the door. Of course, his gun would be in his grip and he'd be willing to use it, if needed.

Sitting at Sullivan's desk, I checked out his stuff: an appointment calendar, a phone number Rolodex, and next to the phone, a framed picture of Vicki. I picked up the photo and studied it for a moment. She wasn't a raving beauty, a little chubby, but kind of cute. Sullivan was a lucky guy I thought, had a wife to share his troubles and dreams. Soon this anguish would be behind them and they could rebuild what they had before Willie and his gang screwed up their lives. It made me think of Deborah. Could we have had a future? One date, not much to build on, I thought.

Picking up the telephone, I glanced at Sol and Jack. "Show time," I announced.

I dialed the number and when a gruff voice answered, I faltered. "This is, ah..." I hadn't thought of an alias.

"Who is this?"

"I want to talk to Willie."

"Who are you?"

I blurted out, "Jack Rabbit." I don't know why I said that. Goddamn stupid. It was the first thing that popped into my head.

"Are you trying to be funny? What's your real name?"

"Jack Babbitt. What's the matter with you?"

"Oh, I thought...Never mind. What do want with Willie?"

"Tell him I'm the new partner at Carriage Trade Distributors in Lakewood. Tell him I'm pissed. Tell him I want to go over the deal."

The line went dead for a few moments before Willie came on. "May I help you?"

Disguising my voice, I said, "Yeah, I'm the new partner—"

"Yes, Dutch told me. Where are you calling from, Mr. Babbitt?"

"The warehouse in Lakewood."

"How can I help you?" he said in a voice as smooth as caramel.

"I don't like the deal. Starting now, we keep seventy-five percent, or I'm going to the cops."

"Seventy-five percent of what?"

"The payroll, I'm—"

"You talking about the payroll for our trainee program?"

"What in the hell do you think I mean?"

"Mr. Babbitt, can I call you Jack?" His friendliness was nauseating.

"Yeah."

"Jack, you get fifty percent from the State, a refund on the cost of our trainee's wages. Can't change that. It's the law."

"Well, we want to keep seventy-five percent of the fifty percent then."

"I don't know what you're talking about." He coughed and continued. "It's a hundred percent yours. But if you have a problem, we'd be happy to send counselors out for a visit. Gonna be there this evening?"

"I'll be here."

"Thank you for your support." The line went dead.

Jack and Sol stared at me. "What'd he say?" Sol asked.

"Nothing, but they'll be here," I glanced at my watch, "in about forty-five minutes."

Sol ran his hand through his hair. "He played it cool, huh?"

"Yeah, I figured he would. The guy's no dummy, but our friends Artie and Flavio will show up ready for battle. You can bet on it."

Chapter Fifty-one

I could hear them stomping down the hallway. Heavy footsteps. Heavy guys.

We were all set. The recorder was on and Jack Fox hid in the storage closet as planned. I sat behind Sullivan's desk perched there like a piece of cheddar waiting for the rats.

Joyce had picked up Sol and they were heading on to Grimes's home. As soon as the cops took Artie and Flavio into custody, I'd call there and let Sol know it was over. Then we'd wait for Grimes to move on Willie and the gang.

The door burst open. Two big ugly bastards came barging in. "Where's Sullivan?" the fat one demanded.

"Out of town. I'm in charge, now."

"Hear you don't like our deal."

"That's right," I said. "We take all the risk and now we want a cut. A big cut."

The strong-arm guys standing before me were just as intimidating as Sullivan had said. The one with the mouth, doing all the talking, had a shiny bald head with bumps. His face was pale, round, and had pockmarks like small craters. His head looked like a tiny moon, a moon with a big fat nose. The other guy was tall like the first one, but his belly didn't hang sloppily over his belt. His muscles were defined and sculptured, as if he pumped iron. His eyes, like serpent's eyes, were beady and cold, shifting rapidly back and forth. Both guys wore black Levi's, black T-shirts, and they had on long dark leather jackets. Their outfits looked like a costume. On stage tonight, The

Goon Brothers. They're going to do a little number—on you.

"Wants a cut, he says. He's a funny guy, Flavio." Moon face gave me a hard look and said, "Do you think we're funny guys, too?"

"Oh, I think you're funny all right," I said. "Very funny. About as funny as an electric chair with a whoopee cushion."

"Whaddya think of this guy, Flavio? Something else, huh?"

"Maybe we'd better 'splain it to him," Flavio, the iron-pumper, said with a slight barrio accent.

"Yeah." I rose out of the chair. "'Splain it to me."

Artie, the moon face guy, lurched forward. "We don't like wise guys." He pounded his fist on the desk. "Are you a wise guy?" He turned to Flavio. "I think he's a wise guy."

Flavio took one slow step sideways, and with a smooth motion of his right hand, slid back the edge of his jacket revealing a sawed-off shotgun dangling in a custom holster around his waist.

"Is that supposed to scare me?"

Flavio didn't say anything. His BB eyes shifted to Artie, the moon-face guy.

"Maybe this will, wise guy," Artie said.

I turned back to Artie. He had his arm stretched out tight and his hand held a .44 Magnum Smith and Wesson revolver pointed straight at my face.

The chrome barrel looked ten feet long and the Magnum had a bore like a howitzer. I could see the deadly hollow-points in the cylinder. I thought the thing would make a hell of a bang when it went off.

Artie sneered at me sideways, staring at me with his bugged out eyes, his finger tight on the trigger.

"Hey, man, stay cool." I brought up my arms. My shoulder began to throb and my toes began to curl. It was getting a little hairy in here.

Artie flicked his head toward the back of the building. "Flavio, go check the warehouse. There's only one car parked in the lot, but make sure nobody else is here."

"What about Dutch?" Flavio asked.

"Should be here by now," Artie said. "Open one of the loading doors. Have Dutch back up the truck and start loading the beer. I'll keep funny man covered."

I didn't like the way this was playing out. Didn't the Goon Brothers know the script? "Who's Dutch?" I said. "What's going on?"

"Shut up," Artie said. He spoke to Flavio out of the corner of his mouth, but his eyes stayed focused on me. "Soon as Dutch starts loading the truck, c'mon back here. Help me take care of this guy."

"Gimme the warehouse keys."

Unintentionally, I shifted my gaze to the keys sitting on top of the desk. Flavio's eyes followed mine and he grabbed the keys, took his scatter gun out of the holster, and held it at his side. He peered around the office door into the hallway and then left the room.

Jack must have slipped back into the closet. He had to figure with Artie's gun pointed at my head, now would not be the time to make a move on Flavio.

"Hey," I said. "Are you guys here to steal the beer? Is that what this is all about?"

"Yeah, and you're going to be a hero, funny man. You're going to try to stop us." Artie laughed.

"Very dumb. Everybody will say you shouldn't have been so stupid." Artie laughed again, a regular comedian, but I didn't like the punch line. "Everyone will say, 'Too bad you got killed trying to save a few cases of beer.'"

I had plenty on tape to have these guys arrested right now, but I didn't have anything that tied them to Willie or the gang.

"Thought you guys came out here to talk about the trainee program," I said. "Tell you what. Forget the seventy-five percent, we'll only take half."

"Hey funny man, you're a laugh riot," Artie said.

"Listen," I said. "You're killing the golden goose. The amount of beer in the warehouse wouldn't cover a month of the phony payroll reimbursements we kick back. Why put us out of business?"

"Sullivan's not outta business. You're outta business. The payroll deal stays the way it is, and when Sullivan sees your dead body he'll get the message."

"Does Willie know about this?" I asked.

"Hell yes," Artie said. "It's his idea. He sent us."

Bingo! I got what I needed. "Help!" I shouted.

Artie's mind clicked. You could almost hear the gears drop into place. "Aw, shit." He turned. Jack stood in the doorway, feet spread, his gun leveled.

Artie moved his shooting hand about a micrometer. Jack fired. The sound was deafening. A blue haze swirled in the air and Artie dropped with a thud.

I grabbed the small caliber automatic out of the drawer, darted around Artie's body and met up with

Jack in the hallway. He stood pressed flat against the wall by the door leading to the warehouse. He gestured for me to get against the wall across from him. I did. Jack crouched down, grabbed the doorknob and twisted the door open a couple of inches.

"Artie, 'zat you?" Flavio shouted.

"Yeah, don't shoot," Jack yelled and closed the door. He urgently waved me back. Jack rolled quickly and moved up the hallway toward the lobby.

I heard the blast. The door shattered. Another blast followed. A hole exploded in the wall where only a second ago I'd been standing. Moving further back, there was another discharge. A blast of buckshot tore through the wall. The walls were only studs and plasterboard. They might as well have been made of tissue paper. I crept farther down the hall until I was protected by the storage closet. I looked up. Jack stood in the lobby by the main office door.

He brought his hand up and pointed at himself, then to the lobby door, and made a circling motion with his finger. Next, he pointed at me, at the ground, and then repeatedly at the opening where the warehouse door used to be. I would guard the hall. Jack would go outside, circle around, and come up on Flavio and Dutch from the rear. He raced out before I could signal him to wait until I called the cops. We both knew that seconds counted. Flavio could charge through the opening, blasting away with his deadly short barrel ten-gauge.

I looked down at the gun in my hand, a .25 caliber Beretta sub-compact. I'd have to get up real close to do any damage with this peashooter. With the barrel cut down and his shotgun loaded with high-powered shells, Flavio could chop down the Chrysler Building. Didn't seem fair.

Standing there a minute, I listened. Not a sound. Jack should be behind them now. I crept back to the opening in the wall and peered into the warehouse. Looking to my left, I saw cases of beer stacked on pallets which rested on racks running the length of the building. The rows had gaps between them large enough for a forklift to get through. A twenty-five-foot wide empty space in the middle had to be the loading area. The area separated the rows of beer on my left from the loading doors on my right.

A forklift was parked in the middle about a third of the way down the building. I didn't see Flavio or Dutch, or even Jack Fox in the warehouse, but that didn't mean they weren't there. Flavio could be plastered on the other side of the wall waiting for me to poke my head through the opening. Funny, but I noticed that the cement floor glistened in the florescent lights hanging from the rafters. They must've put some kind of coating on it, I thought. It'd be easy to mop up the blood. Suddenly the air quivered with the loud crack of a pistol shot. Two rapid shotgun blasts followed.

Without thinking, I charged through the opening into the warehouse holding the peashooter in front of my face. No shots rang out. I was still alive. Score one for me.

Looking behind me, on both sides, and all around I saw no one. I ran to the forklift and ducked behind it for cover. Sweat ran down my face.

God, was Jack hit? The pistol shot came before the shotgun blast, which meant Flavio had to still be alive.

But what about Dutch? Was he here? Was he armed? Most likely.

Seconds passed. I took a quick look over the edge of the forklift. "Show yourselves, you sons of bitches," I said under my breath. Where was everybody? I glanced down the row of loading doors. The last one—at the far end of the building—was open to the darkness outside. But from my angle I couldn't see into the parking lot.

Maybe everyone was outside, or maybe Flavio and Dutch were hiding behind one of the beer pallets waiting for me to pop up like a duck in a shooting gallery.

I had to get to the parking lot to see if Jack was down. It was closer to go directly through the open warehouse door than to go all the way around the side of the building. My nerves were on edge. Exposed or not, I had to make my move.

Darting around the forklift into the open space, I stopped dead in my tracks. A shadowy figure appeared in the darkness attempting to enter the building through the open loading door.

Then I heard a ratchet sound. It came from the other side of the warehouse across from the open door. Flavio stood there fixed, his shotgun shouldered, leveled at the shadow.

I fired a round at him, shot fast without aiming, and missed.

He spun around and took aim at me. I dropped to the floor and heard the roar of his gun. Instantly the warehouse reverberated. The forklift behind me exploded.

Covering my head, falling debris peppered my

body. I heard two fast pistol shots mingled with the clatter of falling metal.

I slowly got to my hands and knees. Flavio lay dead on the floor. Jack was walking toward me with a bit of a swagger.

"That was a hell of a shot you took," he called out.

"I missed," I said.

"Yeah, but the timing was perfect."

I stood coddling my throbbing shoulder. "Dutch?"

"The parking lot. Dead."

Jack and I looked at the forklift. It was still smoldering and red hydraulic fluid pooled on the shiny floor. The machine was destroyed.

"He hit the butane tank. Blew it up. You got to buy Sullivan a new one." Jack grinned.

"It could've been worse. He could've hit the beer."

We walked back to Sullivan's office. I stepped around Artie's body and called the police. Immediately cars were rolling, code three. They'd be at the warehouse within minutes.

"It's going to be a long night," Jack Fox said.

"Yeah, but not as long as the five-minute shootout."

I phoned Sol at Grime's home and told him what'd happened. "It's all on tape," I added.

After he spoke with Grimes, Sol came back on the line and said they were leaving and would be there in less than twenty minutes.

I hung up the phone. Jack sat behind Sullivan's desk and I sat in one of the plastic chairs facing him.

We were silent now with nothing to do but wait.

"Three dead," Jack said softly.

"Yeah," I said.

"Could've been us."

"Yeah," I said again, looking at Artie, lying on his back, eyes open, staring at nothing.

Chapter Fifty-two

We huddled at a large table in a conference room at sheriff's department headquarters in Monterey Park. Earlier, homicide detectives had interrogated Jack and me about the shooting, and the tape recording verified our claim of self-defense.

After listening to the tape for about the hundredth time, Grimes, with strong urging from Sol, finally agreed to raid the halfway house. The raid would go down as soon as the intra- and inter-departmental logistics were firmly in place. This meant that the raid would happen as soon as the cops could get their act together, sometime around noon the following day.

Sol had asked Grimes if he'd be in touch with Sheriff Peter Pitches regarding the gang and the impending arrests.

"No, I can handle it without him. I'll be working with my headquarters staff, the Major Crimes Unit of the DA's office, and Chief Nevins, commander of Field Operations Region III. I'll be in charge and Nevins will coordinate all activities. "Anyway," Grimes said, "the boss is still in Hawaii on a fact-finding mission and asked not to be disturbed."

After a bit more discussion about the complicated logistics of the raid, Grimes seemed to be having second thoughts. "Maybe I should wait for the sheriff to return."

"We can't wait. There are lives at stake. What's the matter with you, afraid you'll blow it?" Sol asked Grimes.

"No, but this could be a political hot potato, Sol. Assemblywoman Mattie Niles is a powerful member of the appropriations committee and she appointed this Willie character as the program director."

"So?"

"Her committee approves contracts worth millions for custodial services we provide the state. She won't like this a bit. It'll piss her off, make her look bad. I don't want to be around when she explodes."

"Tough shit," Sol said. "This is about major criminal activity happening right now, right before our very eyes."

"I'm not saying I won't take down the halfway house, but I'll have to play it cool. We'll have to put a spin on it, get the Media Liaison Office involved, assign a Public Information Officer."

"I don't give a damn what you do, just get it done."

***

The next morning, the phone woke me from a sound sleep. It must be Rita, I thought, as I rolled over and groped for the receiver.

"Good morning, boss. Did I wake you?"

I sat on the edge of the bed. "What time is it, Rita?"

"Eight-thirty. Thought you'd be up by now."

"I got home late, but I'm awake."

"I called Sol's office looking for you. His staff said you moved back to your apartment."

"Yeah, and it feels good to be home. No need for security now that Willie and his gang are going to be out of business today. I guess you heard about yesterday?"

"Jack Fox said you saved his life. Wasn't it supposed be the other way around?"

"That's not exactly the way it happened. But I'll meet you at Dolan's in a half hour and tell you about it while I have breakfast," I said. "Another thing, Rita, before I forget, remind me to call Sullivan. He'll be able to come back tomorrow."

"Jack already called him. Told him what happened and told him you blew up his forklift. "Did you blow up that poor guy's forklift, Jimmy?"

"Afraid so."

"Those things cost a lot of money, I hear. More than a car. But Sullivan said don't worry about it. He's got tons of insurance. In fact, he said he has too much insurance, life insurance, health insurance, all kinds of insurance. Said he had to pay workers' comp premiums for all of the ghost workers, even though they didn't really work there. It's the law and the State didn't reimburse him for that."

"What else did he say?"

"Said thanks for everything you guys did for him. Said he wants to give all of you a lifetime supply of free beer."

Too bad the guy didn't make donuts.

***

I arrived at Dolan's before Rita, and ordered two glazed and a small coffee as I had almost every day for the past seven years. And today, as always, the same Asian guy who owned the place for the last five years just handed me my donuts and coffee without saying a word, no good mornings, or nice to see you again, nothing.

"Don't you recognize me?" I asked, feeling that I deserved to be recognized today for being alive.

"You movie star? I don't go to movies." He moved to the cash register, put the money away, and headed down the counter to begin another batch.

"Hey, what about my change?" I said, raising my voice.

"You always give me change, tip."

"Oh, so you do remember me."

"You Wienie Widow Stud. You always leave change."

It's nice to be remembered.

About the time I started on my second donut, Rita walked in and sat at the table across from me. She smiled, looking pretty, as always.

"Would you like coffee, a donut, Rita?"

"No thanks, but it's good to see that you're eating. Do you feel a little better?"

"Yeah, I guess," I said, rubbing my injured shoulder.

"Don't you want to hear about my meeting with Laura?"

"God, yes."

Rita's smile faded and she became serious. "She was scared, Jimmy, and worried about being seen talking to me. Laura didn't say she was scared, but I could tell. She only talked to me for a minute. But she said Richie was still alive. She's not going to change her mind. Laura's still going to plead guilty on Monday."

I told Rita that if the halfway house raid goes as planned, Willie might cut a deal with the cops and tell them where the gang has stashed Richie. "As soon as we find him, Laura will change her plea. I guarantee it."

Rita left, heading to court, where she had a conference scheduled with the deputy DA concerning her DUI client, Geoff. Sitting there alone, I thought of the dead bodies at the warehouse, and wondered how many more had to die before this was over.

Chapter Fifty-three

Back at my office, I felt depressed. I sat at my desk staring at my law school diploma. It hung on the wall and decreed, with its lofty scrolls and its fancy type: JAMES O'BRIEN, ATTORNEY AT LAW. What a laugh. For all the good I was as a criminal defense lawyer, I might as well be selling shoes at Sears. I had just gotten off the phone with Sol. Supposedly, the details of the raid had gotten to Willie somehow, and the whole thing had turned into a political fiasco involving Assemblywoman Mattie Niles. Willie had been taken for an interview with the District Attorney, where he claimed he was just a victim of a scam. He ratted out Flavio and Artie as the masterminds.

After Willie's meeting with the district attorney, Sol placed a call to a reporter friend of his at the *LA Times*. The newspaperman had a mole in the DA's office who would occasionally leak information to him. The reporter related to Sol the gist of Willie's interview with the DA.

When asked about the Rosenthal murder, Willie admitted that he had been at Moyer's house on the night of the murder. Willie said he had questions about Moyer's payroll reports and stopped by the house, at Moyer's request, to go over the details. Moyer, involved in a poker game at the time, asked Willie to stick around until the game was over so they could hash things out.

When the game ended at 12:30, Willie and Moyer left the house and went to Ship's Coffee Shop on Wilshire Boulevard to discuss the payroll problem. They stayed at the coffee shop until way past the time of the murder.

The police verified Willie's story. They talked to the restaurant workers, the manager, and other witnesses who saw them together that night.

"Sol, are you sure? Maybe the cops missed something. Midnight's an odd time to do business. Willie could've snuck out of the coffee shop."

Sol sadly shook his head from side to side. "Afraid not, Jimmy. I thought the same thing. I had a couple of my guys follow up on the alibi. It's tighter than an iron fist. All of the waitresses remembered seeing him and Moyer together the whole time. Willie made a big ruckus in the coffee shop."

"What kind of ruckus?"

"Willie got into a loud argument with Moyer. He threw his ham sandwich at him. The night manager came over and told Willie if he didn't knock it off he'd have to leave. They stayed another hour or so, way past the time of Arnie's death. The night guy had his eye on him the whole time. Just in case."

"Sounds to me like he was trying to establish an alibi," I said. "I know he's guilty. He could have had one of his goons do the job."

"Yeah, but Arnie wouldn't have let someone he didn't know, a goon, into the house at that time of night. Didn't you figure that Arnie knew the killer and invited him in?"

"That was my theory. Now I don't know what to think."

I turned back and went to my desk. "Dammit." I pounded the desk. "How did I screw it up so badly?" I said out loud. "Dammit, what did I miss? There had to be something that I missed."

My hand hurt now and I rubbed it. I thought about my shoulder and the appointment I needed to make at Gallatin Medical. The hell with it. I didn't care anymore.

Mabel heard the commotion and came into my office. She stood in the doorway with her hands on her hips. "Self-pity doesn't help, Jimmy."

"What do you know about it, Mabel? You've never been in a spot like this."

***

That night in my apartment, I sat in my chair in the empty room and looked around. There weren't any pictures on the walls. None, not even one. No photographs of me smiling with my arm around someone who loved me. Thirty-seven years old and alone. I found someone, Deborah, someone who I was sure I could make a life with, but I screwed that up as well. My life was as empty as the room. If I had a dog, I probably would've kicked him. I kicked my guitar instead.

Richie was going to die, and Laura was going to go to prison for life. It was my fault, and I didn't know what to do. I thought about quitting the law. What good was a system of laws that allowed guilty people to go free, and put innocent people behind bars? But then I realized the thing wrong with the system wasn't the law. The law was good. It created order out of chaos. No, the trouble with our system was that it let guys like me become lawyers, advocates for the defenseless. What a laugh. There ought to have been a law about that.

I got up and went to my car. I drove around for a while and soon found myself pulling into the Regency. I walked up to the bar and sat. "Vodka rocks," I said to Dwayne when he slapped a napkin on the bar.

He didn't say anything. He just brought me a drink. A Coke.

The Coke sat in front of me, but I didn't touch it. Dwayne waited. I stared at him. He stared at me.

I glanced around the bar, all the regulars were there. I looked back at the Coke sitting on the bar. The ice cubes were melting. I glanced up at Dwayne. He was still staring at me.

"Thanks, Dwayne," I finally said and took a sip of the Coke. "I didn't know what I was thinking."

"You're thinking the same thing we all think once in a while."

"Yeah, what's that?" I said.

"We're not worth a shit, and nobody cares."

"You got it," I said.

"Well, somebody cares," Dwayne said.

"Yeah, who?" I said.

"About you?" Dwayne was quiet and somber for a moment. Finally, he smiled. "The Tooth Fairy, and Santa Claus, I guess. That's about it, I'm afraid. Maybe Shirley does, you know, the looker that comes in here, but I doubt it."

I started to laugh, just a little, but I laughed. I might hang a picture of the Tooth Fairy on the wall.

Chapter Fifty-four

The next morning, I skipped Dolan's and went directly to the office. I wanted to comb through Laura's file. Maybe I'd spot something I missed when I figured Willie had to be the murderer.

Mabel wasn't at her workstation when I came in, and now I saw a note she had left with yesterday's mail. She was taking the day off to attend to a personal matter. I didn't know what it was about and the note didn't say. Grabbing the mail from her desk, I noticed a small photo in a gold frame sitting there that I hadn't seen before. I picked it up and looked at the picture. It was an old photo of a little boy of about four with freckles and tousled hair. I held it for a moment and wondered why I had never taken the time to find out about Mabel's personal life.

I put on a pot of coffee and walked to my desk. Pushing the mail stack aside, I opened Laura's file, and scanned the crime scene photographs and the police report. I quickly reviewed my notes. Nothing popped out at me.

The smell of fresh-brewed coffee drifted into my office. I went to the coffee bar and poured myself a cup. It was okay, not as good as Mabel's or Rita's, but it was better than Dolan's. At least I could make a halfway decent cup of coffee.

Frustration consumed me, and it was hard to concentrate so I decided to tackle the mail first. It was mostly ads and a few bills. I felt I could sift through it fast, then get back to the police report. One envelope was addressed to Rita. It was from the business that provided payroll services. She must have sent away for the information, even though we only had three paychecks. I looked at the envelope again, put it aside, and tossed the rest of the ads into the wastebasket. I set the bills in an out-of-the-way spot. I'd give them to Mabel tomorrow. I couldn't stomach reviewing them now.

With the mail out of the way, I started on Laura's file again. All of a sudden, I remembered something. The paycheck company—wasn't that the outfit that processed Farmer Fred's payroll? Rita got the information about them from Farmer Fred's payroll report. I picked up the envelope and tore it open. APR Paycheck Services. They were in Century City, 1900 Avenue of the Stars, suite 1420. I recalled making a crack about accountants' offices being on the Avenue of the Stars.

Fingering through my notes, I found the address, 1900 Avenue of the Stars, David Lawrence's address, Rosenthal's insurance agent. He was the guy who wrote the workers' compensation insurance for the meat company, and he was at the poker game that night. Sure enough, 1420 was Lawrence's suite number. How could Paycheck Services be at the same address? Unless it was a side business owned by him.

He also wrote the insurance for all of those ghost workers. What happened to the money that Lawrence collected in premiums? If he owned the payroll company, what happened to all the tax deductions he took from the paychecks? He wouldn't forward the taxes to the IRS or send deductions from checks for workers that didn't exist, especially workers with phony social security numbers.

Was Lawrence tied into Willie, and could this

be the method they used to steal money from both the State and Farmer Fred's Meat Company?

I got up and paced around the office. My insides were on fire, burning with excitement. I had to calm down. I couldn't make any mistakes now, not after the fiasco at the halfway house.

Back at my desk, I called Carriage Trade Distributors.

"This is O'Brien. Is Mike there?"

Mike Sullivan was instantly on the line. He thanked me and went on about the new life he was going to have now that he didn't have to worry about Artie and Flavio.

I had to cut the chitchat short. I needed answers. "Thanks, Mike, but the reason I called was to ask who your insurance agent is." I held the phone so tight my hand turned white.

"Funny you should ask. The gangsters made me get a new agent. His name is Lawrence, David Lawrence. He's in Century City. Want his address?"

"No, that's okay. By the way, do you use a payroll service to process your paychecks?"

"Yeah, Vicki says we don't need it. Just an extra expense. They charge a dollar a check and with the ghost workers, it runs over a hundred a week. I don't get reimbursed for that."

"APR Paycheck Services?" I said.

"Yeah, how'd you know?"

"Owned by Lawrence? Your insurance guy?"

"Yes, I had no choice."

I must have appeared rude as I just hung up the phone. My heart was racing. I was searching for a motive, and I may have found it. Legally, to imply third person culpability, I needed a plausible motive. I needed a reason to point at Lawrence and then shout to the jury, *reasonable doubt*. It wasn't a smoking gun, but I was on to something. I could feel it.

Grabbing a pencil and paper, I began to calculate. If Farmer Fred's had a thousand ghost workers and Sullivan had a hundred more, there were probably other companies as well, but I'd just figure eleven hundred. With the taxes that wouldn't be paid, the social security, other withholdings, and the workers' comp, the amount pulled out by the payroll company was staggering. I threw the pencil down on the desk and leaned back. I figured it was about forty thousand dollars per week for Lawrence.

Would Lawrence murder Rosenthal to keep forty thousand tax free dollars rolling in week after week? I didn't know, but I suspected a lot of people would.

No wonder he could afford the big yacht he bragged about when I went to his office. He said he met Arnie at the yacht club. They were both members of the same club, but Lawrence had a bigger boat. The yacht club! I was on a roll. Lawrence had a slip right at the yacht club, kept his boat there.

I recalled the name of the boat. Lawrence told me he had christened it the *Double Indemnity*, and I made a remark about the movie. But what was the name of the yacht club? I frantically searched my notes. Bingo! I had written it down, The Gold Coast Yacht Club. . . Lido Isle.

I called information for the Newport Beach and got the phone number and the address, 2901 Bayside Drive, Corona del Mar.

I wrote the address on the back of the paycheck company envelope, and quickly called Sol. I left a message that I was onto something and would call him later.

Draining my coffee cup, I headed out the door. I jumped into my Corvette and swung out onto Lakewood Boulevard. Within minutes, I was driving south on the 605 Freeway. I made the sweeping transition where the 605 curves into the 405 and headed toward Orange County.

This morning the traffic was light, and I zoomed along unrestricted. I slowed to eighty when I saw a Chippie on the side of the road writing some guy a ticket, but a mile farther along I punched it again.

It was a long shot, but if Lawrence was the murderer, he was probably the person who had Richie kidnapped. Maybe he stashed him on his yacht.

I didn't know exactly what I was going to do when I got to the yacht club, but I figured I could snoop around, and maybe get on board the boat. If Richie wasn't there, well, that would eliminate one hiding place.

Chapter Fifty-five

I turned left on Bayside Drive at the end of Jamboree Road and curved along on the rim of Balboa Bay. Magnificent homes edged the waterfront on the right side. On the left, Bayside ran parallel to a bluff. The incline was covered with an abundant crop of ice plant that glistened in the sun.

Continuing south, I shot past the Balboa Bay Yacht Club, and traveled about a mile or so beyond the Harbormaster's station, and turned into the parking lot belonging to the Gold Coast Yacht Club. A sign warned me that parking was reserved for members only and other assholes that parked here would have their cars towed. I pulled into a spot reserved for Vice-Commodore Dr. Jefferies. If I were caught here I'd probably be keelhauled, but I didn't care. I was eager to locate Lawrence's yacht. All the parking spaces seemed to be reserved for yacht club commodores of one type or another. I wondered if everyone was a commodore, who swabbed the decks.

Protruding into the parking lot was a blue arched awning held up by brass poles that led to the main entrance of the opulent clubhouse. Facing south toward the side was a small dry dock overloaded with tiny single-masted sailboats. The little boats were reserved, no doubt, for the peewee commodores. A ramp sloped down on the left side of the dry dock leading to the water where a network of boat slips was located.

Walking along the fence, I hurried toward a gate at the end of the dock. I knew I didn't look as if I belonged here, forgot my yachting togs this morning.

My outfit consisted of a pair of Levis, a checkered sports shirt, and an old leather jacket that I loved.

Two weather-beaten guys with red faces cracked from the wind and sun—too many hours at the helm, or perhaps, too many hours at the outdoor bar—were walking through the parking lot toward the clubhouse. I hoped one of them wasn't the doctor whose parking spot I stole. They turned my way, but continued along without saying anything.

I arrived at the gate with a sign that read, *Members Only*. It was closed, but not locked. I looked around and not seeing anyone, I pulled the gate toward me and slipped into the dock area. I moved swiftly down the ramp to where the big yachts were moored.

Hooding my eyes with my hand, I stared out at all the boats. There had to be forty or fifty of them. Most of the slips had boats in them, but a dozen or so were vacant.

I walked up and down the gangplanks between the vessels looking for Lawrence's yacht. Fancy boats with fancy names like, *Hot Ruddered Bum*, *Busted Flush*, and *Knot a Pheasant Plucker*, were jammed together, but there was no sign of the *Double Indemnity*.

Tied to the side of a nice looking racing sloop, named the *Six to Five Against*, was a thirteen-foot Boston Whaler with the words *Scuba Dooba Yacht Hull Service* painted on the side. Scuba gear and tools used for bottom scraping were lying in a heap inside the Whaler. In the water behind the sailboat, I saw bubbles boiling to the surface. Two or three minutes later a diver emerged from under the hull. He lifted his mask and hopped aboard the Scuba Dooba skiff.

"Hey, buddy," I shouted to him.

He pointed at his bare chest. "Me?"

"Yeah, I was wondering if you could help me." I walked closer to the Boston Whaler.

The scuba diver glanced at his watch. "Kind of busy."

"I'm looking for a yacht by the name of *Double Indemnity*. You wouldn't happen to know where it's moored, would you?"

"Yeah, I know the boat. Belongs to one of my customers; scrape her bottom every week when the boat's here. She's usually over there, by the Cal 40." He pointed to the west. "But, she's gone now."

"Where'd it go?"

"I dunno, but the owner has a can at Avalon, maybe he went there."

"A can?"

"Yeah, you know—a mooring in the bay at Avalon." He gave me a blank look and nodded his head. "Catalina." He nodded again. "The big island out there." The guy said sarcastically pointing out to sea. "Been gone about a week, left in the night. I was supposed to clean her the next morning, but she was gone." He started to toss his junk into the Boston Whaler.

Left in the night, I thought, around the same time Richie had disappeared. Hiding him on Catalina would be even better for Lawrence and the gang. "Oh, yeah," I said. "Sure, thanks." I turned and sprinted back to my Corvette.

A tow truck was backing into the parking lot as I shot back through the gate and dashed for my car. I jumped in, jammed the key in the ignition, and the 350 engine roared to life. I shoved the gear lever in reverse and burned rubber as the car shot backward. Hitting the brakes, I spun around, and swerved to miss the tow truck. Racing past him, I veered north on Bayside, and saw the name painted on the side of the truck, *Jax Big Toe*. God, they must paint funny names on anything that moves in Newport Beach.

On my way to the yacht club, I had passed by the Orange County Airport, and I was heading there now. It was off MacArthur Boulevard, about ten minutes away. I didn't remember if the seaplane to Catalina departed from Orange County or Long Beach Airport, but I had to get there quick.

A blue and white banner—Scenic Flights: Catalina Island to Big Bear—flapped in the breeze on the top of a corrugated metal building at the south end of the field. I parked and went into the structure.

A couple of guys were slouched in a pair of chrome and Naugahyde chairs. They were bragging about their daredevilry while alone at the controls of a Cessna 152. One guy was doing maneuvers with his hands: up, and then it nosed over straight down, twisted sideways, and finally his right hand blasted his left hand completely out of the sky. The Red Baron would've been impressed.

As I walked up to a metal counter that separated the small reception area from the remainder of the building, I spotted a young woman standing there.

I stopped in my tracks. It was Susie, my old girlfriend, and briefly, my flying instructor. Sweat poured from my armpits. I didn't have time for this now.

"Jimmy! I can't believe my eyes. Where have

you been? No calls, no cards, like you fell off the end of the earth."

I started sweating even harder. God, why now? I thought dumbfounded.

"What happened with us? Your flying lessons?"

"Uhh . . . uh . . . I've never been any good at relationships, Susie. Call me a loser, a bum." My chin sunk into my chest with shame. Susie's questions stung like barbs. God, another relationship destroyed. I really am a loser.

"I'm in a horrible bind, Susie. I need to get a seaplane to Catalina right now."

Susie responded, "We fly to Catalina. Charter flights, but our planes are land planes not seaplanes. We land at the Airport In The Sky. It's on a plateau about ten miles from Avalon."

"How long does it take to get to the island?"

"In the 172, about twenty minutes. But then you'd have to take the VW bus down to Avalon from the airport, if that's where you want to go, and that takes another half hour or so."

"Half hour? For ten miles?"

"It's a winding road, but the scenery is worth it."

"When can I leave?"

"I can fly you there right now."

I handed over my credit card and signed a form. In about ten minutes, we were in the small Cessna sitting at the edge of the runway waiting for departure clearance.

It was cramped in the cockpit. I sat next to Susie in the right front seat of the dual controlled airplane. Our legs touched, and I could smell a hint of her delicate perfume. It was kind of flowery and fresh, maybe jasmine or something. Why now? I agonized about our meeting, feeling deflated. Words eluded me. I sat still and stared out the Cessna's windshield at the white line running down the center of the long runway.

Chapter Fifty-six

Susie pulled back the sleeves of her jacket. A ring sparkled on her fourth left finger as she pushed the airplane's throttle. The plane started to move, slowly at first, but quickly gaining speed. At about a third of the length of the runway, when our speed hit sixty knots, Susie eased back on the wheel. The aircraft's nose angled up, the ground fell away, and we were airborne. The small plane rapidly picked up speed, climbed higher, and raced over the remaining runway below us. At the end of the runway, when we were seven or eight hundred feet in the air, the right wing dipped, and the plane turned slightly to the west. The wing leveled out and we continued to soar upward.

"I guess that sparkler on your finger tells your story, Susie," I said with a faltering voice. "When I saw you standing there a minute ago I couldn't imagine how I could have let anything so precious and beautiful slip away."

She looked at me coyly but didn't respond.

"What a jerk I've been," I added contritely. "Who's the lucky guy?"

"He's amazing, Jimmy. A pilot from Continental. We're getting married in Australia next month. I can thank you, Jimmy, for helping me grab him up, not waiting, not overthinking our relationship," Susie blurted out, sounding kind of angry.

"I guess I'm good for something, Susie, even if it is a bad example," I retorted.

In a few minutes the plane's nose dipped level with the horizon, and the velocity increased again. The airspeed indicator needle swung through its arch, and when it reached one hundred twenty-five knots, Susie eased back on the throttle and the speed stabilized.

Farther out I caught sight of the island's rugged silhouette, a shadow looming on the horizon. With one sweep of my eyes, I took in the entire length of Santa Catalina. On the far left, carved into the hillsides, I could see the tiny city of Avalon. The Isthmus, barely visible at this distance, was in the center where the hills sloped down and touched the water, and on the extreme right, just off the edge of the island, I saw Eagle Rock rising magnificently out of the ocean.

"Want to take the controls for a few minutes like old times? It's okay. I don't hold a grudge."

"Sure, I'd love that, Susie. Thanks."

I grabbed the wheel with both hands, and put my feet on the rudder pedals. The Cessna dipped to the left, and started to lose altitude. I moved the wheel to the right and pulled back slightly. The plane seemed to level out, but we were off course and about three hundred feet lower than from where we started.

"Light on the controls, Jimmy. You're doing fine. It's like riding a bike."

I nudged the plane back to the proper heading with the rudder pedal, and continued to hold a little backpressure on the wheel until the airplane was again at twenty-five hundred feet. I eased the wheel forward just a touch and now we were on course and flying straight and level.

"Hey," Susie said, "You're a natural."

Susie reached in to her jacket pocket and pulled out a card. I took it with my left hand, keeping my right hand on the wheel.

"Call me if you want to take more flying

lessons."

My eye focused on the card in my hand. It had a picture of an airplane zooming through the sky. Her phone number, her name and title—Susan Quincy, Certified Flight Instructor—were printed on the bottom. I stuck the card in my jacket pocket. Susie Q, I may just take you up on that offer.

I handed the controls back to Susie when we were about three miles from Catalina. On the radio's UNICOM frequency, Susie called the private controller at the field, informed him that we were inbound from the mainland and would be landing in a few minutes. He said that a helicopter had just landed, and there was no other traffic in the area. She informed him that we would be landing on runway twenty-two from a straight-in approach.

The Airport In The Sky was on top of a plateau scraped out of the surrounding hills. The field hung on the edge of a rocky cliff that rose straight up from the ocean's surface below. We were descending fast and aiming directly down the centerline of the runway about a mile in front of us.

I was a little anxious. From this angle it looked like we were too low and would fly smack into the face of the sea cliff. It looked to me like we'd hit fifty feet or so below the runway's surface.

Susie anticipated my apprehension. "Optical illusion, look at the altimeter. We're at nineteen hundred feet, and the runway is sixteen hundred above sea level. Our approach is perfect."

I looked out of my side of the Cessna at the Coke bottle-green water lapping at the base of the rocky cliff far below us. Turning, I watched Susie prepare for landing.

She lowered the flaps another ten degrees, throttled back, and we gracefully descended closer to the runway. A few feet above the ground, Susie pulled back slightly on the control wheel. The nose lifted, and the two tires of the tricycle landing gear screeched lightly as we touched down. We rolled along the runway, slowing. At a taxiway halfway down the runway, Susie turned the plane and headed toward the parking ramp. She nudged the throttle and swung the plane around with the rudder pedals. We stopped in the visitor's area next to a black helicopter rigged with pontoons.

"You can get your bus ticket in the administration building. Come on, I'll go with you." Susie unbuckled her seat belt and climbed out of the Cessna.

We walked along a gravel path lined with white painted rocks toward a sprawling Mediterranean inspired building attached to a square four-story tower capped with a red tile peaked roof. The building was more of a museum than an airport lobby. Artifacts from the Pimuvits Tribe, the original inhabitants, were on display as well as photographs and memorabilia from the early days when William Wrigley, the chewing gum mogul, owned the island.

Susie paid the airport's landing fee, and I bought a ticket for the bus ride to Avalon. The bus was leaving in five minutes, but the clerk said it didn't matter because I was the only passenger. This time of year was not the island's busy season.

I reached out to take Susie's hand. "Thanks, Susie, it was a great flight."

Her hand felt warm and seemed to linger in mine a moment longer than normal. "Call me. I mean, about the flying lessons," she said.

She gave me a soft smile. "Goodbye, blue eyes."

I boarded the black and red bus, climbed into the front seat next to the driver, and the VW rattled forward, down from the plateau on a road that wasn't much more than a trail. Twice, we had to stop to shoo away a buffalo languorously strolling along our path. The driver told me that a movie company brought the animals to the island in the twenties to shoot a cowboy picture. They left them and, unlike the Indians, the buffalo flourished. Now a whole herd roamed the island.

As beautiful as the scenery was, I needed to regain my focus now. I didn't have a plan worked out. Even if I found the yacht moored in the bay, I didn't know what I'd do, or how I could determine if Richie was aboard. Perhaps I could go to the police in Avalon, tell them what I suspected, and have them search the boat. I knew before they could do that, legally, they would need a search warrant, and it wouldn't be easy to get one based on my suspicions. Hell, I didn't even know how many police were in Avalon.

I asked the bus driver about the police department.

"Don't need any traffic cops, no traffic in Avalon. There is a ten-year waiting list to get a car. Only a few people have them."

"What about other crimes?"

"During the off season, there aren't any. It's only when the tourists come that we have any problems.

We're part of the L.A. County Sheriff's Department and have guys stationed here," he said. "They cruise around in black and white golf carts."

"Golf carts?"

"Yeah," he chuckled. "They're the only cop cars in the world that you can outrun on foot."

Chapter Fifty-seven

The bus dropped me in the center of the village by the Island Plaza a block from the bay. I walked to a colorful tile fountain and checked around. Restaurants and little shops lined the edge of the narrow streets, and pastel colored houses climbed the verdant hills surrounding the village.

Continuing down the palm-lined promenade that curved along the bay, I looked out onto a cozy beach. In the calm water, a half a dozen rows of opulent pleasure boats shone in the sun like newly minted coins. They seemed to be tied to white buoys bobbing in the bay. The buoys must have been the cans that the guy at the yacht club mentioned.

I asked a fellow sitting on a bench if he knew where the harbormaster's office was located.

"It's at the end of the pleasure pier," he said, pointing to a long pier on my right.

Tension mounted in my gut as I proceeded to the harbormaster's office, went in, and waited for the guy on duty to finish talking to an arriving vessel on the radio.

He hung up the microphone and turned to me. "What's up?"

The harbormaster had one good eye and one that wandered to the side. My own eyes kept following the bad eye despite every effort to control the impulse. Perhaps he would mistake my nervousness for just rude behavior.

"Maybe you can help me. I was invited to spend a couple of days on the *Double Indemnity*, and I don't know which can she's tied to, or how to get to the yacht."

His good eye stared at me for an uncomfortable moment. "I'm afraid you got a problem, friend."

"Yeah, why?"

"I know the boat. It's my business to know all the regulars."

I shuddered. "What about the boat?"

"She pulled outta here, let's see, must've been almost a week ago."

My stomach sank. "Where'd she go?"

"I can't tell ya. Are you sure you got the right boat?"

I stood there for a second or two, feeling weak. This was it. This was the dead end, and I mean—dead. I turned slowly toward the door, and started to leave.

"Couldn't have gone far, though."

I stopped in my tracks and turned back to the guy. "What? What did you say?"

"Not far. Two guys on the crew just parked the tender at the dinghy dock, and went into the town," he said. "The yacht's probably anchored in one of the coves on the windward side of the island. Lots of privacy. You know how these rich guys like their privacy. Know what I mean?"

"Gads, how stupid of me. Of course, I was supposed to meet them at the dinghy dock. Can you direct me to it?"

The harbormaster turned, stared out the window, and nodded his head sideways toward the pier entrance. "Down the ramp, 'bout halfway back."

I started for the door.

"Hold it right there, mister," he shouted.

I froze. "What now?"

"You tell your buddies they're not supposed to tie up at the dinghy dock. It's only for boats less than fourteen feet."

"Sorry 'bout that. I'll be happy to move it right now."

I dashed out and ran down the pier toward the beach, practically skiing down the ramp that led to a small dock. A few dinghies were tied there, bouncing up and down with the swell.

Parked at the dock, standing out among several small inflatable rafts and a rowboat, was a brand new seventeen-foot Boston Whaler. It was much bigger than the Whaler the yacht-cleaning kid had. This one had a center steering console and a ninety horsepower Mercury outboard hanging off the stern. Painted on the sides, in big blue letters, were the words: *Double Indemnity Dinghy*. If this luxury runabout was a dinghy, what must the yacht be like? A Boston Whaler like this one cost more than most new automobiles.

Scanning the shoreline, I didn't see anybody watching me or anybody who resembled a thug coming my way.

Jumping into the Whaler, I untethered the bow line and tossed it up front. The boat started to drift away. I scooted to the center console and stood there panic stricken looking down at the controls. "Damn. Where's the starter?" The boat continued to drift sideways toward the shore.

Luck was with me. I located the starter, and the key, tied to a piece of yellow sponge rubber, was dangling out of the ignition. With a twist of the key, the big Merc outboard roared to life. The Whaler's bow shot up, and the boat lunged forward. I jerked the wheel to the left and just missed the dock. "Oh shit," I shouted. My shoulder wrenched along with the boat causing me to almost pass out. I yanked back on the power lever regaining a level of control.

I knew that I would have to creep slowly out of the harbor. Signs all over the place said the limit was five knots. The last thing I needed was to draw the attention of the harbormaster or anyone on shore.

Striving to appear confident, I carefully maneuvered the dinghy around the pier and aimed for the passenger ship terminal at the entrance to the harbor.

Soon, I crossed the open bay and cruised past the immense dock where the Great White Steam Ship moored about fifty feet offshore. A quarter-mile later, I cleared the harbor.

Then I punched it. The bow shot up again as I struggled to maintain my balance and control. Hitting the swells head on, the boat jumped in the air, splashed down, and surged forward like a rocket sending a spray of ocean water all the way back to the console, drenching me. Racing all out with the wind furious in my face, the Whaler pounded my legs. I had no idea where I was going; I only knew that I had just stolen the boat.

Chapter Fifty-eight

Turning the boat into the wind, I raced at the waves head on. The Whaler screamed up a wall of water. The wind caught its bow as the boat leaped over the crest and almost capsized. I had to throttle back. I was rounding the far end of the island. The waves were stronger out here and, with my lack of experience, I was afraid to push the craft to its limits. In a couple of miles I'd turn right again and head up the windward side, away from the mainland. Running parallel with the waves, I'd open her up again.

What if I didn't find the yacht? What if the *Double Indemnity* wasn't even at the island? Or worse, what if the yacht was here, but Richie wasn't on board? Worried that my theory was full of holes, I began thinking it through again. Out here in the ocean, skimming over the waves in a stolen boat, an adrenaline rush made my thinking fuzzy and I didn't fully recall all of the evidence. Was it irrefutable that Lawrence was an embezzler, kidnapper, and a murderer? I was racking my brain. But now a new question nagged at me. Why didn't I bring a gun? There were sure to be armed guards aboard the boat if Richie was being held captive. Not much of a match up in a firefight, I thought.

It was too late for all my fears now. I had already stolen the boat. I should've had Sol do a complete check on Lawrence or taken Jack Fox or Deacon with me before charging out unprepared. And yet, with all of the heat coming down, I knew I had to find Richie before the hearing or before the gang or Lawrence got rid of him.

Before long, I was around the tip of Catalina

heading up the backside of the island. I opened the throttle a bit, wanting to get the feel of the boat before I risked pushing it too hard. The island, with its rocky shore, was off to my right. There was no beach—the land angled swiftly up a ridge about a thousand feet. The surface was covered with undergrowth and scrub. In this setting, surrounded by sparkling clear water, the island was beautiful. God, I thought, if I didn't find Richie, if he wasn't on the boat, could I get the Boston Whaler back before anyone noticed it was missing? Fat chance.

I eased in more power and brought the boat up to a safe cruise speed, holding it there for a while, trying to get the feel of the Whaler. Soon my legs were working like springs on an old buggy. The boat would hit a side swell and shift one way, my legs would bend, and the momentum would carry me in the opposite direction. I was beginning to feel like a pro.

Calmer now, I rehashed the details of the case in my head. On re-examination, it became obvious that Lawrence had to be the financial guru behind the gang. Willie would need someone respectable and politically connected to get the scheme off of the ground. It was Assemblywoman Mattie Niles who pushed the bill through the legislature allowing Willie to set up the halfway house program. And I remembered seeing a photograph of Lawrence, with his arm around her, hanging in his office. That in itself wouldn't be meaningful, but coupled with all of the other evidence, well....

I figured Richie was kidnapped to coerce Laura into changing her plea and ending the police investigation. What I couldn't figure out was why

Lawrence would've killed Rosenthal. Was Arnie in on the deal? Was he stealing from his own company? Trying to get out? Maybe it was just a tax scheme. Or, perhaps, Arnie just wasn't aware of the shakedown and had recently found out. Richie had said Arnie just got back from a long vacation in Europe and had turned over the day-to-day control of the plant to Moyer. Maybe he found out what was going on, and he was going to do something about it. That was a shitload of maybes that didn't add up to one concrete answer yet.

Lawrence had the means to kill Arnie and the gang could have supplied him with the weapon. He had the opportunity to follow Arnie home after the poker game. But, was money Lawrence's motive, or was it a falling out with Arnie?

The boat was now hugging the island and, after a few miles, I curved around an outcropping of boulders perched at the water's edge. I made a wide sweep around a bend in the shoreline, and entered a small cove. The inlet was dish shaped and the entrance was only a few hundred yards wide, but in the center, the diameter of the cove was at least a quarter of a mile. As soon as I made the turn and entered the small bay, the air was still, the water calm and smooth. There were no boats in sight. With the water sparkling and transparent, the lagoon would be a perfect spot to scuba dive. It would also be a perfect place to hide a yacht with a kidnapped victim aboard. Disappointed, I left the cove.

The boat was hugging the island now and after traveling a few miles I veered left to miss a large, golden-brown kelp bed floating on the surface. A harbor seal sunned himself on a rock at the entrance of a small lagoon. The seal scrutinized me almost like a sentry at the gate. As I turned into the lagoon, my heart skipped a beat as I gazed upon the gleaming white yacht anchored there.

Chapter Fifty-nine

The cove, protected on three sides by wave-cut terraces scored into its steep banks was small, but large enough to provide sanctuary to the beautiful yacht floating in the middle of it. I pulled the power back and let the Whaler drift farther into the lagoon.

The yacht was broadside to me, about fifty yards away, and its bow was pointed toward the east end of the island. I didn't have to check the name painted on the transom. I recognized it from the photograph in Lawrence's office.

Easing in the power lever a tad, just enough to keep the Whaler under control without noise, I decided to circle the yacht wide and approach it from the rear.

Fireworks were going off in my stomach. At first glance I didn't see anyone on deck, but then I spotted a man up on the flying bridge sitting at the wheel. He didn't acknowledge me, and from the way he was slumped back in the captain's chair with his feet planted on the panel, I figured he was asleep. If I didn't make a racket, I might be able to sneak aboard the boat before the guy woke up.

Making a gradual turn behind the yacht, I cut the outboard motor, and slowly drifted up to the *Double Indemnity's* transom. I let go of the wheel, rushed to the front of the Whaler, and grabbed the yacht's swim step to keep the craft from banging with a thud. I scrambled over the stern onto the yacht.

Scrunching down behind the live-bait tank in the afterdeck, I listened for the sound of movement or talking. My heart raced and my pulse banged in my ears. I desperately hoped that the guy on the flying bridge was the only person on board, except for Richie, who I prayed was there. He had to be. I figured this was the only chance I'd have.

It was quiet except for the ripples of the bay lapping against the hull and a few squawking seagulls. After a moment or two I scooted across the rear deck, darted around the ladder leading to the flying bridge, and went to the main salon. I peeked in the window. Nothing. I carefully slid open the glass door, went into the cabin, and tiptoed down a teak-lined companionway past the navigation station. First, I checked the two guest compartments. Both of the sleeping quarters were empty. Trash and empty beer cans were scattered about. The rooms were probably used by the crew. I crept to the captain's stateroom. The door was closed. Pausing, I took a deep breath, twisted the knob, and opened the door a few inches. Sneaking a quick look around the gap, I exhaled; nobody was in there either.

The bed was unmade. Three tote bags lay on it, bulging full, with drawstrings pulled tight across the top. They were white canvas bags, the type sailors used to store their belongings when they went on duty.

I turned and went aft down the companionway again and spotted a trapdoor cut into the floor. Bracing myself for the pain that was to come, I yanked the hatch. It hurt like hell, but it was open. It was as dark as a cave down there but, in the light from the companionway, I could see a small stairway. After descending into the engine room, I closed the hatchway door behind me and felt around for the light switch and flipped it on. The compartment was long, maybe half the length of the boat, and there wasn't enough height to stand erect. I had to duck walk to go deeper into the narrow space.

Muffled noises, thumping and moaning, came from an area between the two huge diesel engines mounted in front of me. It had to be Richie. He was alive. I wanted to shout and scream for joy. I made a fist and raised my hand almost to my head, before I remembered the low ceiling. Inching forward on my haunches, I slipped a bit on the diamond-plate floor, but slowly made it to where Richie lay.

He was on his side, bound and gagged. His eyes were as big as manhole covers, full of fear like a cornered animal. Richie didn't recognize me at first. Cowering away, he curled into a fetal position pressing up against one of the diesel's exhaust manifolds. When I got closer, he recognized me and hung his head as his body went limp.

"Richie," I whispered. "Thank God. Are you okay?"

He nodded his head in a frantic manner, struggled with his arms, and mumbled something through the duct tape covering his mouth.

I tore the tape off, pointed upward, and put my finger to my lips in a gesture to hush. "There's a guy sleeping on the bridge."

"Jimmy?" Richie whispered. "Is Laura alright?" He rolled around as I started to unravel the tape that secured his arms and legs.

"Laura's still in jail, but she's okay," I answered in a hushed tone. "We'll talk later. Right now, we've got to get outta here. There's a small boat tied to the stern. Be real quiet." I pointed up again. "Don't want to wake the guy."

"Jimmy, I had time to think here, think about

dying. I knew I was going to die."

"Nobody knows that."

"When I was at my mom's funeral, I saw a seagull. It landed on her hearse."

"So?"

"They say when you see a white bird land on a hearse, you're the next to die."

"What if two people see it at the same time?" I said, still peeling off the tape.

"I dunno, I guess you flip for it."

Richie laughed a little, and so did I, breaking the tension. "C'mon, Richie, we have to get out of here."

His face became hard and severe. "It was Lawrence. He killed my dad. He was here this morning with a couple of lowlifes with shaved heads, and tattoos all over," Richie said quickly. "They were laughing at me. Lawrence told them that he killed my dad, and they were going to kill me too."

I grabbed Richie by the shoulders. "Lawrence was here?"

"Came in a helicopter. Landed in the water next to the boat. They locked me in one of the cabins, but I saw the whole thing through the porthole. They brought some big white bags onboard."

I thought of the sacks in the main stateroom. "Canvas bags like sailors use?"

"Yes, like that. Said the heat was on and they had to get rid of everything."

"Did Lawrence or anyone mention a Mexican guy named Willie, or maybe Guillermo?"

"No, nobody said anything about a Mexican guy. But Lawrence said something about Moyer. Said that when things cool down, he's going to take care of him too."

"How long ago did Lawrence leave?" I asked.

"About two hours ago. Lawrence told the boat crew guys to take the yacht to Cabo, and dump the bags and me overboard on the way."

"How many guys in the boat crew?"

"Three," he said.

"When were they planning on leaving?"

"As soon as Buddy and Donnie—that's two of the guards, the other guy is Ralph; he's the guy you saw on the bridge— well anyway, they're going to leave as soon as they get back with the supplies. They took the tender to Avalon, but first they tied me up and threw me down here."

My brain raced. The helicopter I saw at the airport, the black one with the floats, must have been the one that Lawrence used to come out here. By now, Buddy and Donnie would've noticed that the Boston Whaler was gone. I knew it wouldn't take them long to figure out what was up. All they had to do was ask the harbormaster what the guy who stole their boat looked like. They'd call Lawrence and he'd come back in a flash to finish us off. Donnie and Buddy had probably rented a speedboat by now.

I had to get the bags to the district attorney. All of the evidence I needed to verify Richie's statements was inside.

"Change of plans, Richie."

"What are we going to do?"

"Do you remember how to drive this tub?"

"How could I forget that? My dad forced me to drive his beast of a boat and I hated every minute of it. But I'm thanking him now. We have another problem,

Jimmy. Ralph's got a revolver in his belt, and he has a rifle too. The guys stand on the fly bridge, toss their beer cans over the side, and take potshots at them." A mournful look clouded Richie's face. "Yesterday, Ralph shot a seal, just wounded her. She swam away, but the sharks likely finished her off."

We crawled out of the engine room and quietly skulked back into the main salon. Whispering, I explained my plan to Richie. We'd take the yacht back to Long Beach and turn the evidence over to the police. The Boston Whaler was fast, but the yacht was faster. Also, when the afternoon ocean breeze kicked up in the channel, it would be rough. I didn't know if the Whaler could handle it, and I didn't want to take the chance of capsizing halfway to Long Beach.

To minimize the risk of running into Buddy and Donnie, we'd head back to the mainland by going the long way around the west end of the island. But first we had to get rid of Ralph, and I had a plan for that as well.

I stood out of sight, flattened against the wall under the ladder leading to the fly bridge, and Richie stood at the base of it, next to the salon door.

Richie put his hands to his mouth like a megaphone and shouted up to the flying bridge, "C'mon down and fight like a man, you fat-assed sonofabitch." He twisted into the salon.

I waited.

After a few moments, I signaled for Richie to shout again.

"C'mon down and fight like a man, you big ugly slob," Richie yelled.

Ralph didn't stir.

One more time, I gestured.

"C'mon down and fight like a man, you big fat putz," Richie said retreating to the salon again.

Richie appeared to be enjoying his part of the plan, but Ralph continued to sleep. I was about to signal Richie again when I heard Ralph grunt, "Hey, what's going on?"

Just as I figured, Ralph came down facing forward, holding the revolver waist high, aiming it in front of his body. His other hand was on the rail behind him. Ralph took the steps one at a time. After each rung, he stopped and collied his head like a bird scanning side to side, before starting down again.

When his feet got to the fourth step, I reached through the rungs and grabbed his legs with both hands. I pulled hard, wrenching my shoulder again and popping a few stitches. His body flew forward to the deck, and he landed with a thud. Rushing around the ladder I picked up the gun.

Ralph, still half asleep and now dazed, sat up and rubbed his head. Then he noticed the revolver pointing at him. "Who the hell are you?"

"Neptune," I said. "That seal you shot yesterday was my mother, and I'm really pissed."

"Ahh, I was just having fun. I didn't mean anything, honest."

Either this guy was a complete idiot, or he must have hit his head harder than I figured. "Richie," I called out. "Get Ralph a life vest. He's taking a swim."

Chapter Sixty

Time was crucial now. We had to get the yacht moving before Buddy and Donnie came roaring around the entrance of the lagoon with guns blazing.

"How you coming with the anchor?" I shouted down to Richie on the foredeck.

"The winch is stuck. It won't budge."

I was standing on the bridge, next to the captain's chair, looking down. A Winchester .30/30 lever action rifle lay on the seat behind me. The yacht's diesels—a thousand horsepower each—were idling. Richie had started them, briefed me on the controls, and then ran down to haul up the anchor.

Standing with a befuddled look on his face, Richie stared down at the electric winch bolted to the deck. A taut cable, one end wrapped around the winch's six-inch drum, ran through an open scupper at the deck's edge and over the side into the water. The anchor attached to the end of the cable must have been wedged under some rocks on the bottom.

Richie made a circling motion with his hand raised above his head. "Give it a little slack."

I pushed in the power handles. The yacht surged forward—too much. I yanked them back. The boat shuddered and shot rearward. Richie lost his balance, stumbled, and fell backward. I pushed the levers up to the neutral position, but the boat kept moving backwards. The yacht stopped with a jolt when the anchor line tightened. Richie got up off the deck and shot an evil eye my way. He looked back down at the winch, shaking his head.

Minutes were ticking off and I grew

increasingly anxious. For a brief second, I looked around at the peaceful lagoon with its rocky shoreline and the sun low in the west. I saw Ralph bobbing in the water on our port side. He was trying to dogpaddle to shore, but the bright red life vest slowed him down.

"Hang on tight, Richie. I'm going to try something," I shouted over the chugging sound of the engines.

He scrunched down and grabbed the brackets designed to hold the whaler in place when it was stowed on the deck.

Easing the levers in just a hair, the boat drifted forward creating slack in the anchor line. I counted to five, jerked the power levers back, and the diesels, two thousand horses, screamed. Sixty thousand pounds of yacht jumped backward. Instantly the line strained and I heard a loud bang. The winch contraption, motor and all, broke free. It ripped a jagged hole in the deck and flew into the water. The yacht, now unrestrained, raced in reverse.

I rammed the power levers forward and aimed the wheel for the lagoon entrance. The bow rose out of the water, like a wild mustang, spun sideways, and bolted toward the starboard shore. Frantically I tried to control the boat to keep it from smashing into the rocks at the water's edge. Richie flew up the ladder and pushed me aside. In an instant he had everything in order.

He opened her up and we roared out of the lagoon. We were shooting along the backside of Catalina, screaming like a low-flying missile. The sleek bow sliced through the rough swells, peeled the water back, and created a white foamy wake streaming behind us as we flew forward. The yacht was on a plane, zooming over the ocean, beating out a steady rhythm. As I raced below, I saw the Boston Whaler still tied to the swim step trailing behind us. It bounced along like a flat stone skimming over the ripples on a lake.

Down in the main cabin, I rummaged through the tote sacks. Mingled in with the papers, records, and computer printouts were cement bricks. Lawrence wanted to make sure these bags went straight to the bottom of the ocean. I couldn't blame him. If I were Lawrence, I'd want them on the bottom as well. The evidence was dynamite. There was enough in the sacks to blow his scheme and the careers of a half-dozen government officials to smithereens.

There was more than enough evidence here to send Lawrence to prison for life and put Willie out of business. And there was more than enough to prove that Laura did not murder her husband.

It was all here, all in the bags. In my search I found records of payoffs to politicians, memos about terror tactics used by Willie and his thugs, and a log of meetings between Lawrence and the leaders of *La Eme* and the *Norteños*.

Lawrence was a meticulous record keeper, too meticulous. I could never figure out why people who were engaged in such blatantly illegal activity would keep such incriminating records. The Mafia with their ledgers of skimming in Vegas, the recent scandal involving corporate price fixing, and now Lawrence with the tote bags. How could these smart guys be so dumb?

There were several thick files of businesses that used Lawrence's payroll service, businesses involved in the ghost worker program. Grabbing the Farmer Fred file, I fiercely thumbed through it. My hand shook. I found a memo from Arnie demanding a meeting with Lawrence. It requested that they meet at his home after the poker game. Arnie wanted out of the deal. He knew Moyer was involved, and he wanted Lawrence to cancel the program immediately.

Means, opportunity, and now motive. I had the smoking gun in my hand, and now I just had to keep it off the bottom of the ocean and get it back to the mainland.

I tossed the bricks aside and went back on the bridge. "Richie," I asked. "Do you know how to patch through a call to the mainland from the boat's radio?"

"I'll try," said Richie. "I saw a ship-to-shore radio in the main salon next to the couch. Let me set the autopilot and come down and I'll try."

Richie fiddled with the buttons and finally hollered, "Mobile, mobile," into the receiver before successfully making the connection. Sol's voice came over the air.

"Jimmy, where are you? What's going on? I can barely hear you."

I pressed a button on the receiver to answer. "I'm on a yacht out by Catalina."

"Why? Everything is going to hell. Grimes is out of his mind."

"Sol, listen to me." I held down the button so Sol couldn't interrupt. "I've found Richie, he's alive, and I've got all the evidence we need to break the case wide open. I want to bring it directly to Grimes."

"You've found Richie. My God. And he's okay?"

"Yeah, I'm bringing him and the evidence back from Catalina on a yacht. Can't go into details now, but believe me, the case is over."

"The evidence is that good?"

"Better than good," I said. "Lawrence, the insurance guy, killed Rosenthal. I have Richie's statement, and it's certain that Moyer and Willie are deep into it as well."

"God, are you absolutely sure?"

"Yeah, I have three duffle bags of evidence. Stuff in Lawrence's own handwriting."

"*Got in himmel*! Jimmy, *moch schnel*, hurry!"

"Yeah, Sol, but look, get ahold of Grimes. Have him meet the yacht in Long Beach. I want to give him the evidence before anyone finds out what we have."

"Gotcha, Jimmy. Pull up to the guest dock at the Jolly Roger Restaurant in Alamitos Bay, and we'll be there," Sol said.

"In the meantime, send Rita to Sybil Brand. She's got to let Laura know that Richie's safe," I said. "Also, tell Rita to talk to Webster, the deputy DA, and tell him what's going on."

"This is terrific. I'll send her right away."

"Sol, one more thing."

"Yeah?"

"Bring backup to the dock. I'm probably being followed," I said as the phone clicked off.

Chapter Sixty-one

I heard it before I saw it, an ominous whooping sound pounding the air and getting closer. I jumped up and ran out to the aft deck. Coming up on us fast, skimming over the water behind the yacht, was a black helicopter—just like the one I had seen at the airport.

Charging up the ladder to the flying bridge, I saw Richie steering the boat with both hands, while looking over his shoulder at the helicopter almost on top of us. We were about twenty miles from the mainland going full out on a straight line headed for Alamitos Bay.

"That's Lawrence's chopper. It's got those floats on it," Richie shouted when he saw me.

Looking up, I saw a guy leaning out of the open space behind the two front seats. The door had been removed, and the guy in the opening had a shotgun.

I shoved Richie back. The control panel exploded. An instant later, another shot blew a hole in the side of the bridge, taking out the radio antenna. The helicopter flew forward, directly in front of us, and then it started a wide sweeping turn.

"Get off the bridge, they're coming back!" I screamed at Richie.

"Gotta control the boat." He made a move forward.

Grabbing him I pushed him toward the ladder. The helicopter made its turn and headed back.

"The hell with the boat. Get below."

I followed Richie as he hustled down the ladder. The copter made another pass and blasted two holes in the side of the yacht.

Richie ran inside to the secondary helm below at the front of the salon. He spun the wheel, but it just rotated freely. He pulled the power levers back and forth. The boat didn't respond. Turning, he looked at me. Panic crept onto his face. "Nothing, no control—boat's outta control."

The sea was rough. The yacht raced over the water at fifty knots, unleashed. It ran up the side of a wave, tilted at a forty-five-degree angle, and almost capsized before shooting over the top. The *Double Indemnity* gyrated like a pendulum on amphetamines, running madly over the waves, up one side and down the other. I didn't want to think what would happen when the boat turned broadside at the base of a large wave.

Richie, scrambling to keep his balance, rushed forward to the engine room hatch. "Gotta kill the engines."

Behind us, the helicopter made its turn and, almost immediately, the salon windows on the port side shattered. Double-ought buckshot blasted a hole the size of a basketball in the sofa next to me. Feathers and fiberglass chunks swirled in the cabin. If they kept blasting us with the high-powered ammo, the yacht would soon look like Swiss cheese.

The helicopter raced past us again. Another discharge hit the yacht's bow. The boat swerved, running in the narrows between the swells, and I rolled to my right. Then gravity took over as the boat rapidly turned, flew over the crest, and crashed down on the other side. I was tossed like a wet washrag against the bulkhead, smashing my shoulder. The pain, like a high voltage jolt, stunned my senses as I slid to the floor.

A metallic voice boomed above the sound of the helicopter blades beating the air. "Give it up, O'Brien. Shut the boat down and come to the rear deck."

I crawled to the salon door and looked out. The chopper hovered ten feet above the afterdeck. I could see David Lawrence in the co-pilot seat with a mike in his hand. "You've got ten seconds, then I'm gonna kill you, even if I have to sink the boat."

Another shotgun blast shattered the glass door. The buckshot, whizzing over my head, reduced the salon table to splinters. He could sink the boat with Richie, me, and the evidence in it. I had to figure a way out, fast.

"Five seconds, O'Brien."

"Screw you, Lawrence. Sink your goddamn boat!" I yelled, but no one heard me.

Suddenly, the boat's engines quit. The *Double Indemnity* slowed and the helicopter shot forward. Soon we'd be dead in the water. We'd no longer be a moving target, just an object to take potshots at. No sport in that.

Richie charged back into the salon. "Water is pouring in. The engine room's flooded."

Already the boat was listing to the port side. A few more blasts from the shotgun and the yacht would sink like the *Titanic*.

The helicopter rushed past the starboard side. Two more shots rang out.

"We're sinking!" Richie said. His head swiveled back and forth. "I'll get the lifejackets."

"Richie, listen to me. Forget the lifejackets. In those red vests, they'll hover over us and pick us off like apples bobbing in a barrel."

"What about the tender?"

"No, they'll sink that too."

"We're going to die."

"No! I'm taking you back. Do you hear me?"

Richie nodded his head.

"Get those tote bags out of the main cabin and bring them to the rear of the boat."

Richie couldn't move. Fear had paralyzed him.

"Now! Move it, damn it!"

I ran outside. The helicopter made a turn behind the yacht. It was coming up the port side now. I scampered up the ladder. The guys on the chopper might not have known about the rifle on board. That's why they thought they could just hover and blast away.

The helicopter slowed. The guy with the shotgun spotted me on the bridge. He raised his gun, and I dove to the deck just as he fired. The shot missed by a millimeter and blew the compass to smithereens.

Scurrying on my knees to the captain's chair, I tossed the seat cushion aside and rummaged to find the rifle. I grabbed the .30/30, worked the lever, and took a wild shot at the helicopter. The machine tilted forward and flew off. In seconds, they were about two hundred yards in front of the boat.

Now flat on my belly, I raised the rifle and sighted down the barrel. I had the copter in my sights, but it was an impossible shot at that distance, especially with the boat rocking back and forth. My shoulder throbbed and I had to lower the gun.

The helicopter was getting smaller as it kept flying away. Would they back off and wait until we were in the water, or would they return?

"Turn around, you sonofabitch. Give me one

decent shot."

The yacht listed heavily to the port side, but suddenly now, the bow started to dip. We were taking on a lot of water. I knew we didn't have much time.

"Turn, you bastard, turn," I screamed into the wind.

Wish granted. Thanks to the powers that be, the helicopter was heading back, straight on. They wanted to finish the job. The *coup de grace*.

I raised the rifle, my shoulder gave out, and I dropped the gun. "Dr. Bone, I'm gonna sue your ass if I die out here!" I yelled at the top of my lungs.

The helicopter was dancing in the air, growing larger with each passing second.

I picked up the gun again. Everything moved in slow motion, like a Sam Peckinpah movie. I just hoped the good guys won. The helicopter's windscreen was crystal clear in the rifle sight. "Hold on Jimmy, steady," I said out loud.

The sun was setting behind the helicopter. The main rotor blades spun—back lit—and tilted in my direction.

Strangely, the complex shifting patterns of the blades had a hypnotic calming effect on me.

Holding the gun, I aimed. David Lawrence sat next to the pilot, dead in my sights. The shooter was in the back, slowly leaning out of the side of the copter with the shotgun. Everything was silent now as I slowly shifted my aim and squeezed the trigger.

Crack! I shot the pilot.

The world exploded. The pilot slumped on the controls. The copter twisted sideways; the big rotor blades kicked up a gush of water. The machine hit the surface, and disintegrated. In seconds, the helicopter sank out of sight.

Chapter Sixty-two

Struggling to get to my feet, I stood on the sloping flying bridge deck and dropped the rifle. It clattered and slid forward. The bow of the yacht was almost under, but I stood there, frozen, gazing over the side at the spot where the helicopter had gone down. The copter's floats had broken off on impact and gyrated on the water. There was no sign of Lawrence, the pilot, or the gunman. My stomach was sick.

"Hey, Jimmy, you all right?"

"Oh my God, I almost shit my pants," I said.

Richie had the three tote bags in the stern. He looked at the Boston Whaler tied to the swim step, and started to toss the sacks into the small boat.

Richie panted. "Doesn't look as if it's been hit."

He got into the Whaler and I handed him the last sack.

"There's about a foot of water in the bottom, but it's not a problem with these Whalers," he reassured me.

I climbed over the transom of the *Double Indemnity* onto the swim step and untied the Whaler. "Try to start it," I said.

The big Merc fired up. Richie, grinning ear to ear, gave me the thumbs up. I hopped into the boat.

"Circle around. See if there are any survivors."

Richie maneuvered the skiff around the sinking yacht to where the helicopter crashed. Except for the pontoons, and a small oil slick forming in the wake, there were no signs of wreckage or bodies.

I turned and watched as the *Double Indemnity* slipped silently below the waves to join her owner at the bottom. It brought to mind the myth about the Vikings. When they died, they were buried with their boats so that they could sail to heaven, Valhalla or wherever, in style. Well, Lawrence, you've got a million dollar yacht down there. You and your buddies can sail it to hell for all I care. Richie scanned the horizon to get a sightline to Alamitos Bay.

"We'll have to throttle back," Richie said as he maneuvered the controls. "It's almost dark and the ocean is really kicking up now."

It was then, like déjà vu, that I heard that sound again, helicopter blades whirring, coming closer and closer.

"Richie, I think the stress of this whole mess is making me delusional. Do you hear anything?"

A searchlight scanned the wreckage scene. We both looked up and spotted a police helicopter as it circled overhead. We sat there, vulnerable and shell-shocked, like fish in a pond, reliving the disaster we had just escaped.

"Cut the engine," an amplified voice blared. "And drop your weapons."

"Hell, Richie, the cops don't know if we're the good guys or the bad guys."

Richie killed the engine and we thrashed in the waves as the helicopter hovered over us. In the distance, we could see a Coast Guard vessel bearing down on us. Cold, wet, and exhausted, Richie and I laid there, limp and helpless.

"There's going to be a world of explaining to every agency in town, now," I muttered to Richie. Relieved as I was to be rescued, I just wanted to get to the Jolly Roger to see Sol and Rita, my only family, I realized.

"Someone must have seen the firefight and reported it," said Richie. "You know, Jimmy, I'm glad they're here. My next move was to tell you that we were heading back to Catalina. With the ocean this wild we would have never made it the twenty miles to Alamitos Bay."

As the hundred-foot Coast Guard vessel neared, Richie and I could see at least four guys at various points on the cutter, with guns aimed at us. Two of the crewmen deployed a rubber raft, and started toward our dingy, shouting questions as they neared.

"How many on board? Anyone in need of medical attention? Any weapons on board?"

"There are two of us with no weapons," Richie shouted back. "We have bags of evidence. We can't lose them. We need to guard them with our lives. Please, take them first!"

"Isn't it women and children first?" I quipped to Richie. He didn't acknowledge my stupid remark.

"Don't worry, sir," a sailor replied.

"Mr. Silverman and Mr. Grimes both cautioned us about their importance."

"That Sol," I mumbled to Richie. "Should've guessed he wouldn't trust us to the sea."

"We'll be towing your skiff to the vessel, so prepare for transfer," the sailor continued.

Once on board, Richie and I related our ordeal and the role of Lawrence and his goons in Arnie's murder. About thirty minutes into the trip to Long Beach, I finally found the courage to ask the question to which I already knew the answer. "Would it be possible for you to drop us off at the Jolly Roger dock in

Alamitos Bay?"

"Sorry, sir," an officer replied. "Protocol. We're heading for our headquarters in San Pedro. I'm afraid you'll be spending some time at our Seaside location. The crime scene is in federal waters, so you'll have the FBI to contend with, Catalina is under the Sheriff's jurisdiction, so you'll have the Sheriff's Department to answer to, and since the Coast Guard cutter was deployed, we'll have to investigate as well."

Richie and I stared at each other. "An all-nighter, I assume," I said.

***

Grimes was at the dock to pick up the evidence bags when the Coast Guard vessel arrived. He told us that after our radio call, Sol, knowing we were being followed, had called the Coast Guard, and told them about Richie and the evidence.

"Sol said you'd be handing over the bags. He's letting me take the credit so I can redeem my credibility with the press." Grimes was so excited he was practically salivating. "We're serving the warrants on Willie as we speak." He was eager to put one over on the politicians who embarrassed him after the debacle at the halfway house raid. "Don't worry, Jimmy. I'll make sure the press recognizes Silverman Investigations," he added, sounding kind of annoyed.

Richie was just as annoyed. "The hell with everybody. What about Laura?"

"She's being released in just a few hours, as soon as the court convenes," Grimes answered as he was walking away. "Sol will fill you in as soon as you get done here and they approve his entrance."

* * *

The sun was just rising when Richie and I stepped outside the Coast Guard detention area. Hunger and sleep deprivation made us feel goofy. Our wrinkled up clothes and disheveled appearance made us look goofy as well.

A limo waited for us at the curb. We heard a shriek of joy as Sol and Rita jumped out of the car to greet us.

"*Boitskik,* you're the best looking mess I've ever seen," said Sol, choking back his emotion.

"I was scared out of my mind," Rita yelled as she burst into tears. She was holding up a copy of the *L.A. Times*, with headlines reading: PRISON RELEASE SCAM BUSTED! "You're famous, Jimmy," she gushed.

"Richie's free and as soon as Laura is sitting next to me, that'll be fame enough for me," I answered as I yawned. A big smile came over my face as I entered the limo. "Thanks, guys." I laughed as I grabbed a jelly-filled donut and took a swig of coffee. "Richie, this coffee is called *Life*, created by my own coffee designer, Dolans, for the luckiest people on earth." He raised his cup in a toasting gesture. "Now, I can find the strength to hear the details of what went down on your side this weekend."

Sol gloated as he told us how Grimes had Danny Moyer arrested based on the report from his mole in the wiener factory along with the evidence we were bringing in. The DA cut a deal with Moyer in exchange for his testimony. "Moyer started squealing louder than a herd of pigs at Farmer Fred's," Sol snickered.

Moyer related his involvement with Lawrence in the payroll deduction scam, how it worked, and how they stole money from the meat company. But more importantly, he would testify that he knew Lawrence had murdered Rosenthal. Moyer said Lawrence told him he killed Arnie and told him he would have him killed too if he rat-finked to the authorities.

According to Moyer, Lawrence had a gang of thugs controlled by Willie—ex-cons, skinheads, and bikers. Several of the gangsters hung out at the plant keeping an eye on him. Moyer told the DA he was afraid to come forward before, but now he wanted to come clean and clear his conscience. It's amazing how much a guy's conscience bothered him when faced with a long prison term.

Sol continued, "Willie supplied the fake names and payroll reports, and then he started demanding that Moyer double the amount of phony workers. Moyer, figuring he'd get caught, was reluctant to go along with Willie's demands, and that's what the argument was about at Ships Coffee Shop that night."

With Moyer's confession on tape, Webster and Rita had arranged to have Laura released at the hearing today and officially exonerated at that time.

"Sol, puh...leeze let me read Jimmy the article in the Times," Rita said, bursting with anticipation.

"Go, girl." I laughed.

Congressman Mattie Niles has appointed an overseer from the Bureau of

Prisons to take over operations of the St. Dismas Halfway House work release program

After a routine inspection discovered irregularities in billing and operating procedures at St. Dismas, Congressman Niles launched a sweeping review and has hired an independent investigation firm to examine the scope of the corruption.

Congressman Niles, the chairperson of the Prison Reform Committee, worked tirelessly to pass the Inmate Rehabilitation Act in Congress in 1969. She states, "Finding jobs for our parolees is a difficult but rewarding part of the California Rehabilitation Program, and we make every effort to insure the success of each inmate that is released to the work program."

Inside sources say the corruption is deep and widespread, ranging from intimidation and money laundering to murder.

Undersheriff Robert Grimes, who has been instrumental in obtaining the arrest of Guillermo Chaves, Program Director, said, "This is a case so complex, it'll take a book to unravel the intricacies of the whole scheme. The case has political, gang, and business connections throughout Los Angeles."

"Are you kidding me?" exclaimed Jimmy. "God, this is political ass-saving at its best. Who got the investigation contract?"

"Jimmy, my boy," answered Sol, "those kind of details are privileged. Remember Sol's Rule Number Three, however, that helping others for free often results in greater rewards."

***

The limo made a quick stop at Sol's office before heading to court for Laura's hearing. Sol had asked Grimes and Webster to come back to the office as part of their deal so that Sol could examine the contents of the evidence bags.

"This is a gold mine for the prosecution; notes, ledgers, a political scandal brewing in a bag," exclaimed Sol. "That squares it with us, Bobbo."

"You bet. Now I gotta go, guys." Grimes told his deputies to pick up the tote bags and follow him. He got half way to the door and stopped.

"By the way, O'Brien," Grimes said, "just so you know, we caught the guy who killed Buck Simpson. Wasn't like we figured, wasn't a contract killing after all."

"What? It wasn't a gang hit? I thought Willie had him killed," I shouted, jumping up like a spring. "Who killed him, and why?"

"Apparently Simpson tried to roll his cellmate—the asshole wanted his *Playboy* magazine, for chrissakes! The cellmate, an Asian guy and a grand master Kung Fu expert, took him out with one blow. He set up the hanging to make it look like a suicide."

"The whole Simpson thing was just a coincidence? Shit," I said as I fell back into the chair.

"Are you sure you got the guy who killed Simpson?" Sol said to Grimes. "How do you know he's the right guy?"

"Because the guy confessed, that's how. Willie

might have planned to have Buck bumped off in jail," added Grimes. "But he never got the chance to execute his plan."

"What about the evidence Buck said he had, the gang ties and all?" I yelled.

"It's a moot point now," Grimes answered smugly.

Richie chimed in, trying to cool things down. "In the Eastern culture, Jimmy, there's such a thing as a happy accident. Simpson's death brought about a world of good out of a sad ending and you were the catalyst that made it happen. You took Buck's case—a happy accident. Karma. Don't let it destroy you."

I threw up his hands. "Coincidence. I can't believe it."

***

We drove to the courthouse. Two bums and Rita went to the hearing room. When they brought in Laura she didn't look much better than we did. The judge released her, but turned to me and said, "Your attire is disrespectful to the sanctity of the court. You appear before me looking like that again, Counselor, and you'll be held in contempt."

As soon as we left the courtroom, Laura and Richie embraced. Richie let go of her and twirled her around, scanning her disheveled appearance. "Laura, I can hardly wait to get my hands on your hair." Everyone burst out laughing.

"Does this mean you'll be staying?" Laura asked.

"As long as it takes to get the wieners back in

order," retorted Richie. "Dad forced me drive that damn boat and it ended up saving my life. He also made me major in business, so now I can pay him back in full."

"So, Laura," Sol said. "Tell me, what are you going to do with the ten million dollar insurance check?"

"After I pay your fee, Sol," Laura turned and gave me a beautiful smile, "and of course, Jimmy's fee, and a sizeable bonus for Rita, I'm going to pay off Arnie's creditors. And now that Richie is staying to take over Farmer Fred's, we can try out his new idea to make a line of wieners and hamburgers out of soybeans and mushrooms. We'll call them Veggie-dogs, and Veggie-burgers."

Sol and I glanced at each other. We both clenched our teeth trying not to laugh.

Chapter Sixty-three

I woke up late and was trying to plaster a bandage on my shoulder with Scotch tape. The adhesive tape had run out and the Scotch tape kept bunching up, rendering it useless.

"Son-of-a-bitch," I muttered under my breath.

Rita was due any minute to pick me up to retrieve my car that was still parked at the Orange County Airport, and I couldn't get this damn thing on right. The oozing from my incision would ruin my shirt if I didn't get the gauze secured properly. My shirt collection was limited. Actually, I was down to three; one on, one at the cleaners, and a spare.

Other than Mabel, no one had been to my apartment, and I wanted to get outside before Rita came to the door. Looking around the place, it was as if I had never seen how pathetic and stark it was, worse than a cheap motel.

All of a sudden a perky voice called out. "Morning, boss."

I jumped and shouted, "You scared the crap out of me, Rita. Did you ever hear of knocking?"

"I rang the bell, but it didn't work. Are you mad?"

"No," I answered, embarrassed. "I'm not mad."

"Gads, Jimmy. That wound looks horrible. Those stiches need to come out. Your skin is starting to grow over them."

"I'll go in a day or two to take care of it," I said, a bit peeved.

"Sorry, Jimmy, I'm in charge today. I've got the wheels and the power to make the choices today you know. We're going to the doctor now," Rita said. "Sol told me yesterday, while we were waiting to pick you up at the dock, that all of us would be attached at the hip for years waiting for all the scenarios of the prison scam to get worked out. I guess we'll start immediately."

This was a side of Rita I had never seen. I liked it, bold and take charge.

"Okay, partner." I laughed.

"Partner? You mean it, Jimmy? Partner?"

"You deserve it, Rita. We'll be a good pair. Now with a bit of cash in the coffer maybe we can expand, get some better cases. Hell, with all of the publicity we're getting, we'll have free advertising."

Rita reached over to give me a hug, but my bare shoulder stopped her. "Scotch tape? What the heck?"

"Don't ask, Rita. Please."

Deftly, she bandaged my wound, Scotch tape and all, and helped me put on my shirt. As Rita picked up my jacket, a card fell to the floor. *Susan Quincy, Flight Instructor*. I wasn't certain if she saw the name, but she placed the card back into my pocket, saying nothing.

The morning was a bit foggy and chilly as we walked to Rita's Datsun. Rita reached out and took my hand in hers. It was small, like a child's, but warm and soft, nice to hold on to. We walked slowly, but her demeanor had changed to foggy and chilly like the weather.

"Rita, I was thinking." I searched for the words. "Maybe you can go to the Oak-E-Dokey furniture store with me after the doctor. You know, like, help me fix up my place? Maybe get a desk, some chairs, make it homier."

Rita paused a bit before speaking. "Trying to spruce up the place for Susie?"

"Oh, you saw her card." This explained her foul mood.

Looking down at Rita as she slid into the driver's seat, I could see her smile had been replaced by a sour face. I walked to the passenger's side and climbed into the car next to her.

Rita turned on the ignition to warm up the car. The radio was on and Johnny Mathis bellowed out, "Chances Are." His velvet voice brushed across me and I closed my eyes for a moment remembering the times when Barbara and I would make love to this song. The hair on the back of my neck bristled like a cat does when you scratch her belly. Nostalgia captured me for the moment and I became certain that I wanted this kind of life for myself again.

"Are you in pain? Need an aspirin or anything?" Rita asked, breaking my moment of reverie.

"My arm feels fine, thanks. I'm just indulging myself in a nostalgic moment. You know, almost getting killed three times in a matter of days makes you think a lot about life."

"Like Susie and you at the airport?" Rita snapped back.

"No, Rita, not for Susie," I said, tapping her lightly on the nose with my finger. "Chances are the best things we have are right under our noses."

Rita grinned and her eyes sparkled.

"Come on now, partner. Let's get this show on the road," I said enthusiastically.

Rita reached under the collar of her shirt and

pulled out a thin gold chain with a charm dangling from it.

"Look, Jimmy," she said as she cocked her head to the side like a smitten teenage girl. She held the charm up so I could read the inscription. The charm had the scales of justice on one side and the word "Partner" engraved on the other.

"What the heck?"

"The little white box that Sol gave me after the Busher case," Rita said. "This is what was inside. Sol put in a note. Said we'd be a good pair."

"God," I exclaimed. "Can't I even have a private moment without Sol?"

We both laughed.

ABOUT THE AUTHOR

Jeff Sherratt was a great storyteller. He wrote The Jimmy O'Brien Mystery Series which included The Brimstone Murders, Guilty or Else, and Detour to Murder. He raced against the clock to finish this novel, Cyanide Perfume, but time ran out before the final edits. His loving wife, Judy Sherratt, judiciously completed this novel so it remained Jeff's work.

Anyone who ever knew Jeff would tell you what a wonderful storyteller he was. I hope you enjoy this—his last story.

Jeff was a man with integrity, a great sense of humor, and a heart the size of Texas. He gave good advice, shared his knowledge with whoever would listen, and loved his family more than anything on this earth.

I only knew Jeff Sherratt for a few years, but he felt like a brother to me. He was my mentor and a dear friend. He took me under his wing and led me into the world of fiction. I have him to thank for my success as a novelist.

Sometimes in life, a friend comes along just when you need him, leads you where you need to go, and watches out for you along the way. Jeff was that friend to me— and I expect to countless others who crossed his path.

Teresa Burrell
Author of *The Advocate Series*